# DREADFUL DARK

*Tales of Horror Complete Series*

## DEAN RASMUSSEN

DARK VENTURE PRESS

Dreadful Dark: Tales of Horror: Complete Series

Dean Rasmussen

Copyright © 2022 Dean Rasmussen
All rights reserved.
ISBN: 978-1-951120-31-3

This book is a work of fiction. The characters, incidents, and dialogue are drawn from the author's imagination and are not to be construed as real. Any resemblance to actual persons living or dead, businesses, events or locales is purely coincidental. Reproduction in whole or part of this publication without express written consent from the publisher is strictly prohibited, except as permitted by U.S. copyright law.

For more information about this book, visit:

www.deanrasmussen.com
dean@deanrasmussen.com

Dreadful Dark: Tales of Horror: Complete Series

Published by: Dark Venture Press

Cover Art: Dark Venture Press and Deposit Photos

❄ Created with Vellum

Get a **FREE** short story at my website!

www.deanrasmussen.com

★ ★ ★ ★ ★
**Please review my book!**

If you liked this book and have a moment to spare, I would greatly appreciate a short review on the page where you bought it. Your help in spreading the word is *immensely* appreciated and reviews make a huge difference in helping new readers
find my novels.

Shine House: An Emmie Rose Haunted Mystery Book 0
Hanging House: An Emmie Rose Haunted Mystery Book 1
Caine House: An Emmie Rose Haunted Mystery Book 2
Hyde House: An Emmie Rose Haunted Mystery Book 3
Whisper House: An Emmie Rose Haunted Mystery Book 4
Temper House: An Emmie Rose Haunted Mystery Book 5

Dreadful Dark Tales of Horror Book 1
Dreadful Dark Tales of Horror Book 2
Dreadful Dark Tales of Horror Book 3
Dreadful Dark Tales of Horror Book 4
Dreadful Dark Tales of Horror Book 5
Dreadful Dark Tales of Horror Book 6
Dreadful Dark Tales of Horror Complete Series

Stone Hill: Shadows Rising (Book 1)
Stone Hill: Phantoms Reborn (Book 2)
Stone Hill: Leviathan Wakes (Book 3)

# DREADFUL DARK BOOK 1
## TALES OF HORROR: BOOK 1

THE GARBAGE MAN

Those slimy rat bastards were at it again. Shovels clinked outside Skeeter's bedroom window.

He clutched at his hair and pulled. "I'll rip their heads off."

Soil and stones scraping against metal rose above the erratic whir of his air conditioner. He struggled out of bed and plodded over to the window. Moonlight lit his back-yard and illuminated the outlines of two figures below. Pale ambience reflected off their rotted, gaunt faces. The male figure's black t-shirt and dark gray shorts camouflaged him within the darkness. The woman figure's blood-stained yellow dress stood out more clearly, and she swaggered as if drunk near the hole they were digging. Their sunken postures straightened when they saw him watching them.

They waved at him.

Arrogant bastards. He should have sawed their arms off when he had the chance. They were digging at an older gravesite, one that he had dug two years earlier.

It wasn't bad enough that the neighborhood kids rang his doorbell and ran away on a weekly basis, or stole his water hose, or strung toilet paper across the enormous oak tree in his front yard. But now even his nosy neighbors, Marcus Dipshit and his wife, Mrs. Supreme Leader Dipshit, regularly poked their wide-eyed, sun-browned faces over his fence to feed their insatiable curiosity regarding the nighttime antics in his backyard.

He needed over two hours of sleep. His head ached, and his vision shifted in and out of focus.

The woman in the yard below, Marlene had been her name, stood beside a mound of dirt at the edge of the unearthed grave and turned her smug face up at him. With a large, sweeping gesture she waved for him to come out and join them.

"You'd like that, wouldn't you? I'll pound your bones back to hell." Skeeter's breath fogged the window as he spoke.

Marlene's ratty hair shifted over her face as she swayed. It flowed over her cheeks and down to her shoulders. Even within the dim light, her grin beamed. The wench brushed her hair playfully and blew a kiss.

Skeeter's stomach churned. He'd take one of those shovels and lop her head off with it.

He slipped on a pair of pants, but left his upper half bare. The summer heat and the struggle to get the two back into their holes would have him sweating like a pig in no time. The digital clock next to his bed read 2:44.

He had struggled with them for over an hour the previous night and then filling the holes back in had pushed him to the brink of exhaustion. The damn arthritis in his hands and the pain in his back hadn't subsided after flaring up following the previous night's ordeal. Good thing it was Saturday or he would need to call in sick at work.

Skeeter lumbered down the stairs to the kitchen and crossed over to the garage door. The dirt from the previous night's ordeal still streaked across his floor. Another mess to clean up. Add it to the list.

On his way into the garage he remembered that his ax's handle had broken while struggling with a different set of the devil's demons. The large fat one had given him the most resistance. Skeeter had plowed the ax deep into the fat man's chest only to have the handle snap off when he yanked it back. Waste of a good thirty dollar ax. It had made little difference anyway, as the fat man continued the struggle without pausing. Skeeter had ended the problem by slicing off his head with a shovel.

A shotgun blast would do the trick in a heartbeat, but the neighbors would call the police in a heartbeat. Difficult to keep the evil insurrection down without a lot of noise. If it wasn't for his neighbors, he could blast away all he wanted. Problem solved.

Skeeter surveyed the inventory of his tools to consider the best plan of action. He had chains, shovels, a garden hoe, a rake, and a pile of bricks he'd intended to use to construct a more permanent disposal pit for the bodies. One shovel would do, as it had the previous night. Bits of rotted flesh still clung to the blade's edge.

*Note to self: Clean that shit off.*

Skeeter grabbed the shovel and stormed outside to the backyard.

The fence along his property's edge rose to eye level. It had been the highest fence he could find. Back then, he hadn't foreseen it being a problem.

The neighbor's bedroom light was on.

"Damn nosey neighbors," he grumbled.

He'd rip out that fence and build a new wall ten feet

high. Made of brick. With spikes and barbed wire along the top edge.

Skeeter swung the shovel like a baseball bat as the male figure came into focus ahead. The man's name had been Alan, one of the church members from across town. Skeeter had caught Alan and Marlene in the park fornicating. Skeeter had put an end to that shit. Never mind they were engaged. The park was only a hundred yards from the church. They might as well have been fornicating right in the holy sanctuary itself.

Alan stood waist deep within the hole he'd dug and continued scooping out shovelfuls of dirt even as Skeeter approached. The bastard had the same smart ass smug grin as the night he'd killed him. Skeeter's face warmed.

Marlene was a few feet away to the right, and she waved at Skeeter as if they were friends. Her jaw hung open as if to scream out in terror, but no sound came out of her throat. Skeeter wanted to chop her apart first, but Alan was closer and most likely stronger.

"You won't get to her," Skeeter said to them.

Alan and Marlene paid no attention.

Skeeter had buried the young woman, and everyone else, at least a few feet under. No chance of discovery—unless some asshole went digging in the right place. He'd long forgotten the woman's name. Tina? Tanya? What the hell did it matter? Skeeter's judgment had been just and righteous, and she had gotten what she deserved.

He was doing the town a favor. That's all there was to it. Cleaning up the trash and making the world a better place. Just disposing of all the disgusting filth in the community and doing the service for *free* at the same time. Nobody appreciated his work now, but they would in the future. They'd erect a statue to Skeeter in the center of town one day. Children would grow up praising his name for what he'd done for them.

The community was a better place now without filth like Marlene, Alan and... (Tracy?) creeping around the park at night and committing lewd acts in every corner like a sleazy brothel. The town could be made wholesome again. A family community with no room for immorality, just as it had been for him growing up, and he was chosen to uphold that morality, even if no one else was strong enough. Chosen by the family business he'd inherited.

He was the town's garbageman, after all. Just doing his job. All in a day's work. He'd taken care of the trash. Taken it out and buried it.

But now it came back.

Skeeter rotated his shovel so the blade would slice across when he swung. He was too furious to bother creeping up on them, and besides Marlene had already seen him. He timed it so that Alan's shovel was down in the hole before he swung. Skeeter grunted as he swung, aiming toward the neck.

Alan's shovel shot up from the hole at the last second. Metal clinked and a jolt of vibration raced up Skeeter's arms. Alan had not only stopped his own decapitation, but Skeeter's shovel flew from his sweaty palms and spun off to the opposite side of the grave.

Skeeter ground his teeth. "You piece of shit."

He drew back for a moment, and then a raging fury flooded his mind. He charged forward and dropped to his knees, clutching Alan around the neck. Skeeter would pop Alan's skull from his spine like popping the head from a dandelion with his thumb.

Alan dropped his shovel and grabbed onto Skeeter's wrists. Alan's leathery rotting flesh scratched across

Skeeter's skin and he winced as Alan clamped down harder.

Skeeter sneered and dug his thumbs into Alan's throat. The windpipe collapsed. He pushed harder, straight through the icy strands of rotted muscles to Alan's spinal cord. A few more seconds and it'd be over.

"Hold still," Skeeter said. "Almost finished with you."

One vertebra cracked. Skeeter strained and shook within his rage. Sweat dripped down his forehead. His left hand pulled Alan's neck down and his right hand stretched it up. One of Alan's neck muscles tore and snapped apart. Then another.

A metal object smashed against the side of Skeeter's head. A flash of light as pain exploded in his skull. He toppled over and wobbled at the edge of the grave.

Marlene's shovel rose again and came down hard against his thigh. Pain surged up his spine. Skeeter twisted himself around and the shovel slammed down against the back of his right calf. He didn't stop, and within his daze Marlene grabbed at his legs. She yanked him closer to the grave, but he threw up his aching leg and kicked into the darkness. The sole of his boot slammed into her chest, and she tumbled backwards beyond his sight.

Skeeter grabbed at the clumps of grass and dirt that surrounded him and gasped for breath as he turned himself over and rolled onto his chest. His pulse pounded in his ears as he staggered to his feet. Before he could take his first step a hand clutched at his ankle and he almost fell forward onto his face again. He looked back. Alan was using Skeeter's ankle to tow himself out of the hole.

Skeeter's boot loosened as he struggled to get away. He looked around for anything he might use as a weapon. Nothing.

"Son of a bitch." Skeeter thrashed his foot until he knocked Alan away and scrambled to stand again.

There had to be something in his garage to deal with the problem. Something better than a shovel. Something to send them back to hell once and for all. But without resorting to a shotgun, he didn't have many options. He took in a lungful of air and hurried back to the house.

On his way in through the garage, he grabbed the last shovel and brought it with him into the kitchen in case he needed it. In the morning he'd run to the store and purchase a shitload of axes to chop up those yard bastards. Or maybe something better.

A wood chipper. He'd buy one tomorrow. Why hadn't he thought of it sooner? That'd put the uprising to a rest. The idea perked up his mind, but his body slouched forward. The stores wouldn't open for several more hours.

He flipped on the kitchen light and his eyes narrowed as he searched the counters for any large knives. He found one butcher's knife in a drawer and grabbed it. Next, he walked to his kitchen pantry and dug out two pistols, a rifle, and a shotgun, and scooped up a handful of rounds. He gathered everything, shovel and all, and carried the weapons to his bedroom upstairs.

He dropped everything at the end of his bed. Something clanked outside, and he hurried to the window. Alan and Marlene had continued digging within the grave they had started earlier. Marlene looked up at him, but this time she didn't wave. This time she pointed down into the open grave.

"I'll chop you up into little bite-size pieces," Skeeter said. "That wood chipper will do the trick. And after that's done, I'll dump a few bags of wet cement over you. Squirm your slimy way out of that."

Skeeter went to load his guns just in case he needed to use them, but only as a last resort. One shot and his neighbors wouldn't hesitate to call the cops. A few minutes later he'd have a bigger problem on his hands with the current state of his backyard. It'd be all over. He wouldn't have the time or the strength to fill in the graves before they arrived. Guns were the nuclear option.

He had a right to defend himself against attackers, especially demonic attackers from the bowels of hell, but he doubted a judge would express sympathy in his case.

*"We counted seventeen bodies in your backyard, Mr. Larsten," the judge would say. "How do you explain that?"*

*"I didn't know they were there, Your Honor."*

*"Some of them were freshly dug. You weren't aware of anyone burying corpses in your fenced backyard?"*

*"No, Your Honor, honestly. I never saw a thing."*

*"Some of them were riddled with bullet holes matching guns found in your home. How do you explain that?"*

*"Circumstantial evidence, Your Honor."*

Not good.

As he finished loading his last gun, someone pounded on the back door downstairs. He stopped for a moment and listened. They couldn't get in—except for the garage door. All the entrances and windows were well boarded up with large sheets of plywood to seal himself in. If he wanted to see sunlight, he'd go upstairs and look out his bedroom window.

He'd boarded everything up a few days ago, after seeing the undead digging around in his backyard at night. At first the figures had only stood next to their holes after digging themselves out, and for him to kick them back into their graves had been easy, but now somehow they had found shovels and had dug out the others. The previous night three of them had climbed out and stood watching his bedroom window, swaying in the cool spring breeze.

"Go back to hell!" He yelled from behind the glass. He wanted to scream it from the open window, except for the neighbors. They were past the point of tolerance with him and were itching to make that last call that would send a swarm of officers to investigate his property.

The phone rang. The Caller ID read 'Unknown Number' and he hesitated to answer it. It rang again. He picked it up. Probably his neighbor to complain about the noise.

"What?" he grumbled.

A woman's voice gurgled and croaked back at him. He remembered her name now. It was Twyla. She had made the same noises years earlier when he had wrung the life out of her in the park. Skeeter had caught her one night with a man who was not her husband. The garbage man would take that trash out of town. Bury it a little closer to its home in hell.

"Into the fires of hell, Twyla! Meet your judgment!" He ended the phone call, but it continued to ring over and over. He powered it off, stopping it in mid-ring. He wiped the sweat from his brow and went to the thermostat in the hallway to crank up the air conditioning.

Despite the figures staring at him, he snapped the blinds shut and collapsed onto his bed, gripping his shotgun over his chest. The lack of sleep was catching up to him. His eyes dropped shut and his mind wandered even as the work of the devil's angels continued in his backyard. If they were still there in the morning, he'd deal with it then. He closed his eyes.

~

SKEETER FADED BACK TO CONSCIOUSNESS AS SOMETHING thumped against the side of the house. According to the clock next to his bed, only forty-three minutes had passed. Skeeter trudged over to the window again and opened the blind. Impossible to think they could climb up the sides of the house to the second floor. But since the bastards had discovered shovels, maybe they would also find the ladder in his garage. Had they broken in there? He strained to see anything near the house below his line of sight. Only darkness.

Alan and Marlene were still at it. Alan flung the dirt to the side as the trench below him deepened. It wouldn't take him long now to reach the corpse within it.

Skeeter regretted not burying them all deeper.

*Note to self: Pour cement in the holes next time before covering them over.*

Hell, he'd pound a wooden stake through their damned hearts, sever their heads, and shove a dozen crucifixes down their throats if he got the chance to do it over, and then he'd still pour a foot of cement on top for good measure.

He'd survived two tours in the Vietnam war, attacked by some of the most savage and skilled fighters in the Viet Cong's army, and he'd survived their worst. The last mortar attack had blown through his left knee, shortening that leg by two full inches after the doctors had patched him back together. He'd seen hell, an actual hell, and was ready for those demons outside his house like a tank was ready to battle monkeys with sticks.

Alan stared up at Skeeter's bedroom window as he

stood chest deep in the hole. His mouth gaped open as if to call out.

Skeeter raised his middle finger at them before snapping the blinds shut. He returned to bed listening to Alan's shovel slicing into the soil followed by a thud of dirt dropping next to the grave.

They couldn't get at him, but he didn't take any chances. The weapons he'd carried upstairs would be enough in case the worst happened. On top of that, he stocked his basement with plenty of dried food and water, in case of emergencies.

He closed his eyes in bed until the shoveling ended.

Everything became silent. A ringing in his ears intensified for several minutes before he got up and shuffled to the window. Alan and Marlene were gone, and the gravesites sat wide open. Three in all now.

The doorbell rang and Skeeter shuddered. He clenched his teeth and squeezed the barrel of the shotgun as he lurched toward the door, grabbing the shovel with his other hand. The shovel wasn't the most effective weapon, but it worked well enough for now if he wanted to keep things quiet. He charged downstairs, dropped the shovel to the ground, and stood behind the front door with the barrel of the shotgun aimed waist high at whoever stood on the other side.

The doorbell rang again. Someone pounded on the door.

"Skeeter!"

It was the muffled voice of Mr. Dipshit himself.

"What the hell are you doing? It's 4 AM."

Skeeter lowered the shotgun. "Get the hell off my property!"

"I'll have the cops out here if you don't quiet down,"

King Marcus Dipshit yelled. "What the hell are you doing in the backyard?"

"None of your goddamn business."

"I'll have the cops out here."

The neighbor's footsteps squeaked away across the porch. A moment later someone pounded on the back door. Marcus couldn't have gotten around to the back that fast. And the gate was locked. Alan and Marlene, no doubt.

Skeeter lifted his shotgun again and rushed to the back of the house with wide eyes. He left the lights off, although a hallway light from upstairs spilled down the stairway. He approached the back door with the shotgun held up at chest level.

Something crashed in his basement. He'd boarded up those windows too, although not as well as the larger main floor windows. If they'd somehow gotten in the basement, he was ready for them.

He might have to weed them out of his house like cockroaches. Maybe that was better, anyway. Less commotion to attract the ire of his neighbors.

If he could trap them all in one room, he had a better chance of handling the mess at the same time. The basement would be the best place. Lots of room down there to defend himself and lots of light. In addition, his neighbors might not hear the shotgun blasts over at their house, since the only window to the basement faced away from them. That might be the way to go. The more he thought about it, the more he liked it.

He approached the back door and watched the door handle turn as he steadied the shotgun. If he fired through the door, he might miss and one shot alone might prompt his neighbor to live up to his threat of calling the police.

Something thumped against the door. The walls creaked.

"I know your game," Skeeter said. They were trying to distract him at the back door while someone came in through the basement.

He hurried back over to the front door, picked up the shovel where he'd left it, then headed for the basement. The head of the shovel clanked against the edge of the doorway going down to the basement. He flipped on the light and expected one of them to be waiting for him at the bottom of the stairs, but he was alone. Each footstep creaked as he descended with the shotgun up and ready.

"Yeah, we'll solve this problem right now."

He crept all the way to the bottom of the stairs when the lights cut out. His heart raced and in the darkness something scraped across the tiled floor.

A hoarse gurgling filled the air. Twyla was down there with him. The sounds shifted closer, but he couldn't tell from where.

He stumbled backwards and raced up the stairs.

At the top step he paused and set down the shovel, leaning it against the wall. He fumbled for the emergency flashlight he kept hanging on a nail above the light switch. He gasped for breath when he found it and switched it on.

Twyla was at the bottom of the stairs, staring up at him with sunken, bug-infested eyes. She drifted and straightened her back. Dirt matted her hair against her face and rotting flesh scraped along the railing as she stepped up the stairs toward him.

Her purple and white dress brought back memories of the night he'd killed her. Her cries for mercy on that Judgment Day. He showed no mercy. No room for mercy in the garbage man's judgement.

"Judge... you," Twyla said in a wet, gurgled tone.

"I'm blameless, honey," Skeeter blurted out. "You're the skank who cheated on your husband."

Twyla had been a young woman from his church. The night he killed her and her partner in the affair, his rage had swelled inside his chest. He'd swung at them like the god Thor, striking each of them down with only one blow. He'd laughed while burying them with their lungs still gasping for breath. Strange that Twyla stood there alone. Skeeter scanned the room for her partner, but they were alone. Alan and Marlene must not have had time to dig out Twyla's fornicating friend.

Twyla took another step toward him. Skeeter set his shotgun down and picked up his shovel. She was a scrawny, short woman and he would send her back to hell. No need to make more noise than necessary. The shovel would do nicely.

He moved back down the stairs and lifted the shovel like a spear, holding the flashlight in the other hand. One straight crack to the head should do it.

The basement window caught his eye for a moment before he struck Twyla. He missed his target, and the shovel grazed off the edge of her skull.

He stopped himself within an arm's length of her. The putrid smell of decaying flesh wafted into his face. She reached out at him as he glanced over to the basement window. Someone had pulled away the sheet of plywood he had used to seal the window shut on one side and a man was crawling in—Twyla's fornicating partner.

The man's corpse plummeted and slammed onto a workbench below the window, crashing into an assortment of tools and failed home improvement projects. Skeeter had never discovered the name of Twyla's affair partner.

The man squirmed and climbed off the workbench and stood unsteadily before them.

Skeeter raised his shovel again, but before he could slice it through Twyla's neck, she batted it away and wrapped her fingers around his neck. She pushed forward, and he stopped breathing.

Twyla's partner rushed toward them, but Skeeter twisted around and broke free from Twyla's grasp.

He heaved in a deep breath and knocked away their hands. "You think I'm playing? You think this is a game?"

He stomped up the stairs to get his shotgun. No more playing around. He would get the job done.

Halfway up the stairs his foot slipped and his knee slammed against the edge of a step.

"Shit!" he yelled.

He stumbled and grabbed the railing as footsteps stomped up behind him.

One of them gripped his pant leg and pulled.

Skeeter jabbed the end of the shovel backwards, knocking into one of them. A low growl erupted from the man's throat as Skeeter moved freely until they latched onto the shovel handle. They ripped it away from him, but it didn't matter, anyway. He was only feet from the shotgun. He lunged forward and grabbed it.

Skeeter spun around with the shotgun in his hand and blasted off three shots in rapid succession. Hell with the neighbors.

He fumbled with the flashlight during the blasts, witnessing the upper half of their bodies explode. The first two shots disintegrated the man and the third one took down Twyla. Their mangled corpses tumbled back down the stairs.

Skeeter's ears rang. "Evil, evil, evil." He fired a fourth

shot at them, but his shotgun clicked empty. All his ammo was up in his bedroom.

He lumbered up the stairs into the kitchen. The back door was still sealed shut. The eerie quiet of his house without power sank in on him. He shined the flashlight at each window. No sign of forced entry.

He trudged upstairs, his body weakening with each step. His legs were on fire by the time he got to the top. He caught his breath and steadied himself against the wall.

"The garbage man's got a job to do," he said, trudging into his bedroom.

He took inventory of the remaining firearms and boxes of rounds on his bed.

Something thumped against the wall below his bedroom window.

"Son of a bitch."

Skeeter's head ached as he squinted toward the closed blinds. The bastards couldn't climb the side of his house, so what the hell was out there?

He plodded to the window again, opened the blinds and Marlene's gaunt face met his eyes. She smashed her arm in through the glass, with shards spraying over his face and bare chest. Blood dripped down his face within seconds and he stumbled backwards.

Before he could defend himself, her torso folded in over the top of the windowsill. He retrieved his revolver from the edge of the bed and fired at her, knowing full well that Mr. Dipshit would either call the police or come stomping over to his front door in minutes. The rounds passed through her face and neck. Black ooze drained from the holes.

"Evil woman," he shouted.

She clawed at him without hesitation. "My turn," she said in a low, growling voice.

"Get back in your hole!" He fired the revolver's remaining rounds until it emptied and dropped it to the floor. He grabbed a metal trophy next to his window he'd received as a child for demonstrating exemplary Christian behavior in Sunday school and slammed it into Marlene's face.

It cracked into her skull, collapsing it, leaving one eye and her nose distorted sideways. More black ooze erupted from her nose and mouth and ran down her dress. Some of it splattered over his face and pooled on his forehead. It dripped down between his eyebrows. He wiped it away with the back of his wrist, which only smeared it into his eyes.

Alan appeared beside Marlene and each of them clutched one of Skeeter's arms. Heaving together, they dragged him toward the window. He struggled, but he was too exhausted to resist. He writhed and weakened until they yanked him head-first out into the chilly morning air.

Glass shards along the edges of the window sliced through his body on the way out. The pain shot through him like a blow torch, lit up against his ribcage and spread up across the side of his face. Warm blood soaked down his pants as they lowered him along the side of the house by his feet, his arms flailing below. They didn't let him drop to the ground where he would certainly have broken his neck.

When his fingers touched the ground he clawed at the grass. More hands waited to clutch onto him from below. He recognized some of them in the moonlight. All of them faces of filthy, evil garbage.

"You are all disgusting," he shrieked.

As they dragged him toward one of the open pits, more figures joined the growing crowd around him, and they spun him around so he faced them. They stretched his limbs in all directions over one of the graves.

In one final coordinated effort they released him face up into the pit. He crashed to the bottom. Loose dirt splashed down onto his face, slipping into his nose and his mouth. The chunks of soil and stones pounded against his chest as he struggled to stand up. His lower body sank below the dirt and then his chest. His fingers clawed against the walls of the pit, scratching through worms and plant roots.

A red and orange flashing light gradually lit up the figures above him. Skeeter's eyes widened, and he grinned. His nosy neighbor had finally called the police.

He laughed. "They'll be here in minutes! You're too late. I win!"

His chest filled with exhilaration, knowing that the garbage towering over him would never have their victory.

The dirt piled in. It was up to his chin within a minute, but he only laughed louder.

"Only one way to get rid of garbage," Marlene gurgled. "The incinerator."

He laughed until the heat rose up from below. The orange and red lights from above mirrored the flickering flames from below. His feet and legs burned. The pain grew more intense and spread up his body.

Claws scratched up and down his backside. Rats? His heart pounded as one claw dug into the center of his back and clutched his spine.

His captors dragged him further into the pit. He sank, drowning in the incinerator until it consumed him.

# THE ONE

We were hoping to meet a few fun-loving honeys at the bar, but we met David instead. He was dressed up like a modern-day mobster—something you'd see on one of those TV shows for cops—with slicked-back hair and a stoic gaze that chilled your blood. A fancy black leather jacket covered a gray shirt with some top-of-the-line jeans to catch a girl's eye. The guy had all the looks we would have killed for.

He was there when we arrived, slipping in between two hotties like a knife through butter. One was a blonde chick with a short black skirt and a tight white t-shirt that revealed a piercing in her navel. The other girl had tanned skin and long brown hair pulled together in the back. She wore tight jeans and a red low-cropped shirt that revealed a little cleavage. Neither of the girls seemed to mind as David caressed them openly.

Only ten minutes after we arrived, he swaggered over to us, extending his leather jacket to no one in particular. "Would you be so kind as to watch my jacket while I play a game of pool with these young ladies?"

We all stared at the jacket like it was covered in dog shit. It tempted me to tell him to go fuck himself. Did I look like a coat closet? But he caught me off-guard. Something about his eyes stunned me, and those two chicks were eyeing me up too.

"Yeah." I accepted his jacket and hung it off the back of my barstool.

David strolled back over to his business at the pool table.

"The hell with that guy." Butch glanced at the jacket. "Check the pockets."

Luis laughed and sipped his beer.

I shot a glance toward the pool table. David wasn't paying any attention to us. "You want to get killed? That guy's got to be packing heat."

"Pussy," Butch said.

I expected Butch or Luis to dig into the jacket's pockets, but they left it alone too.

Butch made a crude gesture while detailing his fanta-sized intentions for the girls after getting them into his bed later that evening. Not a chance in hell that would happen. Butch smelled like he hadn't taken a shower in a week. In reality, it was probably more like two.

Within seconds of returning to the pool table, David was showing the two girls how to play the game. We had nothing better to do, so we hung around and watched the master hit on the girls. It was a work of art, actually, the way David ran his fingers along their shoulders and arms as they lined up the pool cue. They soaked it all up, every slick move he dished out to them. A lot of gentle touches with only a quick glance every so often. Most of the time he ignored them. Within minutes they nuzzled up next to him, both of them almost fighting to be the center of his attention.

He sure had the right attitude, and a smile loaded with bright white teeth. Something straight off the cover of a GQ magazine. He strutted around the table before every shot, I guess to see which chick could catch up to him the fastest. After each perfect shot he stood up straight, leaning against the pool cue, with a tall, confident posture.

He shot us a devious grin every once in a while as he worked his magic on the girls. He had to know we were staring. How could we *not* stare? After a while he even maneuvered one girl around, leaning her over the table's edge during one shot so her ass stuck out in our direction. God bless him. Didn't block our view or anything. He must have figured we were losers and wanted to share in the spoils of his conquest. Fine with us. Much appreciated.

We'd gotten there late, so before long the bartender yelled it was closing time and flipped on the lights. The harsh glare blinded me for a moment, but soon enough the reality of our situation hit me. Three losers going home alone again without girls.

David threw his arms around the girls and looked over at us. The girls cuddled up at his sides.

I finished my drink and tried to stand tall, but we couldn't hide our situation. We were going home empty-handed.

None of this shit would have happened if we'd just taken off then. But Butch locked his gaze on the blonde girl and insisted on waiting until she left.

The tanned girl locked eyes with me and smiled. My heart melted. I just about fell off that bar stool—no joke. She walked over to me and I lost my breath as she reached her hand around my back. She smelled like a dozen roses.

"Excuse me." She moved in a little closer. "I need to get his jacket." She tugged on David's jacket.

"Sorry." I leaned forward to free it from my stool.

"What's your name?" she asked.

"Jacob."

"I'm Emily. You up for a party? We're heading out now."

David cozied up to the blonde girl near the pool table. Emily leaned in, rubbing her thigh against my knee.

She was way out of my league, and the last thing I needed was that gangster dude beating me down for messing with his girl. "Maybe some other time."

Emily pouted. "Aw, you don't like me?" Her green eyes never looked away.

"You're beautiful, but—" I glanced back to David.

She laughed. "Don't mind him. I'm not his girlfriend."

I glanced over to Butch and Luis. They nodded with wide eyes.

Emily stroked her fingers across my cheek, pulling my attention back to her. "We should get to know each other. You're cute."

David strolled over a moment later and claimed his jacket from Emily. Instead of putting it on, he swept it over his shoulder. The blonde girl nuzzled up to him. "Thanks for watching my jacket," he said. "You boys up for a party? My name's David."

Butch shrugged without smiling. "Maybe."

David grinned at me. "I see you've met Emily. Don't worry, she's not attached to me." He gestured to the blonde girl. "This is Zoey. She's unattached as well."

"Cool," Butch said.

He shook our hands. Tight grip. I winced until he let

go, and he smirked as if he got a kick out of my reaction. That guy's grasp could have ripped my arm off if he sneezed.

"We're heading to my girlfriend's place," David said. "You'll all get laid. Guaranteed."

Emily elbowed David in his side, her gaze still locked on me.

Butch scanned Zoey's dress. Luis glanced at me.

The blonde girl whispered into David's ear, pulling him down toward her. The edge of his shirt stretched open to reveal a tattoo on his neck, a design that reminded me of the devil. A serpentine red arm snaked up from the collar of his shirt, holding a pitchfork capped with three sharp prongs. A single word stretched out below the image, but I didn't get close enough to read it.

"How far?" I asked.

"Not far," David said. "Ten, fifteen minutes."

"You got beer?" Butch asked.

"We've got everything," David said. "Follow me."

We followed David to the exit. Emily walked beside me in silence all the way to our car before we split off to our separate cars.

"See you there, Jacob." Emily glanced back as she walked away.

Butch and Luis ordered me to drive, probably because they thought I wasn't as drunk as they were. We climbed into our rusting hulk of a car and followed David's white Lexus.

Emily and Zoey climbed into a red Toyota RAV4 and took off in a different direction.

"Where the fuck are they going?" Butch said from the back seat. "Follow them!"

I looked at Luis. He pointed toward David's car.

"Follow the dude," Luis said. "Maybe they're stopping to pick up their friends. Two babes aren't enough to go around, anyway."

"See you later, Jacob," Luis mocked.

"You're jealous," I said.

"Damn right."

"You see Zoey looking at me?" Butch asked. "She wants me."

"Dude, she was looking at *me*, not you."

"Jacob, back me up here. You saw her staring at me, right?"

"I wasn't paying attention."

"Right. That Emily chick was hot for you. Lucky man."

Luis held his palm up for a high five. I slapped it.

"She's The One, Jacob." Luis nodded. "I can tell. You guys had chemistry."

"We'll see." I focused on the road.

We headed around through the winding city streets until turning into a dark residential area a few miles from the bar. Nothing special about the neighborhood. Not the mansions we'd expected from David's appearance, but not a slum either. Just your ordinary suburban row of working-class homes.

As we turned down one long stretch of houses, Luis reached down to the floor between his feet and pulled up a baseball bat. He brought his bat everywhere.

"Slow down." He gestured to a mailbox at the side of the road. The little red flag at the side of the box was up. "There."

I knew what to do. I slowed the car down and came up alongside it. Luis leaned out and swung. The bat cracked against the metal mailbox and the little door flew open, spewing letters of blood.

"Bullseye!" Luis yelled as he sat back in his seat.

"Ready for the big leagues!" Butch patted him on the shoulder.

"I've trained for this all my life."

With the windows down and the stereo pumping out rock tunes, we turned onto a barren street and into an area of the city I didn't recognize.

"He better not bring us to some shit hole," Butch said. "We can hang out at Luis's apartment for that."

"Fuck off. Don't come over anymore if you don't like it."

"You never bring home any girls."

"Says Mr. Casanova, alone in the backseat."

As we drove further, the quality of the houses improved. Maybe it wouldn't be so bad after all. I couldn't read the street names since I guess I'd had one too many at the bar. At that point, it didn't even matter where we were because my mind floated back to Emily.

"What the hell's this dude's name again?" Luis asked. "Dan?"

For a moment I forgot the guy's name, then I remembered. "David."

"Better be some hot chicks," he said.

"And beer," Butch said.

"You'll get laid tonight for sure," Luis said to Butch in the backseat. "I can't believe you're twenty-one and still a virgin."

"It won't be a problem," he answered. "I'll make her scream."

"She'll scream, all right, as she runs away!"

"Fuck you."

David pulled his car over a few blocks down the road. I pulled up behind him. The walkways and streets around those houses in that neighborhood were well lit. A massive rock waterfall sat behind the beaming sign out front. Terrace Gardens Homes. Decked out landscaping everywhere, with a row of red and white flowers bordering the property. If that swanky neighborhood was any sign of the quality of the girls who lived there, we were in for one hell of a good night.

We all climbed out and stood beside the car, waiting for David to come over. He sat there in the driver's seat for a few minutes with the lights on. Making some calls, no doubt, to round up more hotties. He emerged wearing sunglasses. How the hell he saw anything with those sunglasses on in the dark, I have no idea.

"You boys are in for a treat," David said. "This will be a night to remember." He lit a cigarette and dangled it from his lips as he swaggered past us toward the front steps.

David paused at the front door as he flipped through the keys on his key chain. The first key didn't work. Or the second key. Or the third.

"Damn, it's here somewhere," David said. He tried to open the door without a key and it creaked open. He chuckled as he slipped his keys back into his jacket pocket. "Forgot to lock it."

David opened the door slowly, peeking through the crack for a moment before walking in.

"Hey there," he called out, glancing around the house without flipping on the lights. "You home, sweetheart?"

An overwhelming smell of roses filled the air. David flipped on the lights. No flowers anywhere. Must have been scented candles or something.

Paintings of flowers and risque portraits of an attractive red-haired woman hung on the walls. The living room furniture looked clean and new and perfectly coordinated colors filled the room. It looked like one of those model showrooms in a furniture store. They lined the mantel over the fireplace with crystal vases, and everything looked as if they'd designed it to fit in that exact space. Everything was super clean and nothing was out of place, except for our three sorry asses.

David turned to us. "You guys just hang out here," he said. "I'll be back in a minute with the girls. This is my girlfriend's place. Stay out of the bedrooms, though. Don't go snooping. Cool? Hang tight. Chill. Watch some TV. There are beers in the fridge, but I'll get more. Don't you worry."

David slipped past us out the door and he was gone. We stood there looking at each other for an awkward moment until Butch hurried over to the fridge. Luis dropped into the living room couch and turned on the TV.

"Fuck yeah!" Butch said from the kitchen. He held up a bottle of vodka. "No shortage of booze." He poured some in three glasses, mixed it with some orange juice and handed one to me. "He said to chill, so chill."

Butch carried the other two glasses over to the living room and collapsed next to Luis. I sat on a different section of the couch. Luis flipped through the TV channels, stopping on one of those adult channels that only teased the viewers.

WITHIN HALF AN HOUR BUTCH AND LUIS HAD FINISHED their vodka drinks and several beers. I grabbed the last beer and claimed my space in front of the TV, which the others had abandoned.

Luis stared out the living room window toward the street. "What the fuck is taking him so long?"

The portraits of the redhead around the room fixated Butch as if he was in a trance. "Look at those tits. Just perfect."

I went over to get a better look. The girl in the pictures was beautiful, as if a professional had taken the portraits. A model? Just the type of girl who'd fawn over a slick stud like David. Maybe the man himself had taken the photos.

"Very nice." I stepped sideways to view every one of them.

"Nice?" Butch focused on one photo of the girl in a bikini. "She's hot. Beyond hot. She's gorgeous. I'd lay my face right in there and..." Butch shook his head, while making growling sounds.

"Maybe you'll get your chance," I said.

Butch stared at me and wavered with a wide grin on his face. "That David guy better get his ass back here. I'm ready to party *now*!"

Butch staggered away while I checked out the other pictures around the room. He went down the hall and started opening all the doors. I assumed he was looking for the bathroom.

"Hey, dumb shit," I said, "the dude told you to stay out of the bedrooms."

"Fuck that," Butch said. "I'm going to snoop through his shit. Serves him right for leaving us here alone for almost an hour."

"Definitely a chick's pad." Luis munched on a bag of

snack chips in the kitchen. "No guy would ever keep it this clean."

Butch opened the last door at the end of the hallway and his mouth dropped open. "What the fuck?"

"What is it?" Luis asked.

"Get the fuck over here!"

Luis and I hurried over to see what Butch was staring at. I rolled my eyes on the way over, thinking Butch was setting us up for a massive prank. He was a dick like that, so when I got to his side and looked into the room I braced myself for his wild laughter.

But he wasn't joking. My mouth dropped open too. A naked girl was lying on the bed with her hands and feet tied with duct tape to the headboard and footboard. Her mouth was also duct-taped shut and her hair was a mess. The same red-haired girl from the portraits over the walls. Some sheets lay in a heap on the floor, surrounded by stuff you might find on a nightstand. The clock and lamp were smashed as if someone had thrown them there. The girl's eyes were closed, and she wasn't moving at all.

"What the fuck is going on here?" Luis asked.

"Is she dead?" Butch leaned forward.

Her chest rose and fell in shallow waves. "She's breathing."

"Let's get the fuck out of here," I said.

Butch crept toward the girl. "Hey."

No response.

He spoke louder. "Hey!" He reached out and touched the girl's leg.

"Come on," I said. "She must be passed out. Let's go."

"Hold on," Butch said. "Look at those glorious tits." He reached out and touched the girl's breasts.

"Dude, I don't want anything to do with this," I said.

"You want a feel?" he asked us. He cupped his hands around the bottom and squeezed.

"No, Butch," Luis said. "Stop. I think someone raped her. Maybe that David guy."

Butch stopped and gazed at her face.

The girl's eyes opened wide. She stared at Butch, then over to Luis, then at me. Her eyes opened wider as she let out a muffled scream beneath the tape over her mouth. Her eyes were bloodshot, and she squirmed, kicking and pulling against the restraints on her limbs. The tape covering her mouth slid back and forth as she contorted her face to remove it. The whole bed shook just like one of those demon possession scenes in The Exorcist. Butch stumbled backwards.

"We got to go." I nudged Luis toward the door.

Butch stared at her and folded his arms over his chest. "Stop wiggling around."

Luis rushed forward and pulled on Butch's shirt. "Come on."

Butch twisted away and continued to stare. "You don't see stuff like this every day, Luis. Isn't she beautiful? Jacob, get your ass over here."

"No way," I said. "Let's just go now."

Luis pulled on Butch's arm again and this time got Butch out of the room. We left the door wide open and headed for the front door.

"Wait." Luis stopped me as I opened the door. "Fuckin' stop."

"What?" I asked, still holding the door handle.

Luis stepped forward and shut the door. "Listen. I have a bad feeling about all this. Someone obviously raped her. I think this is a setup. That David fucking guy isn't coming back. I can see that now. And thanks to doofus here," Luis gestured to Butch, "she not only saw our faces, but she knows our names. That David guy knew we'd go snooping, and he knew we'd find her. It's a setup."

"We didn't do that shit to her," Butch said.

"I know that, but she woke up with you groping her, dumbass. What is she going to think? That David guy must have drugged her and set us up."

"Fuck, Butch," I said, running my fingers through my hair, "why did you go in there?"

"I was just looking around," Butch said. "It's not my fault. *I* didn't fucking rape her."

"Well," Luis said, "she stared right at each of us. She can ID us. Guaranteed."

"Butch, you're a fucking idiot," I said.

Butch grabbed the front of my shirt and clenched his teeth, pushing me back into the door. "Shut the fuck up."

His eyes and face were red, and I turned my head away to avoid breathing in the warm stench of his beer breath.

Butch shoved me again. "You're the asshole who started talking to that David piece of shit loser. *You* got us into this mess."

"What the hell, guys," Luis said, staring at the floor, folding his hands on top of his head. "What are we going to do?"

Butch pushed me aside, went to the kitchen and started opening drawers.

I found the door handle behind me again. "Let's just go."

"Nobody's going anywhere," Butch said. "I know what to do."

"What are you talking about?" Luis asked.

I opened the door, and Butch came over grasping a large butcher's knife.

"Where are you going?" He slammed the door closed again.

He grabbed my shirt with his free hand and launched me across the floor. My right arm cracked down first, and a sharp pain shot through my back. I caught my breath. Butch loomed over me, brandishing the knife.

"Don't even think of running out on us, you little pussy." Butch slammed his foot down on my chest. He pinned me to the floor for a moment while I gasped for air. "Should I tie you up like that girl?"

I shook my head. "Damn, chill out."

"I'll solve this problem. Got it? I'm not going to prison over this shit."

"Wait," Luis said, "what are you planning to do?"

"Solve the problem." Butch swung the knife in Luis's face.

"You can't kill her."

"Why not? She can ID us now." Butch heaved in and out with each breath.

"Let's think about this."

"You got a better idea?"

"No," Luis said.

"Dead men tell no tales," Butch said, lifting his foot off my chest. "Or dead women."

Butch walked down the hall toward the girl in the bedroom.

I struggled to stand and Luis helped me to my feet. "We got to stop him."

Luis bit his nails. "I got a friend I can call. Come in here and wipe the place clean."

"Dude, we're not murderers. Butch is out of control."

"*I'm* not murdering anyone." Luis was hunched forward, still biting his nails. "I guess it's the only way to get us out of this. He's covering our asses. What choice do we have?"

I put my hand on the cellphone in my pocket. "We can call 911."

Luis looked at me as if I'd suggested we French kiss. "Are you nuts? You don't seem to understand the situation we're in. Butch is right. This is *your* fault for schmoozing with some low-life asshole. I knew right away the guy was a dick."

I scanned the house, as if something miraculous would present a way out of the mess. The TV blared, showing a bunch of lifeguards scrambling into the ocean to save someone from drowning. A gorgeous redhead cried on the shore, comforted by some macho dude.

If I could only get Butch to wait until we came up with a better plan. But Butch never wasted time. He always ran with the first thing that popped into his mind. That attitude was loads of fun in a party setting, but now the party was over. I never wanted to drink another beer in my life. My heart thumped in my ears as everything around me became crystal clear.

I wanted to do something. The image of the girl in the bedroom squirming in terror at seeing us played over and over in my mind. Her muffled cries streamed through the hallway, and chills passed through my chest. I crossed my arms over my chest to keep my hands from shaking.

"We shouldn't do this," I said.

Luis slammed his fist into my arm. "Butch is right. You are a pussy." He crossed around in front of me and got in my face. "Are you going to keep your mouth shut?" Luis shivered and sneered.

"Butch doesn't have to kill her," I said. "There's got to be a better way."

"Not a peep from you." Luis dug his index finger into my chest. "Not another word. We won't ever talk about this again."

Butch was in the bedroom for a long time. Luis glanced at a large clock on the wall every few seconds. The TV show with the lifeguards ended. I leaned forward to turn it off, but Luis stopped me.

"Don't touch anything," he said.

Butch startled me when he came back out.

"Fucking done." He stared at the floor and scowled without looking up. He held the knife out in front of him and stared at it between squinting eyes. "Fucking done."

"Wash it off. Go to the bathtub and wash the blood off." Luis directed him to go back down the hallway. "I'll call my friend to wipe the place clean. We'll need to all chip in to pay him, but it's worth it."

Butch slapped his fist against my back as he turned to go back down the hallway to the bathroom. "You owe me."

"Wait a minute," Luis said. "Don't go in the bathroom. Don't wash it off. Wrap it up. We'll take it with us. We'll throw it in the lake or something. My friend will know what to do."

The bedroom door was wide open. I wanted to run in there and somehow save the girl. Call 911. Anything. But at the same time, I knew it was too late. A chill passed through my spine. I just wanted to run as far away as I could from that house.

"Let's get out of here," I said. "This is fucked up."

"You're in this with us." Butch jabbed his finger in the air toward me. "It's your fucking fault. You brought us here. You owe me big for getting us out of this bullshit."

Butch started wrapping the knife in a kitchen towel next to the stove when the front door swung open.

David stepped inside with Emily and Zoey hanging on his shoulders. Three more girls followed behind them dressed in black leather outfits. He walked in with a grin and locked the door behind himself.

David glanced to the girls. "I told you they wouldn't leave."

Emily dropped her hands away from David and winked at me.

"We've come back for you, gentlemen," David said. "Did you think we forgot about you?"

"You were gone a long time," Luis said. "We thought you might not come back."

"And yet you waited. Good for you." David glanced toward the kitchen. "I see you've made yourselves at home."

Butch stepped forward and unwrapped the knife. "Get away from the door."

David chuckled. "Did you use that on Cassandra? She's the woman in the back room tied to the bed. It appears that you have. What a shame."

"I'll use it on you if you don't get out of my way."

David was unfazed. He leaned in and glanced over at the three new girls. "They always surprise me. Something different happens every time. Sometimes they call the police, and sometimes they indulge themselves, and sometimes they run. Different every time. What should be their punishment for killing Cassandra?"

All five women laughed and approached us. "Drain their blood."

"Excellent idea." David looked at us. "We've judged you guilty for the death of Cassandra, and since you've spilled her blood, we have no choice but to avenge her death. Let the party begin! Who's first?"

"Get out of my way." Butch lurched forward toward the door.

Zoey, David, and one of the new girls attacked him at once, each grabbing an arm or a leg until he crashed to the floor. The knife broke free and slid under a chair. Butch struggled to free himself, kicking and spitting within their grasp, but he was pinned.

Emily rushed over and blocked me while the other two girls cut off Luis's escape. Emily held both of my wrists and stared into my eyes. Her strength overwhelmed me. "Don't fight me, Jacob."

Her scent of roses disarmed me. She smiled as if she were only playing a game.

David leaned into Butch's neck and sniffed. "Yes, I was correct. We're very fortunate tonight. We've scored a virgin, and lots of blood in that large frame of yours. It will be a feast."

No way to escape through the front door, so I broke away from Emily—looking back, I realize she allowed me to run—and shot off to the bedroom where the girl lay on the bed. Nausea swept over me as I viewed the gore from the corner of my eye. Blood covered her pale body and splattered everywhere—the sheets, the floor, the dresser. Luis was right. It had been a set up all along.

I scrambled up the front of the girl's dresser toward the window. I flipped the latch to open it, but Emily and Zoey raced up alongside of me. Their feet didn't touch the floor. They hovered in the air laughing for a moment before Emily grabbed my wrist and pulled me down.

"Don't be afraid, Jacob," Emily said. "Am I so ghastly to you?"

"Leave me alone. I didn't do anything to that girl."

Emily pulled me closer. "I know. It doesn't matter. Stay with me."

David and the other girls dragged Butch and Luis into the bedroom with us, then closed the door. They gathered us together on the floor and stood over us with menacing grins. Emily gazed at me with her soft green eyes.

"You spoiled our dinner." David gestured to the girl on the bed. "I have to admit—I lied to you boys. She's not my girlfriend, but this is her place. Lovely, isn't it? A fine location for a feast. Fortunately, we have plenty of food to go around. We'll begin with you."

"Fuck—" Butch gasped as David pounced on him.

David clamped his teeth around Butch's throat and guzzled the blood that streamed into his mouth. Some blood spurted into the air and splattered across David's clothes. He laughed and moved aside so Emily and Zoey could share in the feast. Butch cried out as the color drained from his face. When they finished, a third girl jumped in and finished him off. Butch moaned one last time and a few seconds later he was dead.

I struggled to stand up. I wouldn't go through that without a fight. Emily pushed me down and whispered in my ear. "It's okay, Jacob, don't fight it. You excite me. I want to keep you for my own."

They swarmed around Luis next, but didn't start their attack until after playing with him for a few minutes. They made a game of it, giggling as they untied the ropes from the dead girl on the bed and rolled her off the side. Her lifeless body thumped to the floor.

Zoey tied Luis's wrists and ankles in the same way Cassandra had been tied.

"You sick bastards are all going to prison," Luis yelled.

The girls laughed louder.

Luis screamed until David descended on him and bit into his throat. Blood spilled over Luis's shirt as he thrashed within the restraints. David backed away a minute later, blood dripping down his chin. He grinned and closed his eyes as if overcome with ecstasy. The girls took turns with him just as they had with Butch.

They turned to me next. David approached and rested his hand on my shoulder. With his other hand he wiped away the blood from his mouth. "Well, luckily for you we've had our fill for the evening, and Emily sees something special in you. She desires to grant you freedom."

I gazed into Emily's eyes. The girl who had flirted with me only a few hours earlier now became my only hope to escape that nightmare. I shudder now to think of what would have happened to me if I had reacted differently to her advances.

"You have a choice now," David said. "You can stay here, if you'd like, and explain all of this to the police. I don't recommend it, by the way, as your DNA and rambling explanation of the truth won't satisfy them. You'd most likely rot in prison for the rest of your life if you choose that path. The other option is to come with us. Emily would like you to join our family as her partner."

Emily moved forward and grinned with blood smeared over her lips and teeth. "I'll take good care of you."

"But you need to make your choice now. What will it be?"

Emily took my hand. Her flesh was cold, but those green eyes pierced me. Magical, soft eyes.

"I'll go with you," I said.

Emily's face erupted in joy and she lurched at my neck. The pain was overwhelming when her teeth pierced me, but it only lasted for a moment before everything faded away. The transformation began and Emily cradled me in her arms throughout the process.

I don't regret my decision. After a year with Emily and my new family, I've found happiness that eludes most people. I found The One.

# THE UGLY TREE

Kayla lifted the scissors to open the last box of clothes, staring out the window at the forest beyond the edge of her yard. The towering pine trees created a darkness beneath them resembling a wide opening to a cave. She would need to make sure Rainy never went in there. Her dad had warned her about wild animals in the area. Rainy wouldn't hesitate to confront them.

"What are you staring at?" Eric's voice blared behind her.

Kayla jumped and turned to the side. Eric stood only a few inches away. "Don't be a creep. You scared me."

"Can I help you unpack?"

"I'm almost done."

He walked to the window. "Why do you get the best room?"

"Because I'm older. You can have it when I go to college."

"That'll be like twenty years from now!"

Kayla rolled her eyes. "Five years, if you're lucky, dummy."

"That's an ugly tree."

Kayla walked over and stood next to him. She knew which tree he was referring to. The one in the middle of the yard with the wide trunk and narrow curling branches that twisted and spread out like tentacles. She'd never seen a tree like that before. It didn't look anything like the other pines and oaks in the area. She'd ask her dad about it—he knew all that stuff.

Running along one side of the ugly tree was a dark reddish patch of bark that stuck out a little like a bulging vein on someone's neck. Some leaves had turned brown, although it was still summer.

Eric tugged at her shirt. "Play hide and seek with me."

She jerked her arm away. "Not now."

"Play." He pulled her arm and growled.

"Fine." She sighed and moaned as she turned toward him.

"You go hide."

Kayla jumped at him, and he squealed as he took off across the wood floors out into the hallway toward his room. Their stomping drew her mom from her room. She scowled as Eric ran to her, and she pushed him away.

"Why don't you play outside? It's a beautiful day. That's why we moved out of the city, so you could play outside. I have a lot of work to do."

Kayla lurched at him, and he screamed as he thundered down the stairs. She chased him out the back door where her dad was cutting wood with a chainsaw across the yard.

Rainy was nowhere in sight. Probably resting somewhere in the house. She had run around like crazy that morning, sniffing and exploring the boundaries of their enormous space. Plenty of room outside for them to goof around. She pictured herself playing catch with her dad, or maybe even target practice with her dad's handguns. Lots of trees to climb. She was the best climber—she could climb anything—or even maybe build a tree house. She'd always wanted to have one.

Her dad had created a stack of wood a few feet high already. That man was a machine. How much did they need for the winter? She'd never seen her dad cut wood before, and sweat drenched the back of his shirt.

She couldn't wait to burn some of those logs in the fireplace. One of the few things she looked forward to about the new house. She'd never had a real fireplace before.

Kayla stayed away from her dad. He was frowning and his face was damp with sweat. Better to leave him alone while he was working.

Eric stopped in the middle of the yard. "I'll count. You go hide." He closed his eyes and started counting. "One... two..."

Kayla crept through the grass and scanned the yard. Few places to hide. One ugly tree stood in the center near the house and several along the edge of the property. Eric would never find her in the dark pine forest, but she'd never go in there alone. Her parents had warned her about wild animals in the area. Even getting close to it might get her snapped up and eaten by a black bear.

She played it safe and circled around the ugly tree.

As she hunched down beside its base, she stared at the thick branch above her. A perfect spot to build a treehouse. The open section stretched out horizontally and the surrounding branches were thick—they could support what she had in mind. She imagined what it would look like. Six feet across and eight to ten feet wide, with a ladder leading up to a trap door in its floor. Her dad would build it in no time. Maybe he could finish it before winter.

Kayla watched Eric as he finished the count. He opened his eyes, and she ducked behind the tree. The forest caught her gaze again. Something moved within the darkness. Swaying branches? Or some wild animals checking out their new neighbors? She hoped whatever animals lived in there never came out. Rainy barked somewhere near the house and she shuddered.

"Keep an eye on Rainy," her mother said from the back porch. "Don't let her go into the woods."

Kayla peeked around the corner. Eric was facing back toward their mom. Rainy charged around the backyard like a madman twice before stopping near her hiding spot behind the ugly tree. Rainy ignored her and instead growled and barked at the tree. She jumped at the wide trunk, scratching it with her claws.

"Rainy, what's gotten into you?" her mom's voice called from near the house.

Rainy barked and continued clawing at the trunk.

Eric walked around the tree and pointed his finger at Rainy. "Rainy, stop that. You can't bite it."

The dog barked several more times, glancing between them and the tree.

Eric wasn't even looking for her anymore. He patted Rainy's head to calm her down.

Kayla grabbed onto Rainy's leash. Maybe something in the tree? She peered up into the branches. No sign of animals. Maybe a squirrel? "Do you see something, girl? What do you see?"

Kayla pulled at her leash, but she broke free and circled around to the other side. Kayla hurried around with her. Before she could grab her leash again, Rainy squatted near the base of the tree and peed.

Kayla rolled her eyes. "No. What are you doing? Don't do that."

Eric laughed. He came over and tapped Kayla on her back. "I found you."

"I wasn't hiding."

"My turn."

He ran off without waiting for her to acknowledge that she would play. His feet thumped across the grass in a zigzag as he scoured out a hiding spot. She started counting out loud with her hands over her face, but kept one eye clear so she could watch her dad slice apart tree limbs with his chainsaw. Her dad cut through the pieces in no time at all, even the larger ones.

"One... two... three..." She finished the count and opened her eyes, turning to look for Eric. "Ready or not, here I come."

With her dad's chainsaw buzzing louder now, she searched for her brother. He wasn't around the ugly tree, so he had to be hiding behind one of three trees at the far end of the yard.

She hurried over in that direction. "Where did he go?" she called out in a playful tone. "Is he out in the forest? I hope not. The monsters will get him."

He giggled from behind one tree.

"Is he behind the tall grass?"

"No," he whispered.

Kayla grinned and followed his voice over to one tree. She lurched around the side, holding up clawed fingers as if to attack him. "I found you." She growled.

He screamed and laughed. "It's my turn now."

Her dad's chainsaw revved down and a piece of wood thumped into the pile.

Rainy let out a high-pitched squeal from near the house, then silenced.

Kayla turned back toward the house. Rainy was gone. She scanned the edge of the yard, expecting her dog to charge out into the open. Maybe she'd run into one of those wild animals her parents had talked about. Something bad had happened.

"Rainy?" Kayla yelled.

Her dad started up the chainsaw and started cutting wood again. If he'd heard Rainy's painful yelp, he wasn't reacting.

Kayla walked toward the house with Eric at her side. "Rainy?"

Nothing.

"What happened?" Eric asked her.

"I don't know."

Rainy wasn't anywhere near her dad. She hurried toward the tree where Rainy had been growling earlier. Maybe a feral cat had attacked her.

Nowhere in sight. She made a full circle around the house before rushing in through the back door.

Her mom was busy doing the dishes in the kitchen.

"Mom," she asked, "what was that noise?"

"What noise?"

"Rainy made a weird sound, like she got hurt."

"I didn't hear it. Isn't she outside?"

"I can't find her."

She groaned. "I hope she didn't run into the woods. I guess we'll need to put up a fence around the yard."

"She yelped near the house somewhere."

"Maybe she ran into a skunk or something. I hope she didn't run away. We don't know the neighbors yet."

"I don't see her anywhere."

"Well, she's not inside. Look out there somewhere."

Kayla rushed outside and circled the yard, calling out Rainy's name. Eric joined her. Their dad joined them after Eric pleaded for help at the brink of tears.

KAYLA GRABBED A FLASHLIGHT FROM DOWNSTAIRS AND trudged up to her room. Hours after Rainy disappeared, still no sign of her. Kayla turned off her bedroom light and opened the window to stare out on the backyard. She strained to see through the screen covering the bottom half of the window, but her light stretched out far enough over the yard to know that Rainy wasn't down there. Maybe her dog would see the light and come running. She swung the beam from side to side like a lighthouse beacon.

"Come home, Rainy."

She regretted not putting Rainy on a leash, but wasn't it cruel to tie her up with so much open space to run? She'd been cramped up in a small yard for years, so letting her go crazy in a sprawling country yard seemed like the right thing to do.

Kayla's heart ached. Even after a few hours of searching the area, she still wanted to go back out there and look for her. She didn't feel right going to sleep while Rainy was lost somewhere in the darkness all alone.

She peered into the darkness.

"Rainy?" she yelled one last time. Mosquitoes buzzed around the window screen that shielded her from their attacks.

Nothing.

She closed her window and the blind too before switching off the flashlight. Her eyes watered up, and she fought back the urge to cry. She didn't like to cry. Her dad didn't like to see her cry either, always turning away as if she was doing something wrong. She couldn't help it. Rainy had been with her as far back as she could remember. A sister, in a way.

Her stomach growled. She considered going downstairs to finish the hamburgers her mom made for her two hours earlier, but the thought of eating anything nauseated her. At supper time, she'd pushed away her plate after only a few bites. Her mom hadn't forced her to finish all her food like she normally would have.

She set the flashlight on the dresser and climbed into bed. Clenching the edge of the sheets, she stared up at the ceiling with her light on. A tear trickled across her temple and through her hair before soaking into the pillow.

Something tapped against the glass in her window.

Bugs? Sounded like a big one. Or maybe a small bird?

Another tap, and then a few more in rapid succession. A swarm of them? Lots of bugs filled a Minnesota summer. Maybe drawn to her light. She should turn it off and go to sleep.

The taps were sharp, like someone's fingertip against a desktop. Something out there really wanted to get in.

Kayla rolled out of bed and lifted the blinds. Darkness. Nothing out there except the ugly tree's branch swaying within range of her bedroom light. The limb was bare without leaves and it swayed in, tapping against her window a few more times before swinging away.

Strange. No wind all day. A few minutes earlier, everything had been calm. Maybe just a gust. Minnesota weather was weird.

The tree bent toward her again. Had it been that close to her window before?

The branches swayed closer, jabbing at the glass like a bony finger. She grabbed the flashlight, aiming the beam out over the tree and down to the yard. It stood closer now by several feet, but that was crazy, wasn't it? It didn't make any sense. She wasn't remembering it right.

The branch slapped forward, its tip cracking against the glass.

Kayla stepped back. Maybe it would break through.

She could reach out and snap it off, except the screen covered the lower window, the section that opened.

The branches swayed in again, scraping against the glass and tapping a few more times before stopping in one spot. The tip stuck, pointing at her.

Kayla inched closer and pressed her index finger against the same place the branch touched on the opposite side.

The limb darted away into the darkness.

Kayla gasped and chuckled.

The branch shot forward, striking the glass with a loud crack.

She jumped away, but the glass shattered and splashed across her floor. The branch burst in, wrapping itself around her wrist holding her flashlight. It clutched her like an angry parent, yanking her forward toward the shards hanging along the edge of the window. She stumbled forward, yanking herself back to avoid stepping on the broken fragments across the floor and along the edge of the windowsill. She pulled back as it drew her closer to the window, and she grabbed the side of her dresser to keep it from yanking her outside.

The flashlight slipped from her hand, slamming against the edge of the window before flying out through the shattered window. It thumped against the ground below. She strained and grunted as she ripped herself back a few inches at a time. Her right foot slipped forward, the tips of her toes touching the pieces of glass strewn across the floor below.

"Dad!" she screamed.

The branch yanked her again, harder this time. She clenched her teeth and struggled to keep from flying out the window. Her fingers strained to cling to the dresser.

A second branch burst in and scraped across the side of her chest as it snaked around her back and up her spine. It engulfed her. She leaned sideways, trying to drop behind the dresser to get leverage before her feet slipped further. The shards cut into the tips of her toes.

The pair of scissors on the dresser caught her attention. She let go and grabbed them, opening the blades wide as she sliced against the wood. She squeezed the scissors together as hard as she could. They cut in deep. Blood smeared over the blades and dripped to the window sill. Had it cut her? She didn't feel a thing. No, the blood came from the branch. Impossible. She crushed the blades together and clenched her teeth until the scissors sliced through. The branch holding her wrist snapped off.

She turned her head to the side. "Dad!"

With blood leaking from its wounds, the injured branch retreated out the window as she sliced at the remaining one. Drops of its blood dotted the floor, mixing in with the glass. Before she could sever off the branch, it released her and pulled back into the darkness.

Her dad ran into the room with wide eyes as she stood there holding the bloody scissors. "What's so—"

Her mom ran in a moment later. She gasped. "My God, Kayla, what happened?"

"Something attacked me."

Her dad stepped toward the window as her mom flew forward and grabbed her wrist. Her mom pulled her away from the glass on the floor.

Kayla embraced her mom as she examined Kayla's face and chest. "Are you hurt?"

"An animal?" His dad inspected the scissors in her hand, taking them away as her mom held her. "What was it? A bird?"

Kayla shook her head. "I was looking out the window for Rainy. Something broke in and attacked me." She hesitated to mention anything about the tree's attempted abduction. Her dad wouldn't believe her, anyway, and she'd get yelled at for lying.

Her mom nudged her toward the hallway. "Go to the bathroom and get washed off. Did you cut yourself with the scissors? Did it bite you?"

"I don't think so."

Her mother inspected Kayla's limbs. "There's blood on the floor. It must have cut you somewhere."

"I think I got a bloody nose," she lied. Better than trying to explain the true source of the blood.

"Did you see what kind of animal it was?"

"Not an animal. A branch from that tree broke through."

"So it wasn't an animal?" her dad asked.

Kayla shook her head. "No, just the tree."

Her dad nodded. "That makes sense. I'm sure nobody's trimmed it in a long time. The previous owners mentioned that the landscaping needed a lot of work. I'll take care of it in the morning."

Her dad was all about things making sense. He'd give Kayla "the look" if she told him anything even resembling a lie. All he wanted to hear was a rational explanation. It all needed to add up. Everything else was bullshit that pissed him off, so no point in giving him a detailed description—a red face and glaring eyes would meet her. Her dad wouldn't tolerate any nonsense. That was fine. She didn't want to talk about it, anyway.

Her dad walked over to the window and gazed at the tree outside. "I'll throw some plastic over your window for the night so the mosquitoes don't get in. Don't worry about a thing, I'll get all this cleaned up in no time. Go into the bathroom like your mom said."

Before leaving down the hallway with her mom, she caught a glance of the ugly tree. A branch waved at her through the shattered opening.

KAYLA THREW THE HATCHET AGAINST THE SIDE OF THE tree as her dad revved up the chainsaw on the ladder above her. The hatchet's blade stuck deep into the bark. She smirked. She'd missed the bulging vein of deep red wood running down the length of the tree, but she would get it next time. Jumping forward, she pulled out the hatchet.

A faint hum came from inside the tree. A moan?

"That hurt?" She stepped back and struck the tree again with the hatchet, this time launching it from several feet away.

Bullseye. She hit the vein right in the thickest part. The vein had grown larger since the day before, looking now like an elongated basketball-sized red grape. The bark covered it, hiding most of the red shading, but it was there. Maybe the lump was its heart.

"I'll cut your heart out."

Pulling out the blade after hitting the target a second time, another sound rumbled within its trunk. A low groan, like a stomach growling.

"Want some more?" She stepped back and launched the hatchet again, remembering its attack on her the previous night. This time, she heaved it as hard as she could.

The hatchet slammed into the same spot. The crimson color fanned out over its surface, then faded.

"How dare you try to grab me? I'll chop off all your arms."

Her dad drove the chainsaw into a branch above her. The main section of the tree angled a few inches to one side. Its branches swayed, but no wind stirred the air.

As the chainsaw ripped across the limb nearest her window, its leaves trembled. Her dad didn't seem to notice.

Kayla sneered as the chainsaw sliced through the thickest part of the branch that had grabbed her. No way would that tree mess with her again. Her grin widened as the chainsaw's pressure tore the bark from its skin. The grinding blade growled, mirroring her own anger.

Her dad stopped. "What the hell?"

A red liquid dripped down the side of the tree where the chainsaw had severed most of the limb.

"That's weird." Her dad leaned in at the cut and then continued.

More blood drained out as the chainsaw whirred louder. More leaves rustled and branches swayed above them. How could her dad not see that?

He stopped again. "That is damn weird. I've never seen a tree do that before."

The chainsaw blasted into the wood again, and a few seconds later, the branch broke off. It plummeted to the ground several feet away from where Kayla stood gripping her hatchet. As the branch lay motionless, she walked over and kicked it. The blood continued to ooze from the open wound at the end.

"Thanks, Dad," Kayla said. "We got it."

She dragged the branch toward the wood pile so her dad could finish slicing it with the chainsaw later. A wide grin spread across her face. She gripped it by its leaves, imagining she was dragging a fallen enemy by the hair. She would enjoy watching her dad chop it up into a million little pieces.

He groaned from the top of the ladder.

"Dear God. Oh, Rainy, how did you get in there?"

Kayla's eyes widened, and she dropped the branch. She glanced around the yard. "Rainy? Where? Do you see her?"

Her dad gazed down into the center of the tree. "You better not see this. I found her. But you won't like it. This is bad, Kayla. Maybe you should go inside."

Her eyes widened. "Where is she?"

"She must have climbed up into the tree and gotten stuck. I'm so sorry, honey. She didn't survive."

Her body went numb. Rainy was dead?

Her dad groaned. "Kayla, I'll take care of this. You should really go into the house now."

She stared at the severed branch. That *thing* did it. She dropped to her knees and slammed the hatchet into its bark. Her eyes welled up with tears. She pulled the hatchet out and cracked it into the wood again and again. "I knew it. It's the tree's fault."

"It's nobody's fault. She was probably chasing a squirrel or a cat and got stuck."

Kayla's face warmed, and she stood again. Walking to the tree, she imagined its bulging red vein to be its heart. She stepped over to it and slammed the hatchet into the target with all her fury. She pulled it out and struck again. Over and over, it sliced in deeper with each thrust. She chipped away at the red wood to reveal a softer, darker interior. Almost as if blood gorged its innards.

She slammed the hatchet into the throbbing crimson pulp.

Something popped.

Blood gushed out over the bark. Gallons of it drained out, along with the body of a decomposing dog. Smaller than Rainy—it wasn't her. Thank God. A neighbor's dog? Other animals followed. A squirrel. A rabbit. A cat. Each of them flushed out in various states of decomposition. Each plopped to the ground like some monstrous animal giving birth. She'd seen dead animals before, but this sight churned her stomach. As the stench wafted across her face, she prepared to vomit.

"Get into the house, Kayla. I'm sorry."

THEY BURIED RAINY IN ONE OF THE HEAVY DUTY moving boxes out at the edge of the yard later that afternoon. Her dad dug the hole, lowered in the box, and covered it over, leaving a mound of black dirt that bulged above the grass.

"I promise I'll put up a real cross as soon as possible." Her dad patted the shovel on the top of the mound. "I'll need to get some better wood from the hardware store.

The one you created will work fine for now. I'm sure Rainy is happy with that."

Kayla dropped to her knees next to the grave. She held out the makeshift cross she'd pieced together only half an hour earlier—two pencils held together by wire. A bit of cardboard sat at the top with 'Rainy' written in thick black Sharpie letters across the front. She stuck her memorial into the mound of dirt, her eyes still wet.

"I can get you some of those branches I cut earlier."

"No." Kayla sneered. "No branches."

"Okay." Her dad stopped and glanced at her. "No branches. I'll get some boards from the store." Her dad walked off with the shovel. "Be back in an hour."

Eric stood at her side with his arm over her shoulder. He sniffed and hugged her. "Is Rainy in heaven?"

Kayla nodded.

"Why did Rainy climb up there?" Eric stared at the tree.

"She didn't."

"Dad said she did."

Kayla glared at the tree. "That thing grabbed her."

"What thing? Dad said she chased after a cat and got stuck. Maybe it's still up there?" Eric glanced toward the ugly tree.

"It doesn't matter. I'll cut that thing down. I don't like it. I hate it."

"The cat?"

"The tree."

"You'll cut down the whole thing?"

"All of it."

"Did you ask Dad?"

Her dad drove away in the truck, leaving her alone with her brother. Her mom was in town getting groceries.

The wind picked up, but the ugly tree remained motionless. Even the leaves didn't waver in the breeze. Something had changed. Had the thing moved closer to the house? She swallowed. No, it had rotated around so the severed limb her dad had sliced off now faced the yard. A fresh, longer branch faced her window.

"Will you play hide and seek with me again?" Eric nudged her.

She shook her head. All she wanted to do was sit beside Rainy's grave. Her mind spun with dark revenge.

Her dad had returned the chainsaw to the garage. She could operate it. Not so difficult to use. She'd watched her dad use it plenty of times. She'd cut off the remaining branches herself and leave that ugly tree with just a bloody stump. And after cutting it apart, she'd chop it up into little pieces of firewood and toss those into the fireplace herself. Did the awful thing feel pain? She hoped so. The thing might even moan again or squeal in the flames. That sounded like a brilliant idea.

Eric continued pestering her. "Play with me. Mom said you have to. We can play hide and seek now."

"Leave me alone."

"Don't be sad, let's play." Eric pulled at her arm.

She pulled back. "I said leave me alone."

"Are you going to sit there all night?"

"Yes."

"You're no fun. Just count to ten. I'll go hide and you come find me. Okay?"

Kayla rolled her eyes. "You go hide then."

She dug her fingers into the black mound of dirt over Rainy's grave. The cold earth housed the one thing in her life she loved the most. Her heart ached, and she struggled to breathe. Numbness washed over her for the second time that day.

A low moan came from somewhere near the house. She gazed at the tree as it bent toward her.

Anger swelled in her chest. She would run over there and cut that damn thing down. She glared at the ugly lumpy tree, and over to the pile of firewood her dad had cut up the previous day.

"That'll be you soon," Kayla said. "I can do a lot of damage before Dad gets home."

"Are you counting?" Eric called out from somewhere near the house.

"One... two... three..." She closed her eyes, but had no desire to play.

The afternoon sun beat down on her and a light breeze blew across her face. Her dad hadn't even let her see Rainy before dropping her into the box and sealing it.

"It's too awful," her dad had said.

After watching the decomposing animals drop from the trunk of the tree, she could imagine how awful. Lots of other poor creatures had suffered the same fate.

Nobody had explained how Rainy had gotten into the tree. Her dad wouldn't give an explanation, because none of it made sense. "Chased a cat up there," was only half an answer. "*How* did Rainy chase the cat up there?" was the other half. Her dad avoided the topic when she questioned him. Rainy couldn't climb more than a few feet, much less the ten or fifteen needed to get trapped in the spot where her dad had found her. But it made sense to him. She had just climbed up there and gotten stuck. Nonsense. *It* had grabbed Rainy, just like it had grabbed her, just like it had grabbed all those other animals. It had eaten them. But it wouldn't eat any more, because she would do something about it.

She opened her eyes again and stared at the mound of dirt in front of her. Broken sections of grass lie around the edges where her dad had tried to blend it in with the rest of the yard. She doubted anybody would talk about it ever again.

Eric cried out.

At first she didn't react, still focused on the mound of dirt in front of her. She turned toward the house, expecting her brother to be peeking out from behind his hiding spot. Maybe he'd fallen down. He was always goofing around. She didn't see him at first, but her heart raced when she did.

Eric was up in the branches of the ugly tree. Near the same spot where they'd found Rainy. The branches gripped his ankles and neck. It hoisted him upside down in the air, dragging him in through the branches and leaves toward the center.

Kayla lost her breath as she jumped up and rushed toward the house. No Mom or Dad to call for help. They wouldn't be home for at least another hour.

Eric screamed.

Kayla snatched up the hatchet lying on the ground next to the ugly tree and slammed it into the trunk. "Let my brother go!"

The thing swayed away from her and then shuddered as if a jolt of electricity had shot through it. Her dad had returned the ladder to the garage. No way up.

Eric called to her, "Kayla, help me!"

She scrambled to the garage and rushed in through the side door. Reaching for the ladder, she stopped. The chainsaw sat next to it. Cut that thing to pieces. She picked up the chainsaw—still warm. Ready to do some damage.

With the chainsaw in one hand and the hatchet in the other, she stormed outside.

The tree was gone.

A long trail of damaged grass stretched across the yard toward the forest as if a tractor had plowed the path. The tree had crawled to the edge of the woods with Eric still hanging upside down, struggling within its branches. His head wavered above the opening where her dad had found Rainy. He screamed over and over. Nobody except her to hear his cries.

Eric's shrieks tore through the air as they disappeared into the blackness of the forest.

She ran as fast as she could across the lawn toward the wall of pine trees. She slowed at the edge, listening for Eric's screams. Something had silenced his voice now.

Her heart beat faster.

The torn up lawn's path revealed their direction, but the light plummeted within the thick pines. Branches cracked ahead, but the noises faded. Too dark to determine where it had gone. All the trees looked the same.

She ran into the darkness, slamming her hatchet into every tree she passed. She listened for reactions. The thing wouldn't escape her.

"Eric!" she called out.

No answer. It couldn't have gotten far. She waited to start the chainsaw. The noise would drown out Eric's voice.

She pushed through the tall grass within the faint sunlight piercing the shifting branches overhead. She followed a trail of collapsed brush.

The thing couldn't hide forever. A gust of wind passed

through and rustled the leaves. One tree swayed out of sync with the others.

That was it.

"I'll get you out, Eric." She clutched the hatchet and chainsaw tighter as a burst of sun lit up her surroundings.

She raced up to the tree and slammed the hatchet into its side.

The tree shook and groaned. One of its branches lashed down at her, knocking the hatchet into the grass.

She fired up the chainsaw. The roar of the spinning blade reverberated through her chest.

Another branch whipped across her neck and tore up the side of her face. She winced as she revved the chainsaw's motor and swung the blade around, cutting across the trunk.

Blood spewed out between the bark and spattered across her face.

She dug the blade into its body as far as she could. Something moaned deep within it, and the leaves rattled overhead. Blood seeped out. Maybe it would bleed to death, but time was running out. She didn't see Eric anywhere. He could only be stuck in its grasp. If she could climb up, she could pull him out. No chance.

The tree backed away. She followed it.

"Let my brother go!"

Her heart raced as she pressed the chainsaw against the trunk with all her strength. More blood spewed from the cuts, and the branches whipped at her face as it moved back again several feet.

She glimpsed its legs. Splayed roots stretched out like tentacles.

It couldn't run away without legs. She dropped to her knees and sliced the chainsaw's blade through anything that moved. More moans boomed from deep within the tree.

A branch whipped around and knocked the chainsaw from her hand. The same branch swung back and slammed into her side, toppling her into the weeds. Before she could recover and retrieve the chainsaw, another branch stretched down. It gripped the chainsaw's handle, lifting it high into the air over her.

The revving engine barreled down at her. The blade slashed into the soil inches from her face.

She rolled out of the way and scrambled toward the hatchet.

The chainsaw whizzed past her ears, smashing into a tree beside her. The chainsaw's engine popped. Sparks rained over the brush as the motor sputtered before smoke poured out. A burst of flames exploded over the surrounding trees and the ugly tree dropped its weapon.

Kayla clutched the hatchet and stumbled back toward the thing's legs as they sprouted beneath it. The tree lumbered ahead, despite its injured legs, and rumbled toward the back of the forest. She lifted the hatchet and attacked.

She let out a flood of curses while chopping away at the bark. Beneath its crusty surface was a smooth black skin. She didn't stop. She hacked harder, faster, even as the tree jabbed a branch into her rib cage. A rush of pain surged through her, but she continued. It wouldn't get away.

Her hands ached as she pounded the blade through its skin. Another gush of blood splashed out. Above her, Eric's shoe and lower leg hung limp over the edge of the main trunk.

Eric moaned.

The fire spread through the surrounding grass. Smoke filled the air.

"Eric!" Kayla crashed the blade into its body again as the tree rotated.

Its mangled open wound came into view—the same spot where dead animals had dropped out earlier. A lumpy, glassy membrane had sealed the opening and a brownish-red pus dripped across the bark below it. Beneath the membrane, the tree pulsed. A clear shot to its innards.

She swung the hatchet toward the wound, but the tree turned, her blade landing inches away from her target. A branch lashed across her face as she pulled the hatchet back and circled around to face the wound again. She pitched the blade in harder this time, crying out until it hit her target.

The blade sank deep into the soft center of the tree. The tree let out a guttural moan that vibrated her body.

Kayla left the hatchet planted in its bowels and stepped back. The tree toppled toward her.

She scrambled out of the way as it crashed down around her. Its branches exploded under its massive weight and the ground rumbled when the trunk hit.

Within the crash, Eric broke free, bouncing a few feet into the air before landing in the brush several feet away.

Kayla staggered to her feet as the tree hobbled on its side toward her. Blood oozed from its broken limbs. Branches crept toward her, even as she hurried to her brother.

"Eric!"

She lifted him as the fire engulfed the nearby trees. She cradled Eric's flopping body in her arms and ran toward the exit. A thick mucus covered his face and chest.

"Wake up, Eric." Her eyes watered.

Eric coughed and gasped for air as she reached the edge of the forest.

Kayla glanced back at the tree. Within the rising flames, blood squirted from its shattered limbs like tiny explosions.

The fire consumed half the forest before the fire trucks and her parents arrived.

Kayla huddled beside Eric watching the blaze. Better than a fireplace.

Even as the firemen dampened the inferno, something within the forest shrieked like an angry old man.

Kayla grinned.


MORE FRIGHTFUL TALES IN BOOK 2! SEE NEXT PAGE FOR info!

# DREADFUL DARK BOOK 2
## TALES OF HORROR: BOOK 2

# CHOMPER

Mikey's eyes watered up as he sat at the edge of his bed in his pajamas. "Give him back."

Rachel stood in the doorway gripping the door handle while holding out Chomper toward him by the tip of his tail. She swung the stuffed alligator like a pendulum. "Get into bed and I'll give him to you."

Mikey did as he was told and pulled the sheets up to his chest. He stretched out his arms. "Now give him back."

"You're too old to have a stuffed animal, anyway." She pulled Chomper away. "Maybe I'll throw him out."

Mikey threw off his blankets and lurched to his feet. "No!"

Rachel pointed at the bed. "Get back there."

"I *was* in bed. You better not throw him out. You're mean." He climbed onto the mattress, but didn't cover up.

She glared at him. "You're such a baby, Mikey. Here's your stupid doll." Rachel hurled Chomper over her shoulder at him like a football. Chomper landed near the headboard and Mikey plucked him up before he could roll off.

He'd gotten the stuffed animal for Christmas the previous year after prodding his parents for weeks following a trip to the Science Center. He hugged the alligator against his chest as if it might have gotten injured, then dropped back onto his pillow.

"Close your eyes," Rachel scolded, "and don't make any noise or I'll take Chomper away again. Got it?"

Mikey sneered at Rachel and opened his mouth to say something then closed it. He'd learned from past confrontations with her to keep his mouth shut. Rachel was nuts with a capital 'N'.

She slammed his bedroom door and hurried downstairs.

Music thumped through the floor. It wouldn't stop until at least midnight—an hour before his parents would get home. Rachel's friends would clear out all the beer and mess. She never got caught. He doubted his parents even cared if she invited friends over, anyway. They believed everything she told them. She could do anything she wanted.

His parents were out at the bar again celebrating *another* friend's birthday. Almost every weekend they celebrated something—a friend's new job, a birthday, a wedding. They would come home rowdy and drunk, say goodbye to Rachel, then go to bed without checking on him. The same routine every night she babysat.

Mikey pulled the pillow in over his ears. How was he supposed to sleep with all that noise? Rachel and her friends partied downstairs while they expected him to just magically fall asleep. She hadn't even read him a story like her parents had requested. She wasn't doing her job at all. On top of everything, it was only 8 o'clock. Not even dark yet. The red glow of the sunset peeked through his blinds. Kindergartners went to bed at 8 o'clock, not him.

Worst babysitter in the world.

He would tell his parents about all the awful things Rachel did if it would do any good, but it wouldn't. Rachel was an angel in their eyes. That charming girl from church who always smiled and sweet-talked them. Just a big scam. They wouldn't believe him even if he took pictures. And he *had* taken some interesting pictures of her friends with his parents' digital camera—drunk on the couch, snooping through his parents' bedroom—but she'd forced him to delete them. Any attempt to get her in trouble would backfire. She'd be back in power again the next weekend to have her revenge. Maybe even put him to bed at 6 o'clock.

He turned on his side, facing into the fading light coming in through his window. He'd much rather be outside playing with his friends. No need for a babysitter, anyway. He was ten years old—old enough to take care of himself. She'd even taken the power cord for his computer, claiming that he'd be up all night playing games—which was true—if she let him use it. Still, it wasn't fair.

Locked in his room like an animal.

A low growl rumbled from his closet.

He froze and stared at his closet door. The music still boomed downstairs. Maybe something had fallen over.

Something thumped inside the closet as if a heavy box had hit the floor.

The loud music was shaking the walls. Rachel's friends would destroy the house. Maybe if they wrecked something valuable, his parents would get a different babysitter.

The door handle rattled.

The music couldn't do that, could it? He held his

breath and fixed his gaze on the door. Was someone in there? Mikey's heartbeat raced and his eyes stretched wide open.

The handle turned.

His heart beat faster. He squeezed Chomper closer to his chest.

The door latch clicked, and the door squeaked open two inches, revealing the thick darkness within. His skin crawled. It was watching him.

"Who's there?" Mikey's words hung in the air unanswered.

He lifted Chomper up and moved him out in front of his face. Chomper wouldn't let anything bad happen to him. Whatever was in there would get eaten up if anyone dared to come near him.

He waited to see the thing emerge. Nothing came out. Either Chomper had scared it away or it wasn't anything. His closet door never shut tight, anyway.

*But the door handle had turned.*

The thumping music from downstairs must have rattled it open... or whatever was hiding in his closet.

He wasn't a baby, but he wasn't about to get up and close it. That's how *they* got you. The monsters. They would lure you out of bed and grab you before you could scream. The ones under your bed would clamp onto your ankles before dragging you down and eating you alive. The ones in the closet would devour you with razor gnashing teeth. If Mikey even got his fingers near that door handle, its claw would swing around and grab his wrist. It would drag him in before he knew what was happening.

He stayed in bed and pulled the sheet up just under his line of sight. Chomper stayed out in the open air to keep an eye on things. He could handle anything that approached.

Mikey couldn't look away from the narrow black opening staring back at him. The shadows churned, but no monster... yet.

Something thumped in his closet again.

This time there was no doubt. Something *alive* had knocked against his closet wall. Mikey didn't move.

But how could someone have gotten in there? He would have seen them. It didn't make sense. Impossible.

The bathroom was behind the wall of his closet. The pipes rattled and whooshed after a toilet flush, so maybe one of Rachel's drunk friends had crept upstairs without him noticing to use the bathroom. It didn't matter that nobody was allowed upstairs. Rachel's friends sometimes snuck into his parents' bedroom and goofed around with the door closed. He cringed thinking about all the things they might have done in there.

The wood floor creaked and his clothes hangars clicked together. Definitely not the plumbing this time. Something was in there. It rustled against his shirts and scraped against the wall—its claw?

His ears picked up every noise, and each breath puffed in and out through his open mouth.

Despite the blankets covering him, an icy chill swept through his body. If something came out, he would scream.

A door slammed at the end of the hallway.

Mikey shuddered.

Muffled laughter followed. Two of Rachel's friends had come upstairs. A guy and a girl. They'd gone into his parents' room. Rachel would be in big trouble if his parents knew what was going on.

At least someone would be nearby to hear him scream if something stepped out of his closet.

The closet door creaked wider and every muscle tensed. He pulled the edge of his blankets closer. He shivered and held his breath.

A strange odor filled his room. A stench that reminded him of a country field in the springtime after the farmer covered it with manure. No, worse than that. More like a rotting dead animal. He winced.

Cool air touched his toes. They were sticking out.

He yanked his feet back from the edge of the blankets. It could have gotten him. Luckily, he'd noticed it in time. He pulled them in a little further, just to make sure the sheets fully protected him.

The dark opening widened further as a footstep thumped onto the carpet. With his view of the floor blocked by the blanket, his imagination ran wild. A thousand horrible nightmares flashed through his mind. He imagined some heavy beast with salivating fangs waiting to pounce after he let his guard down.

Something scratched against the wood door like heavy fingernails. Maybe one of Rachel's friends was playing a trick on him. It wouldn't surprise him if someone jumped out and laughed while he screamed.

"You can't scare me," he whispered. He trembled, wishing whatever was in there would get it over with. It wasn't funny at all. His skin tingled as his muscles tensed.

The door creaked open a little more but he couldn't look away. He fixed his gaze on the shadows shifting in the darkness.

The thing in the darkness moved forward.

Mikey's heart thumped so hard he was sure it would explode. He pressed his eyelids shut and pulled the sheet up over his head, bringing Chomper down with him this time beneath the safety of the blankets.

Another thump on the floor. The party music? No, the thing was coming out. The door creaked again and the thing's foot hit the floor a little closer. It dragged its feet along the carpet between each step as if it couldn't lift them all the way.

If he looked out at that moment he would see it for sure. He couldn't move even if he wanted to. And he didn't want to. If he looked at it, he would die.

*Play dead and lay still.* His only way out.

The air beneath his sheets filled with his hot breath. Not a single opening around the edges of his sheets. He was safe.

The intruder's breath snorted in and out through its deep throaty gargling as if it were struggling to breathe. Not human. No human breathes like that. It sniffed again and again, like a dog on the trail of its prey. The thing smacked its lips, then chomped and slurped as if it anticipated eating a meal soon.

Within the darkness beneath the sheets, Mikey followed its movements as it approached.

The thing bumped his bed. He clutched Chomper tighter. If he could just stay still, the thing would leave him alone. It couldn't get him beneath the blankets.

With the sheets pulled like a tent over his face, something scraped against the sheets. A claw dragged its nails up toward his head as if searching for an opening to dig in at him. It moved up around his head, scratching in a wide circle over his forehead as if drawing a target. Each breath gurgled in and out as it hovered over him.

If it got any closer, he would scream.

He tried to hold his breath, but he gasped and a chill ran up his spine. Maybe it had heard him.

*Go away. Go away. Go away.*

Its claws moved up and dragged along the side of his head.

It would get him any second.

He had to do something.

He drew in a deep breath and screamed. "Go away!" His voice deafened him for a moment beneath the blankets.

He thrust Chomper up into the cool bedroom air with his eyes still sealed shut. His right fist slammed against its flesh. Cold, moist, and solid, like a crab's shell.

The thing recoiled as he lifted Chomper with his other hand and shook him in the air toward the beast.

He wanted to jump out of there and run, but his legs didn't respond. All he could do was scream.

"Rachel!"

He screamed louder this time. The thing stumbled back and knocked against his desk. His trophies clanked together and his desk chair spun around.

He cracked his eyes open for a moment. The inky silhouette of a tall, wide creature stood a few feet away.

Mikey growled, waving Chomper higher into the air.

Instead of running away, the thing lumbered toward him again and clawed at his legs.

He clamped his eyes shut again. He couldn't look. If he saw the thing's face, the terror would kill him. In the darkness, he kicked his feet as hard as he could, slamming his toes into a larger section of its body, a softer, fleshy surface like its abdomen. The thing groaned and snorted. Not human at all. He screamed again and thrashed his legs into the air. He pulled the blankets up to his neck and turned his face away.

While gripping Chomper, he slammed his knee up against the thing's boney upper body shell. Pain shot through his leg, but the thing moaned like a tortured bear. Mikey had hurt it. Good.

But it still didn't back away. It smacked its lips again as if prepping to take a bite out of him at any moment.

Where the hell was the babysitter? Mikey screamed again.

"Rachel! Where the hell are you?"

His face warmed as he aimed his voice at his bedroom door.

"Dammit, Rachel, get in here!"

Mikey kicked again and his bare leg poked out from beneath the sheets, brushing against the thing's claw.

It clutched his ankle and squeezed, lifting his foot toward its slobbering mouth. Mikey couldn't break free. It twisted his leg around, bending it at an odd angle. His leg would snap off it didn't let go. Far from human, that thing could rip him to shreds.

Rachel yelled a torrent of swear words as she stomped up the stairs.

The thing stopped and its grip on his leg loosened.

Michael still pressed his eyes shut, even as the thing moved away from him toward the closet.

Chomper must have scared it away. Mikey shook the animal in the air again and growled, before pulling the blankets over his face again. He nursed his aching leg.

The thing shook the floor as it rumbled back into the closet and latched the door shut.

Rachel stormed in a moment later and flipped on the light. Even after she entered the room, Mikey screamed again, just to make sure she understood it was an emergency.

"What the hell?" she yelled. "What's so damn important?"

He didn't come out from under the blankets. "Get that thing away from me!"

"Get what away from you?"

"That thing."

"What are you talking about? Why are you freaking out?"

Mikey trembled beneath the sheets. His fingers grasped the edges even as the babysitter stepped closer. He couldn't lower his defenses, even if Rachel was there.

"What are you hiding for?" She yanked back his sheets. "What the hell, Mikey? You have a nightmare? The monster under your bed is coming to get you? Well, that's what happens to naughty kids who don't go to sleep on time. They get eaten up by monsters." Rachel made chomping noises. "You better not scream anymore or it'll feast on your little crybaby brain."

Mikey peeked out over the blankets. The closet door was closed, and Rachel stood above him with her arms folded over her chest. His desk chair now faced backwards. His trophies had shifted. "There's something in my closet. Get rid of it."

Rachel growled. "Good God. There's nothing in your closet, you loser. Go back to bed."

"Yes, there is. You don't believe me, but go see for yourself."

She scowled and rolled her eyes as she stomped over to the closet door. Mikey gasped and pulled up the sheets again to the rim of his nose as she opened the door. This time, he forced himself to face whatever lay inside. If the thing was still hungry, it would grab her first, giving him enough time to run away. That would be okay with him.

Mikey held his breath as she poked her head into the closet. He imagined the thing would jump out, take a bite out of her, and drag her inside to consume her in private, but nothing happened.

"Nope," she said. "Nothing here except your stinky clothes. You're just a baby. You don't still believe in monsters, do you? Babies believe in things like that."

"Check behind my clothes."

She mumbled and pushed back a wide section of his shirts. The hangers clicked together, and she stepped back out of the way so he could see the closet was empty. "No monsters."

He pointed down. "Maybe under my stuff."

She let out an exasperated sigh and dug through some clutter around the floor. "Nothing. Maybe you got rats in here. Wouldn't surprise me at all. It's a pig sty. Shit every-where." She lifted out the half eaten peanut butter and jelly sandwich he'd left in their days, or maybe weeks, earlier. "Plenty of food for rodents in your room. Next time I babysit you will clean all this crap up."

Mikey gazed at the empty closet. "It came out and then ran back in."

She grumbled. "You better stop with all the monster talk. You need to grow up."

But Rachel was right. It wasn't there. So where had it gone? It had disappeared. How could it have escaped in those few seconds without making any noise? Had he imagined the entire thing? But it *had* grabbed him. His ankle ached from where it had caught him.

"It's got to be in there. It came out—"

Rachel glared at him. "What did it look like?"

"I didn't see it very well. I was hiding under my sheets."

She sighed. "I don't have time for this, doofus. I can't be running up here every time you have a nasty dream. Just go back to sleep, or I'll tell your mom and dad you stayed up late."

"I'll tell Mom and Dad you had a party."

Rachel sneered and took a step forward. "You don't want to mess with me, kid. If I have to come up here again tonight, no more video games or watching TV or anything. Just remember that, smart ass."

Mikey clenched his teeth and looked away.

Rachel walked back toward the hallway, leaving the closet door wide open. "Go to sleep or you'll be in big trouble. I can't handle your little bouts of dementia right now."

"It was here, right next to me."

"You didn't see anything. It wasn't real. Don't you dare bother me again. I'm busy."

Rachel flipped off the light.

"Wait," he called out.

"What?" she yelled back.

"You didn't close the closet door."

She growled louder. "God, you're such a baby. Do you need your diapers changed too?" Rachel stomped over to the closet door and slammed it shut. "There! The little monster can't come out and get you now, right? Are you good?" She didn't wait for his answer before storming out of the room, slamming the bedroom door shut behind her.

She burst out swearing all the way down the hall. Rachel always swore, but now she didn't hold back. Every dirty word that would get him in big trouble with his parents, and some new ones he'd never heard before. She blurted them out over and over.

Rachel's footsteps pounded down the stairs as she yelled to her friends. "The kid's a big baby. What am I supposed to do? He's got monsters in his closet."

Her friends laughed, then cheered as someone cranked up the volume on his dad's stereo system.

"You're mean." Mikey hunkered down again beneath his sheets.

He wasn't a big baby. She shouldn't treat him like that. It wasn't so easy to fall asleep with that thing in his closet. She should try it if she thought it was so easy.

The creature thumped against the wall in his closet again. Mikey's heart pounded this time. It was back.

The closet latch clicked open and Mikey pulled the sheets up again to the bottom of his eyes. The door creaked wider as a flowing black shadow crept down from his closet's ceiling.

*So that's where it had been hiding.*

Rachel had been right under it. Too bad it hadn't dropped on her head when it had the chance. It could have eaten her instead of him, but now the thing was still hungry, and it would finish its meal.

Mikey sank into his bed as far as he could and covered himself up again. He squeezed Chomper against his chest in the darkness beneath his sheets and held back a scream. No point in screaming for help anymore. Rachel wouldn't show up a second time, anyway. She'd just laugh downstairs with her friends. His pulse pounded in his ears.

*Oh, God, make that thing go away.*

He could run, but his legs were shaking. And it was too late. It would see him jump out of bed and catch him for sure. He needed to keep still, but he shivered.

The creature knocked against his shirts, then thudded

to the floor. No chance of anyone downstairs hearing anything while the music blared.

The thing came right back over to his bed, still smacking its lips and chomping. It hovered over his face and its body bumped against the side of his bed.

A whimper escaped his open mouth as its claw scratched against the stretched fabric until it came to a rest on his forehead. Its flesh was like ice through the sheets. Mikey pressed back further into his pillow as another claw grabbed his arm through the sheets.

He shook. He couldn't help it.

The thing grunted.

He screamed. "Go away!"

It shifted over him.

"Go away, dammit!"

It moved in closer, sniffing near his head. What was it waiting for? The slobbering mouth noises mixed with a snarl as its claw scraped against his pillow. It peeled back his blanket. He pushed back, but he couldn't resist. He closed his eyes and prepared to die. It would get him now.

He cringed as its stinking breath puffed across his exposed skin. He wanted to gag. It pressed a claw against his forehead and clamped its other claw against his shoulder.

The thing grunted. It was laughing.

*No more.* He screamed. "Get away from me!"

He slammed Chomper up into its face, waving him around and kicking at the same time. The creature pressed down into Mikey's shoulder with his head still pinned to the pillow. He swung his foot up, catching it in the side of the creature's chest. A soft spot. The thing loosened its grip on him as it groaned and shook.

Mikey kicked again and again with his face turned

away. He squeezed his eyes shut. The thing couldn't get him if he didn't look.

He broke free and rolled across the bed, throwing the blankets aside. The thing lunged at him as he raced toward the bedroom door. It tripped on the pile of blankets and crashed to the floor. The impact shook his room.

The music stopped downstairs. Rachel had heard the noise. He didn't care. If she took away his video games or not, he wouldn't be around to enjoy them if that thing ate him.

He reached the door as footsteps thundered up the stairs. It would piss Rachel off. Good. She would see he was telling the truth. He wasn't a baby. The thing would get her too. Rachel's friends rushed up with her. Good. They would all see it.

He opened the door and held up Chomper beside his head facing backward to defend himself from the approaching monster. He avoided looking back as the thing stood again and scrambled toward him. Scrambling into the hall, he turned the corner, and met Rachel at the top of the stairs. Her face and eyes were red. She glared at him.

"What are you doing out of bed?" she yelled. She snatched away Chomper. "You're pathetic. Still playing with dolls. No wonder you're such a loser."

"Give him back." Mikey reached for his stuffed alligator. "The monster's behind me. It'll eat me."

Rachel's friends crowded in behind her and burst into laughter.

She dangled the stuffed animal by the neck and squeezed. "There's nothing in your stupid closet. You just want to go downstairs and play games all night."

"Run! It's right behind me."

More laughs.

Rachel pretended she was choking Chomper. "Good. Maybe it will eat you up, so I don't have to babysit your chicken shit ass anymore."

Mikey reached for his stuffed animal again. "You're hurting him."

Rachel wouldn't let go. "You want this?" She tossed it over his head back into the bathroom.

He chased after Chomper.

She slammed the bathroom door behind him.

The hallway erupted in laughter as Mikey picked up Chomper lying on the floor near the toilet and turned back toward the bathroom door.

Rachel screamed first, and then all her friends joined in.

The walls shook as the creature slammed into them. Somebody hit the bathroom door, but it didn't break in.

Mikey lurched forward and locked it.

Moments later, someone tried to get in. A boy's voice. "Let me in!"

Mikey backed away from the door.

The creature must have caught the boy by the throat because his scream was cut short. Blood oozed in under the door.

The monster's disgusting wet mouth noises filled the air. It must've been starving by the way it sounded.

"Dinner is served." Mikey listened as the screams and chaos raged in the hallway. The floor rumbled as the crowd and creature thundered down the stairs.

Mikey waited for the pounding and screaming to move away before opening the door. Three kids dead. It had ripped out their throats and strung their intestines over the railing like a Christmas decoration.

His stomach churned, and he cringed, but he'd warned them. He wanted to yell, "I told you so!", but he held back.

He crept out into the hallway and stepped around the pools of blood. It had sprayed everywhere, even across the ceiling. Streaks of blood lined the walls.

He glanced back toward his bedroom. A fourth victim, a girl, lay limp in the far corner near his door with her arm twisted in some impossible position behind her back. She stared off into nothing with her mouth hanging open and her face white.

Mikey tiptoed his way down the stairs, following the trail of blood, and passed one of Rachel's boyfriends. She had three, now two. The boy was curled into a ball upside down and it had ripped his throat open like the others.

Mikey held Chomper out toward the boy's face and roared quietly. "I'm not a baby," he whispered.

The party music still played despite the chaos. Screams echoed through the house as Rachel's friends scrambled into the kitchen to escape out the back door. Idiots. That door's lock was messed up. It took a lot of effort to open it. Rachel must have forgotten.

Mikey glimpsed the creature from the corner of his eye. A dark, winged creature with baseball-sized black eyes. He avoided meeting its gaze.

Rachel's friends crowded toward the door, but it didn't budge. As they scrambled back in the other direction, the thing blocked their way out. They were all trapped. Their screams hurt his ears, especially the girls. Rachel's scream rose above the others and she called his name.

"Nope," he mocked, "no monsters."

At the bottom of the stairs, Mikey hurried toward the front door, the only way out. Rachel must have seen him now because she pleaded for his help. Mikey raised

Chomper over his head and roared back at them as loud as he could. They stampeded toward him, trying to squirm past the creature, but it was too late. The thing cut them off.

Mikey closed the door behind himself as he ran outside. Muffled screams filled the house. He backed away toward the street, keeping an eye on the front door in case the thing rushed out toward him. A boy threw an object through the kitchen window and tried to climb out, but the monster yanked him back in and finished him. Mikey watched their silhouettes battle the monster as he stopped at the edge of the street.

No cars anywhere, or anyone to call for help. If Rachel's friends had been lucky enough to call 9-1-1, the police wouldn't arrive in time. That thing was tearing them apart faster than opening presents on Christmas morning. Maybe the neighbors would hear the screams and call the police. Probably not though. Too far away.

Something screeched in the air above the house. A large black creature, identical to the one inside, swooped down from the sky and landed in front of his bedroom window. It clawed at the glass for a moment before breaking into his bedroom with a loud crash. It emerged a few minutes later cradling a girl in its arms. She screamed and Mikey grinned. Rachel. Her body fell limp as the thing spread out its angular wings and lifted off into the night sky.

Several more creatures arrived within minutes and flew into his bedroom window, each of them emerging minutes later with their own catch. A boy screamed as a creature pulled him outside dragging him through the window's broken glass. His screams stopped as it flew away toward the first one.

The warm night air soothed Mikey's trembling body. He glanced up the street, then started walking. His best friend lived several blocks away. It would take a long time, but he could call his parents from there. He would need a new babysitter.

## TRICK AND A TREAT

Jackson's arm hurt from the weight of the candy, but it was a good hurt. An aching that surged excitement through his sugar-drenched veins. He'd done well. Better than well. Fantastic. His best year ever, although it would be his last Halloween run with his friends. The candy in his bucket rose to the top edge. Just looking at it took his breath away.

He considered stopping for a piece of chocolate. No time. More prizes were ahead.

He led his friends forward. Each of them had scored massive hauls, but he'd scored more than them. He'd taken advantage of the chaos earlier in the evening as groups of children flooded to an open house. He'd return a second, or even a third time. It didn't always work. Sometimes the adult called him out, and he'd just slink away to the next porch light. It didn't matter if the adult caught him—all just a game. A trick and a treat.

He'd chosen a vampire costume not because he loved vampires, but because no other costume was available during the week before Halloween. It worked just fine, and the best part, no mask to cover his mouth, so munching on a few treats during their run was easy. Just slip out the plastic teeth, toss in some snacks, and keep moving.

Dan's werewolf costume was the best. Realistic fur and claws. His rich parents could afford to buy him the best, so they did, even though he'd only wear the outfit one time in his life.

Emma dressed as a princess with a tiara and a full gown. She always wore princess costumes as far back as he could remember. Nobody teased her about it because she acted like one all the time every day of the year.

Tommy claimed to be a zombie, but he'd pieced it together so poorly he could have been mistaken for a homeless janitorial worker. No thought to it at all. He just messed up his hair, stuck some black teeth wax over one of his front teeth, and tore up some old clothes he'd purchased at a garage sale, but that was it. No rotting flesh or limbs falling off or any of that. Not cool. He'd gotten lucky, though. Emma offered to add some scars using a horror makeup from the previous year, so for the next hour she sat in front of Tommy, sometimes moving in only inches from his sweaty face, as we all watched the prettiest girl in Stone Hill work magic.

Sam wore a Thor costume, the same one he'd worn the previous year, but now he'd gained so much weight the thin fabric stretched to the breaking point over his chest. Like most friends, Sam didn't have a lot of money to buy a new costume. Not that it mattered anymore, anyway. Their last trick-or-treat ritual was at an end.

That realization hit Jackson hard. He'd never trick-or-treat again in his life. Never score free candy again. He had to make the most of the moment, but now it was over.

Jackson glanced back at the rows of houses they'd

passed. Most had already turned off their lights. No other kids around—just them. The stillness of the night sent a wave of dread through him. Maybe they were the last trick-or-treaters in town.

They stood below the final streetlight at the edge of town. The street ended, yet a narrow gravel road extended beyond the asphalt, winding through tall grass and a black forest. A chilly, fall breeze whipped across their costumes, and leaves crackled in the surrounding trees. One light ahead in the distance caught Jackson's eye. One last house?

"There's one." Jackson pointed to the light.

"We don't have to go to every single house, Jackson." Tommy sighed.

"Yes, we do. This'll be the last time we go trick-or-treating. We'll be too old next year."

Sam held up his half-full bucket. "It's not fun anymore. We can just go buy this crap at the store."

"It's not just the candy, doofus. It's the fun. We're having fun, right?"

Nobody answered. Dan took a deep breath. "I just want to go home."

Tommy stuffed another mini Three Musketeers bar in his mouth. "I agree with Dan. My feet hurt."

"No. We can't give up now. You guys are weak. We've only been out here for two hours. Maybe you'd have more energy if you waited until you got home before scarfing down all your candy." Jackson grabbed the edge of his bucket. "Look. It's just a pile of wrappers!"

"I can't wait."

The five of them stood in the middle of the road. Not even a car in sight.

Jackson stepped toward the gravel road. "C'mon, we can't give up now."

"You're wasting your time," Tommy the zombie said. "It's some freaky old woman's house. I think she does farming or something."

"How come I didn't notice it last year?"

"We didn't come out this far last year."

"Her light is on."

"So, what," Sam the overweight Thor said. "Nobody goes out there."

"We need to collect our treat."

"She doesn't have any candy," Tommy said. "I saw her once in town. She walks with a limp, like she broke her leg. Maybe she's a pirate."

"Perfect, so she's in the Halloween spirit all year round. If her light is on for Halloween, she wants visitors."

A bellowing hum came from the forest. The crickets chirped louder in the surrounding weeds.

"I'll just wait here. You go ahead." Emma lifted her flashlight and peered it into her pink pumpkin bucket, stirring the candy around with her fingers.

"I'll stay with Emma." Dan stepped toward her.

"Me too." Sam joined them.

"Guy's, we're a team," Jackson said. "This is our last chance to get Halloween candy. Do you understand what's going on? This is your last chance to do this as a kid. We can't just walk away from this."

"We're not walking away." Tommy straightened his hair. "We'll be right here waiting for you. Get what you want, and I'll just eat a few snacks until you get back. I've never been out there and it's dark. I'd watch out for guard dogs, though."

"I can handle dogs. They love me."

"Yeah." Tommy sneered.

"Don't you have enough candy already?" Emma smirked. "Your bucket's full."

"But my pockets are empty. Plenty of room in there. Always room for more candy."

"Well, I'm not going all the way over there for one little treat. Maybe for a bunch of houses."

"Fine. Stay here and I'll get the goods. You're missing out."

The half-moon above lit the area well enough to see to the edge of the forest on both sides of the gravel road, and along with his flashlight Jackson made his way toward the light. The tall grass swallowed up the path in front of him as he trudged forward. No car had traveled that road in a long time.

He passed the edge of the forest and entered a clearing. A simple stone path wound up to the front door of a neglected single-story house. No light came through from inside the house, but curtains covered the windows.

No car. Not even a garage.

Waist-high grass and weeds surrounded the house. A weak front porch light illuminated half the lawn, and a string of lanterns hung across the roof's overhang. The roof bowed down in the center and smoke drifted up from the chimney.

A low moan, like an injured bear, echoed from the forest next to the house. He pictured a pack of wild dogs charging from around the side of the house at any moment to attack him.

His heart beat faster as he stopped at the bottom of the porch. He cleared his throat as if someone inside the house might hear him. "Excuse me? Trick or treat."

He focused on the windows. Nothing moved inside.

Maybe nobody was home, but he wouldn't give up without making sure.

"If you didn't want visitors," Jackson mumbled, "you should have turned off your light."

He crept up to the front door, pulling back the squeaky screen door, and knocked. A white fabric blocked a small window in the door. He listened for footsteps inside. Complete silence. He knocked again, and the door flew open. An old grayed-haired woman stood in the doorway. Her eyes... glowed? He shuddered and stepped back.

"What's this?" she asked.

A strange smell floated under his nose. Smoke. Candles perched on glass plates hung by chains from the ceiling, illuminating the area behind her. He cleared his throat again. "Trick or treat."

She slumped forward, standing in a loose white robe and bare feet. Her ragged gray hair drooped down over her eyes until she pushed it aside. Deep wrinkles lined her face. A circular metal star symbol hung from her string necklace.

Her eyes widened, and she smirked. "Well, you're my first customer."

*Customer? What a strange thing to say, even on Halloween.*

Jackson scanned the area near the doorway for a bucket of candy. "It's Halloween. Do you have any treats?"

"Oh, I'm aware of what day it is." She chuckled. "You want a treat, eh? What a shame, I was hoping to do a trick instead."

Jackson chuckled awkwardly. "If you don't have any..."

She glanced back over her shoulder. "Oh, I think I can find something. I've lived out here for thirty-two years and nobody has ever stopped by on Halloween."

"Really? Not even one kid?"

"Not one. But you're in luck. I baked a tray of monster chocolate chip cookies. Would you like one of those?"

He lost his smile. "I'm not supposed to eat anything that's not wrapped, like from a store. Do you have any Hershey's chocolate bars or a Snickers bar?"

"I'm afraid not. I don't get out to the store much. Let me get you a cookie."

She turned and limped down the hallway to a back room.

"Oh great," he mumbled, "a cookie."

He frowned and scanned her possessions. Frames dotted the walls, but instead of paintings or pictures, they contained rows of black and white symbols, like some ancient language. He knew some Spanish words, but they didn't look Spanish. Maybe French.

Several large plants snaked up against the wall beneath the main picture window, but with the sheet blocking the sunlight, how did the plants survive?

That smell. Sweet, yet it made him gag at the same time. A mix of sugar and manure. Would the cookies taste like that? No way would he eat anything she brought him. She must not have cleaned the house in a long time. Old people lived that way.

He searched for her back in the darkness. He should just run and tell his friends she wasn't home.

"Here we go." The woman limped back to him, holding the tray of cookies. She stretched it out to him. "Pick one."

Again, that sugar and sewer smell. He hesitated, but the cookies were massive. The biggest he'd ever seen. Almost an inch thick and the size of a small plate. Huge chocolate chips covered every inch.

He leaned toward them and sniffed. Nothing unpleasant about them. Just sweet.

"You'll like these," she said with a grin.

He reached for the biggest one and pulled it away, watching her face. "Thank you. I'll just take it home."

"I know kids these days like sweets. My cookies are the sweetest thing you'll ever eat. Try it."

His mouth watered. He nodded. "Maybe just one bite."

He bit in and within seconds his head swirled. Maybe she put some weird drug in there, but it was so incredibly sweet. The best chocolate chip cookie he'd ever eaten. He wanted to devour the whole thing in that moment. He took another bite. His head reeled, and he smiled.

"Do you like it?" she asked.

"It's delicious. Can I have another one?"

"One per child."

"Can I take one for my friend? He's waiting back there." He gestured toward the main road.

She glanced over his shoulder. "He'll need to come here himself if he wants one."

He stared again at the tray of five more jumbo cookies but turned away as he took a third bite. "Thank you."

"You're welcome. Come back next year if you'd like."

Next year. He wouldn't be out for Halloween next year. Too old. But she *had* invited him. Maybe he'd take her up on it.

He hurried back to his friends. They'd be so jealous when he told them about his treat. He held it out as he approached them.

"What d'you get?" Dan asked.

"She gave you a cookie?" Tommy sneered.

"Not just a regular cookie, guys." Jackson waved it

beside his head and then bit off another chunk. "This thing is so delicious."

Dan reached for it.

Jackson turned away. "Get your own."

"I'm not going in there." Dan frowned.

Jackson teased the cookie in front of Dan's face. "Even for this? It's magnificent."

"Did she put a spell on you?" Tommy asked. "I heard that woman's crazy."

"She's not crazy. She's nice. Go get one. If you don't want it, you can give it to me."

Another low moan erupted from the forest.

Dan shook his head. "I just want to go home."

Jackson took another bite of the cookie, wiping crumbs from the corner of his mouth. He closed his eyes for a moment, relishing the thick chunks of chocolate. How could anyone bake something so delicious? "You guys don't know what you're missing. You need to get in there and get one."

Tommy turned back toward town. "Come on, let's go home."

"You're leaving?" Jackson glared at them. "Are you crazy?"

They stopped.

"It's getting late, Jackson." Emma took off her tiara and hung it from the side of her pink pumpkin bucket. "My parents will be mad if I don't get home soon."

Jackson eyed their costumes. He *did* tell that old woman his friend was waiting for him. Maybe he could use them to go back and get another cookie. "You're just going to let your costumes go to waste, huh?"

"What are you talking about?" Dan asked.

He singled out Dan's werewolf costume. "You guys are

about the same size as me. Lend me your costume, Dan, so I can go back in and get another one."

Dan rolled his eyes. "She'll know it's you."

"How will she know it's me? I'll wear your mask, and that outfit covers your whole body."

Dan held out his werewolf mask. "She'll recognize your voice."

"I won't say a word. I'll just nod and grab a cookie."

Dan slipped off the rest of his costume and Jackson did the same. He slipped on the fur leggings first, then the detailed main body section, then the claw gloves. He slipped on the mask last. Damp.

"Good God, Dan," Jackson spoke through the small air hole near the mouth, "you sweat a lot."

"I'm exhausted. I want to go home."

Jackson set down his bucket of candy and took off toward the old woman's house empty-handed. "I'll be right back."

He stormed up to the front door and knocked.

The woman opened the door with a broad smile. "How wonderful. Two visitors in the same day. This is amazing."

"Trick or treat," Jackson spoke in a gruff voice.

"Would you like a trick or a treat?"

"Treat."

She leaned toward him, staring into his eyes, then offered him the tray. "You must be the friend of that other boy. Did he like his cookie?"

Jackson nodded as he plucked another cookie away from her.

"Have a bite," she prodded.

He shook his head.

"You must try one bite. I know you'll like it."

"No, thank you," he said in his regular voice.

"Hmm, your voice sounds familiar. Have you been here before? Lift your mask and let me have a look at you."

"No ma'am." He spoke in a low voice again.

She leaned in closer and glared at his eyes. "I know I've seen you before. You were here a few minutes ago." She snatched the cookie out of his hands.

He stumbled back. "No."

"I know it's you. You demanded a trick or a treat, and I gave you my best treat. You tricked me in return. No more treats. This time, you'll get a trick."

Jackson turned away. He strained to find the steps of the porch through the small eye sockets in the mask. He glanced back one last time at her.

She raised the star symbol on her necklace toward him and spoke three words.

"As you are."

A flash of light burst out from the necklace and struck him in the chest. He careened down the stairs and toppled to the ground as a burning sensation flooded his body. His face tingled. His body swelled to fill his cloth outfit.

He pulled at the mask, but it wouldn't come off.

"Help me!" he cried out.

The old woman laughed.

He flopped to the side, trying to stand again as his vision spun. What had she done to him? Poison him? He spit crumbs from the edge of his mouth as his jaw stretched out beneath his eyes. His airway opened wider, pulling at the mask's fur as it clung to his skin. No more skin, only fur.

He ripped at his chest to remove the werewolf outfit, but his fingers tore against his own flesh. No more fingers, only claws. The costume disappeared, leaving only an animal's pelt that became his own.

The woman laughed from her doorway, cackling like an old hag as she still held the tray of cookies.

"What did you do to me?" Jackson yelled, but his words made no sense. Growls and grunts came out instead.

"You won't be like that for long, my dear. It's a trick. But remember not to trick an old woman next time." She closed the door on him.

He lurched forward and pounded on her door. "Help me!" Only more growls.

He scrambled away toward his friends, calling out to them as he ran faster than he'd ever run before. His feet pounded through the grass as a howl filled the air. His howl.

He caught up to them within seconds. They screamed and ran in the opposite direction, leaving the candy buckets behind.

"Hey guys, it's me," he yelled. More growling and a howl. "Where are you going? Stop!"

# LITTLE GREEN ALIEN

Ben strained to see the object hovering above them. It was about a hundred feet above the treetops and the afternoon sky reflected off the surface so that from below it looked almost transparent. The only thing that gave it away was when it moved, the air rippled around it, resembling a drop of water splashing into a still pond.

John saw it first and if he hadn't received that green laser pointer from his dad a few days earlier, they might have just ignored it and moved on, but John was eager to use his new toy.

"I think I can get it." John aimed the laser at the object like firing a pistol.

Nothing happened at first.

"It's just a cloud or something. Maybe a sun dog."

"That's no sun dog. That's a UFO."

"Nothing's there."

"I got it!" John's face lit up with a wide grin. "I got that sucker."

"How can you tell?" Ben asked.

"It moved. Didn't you see it jump?"

"No." Everything looked the same, except the clouds shifted behind the strange anomaly.

"I'll do it again, so watch this time. Look for the green dot. There! I hit it again."

Ben spotted the green laser dot jittering against a murky cloud.

John bumped him and held out the laser pointer. "Here. You try."

Ben took it and aimed it into the sky at the same strange shape. The clouds shuddered when the light hit the spot. More than shuddered. They convulsed.

"You hit it too!" John patted him on the back. "Good shot!"

The shapeless form burst, revealing a solid object within it. Something was there. The object appeared in the sky above them in full view, with no environmental interference to mask it. A silver orb. It wavered sideways before coming to an abrupt stop. No smoke or fire to show they had damaged it, but it wobbled like a top near the end of its spin.

John howled with laughter. "I told you guys it was a UFO."

Ben's doubts faded. The object circled in the air, making wide arcs until it careened toward them.

"It's going to crash." Emmie pulled Ben's arm as she stepped back toward the house.

"Holy shit! I shot it down!" John laughed as the thing plummeted.

The ground shook when the object crashed into the woods at the end of the cornfield. A dark billowing cloud rose into the air. It knocked over several trees and the sound boomed through the air like a thousand shotguns had gone off at the same time.

Ben gasped.

"Get in the house." Emmie pulled Ben toward her.

John charged toward the spectacle.

"Where are you going?" Emmie called out to him.

He slowed and turned back. "Over there, to see what happened."

Emmie shook her head. "We should call the police. You better hope that's not a military plane you just shot down."

John rolled his eyes. "So what if it is? Serves them right for flying that thing over our property. Let's go!"

The dust overshadowed the forest. No sign of a fire, but someone might need help. Ben hurried along with John, and Emmie joined them. They crossed the yard and entered the cornfield. Pushing through the cornstalks toward the forest, Ben eyed the skies for any sign of military aircraft searching for the downed object. Nothing yet.

"Do you think it was a military drone?" Ben asked.

"I doubt it. Drones don't hover in one spot. I'm telling you, it's from outer space."

"No such thing." Ben pushed through the field as corn stalks whipped across his face.

"Well, I guess we'll find out then, won't we?"

"You better hope it is," Ben said, "or you're going to prison for downing a military aircraft."

"Can't prove anything." John shook his head. "No proof that I did it. *You* guys won't say a word."

"I hope the pilot's okay," Emmie said.

"The alien pilot," John corrected. "We'll take him hostage, if he survived."

"If it's really an alien," Emmie said, "how are we going to communicate with it? Maybe it'll want to kill us?"

"Of course, it'll want to kill us. We just shot down its

ship. But I think it'll be dead when we get in there. That thing landed hard."

"This is just like that Roswell crash in New Mexico back in the 40s," Emmie said.

"Yep, except this time we'll get to it before the government does. We'll take pictures and post them on the internet before their goons have a chance to threaten us. This will be big news. Everyone in the world will see this."

"Do you have your cellphone?" Ben asked.

"Don't you have yours?"

"No."

"Shit, man, you always carry your cellphone. We'll have to go back to the house and get them."

"Do you think it's aliens?" Emmie asked.

"Absolutely. Be sure to grab as much tech stuff as you can after we take pictures so we can stash it away. The government will take it if we don't."

"Let's just see what it is first," Ben said.

John looked back at him. "It's aliens."

They huffed through the cornfield until coming out on the other side in front of the forest. The dust had dispersed. Still no sign of any fires ahead. No approaching government aircraft, either.

John pulled out the survival knife he carried in a scabbard at his waist. He held it up in front of him as he stepped toward the trees, as if whatever had crashed might jump out and attack him. John was big on knives. He lined the walls of his room with various swords and ancient daggers. He would pull his knife out at the first sign of trouble, whether it warranted it or not. John sliced the blade through the air.

"What are you doing?" Ben asked him.

"Getting ready to kill an alien."

"No, don't kill it," Emmie said. "If something survived the crash, you just leave it alone."

"I won't leave it alone if it attacks us."

"Just don't hurt it. Maybe it'll try to communicate with us."

"I've seen enough movies to know that aliens don't appreciate their ships being knocked out of the sky."

"That's science fiction," Ben said.

"Damn right, and now that shit just got real."

John led them into the woods, following a familiar path they'd created over years of exploring the area. At least the thing had crashed on the side of the forest with fewer trees. A lot easier to get to it.

John used his knife to hack away some stray branches that dared to block his path. He pointed. "It's over there. I can see it."

Ben couldn't see it at first. He followed John and listened for any voices or mechanical noises that might verify its origin as from Earth. The top edge of the object only appeared after they pushed through tall grass. Beyond the grass, a section of the forest floor swelled up from the impact.

John ran up to it without hesitation, holding his knife out at his side like some skilled warrior. "This is awesome. I told you it was aliens. Believe me now?"

Ben didn't answer. If it belonged to the military, they would come to claim it soon. It was an advanced aircraft. Something way beyond any high tech he'd ever seen or imagined. The craft created a small crater with most of it lodged deep into the ground. The domed top half rose to their waists and stretched out a little longer than a school bus, with tapered points at each end like a giant silver football. It had landed horizontally—*if* those points were sticking out from its sides—but it was difficult to tell which end was up. Leaves and branches dotted its surface, and it had flattened dozens of trees on its way down.

No dents or imperfections on its surface. No signs of life.

John moved within a few inches of the object, stretching out his hand to touch it.

Emmie groaned. "I wouldn't mess with that, John. Maybe it's dangerous."

"Of course it's dangerous. Alien technology is dangerous, but I'll need to explain what I saw to everyone on the planet, so I better find out."

"What if aliens crawl out of that thing and abduct us?"

"They might. And then we'll run like hell. Every man for himself."

"John, I'm your sister! You got to protect me."

"Every man for himself, Sis. Ben will protect you if he wants."

Emmie stared into Ben's eyes.

"I'll protect you," Ben said, "but it won't be aliens chasing us. It'll be government agents rounding us up."

"You still don't think this is a UFO? You're nuts." John ran his hand across the surface, then yanked it back. "Oh man. This thing's hot." He stared at his palm. Red like a bad sunburn. "The government doesn't make stuff like this."

"It's a secret spy plane, or an advanced drone." Ben studied the contours. "I bet the feds are on their way right now."

"They'll arrest us if they see us here," Emmie said.

"They might arrest us, but not because it belongs to them." John turned to Ben. "You saw how that thing moved before it came down, right? You see anything fly like that before in your life? Of course not. This thing isn't from Earth."

"Well, we don't have cameras, and I don't see any aliens, so let's get back to the house and get them before the feds show up."

John clinked his knife against its surface as he circled around to the side of it. "I'm not afraid of anything, feds or aliens. Don't you want to find out what's inside this thing? I mean, technically it landed on our property. That means it's ours."

"I think the government would disagree."

"When we get back to the house, are you going to call them?"

Ben paused. "No."

"You'll call them and rat us out, won't you?" John turned the knife toward him.

"I said no."

"Better not say anything. We need to keep this a secret as long as we can. At least, until we record it and reverse engineer their technology."

"Reverse engineer it? You're only seventeen. Did you even pass science class?"

"We'll work on it together. After we figure out how it works and record everything, then we'll post it all online before anyone can shut down the area. As soon as the news is out, the feds will storm in and take it away, just like they did at Roswell. You just know there are aliens in this thing. Do you want the feds to take the aliens away and hide the truth?"

"What do you know about Roswell?" Ben asked.

"I read three books on it."

"You don't know everything."

"Well, I know enough."

Ben grunted and stared back at the object. "It's not doing anything. If there is an alien in there, shouldn't it be coming out now?"

"Just give it some time."

"Maybe it's injured," Emmie said.

John continued tapping the tip of his blade against the surface. "Maybe I should try to cut it open."

"There're no doors." Ben moved in closer.

The surface was smooth without seams. One big hunk of molded metal. "You want to try throwing some rocks at it? Maybe that'll get the alien to come out."

Ben moved in and pressed his palm against the metal where it tapered out to a point. He only touched the surface for a moment before pulling away. Hot like a cookie pan just taken out of the oven. Hot... like it had passed through the Earth's atmosphere. A satellite? "Do you think anybody else saw it?"

John shrugged. "If they did, they'd be rushing over in their trucks right now, but I don't see anybody. The neighbor is a mile down the road, but maybe they're not home."

The object rumbled and hummed to life. Its smooth metal surface lit up, radiating a cocoon of light.

Ben backed away, staring at the thing with wide eyes. "Something's alive in there."

John held out his knife, while Emmie grabbed a baseball bat-sized branch from the ground.

"Good," John said. "I hope it opens the door. I want to see the damn thing."

Ben stared at the mound of black dirt next to the object. A stray worm wiggled its way down toward the ground. The object's hum, like a living being vocalizing, filled the air as they stopped talking. No birds. The gentle afternoon breeze drifted through the trees. All the animals had run away or gone into hiding. Nothing was crazy enough to hang around that object, except the three of them.

"What will we do if aliens come out of it?" Emmie asked. "What would we say to them?"

"Who says they'd want to talk? They're probably hostile." John circled around to the object, peering along the edge where it met the ground and across the top. "There's got to be an opening somewhere. A door or a window."

Ben joined John's search for openings, but he was more concerned that the thing might attempt to lift off or explode.

"I feel kind of weird," Emmie said, "like something is pushing against my brain." Emmie put her palm on her forehead.

"Might be the alien doing that," John said. "Trying to get into your mind to control you. That's what they do."

"I don't like it," she said. "We should go back to the house."

"I have a better idea," John said. "Go back and get our cellphones while Ben and I wait here."

"I don't want to come back here again. I don't feel good."

"You're just scared. Don't you want to see the alien? Nothing cool ever happens in this crappy little town, and then this thing drops right in our backyard. This is so freaking awesome, Emmie. We'll be famous."

"I just want to throw up."

"Feel free." John motioned to the side. "We're in the forest. But why don't you run back to the house, get our cellphones, throw up, then hurry back out here."

"Do you want me to get your rifle?"

"That's a great idea. Better yet, no. Grab that long knife I've got hanging over my dresser. The machete. Maybe that'll come in handy."

"All right." Emmie walked away bent forward holding her head.

"Should we go back with her?" Ben asked.

"She'll be fine. What if something happens after we leave? We'd miss it."

"I don't think you should have shot it down, John."

"Geez, I was just playing around. How was I supposed to know it would drop like a rock?"

Ben stared at the craft. "You must have hit it just right. If there's a dead pilot in there, the government will figure out we had something to do with it. Maybe you shined the laser in his eyes."

"They won't figure it out because the only pilot in there is an alien, and who the hell is *he* going to tell?"

Something cracked on the object like metal striking metal, and the thin outline of a circular door a few feet across separated from the rest of the craft. The door lit up as if on fire, then disappeared. The opening stood black until something moved in the shadows within the craft.

Ben and John scrambled back and hunkered down behind some fallen trees. John gripped his knife as if ready for battle. The opening to the craft was near the ground.

John inched up and Ben pulled him back down. John scowled at him.

"Stay down," Ben whispered to him.

"I want to see it."

Ben shook his head. He glanced back to where Emmie had gone. How would they keep her safe when she returned?

The alien screeched near the open door and Ben glimpsed the top of its body as it flowed from the spaceship. An icy chill ran up his spine as he gasped. Without a doubt, an alien. It didn't walk like a human at all. Its thin gray limbs stretched out as it dropped below his line of sight.

Ben's heart raced. It would come out and find them. They needed to get back to the house.

Nothing to protect himself, except John's survival knife, and that would be no match for the thing that stepped out of the spaceship.

A sinking feeling flooded his chest. No government aircraft. This thing was much worse. Who would believe such a thing existed? He teetered on the edge of sanity as the thing screeched again and rustled through the leaves near the crash site.

The alien thumped against the ground, scratching its limbs through the dirt. It huffed out a breath as a pile of dirt flew into the air and rained down a few feet away. More exotic sounds, low moans and high-pitch screeches, filled the air as it tossed huge piles of dirt away from the ship. Was it digging itself out?

John rose, then ducked again. He moved in and whispered into Ben's ear, "It's digging a hole."

*A hole for what?*

Ben turned back toward where Emmie would enter the forest again. Would she come back before that thing was gone? He considered trying to get out of there and warn her, but the forest floor was littered with twigs—he'd make too much noise. If the alien was violent, they'd be an easy target.

Several more bursts of dirt shot up into the air and across the leaves and grass.

John peaked again. He stared longer this time, then gestured for Ben to look.

Ben rose and witnessed a black hole about the size of a manhole cover near the opening to the ship. More bursts of dirt blasted from the hole.

John leaned in and whispered, "That thing's working fast. Maybe it's trying to build a home."

The forest went silent for several minutes while the thing hunkered in its hole until a branch snapped behind them. Emmie had returned.

Ben gestured for her to stay down and keep quiet. She staggered as if she were drunk.

"Something's wrong with Emmie," Ben said.

John stared at the spaceship. "She's just tired."

Emmie met Ben's gaze and walked over to him holding John's machete. She dropped it on the ground near John and dug out two cell phones from her pockets.

"What's going on?" she whispered.

"It came out," Ben said. "The alien."

Her eyes widened. "It's real?" She handed Ben his cell-phone and gave John the other one.

Ben nodded.

"We should call—" Emmie grabbed his shoulder. "I don't feel good."

Ben pressed his hand to her forehead. "You've got a fever."

"Go back to the house if you can't handle it," John said, putting away his survival knife. He grabbed one of the cell phones from the ground and snapped several pictures of the spaceship. He turned to Ben and gestured at the other cell phone. "You record the video. Just film everything."

"I'll be okay." Emmie stared at the spaceship. "Where's the alien?"

"It went down that hole," Ben answered.

"Do you think it might try to eat us?"

"Probably." John stood up and stepped toward the door of the spacecraft.

"Where are you going?" Ben asked him.

"In there."

"No, John," Emmie said. "Stay away from that thing."

"I need to get a better look. Nobody will believe us unless we get good evidence."

"We can't tell anyone about this if we're dead," Ben said.

John shrugged. He crept around the trees toward the open door. Small branches cracked with each step, but nothing came up from the hole. Maybe the thing had dug so far down that it no longer heard them. He maneuvered around the hole in the ground, keeping the machete's blade between him and the hole. He gestured for them to follow him.

Ben wanted to run, but Emmie stood and wobbled forward.

"Maybe you should wait here," Ben said to her.

"I want to see too."

He put his arm around her and steadied her until they came up next to John.

John stepped toward the open door, shining the cell-phone light into the spacecraft. "You guys keep an eye on that hole while I'm inside looking around."

"You're not going in there, are you?" Emmie toppled to the side, and Ben caught her.

"What's up with you?" John asked her. "Are you drunk?"

"No, John, my head really hurts now."

"Well, stay here then."

Emmie grunted and sneered at John.

"What if there's another one in there?"

"Then I'll hack it to pieces." John waved his machete.

The spacecraft's interior resembled a passenger jet without a cockpit. Thousands of tiny symbols and patterns covered the walls, none of which made any sense. Pulsing colors radiated from every direction, as if the metal in the walls were luminescent.

Not much damage from the impact, except for the surface around their feet. A section of tree had dented the craft's shell.

No flat surfaces anywhere. Or places to sit. The floor circled around so that whatever commanded the spacecraft must have maneuvered around without stepping on the wall symbols.

"Holy cow!" John lit up a mound of gray and purple flesh curled up in the corner.

Ben's heart pounded at the sight of another alien. Its baseball-sized green eyes stared back at them.

John swung the machete inches from its face. A wide, narrow mouth stretched open wider in a snarl, revealing rows of pointed teeth that resembled a shark. With the alien huddled in the corner, it was difficult to know how large it was—maybe the same size as an overweight man.

Ben's eyes went wide and his mouth dropped open. "I want to go."

"Record it." John snapped several pictures of the creature with the machete pointing at its forehead.

Ben fumbled with his cellphone. His hands trembled and his mind blanked out. He couldn't remember how to record anything or even where to start. He pressed random buttons until a red button appeared. Pressing that, he held the cellphone up toward the alien without knowing for sure if he was recording or not. The image on the screen jumped as he backed away.

"You're not scared, are you?"

"Yes."

"Look, it's injured." John focused on the far side of the creature's body. The flesh was torn apart and purple goo spilled out across the wall next to it. "This thing's not going anywhere. Just keep recording."

Ben clutched the cellphone tighter, trying to steady his hand. "Where do you think it's from?"

"Probably a million miles away. I guess there's only two of them. The one that dug the hole and then this one." John reached out his hand and touched the alien's scalp. "God, this thing feels weird."

The alien squirmed as John jabbed his finger into its flesh. The creature's legs sprawled out from under it, snaking out like tentacles, but its motions were slow. John slammed his heel down into one of them.

The creature screeched.

Ben winced. A sharp jolt of pain stabbed at the back of his neck.

John laughed, staring into the thing's eyes. "You don't like that, huh?"

"Don't hurt it," Emmie said.

"I'm not hurting it. I doubt it has nerve endings like we do. This is an alien, remember? But it'll die, anyway. The crash ripped its body open. Just look at it." John moved out of the way so they could get a clear view. "We'll have to kill it to put it out of its misery."

Pain spiked through Ben's head. Nausea churned his stomach as he curled forward. "I don't feel good."

"You too? What's going on with you guys? Did you eat some rotten food?"

Ben touched his cheek. Hot and damp.

John frowned. "Are you going to puke?"

"Maybe."

"Do it outside."

Ben wobbled, and his head throbbed. He pressed his hand against one wall to steady himself as his gaze met the alien's green eyes. The thing was upset. Furious. He didn't know *how* he knew, but he knew. Somehow, it was communicating with him.

"Are you filming all this?"

Ben lifted the cellphone again. "I think so. What are you doing?"

John brought out his knife and brought the blade up to its eyes. "I want to see how this thing ticks."

"Don't kill it." Ben's face warmed.

"I won't kill it... yet. But I won't get a chance like this after the feds clampdown the area. Here's our chance to let the world know the truth about aliens."

John sliced the knife's blade across the side of its head as if gutting a fish. Purple goo oozed from the wound, just like the other side of its injured body.

"I don't think you should do that." Emmie pressed into Ben, then backed away toward the entrance.

John recoiled and grimaced. "Oh, that smells awful." He sniffed. "Reminds me of skinning a deer." He chuckled. "I think it's getting mad at me. Hold the phone up. Make sure you record this."

The alien shrieked and gnashed its teeth toward John's knife, but it strained to lean forward more than a few inches before falling back in place. It didn't lunge at John, or even try to get out of the way. Maybe its insides were too smashed up from the crash.

Ben stared back toward the entrance. Emmie stepped

outside and looked around. She glanced at Ben, then at the hole in the ground. She gripped the side of the spaceship and rubbed her forehead.

"Maybe the other one will come back," Ben said.

"I doubt it. I bet it abandoned ship and went off to hide somewhere. They're afraid of us, don't you see that? I doubt it'll be back."

Emmie dropped to her knees and leaned forward as if to puke.

"I think Emmie's really sick," Ben said as a wave of pain pounded through his head again.

John glanced back toward her. "She'll be fine. She's a tough girl. Probably just one of those female health issues. You know what I mean?"

Ben didn't respond.

John chuckled, then turned back to the alien. "I wish we could drag it out of here and examine it out in the sunlight. I can't get a good look at it." John bent down and grabbed one of its limbs, pulling it toward the door. He strained as the creature resisted him. "This thing weighs a ton. Maybe if we get some rope and we all pull."

Emmie screamed. She staggered like a drunk person and raised her arms over her face like something was attacking her.

Ben rushed toward her. The other creature had come back. Or maybe it had never left. A section of its body was slinking up from the hole. Its legs flowed out from under it like snakes, then hardened into slender rods like a giant spider. It slinked across the surface toward Emmie, its bulbous green eyes locked onto her. It didn't look away or blink as he approached.

Ben hooked onto Emmie's arm and yanked her toward

the house, but she resisted him and turned back toward the spaceship. "John's inside."

"John," Ben yelled, "get out of there. The other one came back."

The creature inside the spaceship shrieked again. John emerged a few seconds later with purple goo dripping from his knife. He jumped toward Ben and Emmie just as the creature outside lurched at him, catching John's pant leg in one of its outstretched limbs. He kicked and broke free.

Emmie staggered toward him before collapsing.

John raced to her side and Ben tried to gather her up, lifting her head. The thing would crawl over to them soon.

"Stand up, Emmie," Ben pleaded, "we have to get out of here."

She didn't answer. Her face was pale and her eyes shot open, then rolled back up into her head as if she'd fallen asleep. A green tint covered her eyeballs. She moved her lips as if to speak, but no words came out.

Ben struggled to lift her, only raising her a few inches before his muscles gave out. Her limp body sank to the ground.

John swung his machete at the alien as it inched closer to them.

"Help me drag her out of here." Ben lifted one of her arms.

Together, they dragged Emmie by her arms through the brush toward the exit.

John smirked. "It's probably pissed off we went inside its spaceship."

Ben's vision reeled as his body weakened. "Call your dad, or call the police, or anyone."

"Yeah." John paused and took one last picture before slipping the cellphone in his pocket. "Soon."

"Emmie," Ben said, "are you okay? We need to get out of here."

Emmie moaned and blinked twice. Ben dragged her a few feet until a wave of weakness flashed through him. They stopped for a moment, and the alien paused at the same time.

John growled and lurched forward, swinging the machete at its face. He stretched out the blade as far as he could but the alien evaded him.

"Damn that thing," John said. "It's like a big insect. I just want to squash it."

"We just need to get out of here."

"Well, go then. I can handle it."

"I can't drag her out by myself. You need to help me and I'm not sure I can walk much further either."

John furrowed his brows. "What's gotten into you? You've got more muscles than me."

"I don't know." Ben could run faster than anybody in school, yet within the last few minutes his strength had drained to where he might pass out at any second. Only during the flu had he felt this bad.

He dragged Emmie a few more steps while John blocked them from its attacks. John gave up and jumped around, grabbing Emmie's other arm. They dragged her along as the alien stalked them all the way to the edge of the forest. At one point the machete in John's hand bumped against Emmie's shorts, smearing in a little purple alien blood. At least it wasn't her blood.

The alien shifted from side to side as it trailed them, its head weaving around as if calculating the best angle to pounce. Its long slender limbs navigated the brush with ease.

As they reached the edge of the forest and moved out into the sunlight, the alien stopped and peered at them within the shade of the trees.

"Get it out into the sunlight," Ben said. "I think it doesn't want to come out."

They moved Emmie away from the trees, close to the cornfield, and Ben dropped beside her.

John stepped toward it and lost his balance for a moment. His arms didn't whip around as fast as they did earlier. "I'll slice that thing up. Take a piece of it home with me and put it on my wall."

Ben heaved in and out each breath. "I don't think I can walk anymore."

John lifted the blade and swung it once before wobbling to the side. "What the hell is going on? Now I feel like shit too."

"It did something to us."

John glanced back and focused in on Ben's face. "What's wrong with your eyes? They're all green."

"I don't know. It's got to be that thing. It poisoned us or something. Now it's just waiting for us to die so it can eat us."

"I won't let it eat us." John faced the alien, raising the machete over his head. "Is that what you're planning? I dare you to step out here." He staggered for a moment. "Well, I guess this is all my fault. I better do something before we all die."

John charged forward and yelled at the same time. The machete's blade sliced clear through one of the creature's stick legs. The thing wobbled and screeched as its mouth widened in a snarl. Its green eyes glared down at John.

As John recovered for a second swing, Ben slumped over to his side. Something in his pocket jammed against his hip. The laser pointer. He had put it in his pocket after the spaceship crashed. He dug it out and switched it on, aiming the beam straight at the alien. Maybe he could catch its eyes and blind it long enough for them to escape.

John's second swing came up short, and the alien moved out from the shade, standing fully in the sunlight with no harm to itself. Its bright white teeth glared in the reflected the light, and its green eyes grew wider when John jumped forward toward another of the creature's limbs.

Ben steadied his hands as the laser's green light darted across the alien's body. He turned and clawed at the grass, struggling to lift himself far enough to aim it. He struggled to keep his eyelids open. Whatever that alien had done was stronger than he was.

A shade of green covered everything around him. The clouds, the sky, Emmie. Ben's face throbbed and warmed in the sun.

The alien struck out at John, sacrificing a limb to knock the machete from his hands. The alien's purple blood spurted across the grass as John jumped to retrieve the machete. When John turned his back to it, the alien seized his legs within its bug-like claws. It dragged John kicking and screaming toward a fleshy pouch near the base of its body.

"Oh shit!" John yelled. "It got me. Grab the machete."

Ben spotted the machete, but it was out of reach.

The alien clutched John's arms and legs and shoved him into its pouch, swallowing him up within its flesh. Nausea swelled within Ben, pushing him to the edge of throwing up. The fleshy pouch bulged as John's muffled screams faded. John's hand poked out from the opening a moment before the alien thrust it back inside.

Ben eyed the machete once more and strained to reach it, but that time had passed.

He used the last of his strength to aim the laser at its eyes.

The green dot hit its target.

The alien shuddered and screeched, lashing its limbs out toward him. One leg slammed into the grass near him.

Ben hit its eyes again. Its torso wobbled as it stepped back. Purple blood oozed from its severed limbs until it turned and retreated into the forest.

Twigs snapped, and the brush rustled as it scurried away. A short time later the spacecraft lifted into the air again, hovering above him for several seconds before darting off into the sky.

Ben regained his strength within minutes after the UFO disappeared.

Emmie groaned and opened her eyes. "Where's John?"

"Gone."

Emmie sat up as something rumbled in the distance.

They focused on the sky to their right. Two black helicopters approached.

Ben dug out the cell phone from his pocket and texted the video of the alien to his dad. A moment later, a message popped up.

*Message send failure.*

Ben groaned as he helped Emmie to stand. "Nobody's going to believe us, except them."


MORE FRIGHTFUL TALES IN BOOK 3! SEE NEXT PAGE FOR info!

# DREADFUL DARK BOOK 3
## TALES OF HORROR: BOOK 3

# BAIT

"I got a great trap this time," Jake said.

"You said that," Tony said.

"I don't know why we didn't think of this before."

"You can tell me all about it when I get there. I'll be there in a minute. I'm turning onto the dirt road now."

Tony ended the call and wound through the forest to the clearing where he'd met Jake several dozen times before. The trap Jake mentioned came into view. Just a metal cage, like a massive dog kennel. A lot less impressive than Jake had made it sound.

Tony shook his head and parked the truck beside Jake's truck.

Jake walked over with a wide grin on his face. He rubbed his hands together like one of those old-fashioned TV villains scheming to pull off the perfect heist.

As soon as Tony opened his door, Jake called out to him, "What you think?"

"No Bigfoot is going to walk into that thing." Tony chuckled. "Well, maybe if he trips and falls into it."

Jake sneered at him. "What's wrong with it?"

"You know the size of a Bigfoot, right? It's too small, and any wild animal could break out of that flimsy thing. How much money did you spend on it?"

Jake glanced back at his genius idea. "I got the biggest one I could find. It won't be stuck in there for very long, anyway. We just need to get it in there and then shoot it with a tranquilizer dart. While it's asleep, we put the cage back on the trailer and haul him out of here. It's perfect."

Tony shook his head. "You didn't think this through. You should have left it on the trailer. After you capture Bigfoot in there, how will you get it back up onto the trailer? You don't have a hoist."

"You're going to help me."

"Hell with that. Do I look like I can move five hundred pounds? You know how big they are. Everybody knows those things are huge."

Jake rolled his eyes. I know what a Bigfoot looks like."

"Good, because all this crazy talk of him prancing by and just stepping into that little cage of yours is all hogwash. Those creatures are smarter than that. They won't fall for your little trap."

Jake's face turned red. "Well, none of your boring ideas have worked yet. We've been scouring these woods for weeks now without a trace of it. Where's *your* evidence? This is a great idea. I told you I had a backup plan, and this is it."

"I'm tracking it down the scientific way. You can't rush these things. We'll only catch him through patience and methodical steps. It takes time to collect the evidence. Bigfoot's a smart creature. It knows how to cover its tracks. Eventually, we'll get him."

"That's what you keep saying, but have you found anything yet? No."

"What the hell are you talking about? We've found plenty of stuff. Remember the cave and all those bones? Plenty of footprints, too. I bet there's more than one of them out there. It just takes patience."

"Your ideas are taking too long. We should try something else."

Tony walked past Jake to the cage. The bars were only a quarter inch thick. Plenty strong to house a pack of dogs, but nothing more. "If you leave that cage wide open out here tonight, you'll find a pissed off black bear trapped inside of it in the morning. How you going to deal with that? You got a plan?"

"Of course I've got a plan."

"Lots of black bears in the area. They're bound to go exploring your little device. How will you get it out of there? You think you'll just open the door and he'll run out and be on his way without ripping your arms off first?"

"I'll shoot him with my tranquilizer gun."

"There you go again. So then you've got a sleeping black bear stuck in your cage. Who's going to help you drag him out? Not me."

Jake folded his arms over his chest. "Maybe some guys from the bar will help me."

Tony chuckled. "They won't help us. They think we're nuts. You know how all those guys tease us. Just think what they'll say when you ask for help pulling a bear from your cage. They'll laugh at you and congratulate you on your "catch". Everyone thinks this is all a joke."

"It's not a joke."

Tony put his hand on Jake's shoulder. "We know that, but nobody will help us. Do you see what I mean? You need to think this thing through."

"Well, what were you planning to do if we caught a Bigfoot?"

"I don't want to catch him. Too much work. I just want some pictures and some video, if I can get it. That's all I'm looking for. Physical evidence would be great, but it's not practical because we don't have anyone to help us."

"Those cameras you set up are worthless. They only caught pictures of deer and wolves."

"At least we know they work. Lots of wild animals in these woods, and maybe only a few Bigfoots. One of these times it'll catch one of them red-handed. We just have to keep trying."

"My cage will work too, because I'll put Bigfoot's favorite food in there." Jake gestured toward the blue-and-white cooler sitting next to the cage. "I brought some tripe."

"Tripe? That's the dumbest idea I've ever heard. What makes you think Bigfoot likes to eat cow stomachs?"

"It'll work. The magazine had a big long article about what they eat."

"What magazine?"

"There's only one. *Bigfoot Hunter*, and the article is in issue 246. The scientists explained exactly how to make your own Bigfoot bait. My cooler is full of it."

Tony winced. "First, the guys in that Bigfoot magazine aren't scientists. Second, the only thing tripe attracts is flies. Bigfoot doesn't want to eat that crap. You should have brought some hamburgers or fried chicken. They eat the same stuff we eat. If you're going to use bait in there, think about what might attract a gorilla or a human."

"Tripe will work. You'll see. Maybe not on the first night, but I think my idea's solid." Jake nodded and grinned. "It's just like fishing, you know. Just set a good bait, and when he bites, that's when you nab him. Reel him in like a big old Northern."

"You're wasting your time with that cage." Tony shook his head. "I'll even bet you a case of beer the only thing in that cage in the morning will be a pile of rotting tripe or a pissed off black bear."

Jake looked away. "I guess we'll find out in the morning."

"I guess we will."

Jake went over to his cooler and scooped out the tripe into a plastic salad bowl. He placed the bowl in the middle of the cage and then set up the door latch so the door would snap down behind anything that tripped the snare.

He inspected it and backed away. "This'll get him."

Tony grabbed the cage's metal mesh and pulled. "These bars won't hold him—maybe a bear or a man, but not Bigfoot."

"You just wait."

"Sure, we'll see about that. I need to get my stuff from the truck."

"I'll get the rifles."

Tony turned back to his truck. "I'll get my backpack. Just a minute."

They prepared for their daily trek through the forest. Each of them carried a rifle, just in case, and strapped on a backpack full of supplies. The entire loop through the woods to each of the seven cameras took a few hours, and they would stop at the third camera to eat lunch. They'd gone through the same process every day for four weeks without a shred of definitive evidence to bring home. No pictures of a Bigfoot, yet. Nothing to spur their hopes they were onto something big. No smoking gun to verify all the sightings of Bigfoot in the area over the last fifty years.

They scoured the trees as they crossed through the forest, keeping their eyes open for broken branches and clumps of fur. Clear, well-defined footsteps were the Holy Grail of Bigfoot hunters, but even just an indentation in the soil was enough to send Tony's heart racing.

They arrived at the first camera and checked the images. Two pictures. Two deer.

"You see?" Jake nodded. "Nothing but wildlife. And that's all we'll get with those cameras of yours. We need to do something different, something innovative, like my cage."

"Yeah, that's fine, Jake. Give that cage a shot. But I think you'll end up regretting it."

They circled around the woods, stopping at each camera with the same results. At the end of the day, the only thing they had to show for their efforts was some clumps of fur they discovered caught in some branches. No smoking gun. No footsteps either, but Tony was willing to spend months in that area, if needed.

When they returned to their trucks, Tony's heart skipped a beat. Something was in Jake's cage. Not as large as a Bigfoot, but something else. It lay on the ground as if asleep or dead. Maybe eating the tripe had killed it somehow.

Jake's face lit up, and he charged forward. "I got something! What did I tell you?"

"Probably a bear." Tony hurried behind Jake. "Don't be scaring it."

"We got a Bigfoot."

Something wasn't right. Not a bear or a wolf or a Bigfoot. The thing was too small.

Jake circled the cage and stared at the animal from all

directions. "It's a Bigfoot all right. Just like in the magazines."

Tony got to the edge of the cage and peered in at the fallen animal. Its chest rose and fell. At least it was alive. Tripe was smeared across its fur and onto the ground. "It looks sick. You only put tripe in that cage, right?"

"Mostly. I stuck some sedatives in there too."

Its face was a mix between human and animal. Like some furry Neanderthal. Brown and black patches of fur covered its body. Dirt and mud covered its feet and its long slender fingers curled into claws. The ground next to the creature was torn up as if it had tried digging its way out. Its mouth was hanging open, revealing sharp white teeth.

Jake's eyes were wide, and he jumped around like a boy on Christmas morning. "I got him, Tony. I told you it would work. You owe me a case of beer."

Tony pressed his face into the metal bars to get a better look. The thing didn't look real. A miniaturized version of what a Bigfoot should look like. "It's no Bigfoot. Too small. Maybe you got one of its children."

Jake squinted at it. "Huh? If that's a baby Bigfoot, imagine the size of a normal one."

Tony scanned the surrounding woods. No sign of an adult Bigfoot.

"Maybe its parents are nearby. Maybe they're watching us right now."

Jake glanced around for a moment, then back to his prize catch. "Ah, let them watch. I won't kill it. I'm just going to take it back to town to show him off."

"We need to get that thing out of the cage."

"What are you talking about? We got the real deal

here. We finally got what we've been searching for, and you just want to let it go?"

"It's just like fishing, right? You said so yourself. Catch and release."

Jake's face turned red again. "No, I'm not doing that. I caught him and now I'll be showing him off to everyone in town. This thing will make me famous. Why would I want to let it go?"

"You don't mess with a baby black bear, right? The momma bear is always nearby, ready to rip your arms off if you mess with its kid, so do you think this thing is just wandering around the forest alone?"

"You're paranoid."

"Think about it. Its parents are probably scheming right now from behind them trees on how they'll kill us."

Jake lifted his rifle to his chest and sneered at the surrounding trees. "Just let them try."

"We need to let it go before they find him caged up like that. They'll probably be here any minute."

Jake narrowed his eyes. "You know, that's a good idea. I don't need tripe to get a Bigfoot in my cage. I got the best bait of all."

Jake smacked the butt of his rifle against the cage. The young Bigfoot gazed at them with half-open eyes, then staggered to a standing position as if it were drunk. It looked at Tony, then snarled at Jake. Its hands formed fists as it attempted to stand tall.

"You're not so tough," Jake said to it.

The animal grunted and wavered for a moment before charging at him. Jake stumbled back just as it slammed its body against the side of the cage. It strung its fingers through the metal bars and shook the whole thing.

"You can't get out of there, baby Bigfoot. We got you and we'll get your parents soon too."

The little Bigfoot thrust his arm through the bars, clawing toward Jake's face.

Jake laughed and glanced at Tony. "Look at that! It's trying to get at me."

"Don't toy with it, Jake. You'll just make it mad. How would you feel being trapped in a cage like that?"

"I wouldn't be stupid enough to climb in there to eat tripe, that's for sure. I told you it would work."

The young Bigfoot grumbled as the cage rattled, then it let out a howl like an angry man in pain. The call echoed through the air, and if its parents were nearby, they'd heard it. As the little Bigfoot raged against its captivity, its eyes burned red as if bloodshot. It gnashed its teeth, then clamped its mouth onto one bar and strained to bite its way out.

Jake howled with laughter and imitated the animal, using his finger like one of the bars. "Aaarrr. Aaaaaarrrrr. Let me out of here."

The young Bigfoot watched him, then threw all of its weight against the metal cage between them with his hand out toward Jake's throat.

"Take some pictures, Tony. This is what we're here for. Now is your chance."

Tony dug out his cellphone and took several pictures, then recorded over a minute of video. Jake posed beyond arm's length in front of the young Bigfoot, but jumped away when it scratched its hand across his back.

His eyes went wide. "Whoa, that was a close one. Did you see that?"

"It's not happy. We should let it go."

"No way." He gestured for Tony to get closer. "You get in here too. Let's do a selfie."

"I'd rather stay back here."

"This is your opportunity to be famous. Last chance before we nab its parents."

"No, thanks."

Jake poked at it with the barrel of his rifle. "Isn't that thing freaky? He looks like a cross between a gorilla and a human. Maybe some gal snuck into the forest one night and partnered with one of those things. You know what I mean?" Jake chuckled. "Maybe this little guy is the result of some gal's wild cross-breeding experiment." Jake tapped the barrel of the rifle against the back of the little Bigfoot's hand.

It recoiled and grunted.

"Stop pissing it off, Jake. I got the pictures. We should just let him go and get out of here before the parents find him. I'll unlatch the door so we can take off. We've got everything we need."

"Take off? We haven't seen the big boys yet. That's what we came here for, right? That's what all this fuss is about. I'm not leaving until I see the real thing. Bigfoot himself."

Tony tugged at Jake's arm. "At least go back to the truck."

"All right, I'll watch from the truck, but I'm not letting him go. I'd be crazy to let him run free before I've seen a daddy Bigfoot."

Tony nudged Jake toward the trucks. "What do you think the parents will do when they can't get him out of there?"

"I don't care. They'll be asleep after I shoot them with my tranquilizer gun."

"You better get it ready."

"It's in my truck. I don't think you understand the opportunity we have here. We just need to get one Bigfoot back to town in that cage, then everything's golden."

Jake walked back to his truck, grabbed the tranquilizer gun from his cab, then climbed into the back of the cargo bed.

Tony climbed into his truck and checked the rifle on the seat. Plenty of rounds, just in case things got messy. He had no intention of killing a creature, but he had to be prepared for anything. He slipped the key into the ignition, but left the engine off. If any problems arose, he could be out of there fast.

The young Bigfoot cried out again as it continued rattling the cage's mesh. Despite its size, that little thing was powerful. The whole cage leaned from side to side as it threw its weight against the walls. Whatever Jake had put in the tripe had made little difference. The young beast showed no signs of drowsiness. It was ready to lunge at them if they dared to release it.

Tony searched the edge of the forest for any signs of young Bigfoot's parents. Nothing out of the ordinary. Maybe its parents were waiting for them to leave before approaching. If they didn't appear within an hour, he would insist they open the cage and head home. Jake would just have to try again another time.

A booming low cry filled the air. Much louder than the young Bigfoot. Tony rolled his window down an inch to listen. Branches swayed and cracked ahead, beyond the cage. A dark figure emerged from the edge of the forest and moved out into the open. Tony's pulse pounded in his ears. It was there, about a hundred feet away—a furry, muscular frame crept toward the cage. It had the same humanoid-gorilla face as the young one. Everything Tony had ever read about the beast was true.

Its gaze locked on Tony and Jake as it advanced, lifting its hands in a defensive pose. Its arms were long and slender with patches of fur torn away in several areas as if it'd been in a recent battle. Maybe a black bear had trespassed on its territory and lost.

Instead of charging toward the cage to rescue its child, the larger Bigfoot slinked forward and crouched down as if ready to pounce on the perpetrator of the crime.

The young Bigfoot howled and stretched out its arms toward its parent. Judging from the larger Bigfoot's breasts, Tony assumed the approaching beast was the mother, which meant the father might be nearby too.

Jake caught Tony's gaze for a moment, giving him the thumbs up signal. Tony considered taking out his cellphone to record again, but his hands trembled too much and he squeezed his rifle.

The mommy reached the cage and comforted its trapped child, while glancing back at Jake and Tony. Jake lifted his tranquilizer gun over the top edge of his cargo bed and aimed. Tony swallowed and held back a desire to yell at Jake. He shouldn't shoot them, even if it was only a tranquilizer dart. Just let the mommy grab the child and go. Tony pressed his mouth shut.

Jake fired one shot, sticking the dart in the mother's lower chest. She recoiled and twisted around before knocking the dart away, but it was too late. The chemicals in the dart started doing their job. She teetered, then clutched the bars of the cage. She snarled at Jake and Tony, her eyes wide and red like her child.

"Got you!" Jake yelled. "Down you go."

The mother Bigfoot wobbled and lurched toward Jake,

but toppled over a few seconds later. The young Bigfoot cried out again and shook the cage.

Jake jumped out of the cargo bed, but another Bigfoot pounced on him from out of nowhere before his feet hit the ground. It grabbed Jake by the neck and whipped him against the side of the truck.

Tony froze. It was the father Bigfoot. The one they'd dreamed of discovering for years. It was at least seven feet tall with limbs like a professional wrestler. Its narrow eyes focused on Jake, and it knocked the tranquilizer gun out of Jake's hands before he could aim it again.

Tony climbed out of his truck and fired three warning shots over the father Bigfoot's head. The beast shot a look at him that sent a chill up Jake's spine. Instead of charging at Tony, the Bigfoot grabbed Jake by the leg and dragged him toward the cage.

Jake stretched toward the tranquilizer gun, but it was far beyond his reach. He screamed and thrashed as it dragged Jake along like a rag doll. When it reached the cage, it stomped its foot down on Jake's leg, pinning him to the ground. Jake squirmed around and tried to break free, but the Bigfoot had him good.

The mother Bigfoot rose to her feet and joined her child in shaking the cage, but the effects of the tranquilizer dart prevented it from doing any damage. She clung to the cage just to keep from falling down.

Jake squirmed and hammered at the father Bigfoot's body as it dragged him to the door of the cage. It must have been watching them earlier because it forced Jake's hands against the latch to open the door as if it understood the concept of the door, but just not how to make it work.

Jake fought against it at first until the Bigfoot slammed

him head-first into the door. Blood ran down Jake's face as the Bigfoot forced his hands up near the door latch again. That time, Jake opened the door. The Bigfoot held Jake by one foot as the young Bigfoot escaped the cage and ran off into the woods. The mother Bigfoot wobbled away after her child.

Jake screamed as the Bigfoot dragged him into the cage and tossed him against the back wall. The cage rattled when his body slammed into the metal mesh.

Tony lifted his rifle and aimed. That would be the perfect opportunity to take it down before it came out and attacked him, but he hesitated. He held the Bigfoot in his rifle scope as it slammed the door shut. He pressed his finger on the trigger, but didn't squeeze it.

The Bigfoot turned toward him and glared at him. With its eyes burning with hate, it grinned at him and took a step forward.

Tony's muscles tensed, but the Bigfoot stopped. It raised its chin and glanced around the area before lumbering away toward the others.

"Take it down, Tony!" Jake called from the cage. Blood covered his face and chest. "Don't let it get away!"

Tony followed the Bigfoot in his scope until it disappeared in the forest. He lowered his rifle and stepped toward the cage, but stopped.

"Tony, I'm busted up good." Jake groaned. "Why didn't you shoot that thing?"

Tony crept forward, keeping his rifle ready. He scanned the woods and listened for branches breaking. Maybe the thing would circle around and approach him from a different angle. Catch him in a surprise attack like it had Jake.

"I'll be right there," Tony said.

"Get me out of here. You should have blasted that thing while you had the chance. We could have taken it back to town."

"I got pictures."

Jake smirked. "Pictures."

Tony moved forward a few more feet until a branch cracked in the woods to his left. He swung the barrel in that direction. Nothing there. Maybe just the breeze.

"Do you think they went home?" Jake asked. "Dammit, Tony, why the hell didn't you shoot. That thing almost killed me. What were you thinking?"

"You caged up its child, Jake. What did you think it'd do?"

Jake swore under his breath. "Just get me out of here. Are they gone?"

"I don't know."

Halfway to the cage, shadows moved within the trees to his right. Maybe just a trick of light, but maybe the Bigfoot never left. Just stalking them within the darkness, waiting for an opportunity to attack.

"Can you stand up?"

"I don't think so. My leg's busted up."

"I think they're watching us."

"Hell with that. Just blast them next time. Don't play around. You saw it almost killed me, right? I'll need some help."

"Stand up, if you can. We'll need to hurry when I open the door, so get ready to run back to the truck."

Jake smirked and groaned. "Yeah, right, run."

"Those things are watching us, Jake. I know it. You've got to stand up. If I come in there with you, I just know one of them is going to run out of the woods and lock me in there with you."

"I'll try." Jake staggered to his feet as Tony approached. Blood soaked his shirt and pants, and he clutched his stomach. "It cut my stomach open, Tony. I can feel it."

"I'll get you to a doctor as soon as we get out of here."

Jake lifted his hand for a moment. A hunk of bloody flesh poked out through his torn shirt. Jake chuckled and winced. "Look, Tony. Tripe."

Tony scanned the edge of the surrounding forest, watching for any approaching Bigfoots, but still no sign of them. He lifted the latch on the cage and stepped inside.

Jake limped toward Tony like a zombie straight out of a horror movie. Jake cringed with each step and groaned.

"I got you." Tony grabbed Jake's arm as Jake stumbled.

"Bring me over to my gun. I bet we can still nab one."

A branch cracked nearby as a Bigfoot came out of the forest. A second one followed behind him.

Tony pulled on Jake's arm. "They're coming back."

"Just get my gun." Jake gestured toward where he'd dropped it.

Tony's heart pounded as he dragged Jake out of the cage. The blood smeared across the ground and soaked into Tony's clothes as the Bigfoots approached within fifty feet of them. If they got any closer Tony would stop and fire his rifle.

"Take them down, Tony. They'll kill us if you don't."

"I got this. I think we can make it to the truck."

"Dammit, let me have your rifle then. I'll do it."

Tony paused. The two Bigfoots continued forward. The father Bigfoot was there, along with another male. How many were there? As soon as the question popped into his mind, grunting and thumping footsteps erupted behind him.

He pivoted as several more of the creatures

approached, swarming out through the brush and trees. All of them were as large as the father Bigfoot, but the faces of each one displayed distinct characteristics. Some old, some young, some muscular and fierce, some weak and wise. They stormed in from all directions, every face full of anger and focus. Jake and Tony were the target of their rage.

When Tony's gaze met their eyes, a few of them charged forward. The others circled in around them as Tony dropped Jake to the ground. He brought up the rifle toward the nearest one, aiming it at its heart, but angling it up above its head to fire a few warning shots first. None of them slowed.

"You missed. Give me that thing." Jake yelled. "I'll do it."

Tony handed Jake his rifle and hurried toward his truck, scooping up Jake's tranquilizer gun along the way. Before he climbed in, he turned back. The two Bigfoot creatures reached Jake before he could bring the rifle up to fire it. They knocked his rifle away and tore at his chest, throwing him back to the ground.

"Tony," Jake said beneath the grunts of the Bigfoots tearing him open.

Tony turned and fired the tranquilizer gun at the two creatures, then shot one into Jake's chest. Blood covered his body. He wouldn't make it. Better to put him out of his misery.

As Tony climbed into the driver's seat of his truck, a Bigfoot jumped up into his cargo bed and pounded on the roof of his cab. The metal banging was deafening as Tony started the engine and threw the truck into reverse with the tranquilizer gun in his lap.

He started backing out when the driver's side window

glass shattered. A pair of gorilla-like hands clutched his shirt and plucked him out of his seat.

The Bigfoot hurled him through the air and slammed him to the ground. He landed on his head, sending waves of pain surging through his spine. The tranquilizer gun crashed on the ground next to him.

Several Bigfoots swarmed in and ripped at his clothes and flesh. They tore open his chest and pulled out his intestines, dangling them in the air like spaghetti.

Tony struggled toward the tranquilizer gun. Maybe he could still get out of there. He touched the barrel, but a Bigfoot stomped its enormous foot down on it.

The Bigfoots howled as they tore out his stomach. They passed it around like a raw steak, with each one taking a big bite of it.

Jake was right. They really did like tripe.

# BIRTHDAY BOY

Wesley came up with the idea to go see Dolores for his cousin's 30th birthday.

"I'm not interested," I said.

"Doesn't matter," Wesley said, "it's not for you, it's for John. What else are we gonna do for him?"

Wesley was right. Not much to do in our small Florida town except go out to the bar or stay at home and invite a bunch of friends over.

"When's his birthday?" I asked.

"Tomorrow."

"What the hell? Why didn't you tell me sooner? I would have planned something."

"No need to plan. John doesn't like big parties, anyway. Not the partying type. He won't have nothing going on. We can just take him out there and drop him off for a couple of hours. I want to do something *special* for him."

"She's special all right."

Wesley laughed. "He won't never forget Dolores."

"I haven't forgotten her, that's for sure."

"Me neither."

"You got sunglasses?"

"Two pair."

"I'm tempted not to wear them."

Wesley shook his head. "Not worth it. Better just keep them on."

"You're right."

Dolores would take John's mind off every problem he'd ever had in his life. She lived alone in the woods about an hour north of Lake Sumter.

"I bet she ain't aged a bit." Wesley held back a laugh.

"Are you sure you want to do that to him?" I asked.

"Hell yeah! Do you regret meeting her?"

The memories flooded back, and I grinned. "No."

"Well, there you go. Me neither. They'll both be whooping it up in no time after she gets Johnny in her arms."

"Maybe she's dead? It's been almost twenty years."

"She ain't dead. I drove in there a week ago, just to check—I did *not* go in, by the way—and her light was on. The place looked exactly the same as it did when we were there."

"It'll be interesting to see her again."

"Yes, it will—through our sunglasses."

The next day, Wesley drove us to her place up north of Lake Sumter to a wooded area. John sat in the backseat tapping his damn foot against the passenger side floor the whole way. He was the nervous type—never sat still.

"She's a lovely lady," Wesley said. "Just lovely."

"Why do you keep saying that?" John asked. "You think I won't like her?"

"You'll love her." Wesley winked at me.

"I saw that. What's wrong with her?"

"Nothing at all."

John insisted on wearing nice clothes and getting all dressed up, even after I told him that Dolores didn't care about that stuff. She'd love him just the way he was, but he went out and bought a new fancy blue shirt for the occasion.

"You're wasting your money," Wesley said to him. "She doesn't care what you look like. But you better bring her something, just to be nice. She loves red roses."

"How do you know what she likes?"

"I just know."

"You've been with her before?"

"I'm not gonna answer that!" Wesley laughed and glanced at me.

"Why not? She ugly?"

"No, not ugly at all, Johnny," Wesley said. "Picture the most beautiful woman in the world. That's what she looks like. That's the truth."

"I get the feeling you're not telling me something."

"You don't love beautiful women?"

"I do." John looked at Wesley suspiciously.

"That's what you're getting tonight. A beautiful woman. What the hell are you complaining for?"

"I ain't complaining."

"Good, because we drove all the way out here just for you. That'd suck if you missed this opportunity."

"We can stop and have a beer on the side of the road before we get there," I suggested, "if that would help."

I craned my neck back at John. He was shaking his head. "No, I want to make a good impression."

"There's a whole case in the trunk. We can chill out for a few minutes. Calm your nerves before we go in."

Wesley shook his head and nudged me. "Best John not drink anything before he meets her." Wesley pointed to his eyes. "It might mess with his sight, if you know what I mean."

"Yeah, I guess you're right. It's probably best you stay sober. You want to see things clearly when you take in the full spectacle of Dolores. She's a sight to behold."

I slowed down along the edge of the highway and pointed to the gravel path leading into the forest. "Her place is in there."

"Where's the road?" John asked.

"It's there. Just that path."

"We need to walk there?"

"We can drive in, but it's overgrown with weeds. Dolores doesn't get too many visitors."

"How do you know this woman, anyway?"

"I told you before. Just a friend."

"A friend from where?"

Wesley grinned and shot a glance at me. "A friend I knew in college." He chuckled.

"If she's so beautiful," John said, "why don't you marry her?"

Wesley scowled and groaned. "Dolores isn't the *marrying* type."

"Wes, you're scaring the guy."

"Sorry."

"So she dates a lot of guys?"

"As many as she can find."

"Oh," John's voice trailed off. "I get it."

"Don't get all emotional on us," I said. "You haven't met her yet. Dolores just likes to have a little fun and move on, but you may be just the guy she's looking for."

"Johnny, my boy, I'm positive you're the guy she's looking for," Wesley said.

"She ain't no prostitute, is she?" John said. "I'm not desperate."

"I know you're not. She's just affectionate. The type of woman to help a guy like you."

"What you mean a guy like me?"

Wesley shrugged. "A guy looking for someone *special*."

I smirked. "She's special all right."

Wesley knocked the back of his hand against my leg. "Don't get him thinking there's something wrong with her."

I turned back to John. "There's nothing wrong with her. As soon as you see her you'll fall in love. I'm sure of that."

"How do you know I'll fall in love if you haven't seen her in years? Maybe she's all old and ugly now?"

"Well, let me just say this. You will thank me."

Wesley steered the Cadillac onto the gravel road leading to her house. The path wound through the trees and he turned on the headlights to see where we were going. The darkness enveloped us even though the sun hadn't gone down yet. Only a few slivers of light broke through the leaves overhead.

One light lit her porch up ahead. The memories came flooding back. I'd been out to her house a few times in my college years, but nothing about her place had changed. Same old run-down shack. I pushed away the nostalgia. Time for John to have some fun.

Wesley parked the car in a clearing in front of her gate. No other cars in sight, but her garage door was closed. If she had a car, nobody had used it in years.

"This is it?" John asked.

"Yep." I grinned.

"What do I do now?"

"Don't you worry. We'll walk you up to the door," Wesley said. "You think we're just gonna drop you off in the woods and drive away?"

"Yeah."

"Hell, I wouldn't do something like that to my favorite cousin."

"Yeah, you would."

We climbed out of the car and Wesley left the engine running so the headlights would illuminate the front porch of her house. Just a single-story house with vines snaking up the siding. A white picket fence ran around the perimeter of her yard, although you could only see the top half of it because the weeds were so thick. Maybe if Dolores cleaned up the place it would look nice, but now it resembled a drug dealer's hangout.

Wesley dug into his pocket and dug out his cell phone. He jumped a few steps in front of John and started filming everything.

"What's that for?" John asked.

"You'll thank me later. I want you to remember everything."

"Oh yeah," Wesley said, "I almost forgot." Wesley took out his sunglasses, slipped them on, then handed me a pair.

"Why are you wearing those?" John asked. "Trying to hide your faces?"

"Nope. I'm sure Dolores won't have any problem recognizing us either way. We just feel more comfortable with them on."

"You bring me a pair?"

Wesley threw his arm over John's shoulder and walked him forward. "You shouldn't wear them. Let her see your baby blue eyes."

"I can barely see anything in here. Shouldn't you take them off? Maybe she'll want to see your eyes too?"

"Oh, no. We're keeping the sunglasses on. Ray and I need to look cool, you know."

"You don't need them."

"Oh, yes we do." Wesley laughed and nudged John forward. "Now, you just go in there and have yourself a good time. Dolores is a little darling. She'll treat you nice."

"Maybe I should have had that beer. I can't talk to girls. Maybe we should go back to the car and have a few."

Wesley pushed him forward. "Now, don't get all worked up before you go in there. You'll need all your strength to handle the love she'll be giving you." He swatted John's back. "Who could resist your charms?"

"Oh, I forgot the flowers." John rushed back to the car and returned with the bouquet of red roses.

"She *loves* flowers."

"Maybe I should have gotten something better."

"Flowers are perfect. Dolores will go crazy when she sees them."

John arranged the roses, then slicked back the side of his hair. "How do I look?"

"Like a handsome guy ready to meet a beautiful woman. She'll jump in your lap in no time. Just hold those flowers out when you walk up to the door. She'll be watching through the window. You want to make sure she knows your intentions." Wesley looked toward the house.

Dolores was peeking out at us between her blinds. Not a light on in the house and I couldn't see her face, but I felt her gaze like a physical touch.

"You look dapper, John," I said. "Just go in there and have a wonderful time. Don't worry about us."

"All right. Here I go."

John walked through the gate, and Wesley and I followed behind him. Wesley filmed John from the side, then moved back behind him after we reached the porch.

"Are you going to be filming the whole thing?" John asked.

Wesley peeked out from behind his cell phone. "Until you go inside. After that, it's all just between you and her."

"You're not going to post that on YouTube, are you? Try to embarrass me?"

"Nope. This is all for you, John. You'll look back on this day and remember it as being the happiest day of your life. You'll thank us for bringing you here. Trust me."

"I guess. What if she doesn't like me?"

"Stop with your nonsense. Of course she'll like you. She will like you a lot. Now knock on that damn door and impress the little lady."

John glanced at the flowers, then at the door. "If she's ugly, I'm running back to the car."

"Stop that shit and knock."

"All right. I guess I can go in there. I guess it'll be okay."

"Sure, it will."

"Hold out those flowers," I said.

He held them out further, then formed a fist up near the door, but he didn't knock. "I'm kind of nervous."

"Take a deep breath. She's the girl of your dreams, man. She's got everything you like. Pretty hair, great figure. Sweet voice. You'll fall head over heels in love."

"What if she doesn't want me to come in?"

"She will. Just shut your mouth and give her all your love, got it?"

"What if I get in there but then mess it up? I always mess up this stuff. Remember what happened with Mary?"

"Don't you be comparing Dolores to Mary. Mary was a lunkhead. She didn't deserve you."

"You told me Mary would be the one."

"Well, I messed up with Mary. This Dolores girl is a million times better than Mary. Quality stuff. I'm telling you right now this is something you won't forget."

"What if—"

Wesley rolled his eyes and raised his voice. "Stop. I'm not telling you again. Just knock and enjoy the night. When she comes to the door, your eyes will pop out. She's the most beautiful girl in the whole world. Your dream girl."

John grunted and shifted the roses again.

Her living room blinds rustled and her face appeared in the window for a moment. Her eyes locked onto me. That's when I looked away. I got a little dizzy for a moment and grabbed onto Wesley's shoulder.

"You okay, man?" he asked.

"Yeah. She's watching us."

Wesley didn't look. He continued holding up the cell phone to record the whole thing.

"You got enough battery power in that thing?" I asked.

"Plenty. We'll be good for a couple more hours, at least."

John heaved in a deep breath, then knocked.

Dolores answered the door a few seconds later.

Her eyes darted between us and then locked onto the flowers in John's hand. "Are you boys lost?"

I cringed at the sound of her voice. I avoided looking at her face but I couldn't help glancing at her. It'd been so long and she still looked the same. She eyed me up and down. She caught me staring at her and grinned. Of course, she remembered me.

John glanced back at us for a moment. A wide grin spread across his face and his eyes were all lit up. His hands shook as he held out the roses toward Dolores.

"We came to see you, Dolores," I said. "My friend here is a bit nervous. He brought you something."

"Some flowers." John held them up closer to her face.

Dolores grabbed them and pulled them back under her nose. She sniffed every single flower, then narrowed her eyes. "What do you want?"

John glanced back to Wesley. "Oh my God. She's beautiful."

"Don't sweet talk me, idiot. Talk to her." Wesley nudged him to face Dolores.

John shifted from one foot to the other. "I was wondering if you'd like to... meet me?"

She moved a little closer to him. "Why, aren't you just the sweetest thing?" She gazed straight into Wesley's cellphone and winked. "Did you put him up to this?"

"We wanted to do something nice for him on his birthday."

"Well, it's your birthday, but you brought *me* the present. Such a handsome young man. You're more than welcome to come inside. In fact, all of you can come in, if you'd like."

Wesley chuckled, still filming every moment. "No, thanks."

She looked past John and caught my gaze. "Take off your glasses, Ray. Come inside and join the party. We had such fun together. I remember every second."

I shook my head. No way was she getting me back in there. "We'll just wait out here."

"What makes you think your friend will want to leave when I'm done with him?"

"He can't stay the night, Dolores," Wesley said, "so don't get your hopes up."

John turned to his cousin. "Why not?"

"You got to get back to your job in the morning, remember?"

"I can call in sick."

"No, you can't. You got to get back home. You come back outside when you're done. We'll be waiting for you in the car."

Dolores chuckled. "I don't think he'll want to leave. They never want to leave."

John mumbled as Dolores reached out and grabbed him by the front of his shirt, pulling him into the house. She blew me a kiss, then slammed the door.

We stood on the porch a few minutes, waiting to see if John might run out screaming, but just as we planned, everything went smoothly. Wesley shut off his video, and we headed out to the car.

"I'm not sure he'll want to leave," I said.

"We'll drag him out if we have to."

"I didn't want to leave either. Remember that?"

"I remember."

We climbed into the car and reviewed the video on the phone. Everything was there. It would have only been better if we could have filmed a little more of John and Dolores's interactions. A few seconds of them cuddling would have been hilarious.

We waited for almost two hours listening to the radio and downing a few beers out of the case in the trunk. Wesley brought up all the stupid shit we'd done in our youth. Our time with Dolores was at the top of our list. We laughed until my stomach ached.

"Maybe we shouldn't have brought John here," I said.

"Are you kidding me? He ain't never gonna forget this. If that guy ever gets married, I'll tease him about it on his wedding day."

"I feel kind of bad for him. Seems like a nice guy."

"Yeah," Wesley said. "John's a good kid. I feel a little bad for him too, but then again, it's a lesson he won't forget."

"He won't ever trust you again."

Wesley laughed. "And for good reason. Serves him right for trusting a devil like me."

"Let's go get him."

"Give him some more time. He's got to be thinking he's in love by now."

"I'm sure he is. That's why we need to go in there and get him."

Wesley groaned, then climbed out of the car with me. We made our way up to the porch again and pounded on the door. It took Dolores a lot longer to answer this time. Wesley started filming with his cellphone again.

She opened the door with a dazed look on her face, like she'd been up to no good, and John was lying half naked on the couch in her living room. She leaned into me and reached for my sunglasses. I swatted her hand away.

"Ow!" She sneered at me. "You don't have to be mean about it."

"You don't have to be grabby."

John saw me slap her hand and jumped up from the couch. "Don't hit her! What's wrong with you?"

"We're here to take you back home."

"I'm not ready to go." John folded his arms over his chest and sat back down on the couch.

Dolores grabbed my hand and pulled me in a few

inches toward her. "Why don't you come in, Ray? It'll be just like old times. Remember all the fun we had?"

"How can I forget?"

I nudged her to the side and yelled in at John, "Let's get going."

"John," Wesley yelled, "get your ass up. We're leaving."

Dolores ran her fingers across my cheek then up into my hair. I cringed. "No sense in flirting with me. I'm happily married."

Dolores giggled. "What does that have anything to do with it? I know how to keep a secret."

John groaned and stood up. He slipped on his clothes and glanced around the room. "I'm thirsty."

"You all can come in for drinks. I have plenty."

"No, thanks." Wesley eyed John. "We have beer in the car."

"I want water," John moaned.

"You can wait till we get home."

Dolores grinned. "I think he should stay the night. We were just starting to get to know each other."

"I want to stay all night." John walked up behind Dolores. "I've got everything I need here. Why do I got to leave?"

"You can't stay. Too much of a good thing isn't healthy for a man like you."

John wrapped his arms around Dolores and pulled her in tighter next to him.

Wesley filmed the whole thing and laughed. "You two get close now."

John put his face up to her cheek and kissed her several times. "Did you get that?"

"Yep."

I reached in and pulled John away from Dolores. His

arm slipped away, but he tugged back. I thought we might be in for a fight to get him out of there, but Wesley joined in and we got him outside before things got ugly. Same thing happened to me when I was in that situation. Except back then, Wesley had to bring a few of his friends to pry me away from her. Thank God he did.

"I don't want to go," John said. "Dolores promised to show me her garden in the backyard."

"I'm sure she did."

"He can stay the night." Dolores reached for John's hand, but I stood in the way.

"I'm staying the night." John pushed past me to go back inside.

Wesley stopped the video then and grabbed John's upper arm. "I can't do that to you, Johnny boy."

"Why not?"

Wesley shook his head. "You'd regret it."

"Why would I regret it? I'm the happiest I've ever been in my life. You were right. She *is* the girl of my dreams."

"Oh, you're so sweet." Dolores swatted her hand toward John.

"You just wait," Wesley said.

"For what?"

"You'll see."

John smirked. "Tell me. Does she turn into a frog in the morning?"

"Nope. No frog."

John lurched forward back into her house.

Dolores blocked me and Wesley from grabbing him again. "He wants to stay the night."

Wesley laughed louder, but didn't chase John past the

threshold. "Okay, birthday boy, if that's what you want to do."

"That's what I want to do," John repeated.

"Have it your way, smarty pants. I'm telling you right now you're making a mistake, but I'll do what you want, and I don't want to hear you bitching at me tomorrow either on the way home. Got it?"

"Why would I bitch about anything?"

"Oh, you will. But seeing as though it's your birthday and I want you to have a real nice time, I'll let you enjoy the evening—both of you."

"You're so sweet." Dolores's grin widened, and she ran her hands down the front of Wesley's shirt.

"Get your hands off me." Wesley stepped back.

John walked over and sat on her couch. "You can come over here and do that to me."

Wesley shivered. "Yeah, why don't you do that to him. It's his birthday after all, right?"

"I'm the birthday boy," John said. "Do you have any more presents for me?"

Dolores giggled and ran over to John as he sprawled out on her couch. "I got lots of big presents for you tonight."

My stomach churned, and I cringed. "Yeah, just live it up, John. Have the time of your life."

"Thanks, guys, I will."

We went back to the car, and it was almost 2 in the morning before we got home. Wesley called me around noon the next day saying he hadn't heard from John yet so we drove over there to take him home.

We parked in the same spot as the night before and, despite being the middle of the day, the forest was dark as ever.

We put on our sunglasses again and knocked on the door. Dolores opened it and John was standing in his pajamas behind her. His hair was a mess, but he smiled.

"Did you just get up?" I asked.

"I didn't get much sleep last night."

Wesley laughed. "Who's pajamas are those?"

John look down at his clothes. "Dolores got them for me."

"Where did she get them?"

"I always have an extra pair in case of emergencies." Dolores glared at Wesley.

"You're wearing someone else's clothes, Johnny."

John shrugged. "Doesn't matter."

Dolores snuggled up next to him.

I chuckled and nudged Wesley. "He looks so happy."

"He does." Wesley nodded. "Just remember this time, John. Enjoy the moment."

John scowled. "You're making it sound like I'm not ever coming back here again. Dolores said I can come back any time, right?" He looked into her eyes.

She snuggled in closer to him. "You can come back any time you want. You want to marry me? Okay."

John stuck out his chest. "It doesn't get better than this, guys. I'm in love."

Wesley stepped toward John, but stopped short of entering the house. "John, we just need you to come back home now. You can return again sometime if you really want."

John kissed Dolores's forehead. "Did you hear what she just said? She said she'd marry me. The girl of my dreams wants to marry me. I'm the happiest guy alive."

"Let's just get you back to the house, lover boy, and let you think things over."

"I don't need to think anything over. Dolores loves me and that's all that matters."

"You don't understand."

"Understand what? What's the problem? I'm happy. Why do you guys want to mess with me?"

"You'll understand better when we get home."

"Wesley, don't spoil our fun." Dolores cuddled in John's arms.

Wesley nodded. "Okay, John. I'll make a deal with you. You come back to the car for thirty minutes with us and after that if you feel you want to go back in the house with Dolores, then fine with me. All I need is thirty minutes to talk with you alone."

John sighed. "I'm not changing out of my pajamas."

"You can leave your jammies on. Let's go talk." Wesley gestured for John to follow us.

"Fine." John put on some brown slippers next to the door and walked outside with us. "I'll be back, Dolores. I need to straighten this man out, seeing as though he insists on ruining our day. Just thirty minutes."

"I'll be here waiting for you." She blew him a kiss. "Just remember that I love you."

"I love you too," John said.

Wesley stood on one side of John and I stood on the other side. I kept my hands up next to his arm in case he spun around and tried to escape back to her. He glanced back several times on the way to the car, waving and throwing kisses before we pushed him into the backseat. Wesley climbed in next to him and I locked the doors.

We took off our sunglasses as Wesley fiddled with his cellphone.

John blurted out, "Wowsy yowsy! She's got it all. I can't believe my luck. This is the best birthday ever. I'm glad you guys got it on video so I can look back and remember this day when we get old. You guys missed your chance with her and now I'm going to marry that girl."

Wesley laughed. "You want to marry Dolores? That's the funniest damn thing I've ever heard."

"What's so funny? Didn't you hear what she said? She'd marry me."

"Nobody will marry Dolores."

"Why the hell not? She already said she would. Who's going to stop me?"

John sneered and brought up his fists.

"Easy, John. No one's trying to start a fight."

Wesley turned around his cellphone's screen so John could see it. "Okay, okay. I got to show you something before you get all riled up."

"See what? You better not have made some awful video of us to post on YouTube. I won't stand for you guys disrespecting Dolores."

"Nobody's disrespecting her. Just watch the video."

Wesley played the video and John watched it expressionless for the longest time. I peeked around and watched it with him. Confusion spread over John's face after Dolores appeared in the doorway.

"Who's that? What did you do to Dolores? This isn't funny."

"That's the girl of your dreams."

"What did you do to her? You put some joke video filter on her face, didn't you? Some special effects from one of those apps that messes up how people look."

"No man. That's how she looks in real life."

"Bullshit. That's not her. Dolores is a beautiful twenty something. You made her look like she's ninety-five years old. That's just mean."

"She might be ninety-five, or maybe even older than that. Dolores is a witch. I just wanted you to have a fun time and there's no shame in that. We did the same thing when we were young. We got taken in just like you did. You had fun though, didn't you? You had the time of your life?"

John just stared with his mouth hanging open.

"You had fun. That's great and you deserve it. You're my favorite cousin, John, so I hope you had a wonderful birthday. Dolores puts a trance on anyone who sees her and whatever you want her to look like, that's what she looks like. No shame in what you've done. I just wanted you to have a great birthday."

John continued to stare and shook his head. "No, that's not her. That woman's uglier than a rock."

Wesley nodded. "Yep. She tricked you and me and Ray, and anyone else who looks at her. She would've tricked us last night too if we weren't looking at her through these sunglasses. Something about polarized sunglasses messes up her trance. Doesn't work when they're on."

He gazed at me and then back to Wesley. He furled his brows. "You mean, she's really not pretty? She really looks like that old hag?"

"She's not bad or anything—at least, I don't *think* so. Maybe if she were sixty years younger, we might work something out, but I'm afraid that's the way things are. I tried to get you out of there last night before she dragged you deeper into her spell, but you didn't listen. I made the video so you would believe me and we could all have a little laugh. You had a good time, right?"

"We've been through it too, John. It's just a little prank. Hope you're not mad."

John slowly shook his head. "No. I'm not mad. Give

me those sunglasses."

"What for?"

"I have to see it for myself."

Wesley nodded. "We did the same thing. We didn't believe it either, at first."

I handed John my pair of sunglasses and he slipped them on.

"I'll be right back," he said, climbing out of the backseat.

"Don't take them off," Wesley said.

He didn't answer. He slammed the door and hurried back to Dolores's front porch. She stood in the doorway as he walked up to her.

"Maybe we should go over there," Wesley suggested.

"Do you think he might try to hurt her?"

"He might. He's a good kid, but I think he's pissed."

We stepped out of the car and walked toward the house.

I avoided looking at Dolores, forcing myself to only see her from the corner of my eye. John ran his hand along the side of Dolores's face and they talked for a moment. He pulled her inside the house, then emerged a few minutes later still in his pajamas. He took off the sunglasses and tossed them out toward us.

"You guys go home." John gestured for us to leave.

We stopped. "Are you sure?"

"Yeah, I'm staying here. I'll call you later."

I picked up the sunglasses and the front door slammed shut.

"Well, that ain't what I expected." Wesley's eyes widened. "Should we go in there and drag him out?"

"What for? Let him have his fun."

Wesley laughed most of the way back home.

# CASSETTE

Blair hovered over Jake as he slipped the black cassette tape into the player.

"What are you doing?" she asked.

"What does it look like I'm doing?"

"Wasting time listening to a bunch of cruddy old cassette tapes. You might as well just throw those things out."

"That's your solution to everything, isn't it? Just throw it out."

"You're so defensive, Jake. I'm your wife, remember?"

"You always remind me." Jake rewound the tape. "These are valuable. Some of the last items from my childhood."

Blair dug into Jake's tote of childhood possessions and pulled out an old leather gun holster. She held it up with two fingers as if it were a piece of rotting flesh. "What's this thing?"

Jake glanced at it. "Something I used to play with."

"You wanted to be a cowboy?"

"Anything wrong with that?"

"I guess not." She dropped it back into the tote. "Seems kind of silly, considering you grew up in New York City."

"I just wanted to get out of there and have an adventure. I was a kid."

"Can't hang on to the past forever." Blair grunted and left the room.

After the bedroom door clicked shut, Jake hit play on the tape deck. His cousin Logan's voice blared out the name of their imaginary radio show, the "Jake and Logan Mystery Hour," as if they were famous entertainers. Without a pause, they jumped into their first skit. Jake's youthful voice brought a smile to his face. Even back when he was eleven years old he knew he wanted to entertain people.

It surprised him that any of his old cassette tapes had survived for so many years. Most of his childhood possessions had gotten thrown out by his minimalist parents after he'd left home for college, and he'd adopted the same habit of clearing clutter on a regular basis. Only one plastic tote left.

He grinned as he listened to the tape. Two decades had passed since he and his cousin had filled up several tapes with goofy, ranting sketches. Most of their antics made no sense now, but back then it had been magical. They recorded some of the best times of his life during those carefree summer days. Listening to his childish voice now was almost surreal. Familiar, yet like listening to a complete stranger.

The audio played and transported Jake back to that summer afternoon.

*Logan: "Here's the train, Jake, it's coming over the mountain. Are you watching?"*

*Jake: "Aaah, lookout!"*

*Logan: "Get out of my way, you moron."*

*Jake: "Turn!"*

*Logan: "I am turning. I can't stop! All the way up the mountain, then down the other side. Aaah, I can't stop! I'm going to crash!" (crash and explosion sounds)*

*Jake: "All fourteen passengers are presumed dead after smashing through the side of a building at the base of the railway. Seven additional bystanders were killed in the collision."*

*Logan: "Someone call an ambulance! I think they're dead!"*

Jake furrowed his brow. That was strange. He and Logan had said a lot of crazy things in the tape recordings —that's just how eleven-year-olds talked back then—but Jake didn't remember saying anything so grown-up and morbid.

The urge to call his cousin popped into his mind, to ask him about what they'd recorded, but that time had passed. Logan was gone. Dead from a car accident a few days earlier. Jake hadn't even bothered to tell Blair about his loss. She wouldn't care, anyway. That's how their relationship had developed the last couple of years. He'd gotten used to it.

Jake glanced at the digital clock on his desk. 6:36pm. The funeral would be over by then and his cousin was six feet under. He would have been at the funeral, but he'd had too many other things to take care of—one of them, to prepare for Blair's birthday party.

The doorbell rang and Jake stopped the tape. He went out into the living room just as his wife answered the door.

Victor Thompson and Steve Barlow had arrived early.

Two guys always looking for a good time. Blair greeted them with her usual over-enthusiasm.

Victor spotted Jake standing behind Blair and formed one of his usual phony smiles—a smirk—then handed Blair a bottle of champagne with a bow around the neck.

"Happy Birthday!" Victor switched to a more genuine smile when Blair gave him a hug.

She wrapped her arms around him and held him a little too long.

Jake rolled his eyes and approached Victor when Blair took the champagne to the kitchen.

"Are we going to have a good time, or what?" Victor stepped inside and took off his shoes.

"I hope so," Jake said.

"You hope so? You don't sound too sure."

Jake shrugged.

Steve Barlow walked around Victor and headed straight to the living room. He switched on the TV and dropped into the couch. "You guys need to get a bigger television. 40 inches doesn't cut it anymore."

"Sorry, Steve," Blair said from the kitchen, "I know you like your big screens."

"Just for the games."

"Jake insists we don't need a bigger one."

"Blame it on me." Jake turned to Victor and shook his hand. Cold and clammy. "Enjoy the party, Victor."

"I intend to." Victor nudged past him to get to Blair, who was digging out food and beer from the fridge. He rattled off a crude joke and Blair broke out laughing. She was always laughing at his stupid jokes. Nobody else would listen to them, and they were *stupid* jokes. Not even something a child would think was funny. Not a single intelligent bone in Victor's body.

A short while later, the Crane twins arrived, Alivia and Alice. Brazilian girls who Blair had met while getting her Masters Degree in Communication Studies at the University of Minnesota. They presented her with a small, pink gift bag. Blair opened it right away. An assortment of body lotions. Blair raved about the gift, set it on the counter, then set them up with drinks.

Another couple arrived an hour later. Danny and Amy. Everyone was single, except Jake and Blair.

Jake hovered between them, striking up brief conversations to hear what they'd done since their last party. He downed two beers, watching the interactions with feigned interest. They were Blair's friends. He was the outsider, even after three years of marriage.

Victor moved in and flirted with Blair again. Same maneuver every party. He slinked in toward her during their conversation and tapped the side of her stomach. Tap, tap, tap. She giggled, then talked a little louder. Not too obvious, but Jake had noticed Mr. Slick months earlier.

It made no difference anyway. Jake and Blair had long since gotten past the jealous stage in their marriage. She could do whatever she wanted with that unfunny slime ball.

Jake helped himself to another beer in the refrigerator while Victor poured Blair a glass of the champagne he'd brought for her.

So smooth, Victor.

Despite the abundance of alcohol in their house, Danny and Amy brought a bottle of wine, and Steve Barlow brought a bottle of Captain Morgan rum, but he would consume the gift soon enough.

The Crane twins wore tight skirts, Alice in blue and Alivia in purple, as if they were in for a night on the town. They wiggled and danced in place at the slightest sound of music. Danny and Amy talked with them at the edge of the living room until Steve broke away from the TV and lumbered over to join their group. He threw his arms around both twins and juggled his attention between them as they laughed. Steve's jokes were actually funny.

Jake crossed into the kitchen and grabbed a beer before sitting down in his usual spot on the couch in front of the TV. Alivia caught his gaze and broke away from the others. She walked over and sat down next to him. Jake breathed in her rosy scent and smiled.

She leaned in close, rubbing her knee against his leg, and talked about the joys of her new job in marketing, but he had little interest in listening to stories about anybody's job. He only wanted to forget about life's problems, his cousin's funeral, and just get drunk. Any talk of work brought his mind back to his own job—graphic design—and all the headaches waiting for him on Monday morning.

Jake glanced back toward the kitchen. Victor's voice boomed across the room. The life of the party, the driving force behind their frequent get-togethers. Victor rattled on about the successes of his gaming company, and all the celebrities he'd met while recording their voice-over for various characters. Elijah Wood, Mark Hamill, Ellen Page, and Samuel L. Jackson.

Jake had listened to all the stories several times now, but Blair still insisted on hearing them all again. She hung on Victor's every word.

Victor vented another poor joke, followed by Blair's laughter. Jake glanced back at them just as she touched Victor's arm.

"Oh, you should take your jokes to the comedy club,"

Blair said. "I love the stories you tell. You could be a standup comedian."

So much bullshit. Why did she keep encouraging him to tell those same stories over and over? Jake would need to have a long conversation with Blair in the morning.

"Are you and Blair planning anything special for your anniversary?"

Jake paused and shrugged. He'd forgotten all about it. Only four days away. "She has to work."

"Have you thought about taking a trip to Brazil? It's so beautiful."

"Maybe someday. Blair doesn't get much time off."

"I travel back there every year to visit some family. I could meet you down there and take you to the best places away from all the tourists."

Victor's voice rose and fell in the background.

Alivia's brown eyes calmed him. "That sounds good."

Steve flipped through the TV channels, pausing on a breaking news story. "... The cable used to tow the tourist trolley to the top of Corcovado mountain in Rio de Janeiro broke free, sending it hurling to the bottom at over 90mph. All fourteen passengers are presumed dead after smashing through the side of a building at the base of the railway. Seven additional bystanders were killed in the collision."

Alivia gasped. "Oh God!"

Jake paused. The news stunned him. Not just the news, but the exact words the announcer had used.

*All fourteen passengers are presumed dead after smashing through the side of a building at the base of the railway. Seven additional bystanders were killed in the collision.*

He'd heard those words somewhere before.

"So horrible!" Alivia gazed at him. "Are you okay?"

Jake glanced around the room. "That's weird. I think I'm having deja vu."

Alivia's brow furrowed. "Really?"

Jake nodded. "What that news guy just said—I've heard it before."

Alivia nudged him. "Too much beer."

"Not this time. Something's different. It feels strange, like everything's a dream. Maybe I'm going nuts."

"You got that right," Blair said from the kitchen.

Jake sneered. "Don't be a smartass, Blair. Just drink your champagne."

Alivia touched his hand. "My mom said that when someone has deja vu, they're remembering a dream they had. Or maybe you're repeating a conversation you had in a previous life."

Alice jumped in and corrected her. "Reincarnation is bullshit, Alivia."

"Well, *I* believe it. Whatever it is, it's strange."

The deja vu faded as Jake downed the rest of his beer. "I know I've heard that line before."

"Maybe you're psychic." Alivia squinted as she gazed into his eyes.

Jake shrugged.

"What am I thinking?" The corners of her mouth rose as she leaned closer.

"Naughty things, I'm sure."

Alivia slapped his arm, but didn't pull away. "I was thinking you should get me another drink."

"Jake," Blair said from the kitchen. "Don't be flirting with the twins."

Alice and Alivia laughed.

"It's okay," Alivia said. "We've gotten used to Jake by now. He's harmless."

Jake glanced back at Blair. Victor continued with his story and put his hand on her arm.

Jake grunted. They would need to talk in the morning.

The TV news reporter's strange sentence ran through his mind again. He'd heard that line before. Not just deja vu or remembering it in a dream, but from somewhere else.

The tape. He'd heard those same words on the cassette tape. His own eleven-year-old self had said those exact same phrases twenty years earlier, but how was that possible? Just a circumstance? Why would an eleven-year-old kid say something like that? But maybe he remembered it wrong. He couldn't get it out of his mind. He had to go back to the stereo and listen to it again. The beer wasn't screwing with him—it was on the cassette tape for sure, and he'd prove it.

Jake repeated the words of the newscaster over and over in his mind as he got up and went into his office.

*All fourteen passengers are presumed dead after smashing through the side of a building at the base of the railway. Seven additional bystanders were killed in the collision.*

He closed the door and sat in front of the stereo system. He rewound the cassette, skipping back, then a little forward to find the exact moment he'd said the line.

*Jake: "I'm almost done."*

*Logan: "Here's the train, Jake, it's coming over the mountain. Are you watching?"*

*Jake: "Aaah, lookout!"*

*Logan: "Get out of my way, you moron."*

*Jake: "Turn!"*

*Logan: "I am turning. I can't stop! All the way up the mountain, then down the other side. Aaah, I can't stop! I'm going to crash!"*

*Jake: "Who knows what a crazy person might do with a weapon like that?"*

*Logan: "Put the gun down, you psychopath!*

*Jake: (sound of gunshot) "Aaah! You shot me!"*

*Logan: "Someone call an ambulance! I think he's dead!"*

*Jake: (death noises) "How could you do such a thing?" (body collapsing)*

Not the same line. Not even close. He'd remembered it wrong. Alivia was right, it must be the beer.

The new conversation made even less sense than the one he'd originally heard. The words streamed through his thoughts again and again. Such a strange thing to say for an eleven-year-old. But he'd said and done so many stupid things back then. Anything was possible for an imaginative child.

The sense of deja vu flooded back to him. What was going on? Something straight from a Hitchcock movie. In the morning, he would listen to the tape again, and maybe then it would all make sense.

Jake shut off the stereo system and walked out of his office.

Blair cut him off on the way to the living room. "Where were you?"

"I had to take care of something."

"You were gone for thirty minutes."

"Was I?" Jake looked at the time on his cellphone. "It seemed like just a few minutes."

"Did you take a nap? Don't crash yet. It's my birthday, remember? And we have friends over."

"I wasn't asleep." Jake pressed his palm to his forehead. "I feel weird."

Blair eyed him with concern for a moment, then sneered at him and sniffed his shirt. "Did you smoke a little weed while you were in your office? Are you high?”

“Not this time. I feel kind of... out of it, like things aren’t real.”

“Put down the beer.” Blair grabbed at his beer, but he pulled back.

“It’s not the beer.”

“Did you guzzle some shots of Jack when I wasn’t looking? Are you drunk already?”

“I’m not drunk at all. Well, not yet.”

“Just don’t embarrass me again, okay? Drink some water for a change.”

Blair gazed into his eyes, then went back to Victor Thompson’s side. Within seconds they were laughing it up. Blair whispered something to Victor, then he glared back at Jake as if he’d done something wrong.

Jake lumbered into the living room and returned to his spot on the couch next to Alivia.

“Do you feel better?” she asked.

“A little.”

“Maybe you should go lie down.”

“I’m okay.” He finished another beer and stared at the television. Someone had turned the channel to a football game. Steve hoarded the remote next to Amy and sat fixated on the screen.

Danny emerged from the bathroom waving a silver pistol over his head. “Look what I found.”

Jake’s breath stopped at the sight of his antique .45 Colt revolver in Danny’s hand. How the hell had he found it? It was safely stowed away in Jake’s office closet.

“Put that down!” Alivia put up her hands.

Jake stood and approached Danny. “What are you doing? Are you drunk?”

"No, but you are."

"I'm not."

"You are definitely drunk, Jake. I can see the future. I predict you'll be curled up on the floor in a corner by the end of the night."

Jake reached for his revolver. "How did you get that? Were you snooping in my office?"

"So, it's yours then?"

"Yeah, it's mine. Give it here."

"I wasn't in your office, Jake. I found it in the bathroom next to the sink. Do you always keep your guns lying around like this?"

"Oh no. That's my fault," Blair said. "I left it there by accident. Jake left it out on the coffee table this afternoon after he spent *way* too much time cleaning it. I meant to put it back in his office, but I forgot. Sorry about that. I must have gotten distracted and left it in the bathroom. I hope it's not loaded."

"I never leave it loaded," Jake said.

Danny stood several inches higher than Jake and used it to his advantage to keep the revolver out of Jake's hands. "Is it loaded, Jake? Did you leave a loaded gun out on the coffee table?"

"I don't leave loaded guns lying around. Give it back." Jake lost his smile. "I'm not goofing around."

"You're not?" Danny chuckled and examined the pistol. "This thing's old."

"It's a .45 Colt Single Action Army Revolver. The gun that won the west."

Danny spun it around his trigger finger twice and backed away as Jake reached for it. "Is it a real Wild West gun?"

"What do you think?"

Danny nodded. "I like it. Maybe a cowboy killed some outlaws with this thing. Where did you get it?"

"I inherited it."

"So maybe your descendants killed some people with this."

"Maybe."

"Cool." Danny pointed the gun at Jake's face with a wide grin. The barrel's tip wavered only inches from Jake's forehead when Danny pulled the trigger.

Click.

"What the hell?" Jake grabbed the barrel and yanked it away. "You better knock that shit off."

"You're right. It wasn't loaded." Danny laughed. "Don't worry, I checked it before I came out."

"You're a fucking psychopath."

"Don't get all testy. I wouldn't have pranked you unless I knew it was empty. You think I would point a loaded gun at you without checking it first?"

"Yeah."

"I wouldn't. I'm not that stupid. Don't get all severe on me now. It's just a joke, okay? We're having a great time for Blair's party, so chill out."

Jake's face warmed. "I'm chilled out just fine, but you better not point that gun at me again or I'll beat your ass with it."

Danny raised his eyebrows. "Beat your ass. What a drunk thing to say."

"Dickhead."

Danny walked past Jake, laughing on his way to the living room. "You should probably lock that gun away, Blair. A dangerous person might get his hands on it. Who knows what a crazy person might do with a weapon like that? Do you agree?"

Those words. Deja vu rushed in again.

*Who knows what a crazy person might do with a weapon like that?*

The cassette tape. A chill passed up his spine. He'd said those same words on the tape.

"What's wrong, Jake?" Danny asked him. "You look like you just shit your pants."

Everyone laughed, except Alivia and Alice.

He tried to smile. "I think I'm having deja vu again."

Danny whistled an eerie melody. "Maybe you're dreaming. This is all an illusion, Jake," he said in a hypnotic voice. "Soon you'll wake up and discover yourself sitting on a tropical beach."

They laughed again.

Alivia walked over and pressed her palm on his forehead. Her warm hand comforted him for a moment. She stared into his eyes. "You don't have a fever. But I think you should lie down for five minutes. Your face is pale."

"I'm okay."

"Jake, stop flirting with Alivia."

"He's not flirting with me, Blair," Alivia said. "I told him to go lay down."

Blair sneered at him. "I suppose."

*Who knows what a crazy person might do with a weapon like that?*

Jake hurried back to his office clutching the revolver and closed the door. He rewound the tape again and played it back near the start of the section he'd listened to earlier. He needed to hear those words again, just to make sure he wasn't going crazy.

*Logan: "Hurry up, Jake."*

*Jake: "I'm almost done."*

*Logan: "Here's the train, Jake, it's coming over the mountain. Are you watching?"*

*Jake: "Aaah, lookout!"*

*Logan: "Get out of my way, you moron."*

*Jake: "Turn!"*

*Logan: "I am turning. I can't stop! All the way up the mountain, then down the other side. Aaah, I can't stop! I'm going to crash!"*

*Jake: "Don't do anything stupid, stupid."*

*Logan: "Put the gun down, you psychopath!"*

*Jake: (sound of gunshot) "Aaah! You shot me!"*

*Logan: "Someone call an ambulance! I think he's dead!"*

*Jake: (death noises) "How could you do such a thing?"*

*Logan: "I shoot bad guys. That's what I do."*

Jake switched off the cassette player. Different words now. His stomach churned and he wiped his damp forehead. If the previous version of the lines had come true, then someone was about to get shot. No, that couldn't be right.

Jake glanced over at the pistol on his desk. No need to panic. He had the only gun, and if the words came true, someone might say them on a TV show just like what had happened with the trolley crash on the news.

*Someone call an ambulance! I think he's dead!*

Jake slid the pistol into the bottom drawer of his desk. As long as it remained in there, nobody would get shot in his house. Everything would be fine. The strange sense of deja vu didn't mean that the lines had to happen in actual life.

He lumbered out to the living room and forced a smile.

"Are you okay?" Steve asked him from the couch. "Your face is white like you just saw a ghost."

"Nobody has a gun on them, right?"

Everyone stared back at him with blank expressions.

"Why?" Alice asked.

Danny turned away from his girlfriend Amy and took a step forward. "You lookin' to pick a gunfight? I'm ready for ya." He scowled as he held the TV remote at his waist like a gun in a holster.

Jake shook his head. "I'm serious."

"I am too. Now *draw*!"

"I've got this one, Jake," Steve jumped up from the couch, also with a pretend gun at his side, and faced Danny. "Don't do anything stupid, stupid."

Danny sneered at Steve. "Put the gun down, you psychopath!"

Steve drew his imaginary pistol and fired.

"Aaah!" Danny recoiled as if someone had shot him in the chest. "You shot me!" He tumbled back onto the couch and faked his death.

Alice jumped in beside him and raised his limp arm before dropping it again. "Someone call an ambulance! I think he's dead!"

Danny choked and gasped for air. He sprang back to life and reached out his hand toward Steve. "How could you do such a thing?"

Steve blew smoke off the tip of his imaginary pistol. "I shoot bad guys. That's what I do."

Everyone laughed.

Jake's mind reeled. The exact words from the tape. At least nobody had gotten hurt.

"Nobody's packing heat at Blair's birthday party." Victor held up his hands. "Want to frisk me?"

Blair pushed Victor's hands down. "Don't mind Jake. He's drunk."

"Should we go home and get our weapons, Jake?"

Danny asked. "Something going down soon?"

"No, I... never mind. I'm just a little tired."

The football game blared on the TV as Jake walked to the kitchen. Victor and Blair veered out of his way as he poured himself a glass of water.

"What's this all about?" Victor asked. "You worried we might start something? We're all friends here, right?"

"Yes," Jake said, "nothing like that. I'm just having that deja vu again."

"Go lay down then." Blair turned away from him.

He walked back toward his bedroom with his head throbbing, then stopped. What would the tape say now? He paused and stared at his office door a few feet down the hall. Everything on the tape had come true, although strangely. Maybe now he'd hear the playful voices he and his cousin had truly spoken twenty years earlier.

He turned into his office and closed the door. Blair wouldn't bother him now. He wouldn't be able to calm his mind until he knew everything was back to normal.

He sat down and rewound the tape. Hitting play, his body tensed.

*Logan: "Let's go to my place."*

*Jake: "He's right outside. He'll see us leave."*

*Logan: "He won't see anything. He's drunk. He'll pass out on the floor again."*

*Jake: "It is my special day, but not yet."*

*Logan: "We'll wait until he's asleep."*

*Jake: "You two look like outlaws to me. Get ready to draw."*

*Logan: "Don't point that thing at us, you psychopath!"*

*Jake: "I'm the new sheriff in these parts. You two varmints are under arrest."*

*Logan: "Stop goofing around. That thing better not be loaded."*

*Jake: "Put that away. Not—"*

*Logan: (sound of gunshot) (scream) "Oh, my God!"*
*Jake: (sound of gunshot) "Shit!"*
*Logan: (death noises)*
*Jake: "What the hell?"*
*Logan: "What happened? You shot them!"*
*Jake: "I... He said it wasn't loaded."*
*Logan: "Call an ambulance!"*
*Jake: "I didn't mean to."*
*Logan: "What were you thinking?"*
*Jake: "We have to stop the bleeding."*
*Logan: "Check their pulse."*
*Jake: (crying) "It's too late. They're dead."*

Jake stopped the tape. His eyes widened and his jaw dropped open. What had just happened? Not only had the words on the tape changed but no child could have imagined such a horrific scene during an afternoon playtime. Despite the strangeness of the dialogue, the cowboy references were undeniable.

Jake stared at the pistol on his desk beside him. How could something so specific and horrible happen in the future? His pistol wasn't even loaded.

He sipped his water and stared at the handwritten names across the front of the cassette tape in the player. Jake and Logan's Mystery Hour.

He couldn't have said any of those lines as an eleven-year-old. He'd said many strange things back then, but those words had never come out of his mouth. Yet there they were on the tape. And if the previous versions of the lines proved anything, they would come true.

But how could they come true? He never loaded his pistol in the house. Ever.

The words of his wife came back to him. Can't hang on to the past forever.

But he loved her. Did he?

He'd rid himself of the mementos from their early romance and marriage. Nothing in his office to remind him of her. And they'd long given up on date nights or talking about having a child.

Jake picked up the pistol and turned it over in his hands. Clean and ready to go. There would be witnesses and no chance of anyone to suspect him.

He set the pistol down again and dug through the bottom drawer of his desk. A box of rounds sat in the corner. He opened the box and picked out six. The metal cooled his palm. He only needed two if the recording was right. No, better to have six for the inevitable investigation. He placed the six rounds end-up on his desk and closed the drawer.

A faint grin stretched out from the corners of his mouth. Was he evil? *He* wasn't doing anything wrong, technically, except allowing fate to take its course. Maybe nothing would happen anyway. No chance to know for sure if the tape's conversation would come true, but the others had. And this one was so *specific*. All too perfect. How could he pass it up?

Jake loaded the rounds into the revolver's chambers and snapped the cylinder shut.

He wouldn't need to do anything. Just set the pistol on the desk like before and let fate do its thing. Everything would take care of itself.

Someone knocked on the door. Jake shuddered. Alivia opened it and peeked in at him. "Are you okay?"

He got up from his desk and stepped to her. "Sure, I'm fine."

"Would you like to get some fresh air?"

A devious grin passed over her face. His heart beat

faster. He would love to see that grin every day for the rest of his life.

Jake nodded. "Let's go."

She grabbed his arm and glanced back at his desk. "Shouldn't you put your gun away?"

"No, nobody comes in here."

"We can go out the back."

He paused and gazed into her eyes. "I'm glad I have you in my life, Alivia."

Her eyes widened as she beamed. "I feel the same way." She pressed her head against his shoulder.

She led Jake out through the living room toward the back door. Neither Blair nor Victor noticed. Alice and Steve were snuggling closer on the couch in the living room. Amy stood next to Danny near the kitchen table.

Danny guzzled his beer and pretended to pull a pistol from his imaginary holster. "Gotcha. Where are you guys off to?"

"Get some air." Jake feigned nausea. The butterflies in his stomach multiplied with the excitement building in his mind.

"You look a little better now."

Jake shrugged. "I think I'll feel better tomorrow."

As he headed out the door with Alivia at his side, he glanced back to Blair and Victor. One of his hands moved across her waist.

Can't hang onto the past forever.

Jake and Alivia moved out into the cool night air.

She snuggled in closer to him and stared up at the night sky. "I'd like to travel the world someday. Have you ever thought about doing that?"

"I love adventures." Jake walked until he heard the

gunshots and the screams. He didn't even flinch as Alivia turned back in confusion toward the house.

"What was that?" She stared at him with wide eyes.

Jake covered his mouth to hide his wide grin. "I don't know. Let's go see."


MORE FRIGHTFUL TALES IN BOOK 4! SEE NEXT PAGE FOR info!

# DREADFUL DARK BOOK 4

## TALES OF HORROR: BOOK 4

# RANDALL'S BETTER HALF

Randall hunkered along the edge of the cabin's window frame next to his friend, Michael, with the lights off and their fingers grasping the top of the windowsill. Michael wasn't one to hide from anything, but they poked their heads up and stared outside into the moonlit lakeshore that had been their fishing grounds only hours earlier. The tattoo of a shark covering Michael's forearm caught Randall's eye. A fitting symbol of his friend's personality.

"That's where I saw her." Randall pointed near the beach.

"You're full of shit," Michael said.

Randall shook his head. "I'm not lying. She was really out there."

"You're making it all up. I'm too smart for you, Randall. Did you finish *your* college degree? No. You've got to remember that when you try to pull shit like this."

Randall's eyes went wide. "I'm not joking. She walked out of the forest, naked and everything, except something about her head looked... off. Too big for that petite body of hers."

Michael stared at him. "Are you drunk?"

"No, sir. I stopped drinking..." Randall glanced at the time on his cellphone. "...five hours ago."

"Bullshit. Why are you wasting my time like this?"

"I'm telling the truth. She walked right out of those trees and went into the lake."

"Swimming *and* a big head? At 10pm? *And* it's only fifty degrees out there. You're just making this shit up, aren't you?"

"No, sir. I saw her right out there." Randall pointed.

Michael scanned the darkness once again and then stood up. "You're so full of shit. You just want me to go out there so you can have a good laugh at my expense. I'm going back to my room."

Randall motioned for Michael to get down. "She'll see you!"

Michael scoffed. "Does she have x-ray vision too? Nobody can see us in here, and I don't care if she does, because nobody's out there, anyway." Michael stood in front of the window now without even trying to be careful.

Randall looked along the beach and waited for the pale figure to emerge from the water. She *had* to show up again and prove to Michael that he wasn't a liar. The trees swayed outside and shadows moved below the rustling branches. "Something's moving."

Michael sighed and turned back. "Where?"

"Near the water."

Michael leaned forward and squinted. "That isn't a woman. That's some weeds."

The water shimmered where the woman had gone in.

Randall hoped she would come back out so he wouldn't look like a lying idiot.

"I'm done fooling around." Michael turned toward the bedroom door. "I'm tired as hell and you're full of shit. How many beers did you have this afternoon?"

"I don't know. Only five or six."

"See? That's your problem. Not enough beer. Your brain is still stuck on that Marcy girl who dumped you last week. You're hallucinating now about big-headed mutant naked women."

Randall glanced out the window. "She looked real enough."

"Nope, just a mirage. Tomorrow I'll see that you down a twelve-pack, at least. Erase that woman like deleting a file from your hard drive."

Lightning crashed nearby, and the sky flashed. Michael yawned. "It's going to rain soon. Nobody would be crazy enough to swim during a storm, anyway."

Randall gazed out toward the beach again. "She didn't look like she was swimming. Not like a normal person, anyway. Maybe she's drunk and got lost."

Michael smirked as he turned to leave Randall's room. "How could she be lost with that big brain of hers?"

Randall sighed. "I guess I shouldn't have said anything."

"Maybe not." Michael left, closing the room's door behind him.

The wind picked up, triggering the motion lights on the cabin's porch to turn on. The front yard lit up, but only a little light stretched to the beach. Darkness shrouded the shoreline, but something moved in the shadows.

*The woman.*

Randall's mouth dropped open. Michael had left the room too soon. She was back, and now her upper body rose from the water. Her white skin stood out from the black background. She stepped onto the beach, revealing her drooping bare limbs, perfect breasts and ass, but damn... that head. Not just the head, but her neck—too wide—it stretched out almost to her shoulders.

The air howled through the cracks in Randall's window as he fixated on her slow, graceful movements. Maybe he wasn't seeing her right. Maybe it was just the poor lighting, and the shadows playing tricks on him.

Lightning flashed and boomed. Three second delay between the flash and the boom. The storm would hit soon. What was she thinking going into the water right before the storm? No clothes on the ground either. An evening skinny dip? Bad timing. She must have walked a long way to go skinny dipping. No other houses within a couple of miles.

Randall opened his mouth to call Michael again, but stopped. The woman turned toward him with her hands out, gesturing for him to go out there.

He ducked down, his heart pounding. She'd caught him watching her. She'd tell Michael, and he would tease the living shit out of him about it for months. *Should have gone to bed.*

He moved off to the side of the window and reached up, grabbing the string to lower the blinds. He pulled, but hesitated before closing them, peeking around the corner first.

The woman stepped toward the cabin with her arms stretched toward his window. No doubt—she knew he was there. She made a wide gesture with her arms for him to go out there with her.

He would never go outside with her. His fingertips dug into the edge of the window frame. He shook his head and trembled as his heart thumped louder, but he couldn't look away.

Her graceful white silhouette sharpened within the cabin's porch light as she made her way across the grass toward him.

*Beautiful body. Just that big head, and something wrong with her hair. Not... right.*

He released the blinds, and they cracked down over the against the windowsill. No doubt, she had seen that too.

He winced. *Just stay quiet, keep the blinds down, and she'll go away.*

With his heart still pounding, he crawled over to his bed and slinked in under the covers, pulling the cool sheets up over his face. His breath heaved in and out in the darkness.

For the longest time, just the wind pushing against the side of the house. The wood creaking and rumbling storm clouds in the distance.

Something tapped at his window.

Tap... tap... tap...

*Aw, shit.*

*Bugs, just bugs.*

A gentle, whispering voice came through the glass. Her voice wasn't right either. Behind the faint words, a gurgling sound.

She tapped again, harder this time.

*Oh, God. This isn't a Marcy mirage. This is some real shit.*

Each knock sent a chill down his spine. His muscles tensed, and he wanted to scream.

"Just go away," he whispered, pulling his knees up into

his chest forming a ball. He pulled the pillow in over his ears. No more gurgling sound, but he still heard her tapping against the glass.

*Go away.*

"Oh, God, oh, God." His pulse thumped in his ears.

Tap... tap... tap...

*No way in hell I'm letting you in.*

Then silence.

Just his breath and the storm outside again for several minutes as he trembled beneath his sheets. He loosened the pillow over his ears and listened to the wind whistling through the cracks in his window.

He calmed and stared at the blinds over the window. How long could she stand out there in the cold naked?

She had to have given up by now, or passed out drunk. Was he responsible now to get her home? Or leave her there to freeze?

*She will die, you know, if she passes out on the lawn, exposed like that, and it rains.* Hypothermia would get her, and then he'd have a bigger problem to deal with in the morning.

*Dammit.*

He crept out of bed and made his way toward the window again, pulling back the edge of the blinds—just a little—and peeked out.

No sign of her. *Must have headed back to the forest... or her car... or wherever the hell she came from.* Randall scanned the yard and raised the blind a few more inches, then halfway up to get a better view.

She rose from the bottom of the window, her face now wrapped in the white scarf she'd played with earlier. Blue eyes peered at him between the layers of cloth and tufts of brown hair jutted out from the top. Her ivory skin and breasts were flawless, and as his eyes darted from her chest to her face, she laughed at him—a strange, broken cackle. She reached toward him and clawed at the glass like a hungry cat pleading for food.

Randall's muscles froze and gasped, but nothing came out.

She thumped her palm against the glass. "Come out and play."

He knocked his foot against a metal trashcan and teetered back, catching himself before falling. A guttural moan escaped his throat.

She tapped louder. "I need you."

He fumbled with the cord to close the blinds again, but something had jarred it open. *Hell with it.* He turned and ran out of the room.

What had he gotten himself into? If the woman tried the cabin's front door, she might get in. But Michael had locked it, hadn't he? *God, I hope so.*

Randall rushed down the hallway to Michael's closed bedroom door and hesitated a moment before he knocked. Michael would be pissed, but he had no choice.

He knocked. No answer. He pounded. "Michael?"

"What the hell is wrong with you?" Michael yelled.

"She's out there right now," Michael whisper-yelled. "She came up to my window."

Michael cursed, stomping to the door, then threw it open and stood in just his underwear. His body was damp, as if he'd been working out. He flexed his chest muscles and sneered with a red face. "Good God, what's your problem?"

Randall pointed to his room. "She's out there now."

"Do I look like I care?"

"Last time. Just come and look, and you'll see her."

Michael grumbled, but got dressed and followed

Randall to his room. "You're really losing it, you know that? No girl is worth losing your mind over."

Randall stayed back as Michael walked straight to his window and yanked the blinds open all the way. "I don't believe—" He glanced back with a big grin spread across his face. "Oh, man. Is that her?"

"Do you see her?" Randall came up alongside him. The woman was at the beach again, walking gracefully in circles, stretching and twisting like a ballet dancer. The scarf was now draped over her bare shoulders. Randall sighed. At least she wasn't near the cabin anymore. "Yeah, that's her."

"Holy shit, you weren't kidding."

"What do you think she's doing out there like that? You think she's drunk or crazy? Should we call the cops or something?"

Michael glared at him. "You're not bringing the cops out here. You know I've got a warrant. Are you really *that* stupid?"

"I don't want her to freeze."

"She won't freeze." Michael scoffed. "Her clothes are probably laying on the grass or in her car up the road." He whistled.

"She came right up to my window a minute ago. She was trying to lure me outside with her."

"You?" Michael furrowed his brows. "Are you kidding me?"

"What do you mean by that?"

"Nothing, Randall." He watched her sway and turn. "But we can't turn down her invitation. If she wants to party, we better get out there and do something about it. Who are we to judge her for enjoying an evening by the lake? It'd be a shame if we disappoint her, right? You know, there's that college up the road, so I bet she's from there. Probably just some lonely heart looking for a little action." He hurried toward the door.

Randall followed him. "Where are you going?"

"Outside. She must be drunk. I'm going to talk with her, and you're a fool if you don't come with."

Randall grabbed his wrist and pulled him back. "I wouldn't do that. Something's wrong with her."

Michael pulled away, but paused. "Yeah, you said that. Big head, right? Big deal. I'll just say hello."

"Can't we just call the police? She might be dangerous."

Michael rested his hand on Randall's shoulder. "Listen, wake the hell up. Big head or not, she looks good from back here and she's naked, so how can she be dangerous? You didn't see any weapons, right? Any pistols tucked under that scarf? No, so I'll just talk to her. Get her name and phone number." He laughed.

Randall gripped the edge of Michael's shirt, but Michael broke away and hurried through the cabin toward the front door.

Michael threw on his jacket and grabbed a flashlight near the door. "Just stay here, if you want. I don't care. She's probably got friends nearby and this would be the perfect chance for you to forget all about that Marcy girl. Either way, just don't mess it up for me. Got it?"

Randall's eyes widened. "You're really going out there with her?" Randall shook his head. "She's not normal."

"I can see that. Good. I like weird girls."

Michael flipped on the porch light and opened the door. The cool air rushed in around them as they stepped outside together.

The woman had moved off over near the forest now, but she was turned away, and now she fluttered the scarf above her in the wind. Her silhouette stood out against the darkness.

Randall hunkered behind Michael and followed him across the yard. As they approached, the woman backed away further toward the forest. The gentle lapping of the water against the lake's shoreline did nothing to soothe his nerves. The smell of dead fish blew across his face.

Michael's flashlight wasn't strong enough to light more than a few yards ahead of them, but he kept going. "Hey there, what's up?"

The woman swung her hips side to side in exaggerated poses and moved into the trees, fading beyond the flashlight's reach.

Randall cleared his throat. "I don't think we should go over there."

"Nonsense. She's beautiful."

The woman gestured for them to follow her.

Michael chuckled and spoke up. "You got a party happening out there in the woods? I didn't think anyone lived around here. You got a cabin nearby?"

She didn't respond and continued swinging the scarf around, weaving between the trees.

"You got a name?" Michael asked her. "Go to college near here?"

The woman moved into the deep grass, stepping over the brush toward a chain-link fence. She dipped down and slinked through a hole near the ground, then came up on the other side.

"Oh yeah, she's looking for some action, all right." Michael rushed ahead.

Randall struggled to keep up. "Wait, Michael."

Michael glanced back. "If you can't keep up, go back to

the cabin. I'll tell you what you missed in the morning." He laughed.

"Aw, hell." Randall raced up to Michael's side and caught his breath.

Michael patted his back. "That's more like it. She's bound to have some friends, Randall, and I bet by morning you won't even remember that Marcy girl."

Another crack of lightning broke through the night sky. It would suck if they didn't get inside before it rained.

The breeze picked up as Michael reached the fence. "She went in through here somewhere. I see it." He leaned down and pulled back the bottom edge of a large bent section. "You go first."

They hurried through.

The woman kept her distance as she waved them forward toward a distant light.

"Must be a cabin back there." Michael hurried.

"How come we never saw that place before?" Randall struggled to keep up.

"We never went into the woods this far before. Let's just see where she's going." Michael shouted at the woman, "You have a party out there?"

No response.

After a few minutes of a brisk walk, they came out into a clearing and stopped. A run-down cabin stood about thirty feet away with only one faint porch light to illuminate the area. The windows were boarded up and weeds covered the driveway. Only one car in sight—a rusting white two-door hatchback.

The woman had disappeared.

"Where'd she go?" Michael scanned his flashlight over the area.

"Can we go back now?"

"Just a minute. Did you see her go inside?"

"No."

"Well, *somebody's* here or there wouldn't be a light on."

The wind swept through the trees as another crack of lightning hit nearby.

"Shouldn't we get inside?" Randall scanned the edges of the property.

"Good idea." Michael stepped toward the cabin's front door, then stopped.

Someone emerged from the darkness at the side of the house. The woman with the scarf. She inched forward and gestured for them to go to her. At that distance, her enlarged head was clear. Way too big for her petite frame. But now he gagged at the hideous details he hadn't seen clearly before. Her brown matted hair clung to one side of her face, and a thick scar circled the bottom of her neck where her creamy white skin ended. Those same bulging white eyes that had peered at him through his bedroom window now widened even further as she formed a malicious grin.

Randall caught his breath. "Get away from there, Michael."

"Come closer." She slid the scarf up and down her body seductively.

"Oh, God, what is that?" Michael leaned toward her.

"She isn't *right*. Let's go." Randall cringed, but he couldn't look away, trying to make sense of what he was staring at. Her head belonged to someone else. Some other woman. And whoever had joined them together had horrendously mangled the surgery. His stomach churned.

Michael stepped back, bobbing the flashlight's beam up and down her body, then stopping at her face. "She's a freak. Is this a joke?"

The woman opened her arms wide, as if to embrace him, but remained at the edge of the darkness. "Lots of girls inside. Take your pick."

Michael groaned and took another step backwards. "No way."

A taller woman peeked out from around a tree near the house. She was nothing like the first one. Her bloated body jiggled, and when the flashlight focused in on her torso, his stomach churned—a thin pink t-shirt, one size too small, stretched over her deformed chest. Her shorts failed to cover pale, fat legs with a network of veins spread over them like a spider's web. Like the first woman, she too had a mis-matched head, but she was far uglier with a rat's nest for hair and bugged-out eyes. Her stench grew stronger as she approached them, and Randall held back the urge to vomit.

"Just in time." The taller woman chuckled, her flabby chest jiggling. "I couldn't have lasted another day. Are you boys here for the party?"

Michael backed away, mumbling a string of curse words before stumbling and falling backward onto the ground. He scrambled to stand again. "Shit, what the hell is that?"

Randall couldn't move. His legs no longer worked. He screamed inside, but he couldn't open his mouth. A horrible stench drifted past him, like hundreds of dead animals.

Both women stepped toward them, pushing through the tall grass with their arms outstretched as if to comfort them. Gurgling, wet huffing noises escaped from their throats. The better-looking woman stopped and laughed, while the taller repulsive one approached faster.

Randall and Michael turned and ran.

*Crack.*

Michael screamed out in pain. Only a few seconds into their escape, Michael tumbled forward, a metal chain jangling at his feet, and landed flat on his face. The flashlight splashed into the weeds just out of his reach. He clawed at his foot. "It's got me! Son of a bitch!"

"What's got you?" Randall pulled on Michael's arm in the darkness.

"A clamp or something. A trap. An animal trap." He groaned and cried out.

The ugly woman approached faster, her flabby frame gyrating in the dim light.

Randall yanked at Michael's shoulder. "You've got to get up."

"I can't." Michael knocked Randall's hands away. "Don't pull on me, you idiot, pull the chain!"

Randall squatted and followed the chain to a cement block. "I can't." He glanced up at the woman. "She's coming, and I can't move it."

"Yes, you can. Pull that damn thing out of the ground." Michael wobbled to his feet and limped backward, pulling the chain with him. "Call the police."

Randall felt his pockets. "I don't have my phone."

Michael pointed to the taller, ugly woman. "Knock her out then!"

Randall scanned the ground. "How?"

"Do I have to explain everything?" Michael strained and cursed as he pulled on the chain.

Randall scooped up the flashlight, then the largest branch he could find in the moment. The taller woman's arms flailed as she hurdled toward them. His heart pounded, but he lunged at the woman, whacking the branch across her neck as hard as he could.

She recoiled and paused, whipping her thick arms

against him and knocking the branch out of his hands. Their flesh intersected for a moment. *Like cold, wet fish skin.*

The flashlight's beam hit Michael's trapped foot. It was an animal trap, all right, just like the ones used to catch bears and coyotes. Blood saturated his ankle and shoe. "Get me out of this thing!"

The ugly woman pounced on Michael as he tried to stand, slamming him to the ground as nauseating guttural noises filled the air.

Randall cried out and threw himself on her back, batting the woman's torso with the flashlight and his forearm. Despite the flab and putrid stench of her body, her strength matched his own.

A nauseating churn of black goo erupted from the incision around the woman's neck as she held Michael down. The crud drained down over his chest and arms as his fists pounded up into her face. He screamed at the top of his lungs until she clutched his throat and silenced him.

"Michael!" Randall winced, straining to pull her away. He caught sight of another, larger branch, and leaned toward it when the cabin's front door swung open.

A tall, thin man in blue jeans and a white t-shirt stepped out holding a rifle. "Caught you, Gracie! You cheating on me again?" Even within that dim light, his eyes stood out against the darkness—wide circles of white. He raised his rifle, then aimed it at them.

"Nobody's cheating on nobody." The ugly woman answered with her hand cupped over Michael's mouth. She gestured to the other woman. "Pepper brought in two more."

Behind the man, against the far wall, were a line of wall-mounted human heads, displayed like trophies, their eyes and mouths wide as if caught in an eternal scream. Randall counted seven—two men and five women—before the door snapped shut.

Randall stepped back and screamed.

"We need a woman, Gracie, not more men." The rifle's barrel targeted Michael first, then turned to Randall. "You want a man's body this time? That doesn't work for me." A rifle blast exploded into the ground near Randall's feet.

Randall shuddered and stumbled over a branch.

"I don't want a man's body, you dope! You know me better than that." Gracie rolled over, still pinning Michael down. "I'm only thinking of Pepper. She's so lonely."

"Two in one night, Daddy." Pepper moved toward the porch. "I thought you'd be happy. Can I keep one?"

The man aimed his gun at Randall's chest. "Keep the healthy one, then."

Randall lurched sideways as a second blast ripped past him, meeting Michael's eyes for a moment.

Michael's face was pale and his eyes were full of fear. He trembled with his hand stretched out. Beneath Gracie's hand, his voice came through. "Run."

Randall rushed away, switching off the flashlight. His pulse thumped in his ears as he tried to catch his breath. His footsteps crashed through the branches and leaves as he sprinted back in the cabin's direction.

No more shots fired, but one of them chased him. He didn't stop to check which one. Panting and scanning the darkness for the cabin's porch light, he charged ahead without direction.

He must have gotten disoriented during the escape. *Where the hell am I?*

Nothing looked familiar as he pushed through the brush with only the flashes of distant lightning to light the way. His legs cramped and burned, but he didn't slow down. He held the flashlight out and flipped it on for a moment. A narrow path lay ahead through a clump of trees. *Had they entered the forest through there?* He paused, then followed it anyway. *Damn, all the trees look the same.*

The faint sound of churning waves came through the forest to the right. *Or was that just an echo?* He turned around. Impossible to know for sure—the sound came from every direction. The wind stirred the branches, and the leaves rustled. The cabin couldn't be too far away—they hadn't walked more than ten minutes beyond the edge of the property. Not slowing down, he crashed forward, the branches cutting across his arms and face, and his heaving breaths blocked out any sounds of his hunter. His body ached—he couldn't continue.

A massive fallen oak tree blocked his path. He paused, grabbing onto a branch to balance himself.

"Where's the cabin?" Randall's teeth chattered. The cool air chilled his shivering body.

The flashes of nearby lightning illuminated the sky, but provided no help in finding his way out of there.

*I don't want to die out here.*

The clouds rumbled overhead. It would rain soon. Maybe his pursuer had given up, but he needed to get help for Michael. He cursed himself for not grabbing his cellphone earlier.

Branches cracked to his left, followed by a woman's deep groaning sounds.

He shivered again. *Gracie. She's nearby.*

He scanned the fallen oak tree in his path for the best place to hide, then staggered around to the back of it, pushing in beneath an overgrown section. The ground was damp beneath the log, but he hunkered down as low as he could go.

His own breath startled him. *Too loud. She'll hear you. Calm down.* He took in a deep breath, then held it as the woman approached, cracking through branches straight toward him.

The wind ruffled his hair as he crouched even further beneath the downed tree. He folded his arms over his chest to keep warm and keep still.

More branches cracked only a few feet away now. He didn't dare even move.

Tense and trembling, he considered his options before the stalker closed in further. *Run like hell or keep hiding like a coward. What would Michael do?*

*Michael would run.* He glanced down at himself in the darkness. His muscles burned and his heart still pounded just from the short run to that hiding spot. *All those years of not exercising came back to haunt him. But I'm not a coward.*

He would run. *Okay, in... 1... 2...*

The footsteps moved away. He paused his escape. The relative calm surrounded him again, and he heaved in a deep breath. Rising above the edge of the log, he stared into the darkness, but nothing moved. *Lucky as hell.*

No signs of anyone. He crept out into the open again, flipped on the flashlight, and ran. The edge of the forest couldn't be *that* far away. Thunder crashed overhead as the wind picked up, and the trees creaked and swayed. Seconds later, the stench of dead fish blew across his face, and he cringed. *Thank God—the lakeshore is nearby.*

A little further and the sound of waves splashing against the shoreline grew louder. Relief surged through him.

*Not too far now. Only a little further to the cabin.* Lightning flashed across the sky.

"Almost there," he mumbled.

When the cabin's porch light came into view, a rush of adrenaline propelled him forward. The opening in the fence where he had entered was just ahead. *I'll come back for you, Michael. I won't leave you behind.*

Emerging on the other side of the fence, a woman's voice startled him.

"I want him, Daddy," she pleaded. "He's cute."

"Let her have this one, Doc," another woman added.

*Cute?* Randall turned his head to look for the source when something struck him in the back of his arm. A wasp? His palm covered the sudden wound and found the feathered tail of a tranquilizer dart. He removed it, but the needle had already released its drug in his muscle.

Gracie, Pepper, and Doc approached from the edge of the forest.

Doc grumbled and scowled at him. "If he survives, honey."

Randall's eyelids drooped, and his body crumpled as he passed out.

He awoke strapped to a wooden table. Ropes held him down by his arms and legs. No windows or clocks in the room, but he felt as if he'd slept for days. A bright light overhead blinded his view of the ceiling.

Mounted heads circled the walls, but not the same ones he'd seen earlier through the open doorway to the cabin. More victims displayed like prizes. Who could do such a thing? Men and women of all ages frozen in a ghastly cry of terror.

The older woman—what was her name?—Gracie. She held an empty plague against the wall next to the others and shifted it left and right until stopping with a nod.

Would that be his new home?

To his left, he spotted an open ice cooler only a few feet away. Michael's head lay in the center with blood splashed over the ice like cherry slushie. His body was nowhere in sight.

Aside from the heads, the room resembled an operating room. Medical equipment surrounded him, and some of them were functioning. The familiar beeping of a heart monitor repeated beside him.

Terror swept up his spine, but before he could scream, Pepper's voice whispered in his ear.

"You'll be mine." She nuzzled closer and ran her hands down his chest and legs. "I couldn't just let you end up on the wall like the others. We'll have great fun together, but you'll need to stay in shape if you want to keep me happy. I exercise all the time. Can you tell?" She posed for him, still naked, twisting and turning like a fashion model.

Randall screamed now, but it came out as a weak moan. His throat ached.

"Don't struggle, my darling." She eyed the full length of his body and reached for his crotch. "Daddy did a good job."

"Leave him, Pepper." Doc stepped into the room from somewhere out of sight. "You'll have your fun later."

"He won't scream. I can tell." Pepper leaned in and whispered in his ear again. "You aren't a screamer, are you?" She laughed.

She patted his face and left the room.

The doctor was busy with something on another table beside his own.

Randall's neck itched like never before. He moved, and pain shot up his spine. An IV drip line ran into his hand. He whispered, "What's this?"

"It will take time to heal," Doc said without turning around. "But I'm the best. You won't be unhappy with the result."

*Result of what?* He tugged his hands, but the ropes around his wrists didn't budge.

He was stuck and caught sight of the ice cooler again. "Michael," he moaned.

"This is your lucky day," Doc said, glancing back at him. "What's your name?"

Randall didn't answer.

"Shy? It doesn't matter. We'll get to know each other quite well. You're family now, so just call me Doc. You won't try to escape, will you? That would be a grave mistake. But you don't need to be afraid. Pepper has chosen you as her partner, and you'll be happy with us. Do you believe in eternal life, Randall?"

Randall stared at him for a moment, then nodded.

"I'm not talking spiritual. Forget that. It is physical life you've won. Not only does it exist, but you now possess it... as long as you don't betray me. Understand?"

Randall winced at a sharp pain shooting down from the back of his neck to his feet.

The Doc grinned. "The pain will fade away within a few days. I'm very good at nerve management. You just need to know which wires go where. Your friend is gone, but, in a way, he lives on through you." Doc tapped Randall's chest.

Randall strained forward and stared down at his chest. Muscular and more hair than he remembered. Unfamiliar, but he felt... better. Better than he'd ever felt in his life. He took in a deep breath. He spotted something on his left wrist. A tattoo of a shark.

"Pepper will be so happy with you, and you'll get to enjoy her new vessel as well. By far, the best one she's ever had. Plenty of time to run before it'll need to be replaced. Gracie is long overdue, but she'll get an upgrade soon too." Doc patted Randall's shoulder. "Enjoy."

## MR. WHISKERS

John met the Pomeranian's gaze and cringed. The little beast was long dead, yet its beady glass eyes glared at him. Mary had stuffed the damn thing, and for twenty long years it had watched over his every move from the top of her dresser.

"Your master's gone," John said. "What'll you do now?"

Time to make some changes. He'd toss that stuffed ankle-biter first thing in the morning, along with all the other piles of crap she'd accumulated over the years.

He didn't want to think about all the work ahead of him now that she was gone. She'd hoarded everything, stuffing box after box and piling them anywhere she could find the room—in the closet, in the garage, under the bed, and even under the kitchen table. Couldn't even see it anymore behind all the boxes, much less use it.

No more storage unit either. Twenty years of paying a hundred bucks a month to store a pile of crap worth less than a good meal at McDonalds. He avoided doing the math in his head. It would just make him upset again. He took a deep breath. It was over. He'd pull a dumpster up to the side of the house and chuck everything out. Fire Sale. Everything Must Go.

Her damn little devil-dog sat up there on her dresser, staring back at him like everything was all fine and dandy. Its gaze followed him everywhere in the room, watching over him like The Great Protector. Nothing behind those glassy eyes anymore. The taxidermist had done a damn fine job to his wife's delight. As good as new. Whatever the man did in his magic lab to bring it back to life was incredible. You'd never guess the little monster had stopped blinking twenty years earlier after a nauseating battle with bladder problems. Such a relief to not have to clean up pools of pee every morning, noon, and night.

But you couldn't tell no gears turned behind those big, bug eyes. Mr. Whiskers had lived on in that gallant pose, brandishing teeth that had chewed apart his shoes plenty of times. Razor teeth that had drawn his blood several times with Mary jumping to defend the animal's action.

"What did you do?" Mary always scolded him, as if it were *his* fault the dog attacked him.

What could he say? Nothing. The little devil liked to bite him. That was it.

Never again.

"Your master is never coming home again. Who'll protect you now? You'll rot in a landfill. In fact," John climbed out of bed, "I'll do it right now."

John stood up, his joints cracking as he lumbered across the bedroom to the dresser on Mary's side of the bed. Only a few precious items had earned their place on her dresser over the years. Their wedding photo from fifty-three years earlier, a photo of their two kids when they were much younger, a vase stuffed with plastic daisies, and her cherished-more-than-her-husband Mr. Whiskers.

He plucked the dog from the dresser, gripping it by its hind legs as he walked over to the closet. He held it away from his body as if it were a piece of rotting meat.

"I should have done this years ago, you little shit."

He opened the closet door and tossed the dog to the back of the closet, behind a stack of his wife's old clothes. The figure thumped against the back wall. A tiny gasp of breath filled the closet. Not his own.

He stopped and listened. Someone's breath? Some *thing's* breath? Ridiculous. Nothing more than his imagination. He was a rational guy. His old mind was playing tricks on him. He slammed the closet door and chuckled.

"I feel better already."

He stared at the empty spot on Mary's dresser. A fluttering sensation filled his chest and his heart beat a little faster. Something was wrong.

*Shouldn't have messed with Mr. Whiskers, Johnny boy.*

John smirked. "She's gone. What's she going to do about it now?"

He climbed back into bed. 10:32pm. Long past his regular bedtime, but no need to keep Mary's early to bed, early to-rise schedule anymore. He could stay up all night if he wanted.

"Just like the old days."

He pulled the covers up to his chin and glanced over at Mary's dresser where the dog had sat. Much better. Finally, he'd get his life back to normal. Move past all the craziness and clean the slate. Dump all the crap she'd crammed into every corner.

On Mary's deathbed, she'd grabbed his wrist and squeezed. "Watch over little Mr. Whiskers. Keep him right there on the dresser, so he can protect you. Keep you safe when I'm gone."

He'd struggled to hold back his disgust. "Wouldn't it be better if I put him... with you? To keep you company?"

She'd scowled at him. "What a horrible thing to say. Lock our Mr. Whiskers deep in the ground? That's so mean."

So he hadn't touched her precious little animal. The damn thing wasn't doing anybody any good up there, staring at him with those bug eyes.

The little rodent had made his life miserable for fifteen years before it had keeled off. Fifteen years of that damn thing yipping at all hours of the day. Putting up with its random attacks against his feet. Dozens of destroyed shoes torn up by its razor teeth. All the time Mary defending the little bastard.

"You must have done something to make him so mad."

He hadn't. Mr. Whiskers was a psycho little devil and now it was supposed to be his protector? Protector from what?

Mary had never understood his disdain for her precious animal—always a point of contention between them. Nothing he could do about it. She got everything she wanted, and he kept his mouth shut.

At least its damn yipping had stopped. That thing had yipped morning, noon, and night.

John took a deep breath and listened to the silence. Wonderful.

At the funeral, Mary's sister had the brashness to suggest he get another dog to fill the companionship void. No chance in hell. One demon in a lifetime was enough torture. No more dogs. No more animals.

"Maybe we can clone Mr. Whiskers," Mary had suggested days after finding the furry hell beast dead beside its silver water dish. "They can do miraculous things these days."

"No." He'd fumed without looking at her. "No more dogs. No more animals in this house."

So she'd gotten him stuffed instead. An eternal resting spot only inches away from their bed.

So every night before bed, she'd kissed the damn thing on the forehead, even before kissing him. Its unblinking eyes and gaping mouthful of shark teeth were the last thing he saw before switching off the light.

She'd never turned it away. Not even during their intimate moments. It always stared at them. He assumed he'd get used to it over the years, but it was like Mr. Whiskers had never left. So damn lifelike. Whenever he'd gotten the chance, he'd moved it off to the side or turned it around backwards, hoping she wouldn't notice, but she'd always returned it to the same spot soon after.

"He's watching over us," she'd said, "protecting us."

From what? He wanted to scream at her. What was it protecting him from? Bullshit. The damn thing needed to go in the trash.

His heart raced now thinking about it. He closed his eyes and caught a whiff of his wife's pillow as if she hadn't left the room. He hadn't changed the sheets since she died. Lots of things around the room reminded him of her. It would take time for all of that to fade away before he could get the quiet he deserved.

He turned off the light next to his bed and his mind drifted off. The traffic from the nearby highway faded away as sleep flooded in.

*Yip, yip.*

John's eyes shot open. The traffic's steady drone faded

back in. A car's horn jarred his silence. Crazy drivers out there.

*Yip, yip, yip.*

What the hell was that? A dog?

He switched on the light. Mr. Whiskers? That was nuts. Why would he even think something so crazy? But the sound had come from his room. A neighbor's dog had snuck in? But how? He locked the doors downstairs. He made sure of it as he did every night.

Just a dream. The traffic noises had spurred his imagination. Just a trick of his mind.

*Yip, yip.*

No dream. He gasped. Wide awake now. Something scratched against the closet door.

Rats? Or the neighbor's dog had gotten into his closet? But their dog was a Border Collie mutt, not the size of a dog he'd miss sneaking around in his house. So how the hell could anything except rats be in there? Maybe he'd left the door open earlier in the day and something else had gotten in. A cat? Yes. The neighbor had a cat too. Some time during the day their cat had snuck in. That made sense.

Something scratched again.

A cat or a rat. Either way, it had to go. The rat theory made more sense. So much junk packed into the house. The walls were probably teaming with the little rodents.

He groaned and climbed out of bed again. "Whatever's in there, you're about to catch my shoe in your ass. Damn neighbors can't keep track of anything. I'll have animal control stop by to pick you up."

He hesitated before opening the closet door. "If you scratch me, I'll knock your ass to kingdom come."

John opened the closet door and stepped back, expecting *something* to dart out. Nothing came out.

He opened the door a little further. Mr. Whiskers was on the floor standing up facing out.

"That's different." The dog must have rolled off the stack of clothes and landed in that position.

No sign of any rats or cats. He thumped his foot against the side of the door. "Hey. Whatever's in here better get the hell out."

He kicked harder this time. He winced. Pain surged through his bare foot.

Nothing. No movement, no scratching, no signs of life. Whatever had scratched the door earlier was either hiding behind all the clothes and boxes, or it had raced away through an unseen hole in the wall.

He kicked into the pile of clothes and pushed aside some of them to get a better view.

"Better get out now before I get pissed. Here's your chance to run. Do you hear me?" He kicked against the side of a cardboard box labeled 'dresses' along the wall. Again, nothing.

No sign of the neighbor's cat. Had to be rats. He'd need to clear everything out to find it. He winced. Paying an exterminator to flush out all those rodents wouldn't be cheap, and he didn't have the money for it. Maybe if he kept the closet door locked at night, they wouldn't run helter skelter through his house.

He dug his foot in around the back of Mary's clothes and nudged the stack away from the wall. No holes as far as he could see. It had to be there somewhere behind those boxes.

Mr. Whiskers stood at his feet, staring back toward Mary's dresser. So lifelike in that darkened area. A chill passed through him. He expected the damn thing to come to life at any moment and clamp its jaw around his ankle.

He bent down and held out his index finger in front of the dog's face as if offering it a bone. "You want a piece of me now? Mary said you have to protect me, remember? Can't bite me anymore. But I'll give you one chance. Do your worst." He dangled his fingers in front of the dog's eyes.

John chuckled. "I knew you didn't have it in you. What good are you? Can't protect shit. Don't even want you in my house anymore." He scooped up Mr. Whiskers by its neck, lifting it off to the side as he stepped back. "I can't even look at your ugly face anymore. I don't know what Mary ever saw in you."

He plodded down the stairs to the kitchen and over to the back door. Locked tight, just as he remembered. Nothing could get in. Definitely rats.

He unbolted the door and walked outside in his flannel pajamas. Never mind the neighbors seeing him dressed like that.

He marched straight over to the garbage cans next to the garage and lifted the lid. Without hesitation, he flung the dog into the trash and snapped the lid shut.

"Good riddance."

He checked the lid before walking away. A little loose. Better make sure... Make sure of what? That he doesn't get out? Lunacy. Well, raccoons prowled the area at night. Better make sure no raccoons get in there and dig him out.

He spotted a stack of bricks left over from a garden project against the garage. They would do just fine. He grabbed a couple and stacked them on the garbage lid.

Wiping his hands on his pajamas, he walked back toward the house.

"Done." He went inside and locked the door behind himself, making sure the deadbolt was in place. He passed by each window and checked their locks. All of them were closed. Why would any of them be open? They hadn't opened any window in at least ten years.

He returned to his bedroom upstairs and paused before climbing into bed again. The closet door was still open. Maybe whatever was in there had scrambled out while he was downstairs. He kicked his foot against the door one more time with a loud thump, but nothing scurried away.

He shut the closet door and went to bed. His mind whirled at the thought rats might share the same room. The potential points of entry for them were endless. It was an old house. Lots of cracks and holes. So much space between the walls, and an enormous attic full of rotting family clutter. It would take a long time to secure everything.

The air in the room shifted as if someone opened a door. Something clicked at the bottom of the stairs. An intruder? He'd checked the locks, but maybe someone had gotten in while he was outside. Or maybe the thing in the closet had run downstairs.

John sighed and his head hurt. Too much to think about.

His heartbeat picked up as something pattered up the stairs. Tiny footsteps of a small animal. A rat wouldn't run up the stairs.

"It's that goddamn cat."

Through the light coming in under his bedroom door, he watched the shadows move. Something pushed against the door, but the latch held it closed. Whatever it was, it couldn't get in. It thumped against the door and scratched at the wood. The same animal that had been in his closet.

The thing let out a low, pained whine. A familiar sound. It scratched again and again. That thing really wanted to get in.

"Come back for more? I just want to get some sleep now. Go away."

The thing scratched faster, and the door rattled.

"Oh, what the hell." John tossed the blankets aside and stood again. He scanned the room for something he could use to scare the animal away with. He'd smash the damn thing. His body tensed and his eyes narrowed, focusing on the end table beside his bed for his glasses. Gone. Where had he put them?

No chance to avoid the problem. He'd need to deal with it right then if he wanted to get some sleep. The damn thing would just keep waking him up.

He grabbed one of his old shoes, one with a thick heel, and raised it before resting his hand on the door handle. He shook the handle. Maybe the jarring noise would scare the little bastard away.

The animal whined again and scratched faster.

"Go away."

It responded with a low guttural growl. Not a cat.

"Good God."

He turned the door handle. The thing thumped against the door even as he opened it. He raised the shoe a little higher and calculated its trajectory to strike it dead with one blow.

He gasped. Within the light of his end table lamp, Mr. Whiskers stood frozen, facing in toward his room. Its eyes glared ahead as if waiting for him to pick it up. Its jaw opened wider as he stared at it, pushing back the corners of its mouth into a wild grin.

He couldn't breathe. An icy chill swallowed his lungs and his heart pounded. "How did you get in here? Did someone let you in?"

A ridiculousness statement. He was talking to a stuffed animal. A practical joke? Yes, someone had broken into his house to play a joke on him.

"Ha ha. Not funny assholes. Come out now before I call the police."

They could hide anywhere. Maybe even in his own bedroom, or downstairs waiting to surprise him after going to investigate. Had they hidden in his house all day?

"This isn't funny." John shouted. "When the cops get here, they'll blast your ass."

He bent down and slammed his shoe's heel into Mr. Whiskers's side. The dog tumbled into the hallway and thumped against a far wall as he hurried toward the bathroom. He'd left his glasses in there earlier.

He found them and looked at himself in the mirror for a moment. His pale face reflected his fear. He swallowed. He should call the police. The phone was next to his bed.

On his way back, he stopped before arriving at his doorway. Mr. Whiskers was gone. He scanned the darkness and crept back into his room, still holding up the heel of his shoe. He'd always meant to buy a pistol. Too late now.

He looked around the room for the intruder. Mr. Whiskers sat on his wife's dresser again in the same spot he'd sat for twenty years.

John trembled. It wasn't funny. Not funny at all. His pulse thumped in his ears as he struggled to breathe.

He stumbled toward the phone. He'd call the police, but what would he tell them?

*Someone broke into my house and they're playing a prank on me.*

They'd laugh. *Is the intruder armed? What do they look like?*
*I don't know, but they keep messing with my stuffed dog.*

Oh yes, they'd get a big kick out of that conversation. And after they arrived, what would they do if they didn't find anyone?

They'd send him to a mental hospital. He couldn't explain any of it.

He rubbed his forehead. Dementia? At seventy-eight years old, it was a genuine possibility. Maybe all of it just a hallucination?

His eyes locked onto Mr. Whiskers. The jaw had opened a little further and the corners of its mouth pulled back a little wider.

Its head moved. Just a little, a slight motion toward him and a subtle movement in its eyes. The damn thing was laughing at him.

Prank or not, he would get rid of that thing. No need for the police. If he said anything to anybody, they would lock him away in the looney bin. He wasn't crazy, just beyond exhausted. A good night's sleep would do him a lot of good, but that would have to wait. He needed to take care of the Mr. Whiskers problem once and for all.

He circled around the bed and plucked up the stuffed dog again, clutching it by the neck, squeezing it as if it might get away if he loosened his grip. Clutching his shoe in his other hand, he stomped down the stairs to the kitchen.

He could chop it to pieces, but what would he do with the pieces? He needed to get rid of it. Annihilate it.

Burn it.

He switched on the outside light and slipped on a pair of boots next to the door before hurrying outside to the garage. The garbage can lid he'd sealed shut earlier was wide open. The two bricks lay on the ground next to the can. He shivered in the warm summer air.

He opened the garage door and pushed aside an assortment of broken brooms and mops to get to the grill. No gas to start any flames, but the lighter fluid sat on the shelf. Perfect, and a box of matches sat right next to it.

He dragged everything into the driveway, the wheels of the grill squealing all the way. If the neighbors looked out their windows, they'd see a crazy old man lighting his grill at close to midnight, but to hell with them. They didn't understand. A stuffed dog needed to burn.

He slammed Mr. Whiskers on the grill and held it down with one hand as if by letting it go the thing would scramble away. He stuffed the lighter fluid's nozzle into the dog's mouth and squeezed. Not much fluid went into the beast, but that wasn't the point. The excess drained out of its mouth and pooled at the bottom of the grill. Without looking away, he squirted the lighter fluid over its body, saturating its fur.

He grinned. "Cremation time."

He took a match out of the box and struck it on the side of the grill to light it. A flame burst from the match's tip, then puffed out. He pressed the smoking matchstick against the dog's fur, but it didn't ignite.

He grabbed three matchsticks and lit them all at the same time. None of them stayed lit for more than a second.

He looked around. No wind. Maybe the matches were outdated. Did matches get too old?

Four at a time. The same result.

"Well, good God. Am I going mad?" His hands trembled as he tried one last time.

No fire.

The lighter-soaked dog stared off into space as he considered his options. Bury it? Too much work. Dump it in the lake?

Sounds good, but the damn thing might float back up. Got to weigh it down.

He grabbed Mr. Whiskers—couldn't let him out of sight for a second—and walked back into the garage. A rusty chain hung near the door. He grabbed it and wound it around the dog's torso. That would do. As lighter fluid dripped off the dog and through his fingers, he carried the ball of rattling metal back into the house, grabbed his keys, and went out to his rusting Honda Civic. He set the shackled dog on the seat, not bothering to put anything under it. He would clean up the mess in the morning.

Half-asleep, he darted out of the driveway still in his pajamas and made his way across town to the beach. The crickets chirped as he climbed out of the car holding the captive Mr. Whiskers.

"I'd like to see you get out of this one."

The swimming dock wasn't too far away, and it stretched out over the water far enough. If anyone found it later, only a coil of chain would survive.

Cradling Mr. Whiskers like a cannonball, he trudged out to the end of the dock and within the light of a half-moon he hurled the rattling ball as far as he could. It splashed into the water several feet away.

That was it.

He stood there for a moment before turning around and going back to his car. The smell of lighter fluid wafted into his face. He winced, wiping his fingers onto his pajamas.

The odor of lighter fluid permeated the air on his drive home. Nothing a long shower couldn't wash off.

Worth all the trouble to get rid of that dog.

He turned the corner toward his house, his fingers still slick from the lighter fluid.

*Yip.*

He shuddered. The steering wheel slipped through his fingers, shooting to the right into the path of an oncoming truck.

A flash of light, then black.

He awoke in the driver's seat, leaning to his right, pushed down by the collapsed roof. His head pounded and a wall of heat surrounded him. Flames engulfed the passenger seat and the engine. The truck he'd hit was nowhere in sight, although someone screamed in the darkness. Fire raged across the seat toward him as he unbuckled his seatbelt.

The car door cracked open, but everything was a blur. He'd lost his glasses.

"Help me." He struggled to move away from the encroaching flames, but every move sent needles shooting through his spine.

No response.

He wrestled to lift one leg, but the steering wheel prevented it. He teetered on the edge of consciousness.

*Yip, yip.*

Oh, God. No. Impossible.

Something tugged at his left ankle. Someone to rescue him. He couldn't see that far.

"Please, help me. Mr. Whiskers? Is that you?"

He lifted his head high enough to see his rescuer.

A Pomeranian engulfed in flames.

It stretched open a mouthful of razor teeth and clamped onto his lower leg. Blood soaked his pajamas.

He screamed as it dragged him out of the car with supernatural strength.

"No! Go away! Bad dog!"

The flames ravaging its tiny frame spread to his boot, then caught the end of his pajamas. A searing pain stabbed at his brain as the fire moved up his leg. It dragged him several feet across the asphalt, far from the raging fire of the crash.

As John squirmed within excruciating pain, Mr. Whiskers pranced up his body and came to rest over his heart. The dog's body burned like the sun as the flames spread through his pajamas and into his chest.

His protector.

*Yip, yip.*

# MRS. TUTTLE'S ROOM

Matt Bailey stepped out of his car, and before he shut the door, the ground shook. He clung to his door's edge as his car and everything around him wobbled.

*An earthquake?* Or maybe just the fallout from driving ten hours straight, his brain still frozen in high gear from the car's constant motion. He paused and balanced himself. Several dogs barked in the distance. *Definitely an earthquake.* Palm trees swayed along the edge of the motel's property. *Just a minor earthquake. 4.5 at the most.* It only lasted for a few seconds before it faded away.

No surprise. Fault lines snaked across the California landscape like a spider's web. He grabbed the two suitcases from his trunk and dragged them across the parking lot to the motel's main entrance.

A sign beside the door read "Press buzzer for entry after 9 PM." He checked his cellphone. 9:05. *Damn.* He pressed it and waited.

Through the glass door, Matt spotted a rack of tourist brochures and framed photos of the San Diego skyline lining the walls. A coffee maker and other breakfast appliances sat neat and ready in the corner, and a little further over a large screen TV hung on the wall switched off.

He'd made it. First vacation in nine years, and first vacation ever without his wife or family. Paradise.

The motel wasn't a total dive, but he wouldn't have stayed there normally, except that it was cheap and one of the last rooms in San Diego because of a convention. Too late to change his vacation plans. *That's what you get for booking late.* Sure, it would've been better if he'd planned ahead, but life had gotten in the way and his wife demanded a divorce, and she always got what she wanted. But now that was over and it was good to be away from home. Far, far away.

The front desk clerk emerged from an office behind the front counter—a thin, middle-aged man wearing a flannel shirt and thick black glasses. He buzzed Matt through the security door, but then he disappeared again into his office.

Matt lugged his suitcases across the lobby's faded tile floor, dropping them at his feet when he'd reached the counter.

The clerk re-emerged again from the back room. Matt focused on the man's name tag. Charles.

"How can I help you, sir?" Charles asked.

"I have a reservation for five nights. Matt Bailey."

Charles nodded, then flipped through some paperwork. "You're here for the convention?"

"No. What convention?"

"Comic Con. It's a pop culture thing that happens every year. My ex-wife was a huge fan of the event, but I never found it interesting in the least." He pointed to a framed photo on a shelf behind him. "That's her. Gone for six years now, rest her soul."

The woman in the photo had long black hair and a wide, bright smile. Matt glanced at the other photos on the wall behind the counter. In one, Charles stood with his arm around a pretty Latina woman. Another frame displayed the motel's business license with the owner's name: Charles and Rita Redding.

Matt checked the man's name tag again. "You're the owner?"

Charles looked up. "Yes, sir. My wife and I own it. A small, family-owned business among all the other corporate options. We like it that way. Are you here on business?"

"No. Just here to get away and relax."

"Good thing we had a room available. Every room is booked this week. We're full of Con goers. Somebody cancelled an hour before you called."

"Lucky me."

The clerk handed him the keys to the room, but circled around and came out from behind the counter. He called out to someone in the back room, "Rita, watch the front desk. I need to show a guest his room."

"Yes, Charles," a woman's voice answered.

Matt shook his head and held up his hand. "I'm sure I can find it myself."

Charles grinned. "I'm sure you can, but I need to point out a few things inside the room. We had a long-term tenant staying there, and she recently passed away. That's her picture there." He gestured to a photo on the wall. It showed a red-haired old woman wearing a dark dress while standing next to a man in a business suit. "She had quite a history with this hotel. Have you heard of Margaret Tuttle?"

"No."

"Famous psychic, known for talking to the dead. You believe in that stuff?"

"Not really."

"Me neither. I thought she was a nut, personally, but she grew quite popular in the last year of her life. Rita was quite close to her, unfortunately. People would schedule a visit for a reading with her months ahead of time."

"A reading?"

"A communication. Like a seance, except that she never let anyone watch her do it. They'd show up at her door and wait outside for hours sometimes just to hear what she had to say."

"People will believe anything, I guess."

Charles chuckled and led Matt outside. "I guess. She lived in our motel for over half a century, which is why we haven't renovated her room like the others. You'll see. It still has that 1950s nostalgia, since we haven't had a chance to get in there and renovate anything yet, but it's clean."

"She died in the room?"

Charles laughed. "No, nothing like that."

Matt narrowed his eyes. "So what's wrong with it?"

"No, nothing wrong. Just some... quirks."

"That doesn't sound good." Matt dragged his suitcases along as he followed the clerk around the side of the single-story motel to the far end of the complex.

"It's a very nice room. I'll go over everything, so no need to worry. Just some unique details to make your stay more enjoyable. You're only the third guest to stay there since she left it vacant."

Matt's legs ached as he trudged along.

Charles gestured forward. "Your room is at the end, the last one. A bit of a walk, but maybe a little quieter too."

Matt cringed halfway there. A nauseating smell filled the air, like unregulated pollution escaping a manufacturing plant. "Is that what you needed to explain? That smell?"

"Oh yes, that. I'm very sorry about that. Nothing we can do about it. There's a drilling operation next door. We've done everything we can to alleviate the smell, filter it out inside your room. I advise you to keep the windows closed."

"I don't know if I'll be able to sleep with that."

"The previous guests admitted they hardly noticed it once they closed the door. You should be fine."

They stopped at the last room in the long complex. 145.

Beyond the edge of the motel, a thick row of bushes and small trees obscured a tall brick wall.

"Not much of a view." Matt gestured to it.

"Our motel caters to the budget-minded. The facility next door put up the wall. We had no choice in the matter."

"What are they drilling for over there?"

"I've never bothered to find out, but I'm sure it's making someone rich. As long as you keep the windows shut, you shouldn't have a problem. We've installed the best filters to keep the air inside clean and fresh." Charles opened the door.

The room was far from ordinary. A little larger than he expected, the odd colors and furnishings resembled an old sitcom set from his childhood. Bright orange painted walls, except for a small section of yellow-white flowery wallpaper near the bathroom. A small rustic desk sat to the right next to a vintage TV complete with a rabbit ears antenna perched on an antique wooden stand. Everything one would need fifty years ago.

But it still resembled a motel room. A small kitchen area was straight ahead, including a turquoise stove and a full-sized beige refrigerator. An open closet door revealed plenty of space and a line of empty clothes hangers. The bathroom was in the far left corner, and a king-sized bed filled the space to his left. The headboard was a massive piece of hand carved dark wood.

Charles stepped into the room. "Again, we plan to renovate at some point in the near future, but the budget hasn't been approved yet. You may like the charm of its retro style. Mrs. Tuttle lived here alone for sixty-nine years. Can you believe that?"

A flood of questions popped into Matt's mind. "Why?"

Charles shrugged. "The place was a lot nicer back in the '50s when it was built. I guess she wasn't one to move around."

"That's a little weird."

Charles nodded. "I agree, but she was a very sweet lady." He ran his fingers over the desk. "This is where she sat to go into her trances, so I've been told."

"Maybe I'll try it out later." Matt smirked. Nothing special about the desk. It was well worn, but wouldn't have stood out against any other desk found in an antique store.

Charles tapped the top of the TV. "Everything is original, except for the mattress, of course. I don't think she's ever renovated anything."

"As long as it doesn't stink and everything works, I'm fine."

"Glad to hear you're open-minded. That's why you received a discount on your stay."

"Lucky me."

"It *is* the last room in the motel and I'm not sure you would find another available room within thirty miles this weekend. The convention takes over the city, you know."

A circular patched section in the wall, about the size of a manhole cover, lay partially hidden behind the TV. Matt gestured to it. "What used to be there?"

"I'm not sure. The drilling company next door had owned this property for decades before they sold off the land and built a motel back in the early '50s. Things were very different back then, but it does add a certain charm, don't you think?"

"Charming might be an overstatement, but it'll do."

"Fine. I hope you enjoy your stay then. I'll be in my office throughout the night. If you need anything just dial zero on the room's phone."

Matt glanced around the room. "So that's it? That's all you wanted to tell me?"

"That's all. Just keep the windows closed, and I've been told the pipes rattle a bit. Sorry about that."

Matt lifted his suitcase and dropped it on the bed. "You had me scared for a moment. I thought you were going to tell me something was really messed up in here, like rats, or no running water, or some crazy shit like that."

The clerk chuckled. "Just some mild inconveniences for the reduced price. We've done everything we can to make your stay as pleasant as possible, Mr. Bailey. I'll be in my office."

The clerk left and Matt wasted no time in unpacking his clothes into the scratched and worn brown dresser against the wall to the right. He switched on a small Art Deco desk lamp sitting on the desk by yanking a short chain hanging underneath it.

*Some of that charm Charles had mentioned.*

The distinct smell from the facility next door hung in the air despite the clerk's assurance about the filtered ventilation. Not a terribly strong odor, but enough to ruin his appetite.

A vintage white lace linen covered a thick white comforter. A setup that reminded him of something he would expect to see in his grandparents' guest room. The bed's headboard was hand-carved with flowers and intricate organic designs around the edges, but some of it had worn down or chipped off.

Matt glanced down along the edge of the mattress. A white t-shirt was jammed between the mattress and the wall.

*Charming.*

He walked to the bathroom and cringed. *Definitely in need of renovations here.* The turquoise laminate countertop was a web work of cracks, although someone had patched them up. Brass handles on the sink, but someone had left them tarnished and smeared with a black substance like mud. A dark ring of mildew circled the edges of the tub, and the only towel was wadded up and stuffed into the drain. Flowery red and white wallpaper covered the walls. The motel's owners desperately needed to tear down and burn everything.

His cellphone dinged, maybe the tenth time that day. Checking his cell phone, he walked back out into the main area and read through his text messages, one from his ex-wife's lawyer.

"I'm on vacation." He groaned and skipped over it to the more important messages regarding his vacation schedule. *Not going to let anything ruin my time here.*

He finished using his cellphone and caught sight of the items on the desk. A small notepad, a pen, and a scattering of restaurant flyers lay beside a coffeemaker. He would use it in the morning, except...

Someone had opened all the cream and sugar packets, and the paper cups were used. One of them even showed bite marks along the top edge, as if someone had chewed on it. A closer inspection of the coffee pot revealed a black layer of grime along the bottom.

"What the hell."

A box of facial tissues sat next to the mirror. Empty.

*Why hadn't he noticed that when Charles was in the room?*

*Too distracted by all the other* charm.

"Dammit."

Better check everything. He grabbed the TV remote and hit the power button. Nothing.

"Dammit!"

Following the cables to the back of the TV, he located the problem—someone had unplugged it. But he also located the missing facial tissues. Someone had stuffed all of them into a baseball-sized hole next to the outlet.

*Rats. Of course.*

He scoured the floor for any signs of rodent droppings. None that he could find. At least someone had *tried* to block the hole.

He shook his head and clenched his teeth. What the hell had he gotten himself into? In a normal situation, he wouldn't hesitate to check out and demand a refund. But Charles was correct—no other rooms available within an hour's drive.

*But better to drive an hour or two out of his way than to put up with that shit, right?*

He shivered at the prospect of waking up with a rat running across his floor. But his body weighed heavy, and the bed lured him.

"I'll make them clean it, then demand a refund in the morning. Charming, my ass. Run down, rat infested hellhole."

He scoured the room further and spotted dried blood stains on the lower edge of the mattress.

"What the hell?" His stomach churned.

He picked up the faded beige phone next to the bed and dialed the front desk. His face warmed.

Charles answered. "Front desk."

"This is Room 145. This place is disgusting. The coffeemaker hasn't been cleaned, and I'm pretty sure there are blood stains on the mattress. Where the hell did *that* come from? I can't sleep in this mess."

"We're very sorry, Mr. Bailey. We'll be right over there to clean it up. I'm sure it's not what you think it is. Perhaps someone spilled their food or drink. I'll get house-keeping to thoroughly clean your room right away."

"And it looks like you have rats too. There's a hole behind the desk stuffed with facial tissues. Any complaints about rodents?"

"Certainly not, Mr. Bailey. I would not have checked you into a room with a rat problem."

"Move me into a different room."

"I'm so sorry, Mr. Bailey, but I don't have any other rooms available because of the convention."

"I'll need some compensation for this."

"Of course, Mr. Bailey. We'll work something out when you check out. It's an old motel and we acknowledge the need for refurbishment. I'm sorry the housekeeper failed to clean the room properly. The history and charm of the motel is what our guests appreciate. I think once you explore more areas of the motel you'll find you made the right choice."

"I didn't have a choice."

"Very sorry, Mr. Bailey. The housekeeper will be there soon."

Matt hung up the phone and sat on the bed waiting for the housekeeper to arrive. The circular patched hole in the wall above the desk caught his eye again.

*So that's just an old section of ductwork—leading where?*

He stood up and pushed aside the TV on its stand to get a better look. Not just a cover, but a metal door. Someone had painted over it, although they'd done a poor job. A hairline crack circled its perimeter. Had someone opened it recently?

He unlocked the latch on the right side and dug his fingers into the door's edge. It squeaked open without much effort. A dusting of drywall and wood particles sprinkled across the floor. A wave of sweet, musky air poured out around him. He gagged and stared into the metal tubing. Someone had stuffed a dirty white bed comforter in there. Matt smirked. "I guess this is where they keep the linen."

He pulled it out and dropped it on the floor. The sweet smell from the hole faded, and another smell took its place —a sickening, bitter stench. He cringed. The housekeeper could take it to the trash.

With the comforter out of the way, another obstacle blocked the metal shaft a few feet away. A crumbling red brick wall. The mortar holding the bricks together had oozed out and dried in clumps along the seams. Most of it had cracked and toppled over, exposing a gaping darkness beyond it. Plenty of room for a stream of rodents to pass through.

"Nothing charming about rats, Charles," Matt called

into the void. His voice echoed and reverberated off the duct walls for a few seconds.

*The room's walls had more holes than a slice of Swiss cheese.*

The smell grew worse. "Good God." He groaned and snapped the cover closed again, latching it and leaving the comforter on the floor. "I might as well just sleep outside."

Within minutes, a young Hispanic woman arrived at his door with a cleaning cart and gloved hands. Her name tag read 'Rita'. No smile as she greeted him, but apologized as she stepped inside. "I will clean everything."

"Thank you." He closed the door behind her and studied her face. The woman from the photo in the office?

She glanced at the comforter he'd dropped on the floor, then met his eyes for a moment before her eyes widened. "You removed that?"

"It was stuffed in there." He gestured to the ductwork cover.

"I know. Mrs. Tuttle put it there. You shouldn't have touched it."

"Why not?" Matt narrowed his eyes.

"It's not good in here."

"No, it doesn't look like anyone's cleaned it."

She shook her head and used her feet to kick the comforter toward the door. "Maybe you can get another room. This was Mrs. Tuttle's room."

"Charles told me, but she's dead, right?"

Sadness spread over Rita's face. "Yes. She passed away two weeks ago."

"Then what does it matter?"

"She was a wonderful woman. My husband didn't like her, but she was blessed with a gift to speak to those in the afterlife. You should find a different room."

"I'd like to, but the motel's full."

Rita sighed. "You won't sleep."

Matt tried to catch her gaze again, but she avoided eye contact while stepping closer to the door. "What do you mean? Does this room have rats? I saw someone stuffed all the holes with towels and tissues."

"No rats, but leave the holes plugged." She gestured to the comforter on the floor. "Maybe you can put this back."

"What for? What's in there?"

"Keep all of them closed, or stay somewhere else. It's not good here. Charles does not listen to me. I'm so sorry." Rita hurried around the room, scanning the bathroom, bed, and desk. She sighed. "I'll clean the room. Come back in an hour. I'll finish by then."

"I wish I could go somewhere else, but I'm stuck."

"Go back to the main lobby. My husband will talk with you."

"Your husband?"

She barely smiled. "Yes. Charles can tell you about the city." Rita picked up the comforter and put it on the bed on her way out. She gathered some cleaning equipment and spray bottles, then returned. "Please wait an hour. I'm sorry for this inconvenience."

"Where should I go?" He was in no mood to drive anywhere.

She shrugged and gestured to the door.

He stepped out onto the sidewalk for a moment, debating where to go. Too tired to eat. He could go sit in one of the chairs in the main lobby, but first...

*A chance to see what's behind the motel.* He turned in the opposite direction. The parking lot's lighting illuminated the brick wall separating it from the drilling facility, and it stretched back through a narrow corridor between the two properties. He calculated where the other side of that ductwork might come out the other side. A dimly lit brick structure extended out from the wall connected to his room, but it stopped well short of the facility's wall. No connection between the two.

So the opening could only lead underground. Maybe as far as the sewers. A highway for the rats to find his room. He wanted to go back there and explore it further, but tall weeds and darkness enshrouded the area.

Instead of going to the lobby like Rita suggested, Matt walked to his car and sat inside reading the news from his cellphone. From the driver's seat, he watched the shadows move within the light from his room's open door. His eyelids drooped as he shrugged to stay awake.

If she didn't finish soon, he'd just sleep in his car. *Should have thought of that before paying for a room.*

He closed his eyes and drifted on the edge of sleep, waking forty-five minutes later. The door was shut now and Rita's cart was gone.

*Done.*

*Hallelujah.*

He dragged himself out of the car and over to his room. Before stepping inside, that nauseating smell from nearby caught his nose again. It awakened him a little. The stinging odor reminded him of ammonia or sulfuric acid. A stink that brought up images of sweaty laborers mining at the bottom of a volcano. Whatever they were drilling for next door, it wasn't meant to be brought to the surface. He hurried inside again and locked the door.

The smell faded inside the room and the housekeeper's improvements were clear. New linen. New coffee supplies. She had even straightened the pocket change he'd sprawled across the desk.

Mrs. Tuttle's desk.

He sat in the chair for a moment and lay his palms flat on the desk's surface. "Any dead people feel like chatting?"

No answer.

"I didn't think so."

Silence. Not even any noises from the neighboring room. It was late and everyone would be in bed by then.

He stood and checked the refrigerator. They had stocked it with the usual overpriced mini-bar, although if he really needed a drink he could drive to a store a few minutes away and save the money. Despite the high price, it tempted him to indulge this once after such a long drive. A reward for enduring the grueling highway journey. And the motel's cleanliness issues.

*Not tonight.*

He kicked off his shoes, slipped into his pajamas, and lay back on his bed. He sank down, both physically and mentally, letting out a grumbled, "Finally."

His eyes snapped shut.

His body shook sometime later, and he lurched forward. The digital clock on his nightstand read 2:14.

Without thinking, he dragged himself out of bed and over to the bathroom. The soapy smell from the sink and the sight of clean towels erased some of the bitterness at having to complain earlier. Two smaller towels still plugged the hole in the tub and the sink.

*Leave them plugged*, Rita's words came back. *Not good here.*

For a moment he considered leaving them that way. Rita had left a stack of towels behind. Plenty to last him a couple of days, and it must have been there for a *reason.*

*Cockroaches or ants?*

He removed the towels and dropped them to the corner of the floor.

*Keep them plugged.*

The thought floated away as he washed his hands. On the way back to bed, the sight of himself in the mirror startled him. He chuckled. *Why so jumpy, Matt?*

*You know why. A giant rat or something awful is going to crawl out of those holes.* He cringed.

*The long drive traumatized you, little man. That, and the divorce.*

*You're a nervous wreck.*

*Yep.*

Matt trudged back toward his bed and stopped. The mini-kitchen's sink gurgled. She'd stuck a towel in that drain too. He removed it and flipped on the small overhead light to reveal a reddish-black sludge churning its way up the drain. The mass slurped down again, followed by several guttural gasps from the pipes somewhere below. Small hairs remained stuck against the bottom of the sink as the rest of the sludge drained away.

An animal must have died down there.

*All those damn holes, it's no wonder.*

Rats or mice, or something larger?

*Where there's one...*

He searched the floor and shelving beneath the sink for any signs of more animals. The pipes led back into the wall.

"This place is probably crawling with them." He continued the search around the perimeter of the room.

Nothing behind the chair or refrigerator. He looked behind the desk. The wad of facial tissues still clotted the baseball-sized hole near the floor. Rita hadn't pulled them out, but she had replaced the empty facial tissue box.

The cover over the ductwork was still latched.

No sign of anything *alive*, anyway.

Something scratched against the wall nearby. He turned his head and focused in on the source. *Something's in here. Under the bed?* He dropped to the floor and pulled up the bed skirt. Nothing.

*More holes?* Only one area he hadn't checked yet. The closet.

Rita had left the closet door cracked open a few inches and the room's light illuminated the shirts he'd hung earlier, but deeper inside they wavered in the shadows.

He listened for an air conditioner. Nothing, not even a fan. The air was still, but they *moved*. His heart pounded as a chill rushed up his spine.

Not an animal—an intruder. Someone waiting to rob him after he'd fallen asleep? He'd read plenty of tales of motel thefts, but now the reality struck him. A criminal stood in his closet. A terrifying vision of someone jumping out waving a handgun paralyzed him. How had they gotten inside?

He glanced back at the lock on the door. Still chained shut. His mind jumped back to the housekeeper.

*They'd snuck in while she cleaned the room.*

*How? He'd watched the door from his car.*

*Not every minute, Matt. You missed him.*

*Get out.*

He took a step back.

A stranger's breath filled the closet's darkness—a subdued inhalation, coarse and slow.

*Definitely not an animal. Holy shit.*

*Run.*

Wide awake now, he would scream if they jumped out. He forced himself to move slowly back toward the door and open it, twisting the squeaking locks with every ounce of patience he could muster. His heart beat faster than he thought possible.

*I'll have a heart attack.*

*Just get outside.*

The door cracked open, and he scrambled out into the cool night air toward the front office. Never mind that he only wore pajamas.

He shook his head as he ran, muttering under his breath, visualizing how the intruder must have slipped past Rita. They must have gotten in while she was cleaning the bathroom. The closet provided a perfect hiding spot— no cleaning necessary in there. All they had to do was creep in there, stand still, and wait.

*Call the police.*

Yes. Why wait for Charles to take care of it? But... the pajamas. Matt placed his hand where his cellphone would have been. No cellphone. He'd forgotten it on his nightstand, along with his wallet.

He cringed. *You just gave the thief a nice little gift, Matt.* "Dammit!"

He stopped and looked back. No sign of anyone leaving the room. Maybe the thief hadn't noticed yet that he'd snuck out.

*Not too late.* He was still closer to his room than the motel's front desk.

He had to go back. Standing in his pajamas in the motel lobby begging Charles for help would be humiliating enough. He hated himself for not grabbing the items on the way out. So much vital information on his cellphone— all his contact info for friends and family.

The items weren't far from the door. He would just reach in, grab them, and run. *Run like hell*. He could even dial 911 on the way out. Faster than waiting for Charles to react.

He backtracked, eyeing the door for any movements. He hadn't closed it all the way after his hasty escape. Clutching the door handle, he peaked in. The lights from the parking lot lit half the room well enough to locate the nightstand next to the bed. His cellphone and wallet were still there. *Thank God.* Only about ten feet away.

He stepped inside. No sign of the thief. The closet door was still open, but something was different. Maybe open a little wider than before?

He crept around the bed, moving inches at a time to minimize the floor's creaking. His skin crawled as he imagined the intruder listening to his footsteps from across the room. Were they watching him now too? He pictured a pair of menacing eyes staring back at him from the darkness of his closet, calculating the best moment to jump out and strike him down.

He moved within an arms length of his items. *Just grab them and get the hell out.*

He lifted his cellphone first, then his wallet, and turned back toward the door.

A dark figure stood swaying next to the TV. A mangled woman, choking and clutching at her neck, her eyes white circles and her mouth gaping far too wide. Her clothes were shriveled and wet, the edges eaten away. The woman gasped for air as thick, slimy liquid oozed from the corners of her mouth.

Matt froze as adrenaline surged through his body. His mouth dropped open, and he screamed long and loud. Heaving in his next breath, he broke through his paralysis and charged past the intruder toward the door. His foot hit the corner of his bed and he stumbled, slamming his shoulder against the door's frame as he rushed outside.

He didn't look back. Someone's room door opened behind him as he rounded the corner to the motel's main lobby.

"What the hell?" a man's growling voice called out.

At the motel's entrance, Matt swatted the buzzer beside the security camera. "Open the damn door!"

No sign of Charles through the glass. He forced a smile into the security camera and tried to calm himself. He wouldn't get help by looking like a raving lunatic.

Matt pressed the buzzer again, just once this time. A moment later, Charles stepped out of the room behind the front desk.

Charles's tired expression changed to confusion as he walked over and opened the security door for Matt, eyeing his pajamas. "May I help you?"

"I need the police." Matt's hands trembled as he gestured toward his room. "There's a woman in my room."

Charles furrowed his brows. "A woman? Take a breath. Someone broke into your room? Please calm down."

Matt shook his head. "I can't. I don't know how she got in. She's just *there*. Call the police."

Charles lifted his cellphone, but hesitated. "What did she look like? Any weapons?"

"I don't know. It was dark. She must have been hiding in there, in my closet." Matt rubbed his forehead and muttered, "I don't know how I missed her earlier."

Charles stared expressionless at Matt. "You're in 145, right? Yes, I remember. Please have a seat while I get something." He gestured to the chairs in the lobby.

Matt caught his breath. "I'm not going to sit down. Get the police over here right now." He glanced back at the front entrance. "Maybe she followed me. She might try to come in here."

Charles answered calmly and stepped toward the office in the back. "Nobody will get in here. Just a moment." He disappeared behind the door and returned with a silver .9mm pistol.

"What's that for?" Matt asked.

"Our safety." Charles came out from behind the desk.

"Did you call the cops?"

"I can handle it. Lots of homelessness in this area. I know how to deal with trespassers." Charles winked as he swaggered out the door.

Matt followed him. "Can't we just call the police?"

"Probably just a vagrant. I'm very sorry for your trouble."

"And why the hell does your housekeeper keep telling me to keep the drains plugged?"

Charles scoffed. "Rita? Never mind her. She believed everything Mrs. Tuttles told her—a gullible and superstitious woman."

They circled around the motel back toward Matt's room.

A few doors before they arrived, a shirtless, muscular man in pajama bottoms stepped out from a room and glanced around. He squinted at them. "What the hell's going on? Was that you running past my room just now? Woke me up."

"Sorry about that, sir," Charles said. "Nothing to worry about."

The man's gazed fixed on the pistol in Charles's hand. "What the hell? What's up with that? You got trouble?"

"No troubles, sir. Please stay in your room."

"Hell with that. I've got eight years in the Marines. I

never walk away from a fight. I'm wide awake now, anyway." He walked out behind them.

Charles didn't object.

They arrived at Room 145 within seconds. The door stood wide open, and a light was on now that had been off before.

"What are we looking for?" the Marine asked.

Matt peeked inside. "Someone was hiding in there."

"A perv?"

"Let's not jump to conclusions," Charles said.

"A woman," Matt said.

"Got it." The Marine pushed in front of them and made his way into the room first. He spoke loud and booming, "All right, now who's causing problems in here?"

Charles held the gun out and flipped on the main light as they searched the room. "Come out with your hands up."

The Marine looked back at Matt. "Where did you see her?"

Matt gestured to the area in front of the TV. "She was standing right here."

The Marine nodded once then searched the closet and under the beds. He grinned. "Nobody here, man. You must have scared her away."

"I hope so."

"What did she look like?"

"I didn't see her very well, but she was right here."

Charles lowered the pistol. "Whoever it was, they're gone now."

The Marine threw his arm around Matt. "If she comes back, you just knock on my door and I'll take care of it for you. Room 139. Got that?"

Matt nodded. "I just want to get some sleep."

Charles checked the locks on the windows and door. "No sign of a break in."

The Marine laughed. "See, nothing to worry about. We've got your back."

"Yeah." Matt circled around the room, double-checking every corner. He ran his fingers through his hair. "At least, she didn't get my wallet." Matt waved it.

"It's a safe neighborhood." Charles stepped toward the door. "Probably some transient taking advantage of an unlocked door. I'll remind Rita to keep an eye out for any suspicious persons. Just make sure you keep your door locked at all times."

"I will. Shouldn't we call the police anyway?"

"We could, but what's the point now? Nothing was stolen, and she's gone." He chuckled, holding up the pistol. "They see me coming and run."

"This has happened to other guests?"

Charles lost his grin. "No, not really. It's a safe area. Just sometimes riffraff wander by. Nothing to worry about, I assure you."

Matt's head ached. *Too tired to argue.* "Okay."

"There are drinks in here." Charles peeked into the mini-fridge. "Might help calm your nerves. No charge. Help yourself."

Matt sat on the edge of his bed. "Yeah maybe. Thanks."

"Take advantage of the free drinks, man." The Marine folded his arms over his chest and chuckled. "You here for Comic Con?"

Matt met his eyes. "No."

"Me, neither. We're probably the only ones in the motel who aren't going." The Marine stepped forward and extended his hand. "Name's Patrick Gleason. Room 139. Don't hesitate to stop by."

They shook hands. Patrick's palms were sweaty. Matt tried not to cringe. "Matt Thorson."

"Well, looks like everything is squared away." Charles stepped toward the door.

"Thanks for your help." Matt closed the door behind them and locked it.

Silence and stillness filled the room after they left. Matt checked the windows again—secure. He dragged over the wooden desk chair and jammed the top edge up under the door handle, just to be sure. No way to break in now without making a lot of noise.

The free drinks sounded good. *Yes,* really *good about now.* He grabbed two mini-bottles from the refrigerator and downed one of them, a bottle of rum, before he climbed into bed. The buzzy warmth moved through his body. He sipped the other bottle, a popular vodka, as he climbed under his sheets and sat upright, considering all that had happened.

*Too much drama.* He had enough shit to deal with in his personal life. He'd come there to *get away* from the stress. His eyelids drooped as he hovered on the edge of sleep and placed the half empty mini-bottle on the nightstand.

The desk's mirror reflected his frazzled face, and he cracked a smile. What a story to tell his wife and kids.

*Ex-wife, Matt.*

*Yes, I forgot.* They wouldn't want to hear about it, anyway.

His buddies would listen to him after he returned home. They'd have a good laugh about all this over a few drinks—a lot of drinks. A wild tale to share when the conversation needed a little zing.

Something thumped in his closet. He gasped. His eyes widened. They had *all* checked the closet from top to bottom. Just his damn clothes in there. Matt held his breath as he listened.

*It couldn't be an intruder this time. It had to be something else. Maybe just the building's structure settling.*

*Still settling after sixty-nine years?*

The closet door was closed now. A second, softer thump shifted the door forward far enough to hit its latch.

No sound of anyone breathing this time.

*Just a change of air pressure.* But the fan wasn't running.

Matt forced a laugh. "If someone's in there, a U.S. Marine is about to kick your ass."

The closet door handle turned and an icy paralysis rushed through his spine. A sickening groan pushed up his throat. He would scream, if he could, but his breath cut off.

*Someone's in here. The woman never left—in here all the time.* But how could they *all* have missed her? A trap door? A ceiling vent?

Matt clutched the bedsheets and whipped them aside before charging toward the door. His heart pounded in his chest. The chair that he'd jammed against the door now blocked his exit, but he knocked it over and rushed outside. Never mind his cellphone or his wallet.

But he stopped outside the door and turned back. He wouldn't run this time. Better idea—he grabbed the door handle and slammed it shut, trapping the intruder inside.

Thumps and footsteps shook the floor of his room.

He gripped the door handle with both hands and squeezed it, focusing all his anger and fear into his hands as he shuddered. The intruder turned the door handle a bit, despite his grip. The door frame squeaked under the weight of the intruder's pressure from the other side.

A strained call for help escaped Matt's throat. "Help..."

*Not loud enough.*

Again, this time he yelled, "Help me!"

The windows rattled next to the door, and the curtains swayed. Maybe the intruder would try to break through the glass to escape, but for now all he could do was hold the door shut.

A few seconds later, the Marine, Patrick, opened his room's door and poked out his head. "What's going on over there?"

Another room's light further down also switched on.

"I got her." Matt's hands ached as he strained to keep the door handle from turning any further. "She's in my room again."

Patrick rushed over in his pajama bottoms and bare chest. "She came back?"

"Yes. She must have been hiding in there when we searched it."

Patrick furrowed his brow and grumbled, "No way. It was clear."

"Well, she's in there now."

"You see any weapons?"

"No."

Patrick gestured to the door handle. "I can take over for you. She won't get past me. You run back and get that front desk guy."

Matt released the door handle for only a moment before Patrick pushed in front of him and grabbed it.

"She's not going anywhere." Patrick sneered.

Matt hurried back to the front desk and returned with Charles a few minutes later.

Patrick still held the door, but now he was peeking into the room through the window. He glanced over at them as they arrived. "Are you sure there's someone in there, man?"

Matt nodded. "Absolutely."

"What the hell did she look like? I don't see anybody."

Matt's face warmed. "I'm not making this up. She was in my closet."

"But we searched in there," Charles said.

"Well, I don't know how she got back in the room, but she did."

"Let me handle this." Patrick pushed ahead and opened the door while Charles held the gun at his side, although this time he didn't raise it.

They crept inside and flipped on the lights. No sign of anyone as they made their way across the room toward the closet. Matt scanned every corner and checked under the beds again. His wallet and cell phone were still there. "I'm going to call the police."

Charles raised his hand. "Hold off for a minute. Let's check it out first. You said you saw her in the closet again?"

"Yes, that's right."

Charles walked over and opened the closet door, then pushed the shirts aside as he scanned every corner. Matt came up behind him and peeked in at the same time. "Nobody's here."

"Maybe she didn't get in through here, but that's where I saw her." Matt walked over to the bathroom and followed the contours of the ceiling and vent at the top of both the sink. A large opening in there but not large enough for a person to climb through.

Patrick walked over and looked in but only for a second. "Nobody's in the room. I don't know what to say."

Matt rubbed his forehead. "I don't know either. Where could she have gone? There was somebody here. I'm not making it up."

"We already searched the place twice now." Charles shrugged. "Do you have a camera on your cellphone?"

"Yes."

"Okay, then maybe get a picture of them next time, and we can use that to show the police." Charles headed back toward the door and mumbled something to Patrick.

Patrick nodded and followed him.

"You aren't leaving, are you? We haven't found her yet."

They stopped and turned back. Charles's face reddened. "Look. I wasn't going to say anything, but do you think maybe your medication is causing you to...?"

Matt clenched his fists. "Hallucinate?"

"I don't want to jump to conclusions, but some medications have that side effect. I saw your prescription bottle earlier, and I looked up the medication after I got back to the office. One of the side effects is hallucinations, although it's rare."

Matt crossed his arms over his chest. "So you don't believe me?"

"I'm just saying, sir, that it's a possibility."

The circular ductwork's cover near the TV caught Matt's eye. He pointed to it. "What if she was hiding in there?"

Charles smirked. "In the vent?"

Matt climbed onto the desk and unlatched the door.

"What are you doing?" Charles moved toward him.

"Maybe she came in through here."

Charles scoffed. "That doesn't go anywhere, and you'll probably find a brick wall if you open it."

"I opened it earlier." Matt gripped the metal cover by

the edges and pulled it open. Now the latch broke, and he caught the cover in his hands. The same comforter he'd pulled out earlier was there again. *The housekeeper must have put it back.* "That woman must have come in and out through this opening." Matt placed the cover onto the desk. "No other way."

"What are you doing?"

"You're right. There *is* a brick wall behind here, but it's falling apart. A smaller person could easily get in and out through this opening, just the size of the woman I saw."

Charles shrugged. "Look, I understand people are tired after a long drive. Your mind is spinning, you're exhausted. Sometimes people even have strange dreams. It's very common."

"This wasn't a dream. This was real."

Matt dragged out the grungy comforter again and tossed it on the floor. The black hole in the brick wall now stared back at him. Again, a burst of sweet, musky odor blew over his face followed by a stronger rancid smell.

"I didn't know it was there." Charles moved closer and peeked in. "It's an old building needing renovations, which are coming soon. Looks like discarded ductwork. Nothing out of the ordinary."

Patrick winced and waved his hand in front of his face. "Stinks in there. Reminds me of the smell coming from next door. Are these places connected?"

"No, they're not."

Patrick nudged Matt with his elbow. "Well, if anyone is camping inside that tube, they wouldn't survive long. The air is foul."

Matt crawled inside the ductwork and pulled at the bricks, tossing them aside as he peered into the darkness ahead.

Charles grumbled. "You've damaged the motel, sir."

"I'll put them back after we catch this woman. You should thank me for discovering this."

Charles pulled at his ankle. "You haven't discovered anything. Please get out of there."

Matt stopped and focused on a shifting shadow on the other side of the wall. The silhouette of a head and upper torso rose from the darkness several feet back, then dropped again.

"There!" Matt pointed and looked back. "Did you see her?"

Patrick stared inside. "Where?"

Charles glanced in for a moment, then met Matt's eyes. "Nobody's in there, sir."

"At the back. She's probably just waiting for you guys to leave again. I think she's taunting me."

Charles groaned. "I doubt it."

"Get your gun ready." Matt banged his hand on the side of the ductwork just inside the opening, and called out, "Whoever is in there, come out with your hands up."

No response.

"Hey, man," Patrick said with a chuckle, "think about it. Why the hell would anyone hide in there? Not even a homeless person would slink into that shithole."

Matt's gaze jumped from the hole to the faces behind him.

Charles pulled out his cellphone and lit up the opening in flashlight mode. "You see? No sign of anyone. Let's all just relax and close this up now. The stink is nauseating, and it's getting ridiculous."

Patrick yawned and turned back to Matt. "He's right. Long day tomorrow."

Matt relented and backed out of the ductwork. He brushed himself off after standing again next to the desk.

Charles headed for the door. "I'm sure if you just get some sleep, sir, you'll be fine."

"So, you won't do anything?" Matt stepped toward him.

"There's nobody here, sir. Feel free to drink more bottles from the mini fridge. I see you've started on them. Finish them all off, if you want, and if you need more just dial the office. No charge, again."

"I don't need more alcohol. I need you to do something about this person getting into my room. How am I supposed to sleep now knowing that someone keeps breaking in here?"

"Please take a photo next time, sir. That will help the police identify the perpetrator."

"You want me to stop the guy and get a selfie with him?"

Charles raised his voice and rolled his eyes. "We didn't see *anyone*, or even any animals, but I can drop off some earplugs to block out the noises, if that would help. I'm guessing what you saw and heard has something to do with the outdated ventilation system. I suppose it's noisy, and maybe a little shadowy dust cloud formed in the room with a change in the air pressure. Maybe in your dream state you mistook that for an intruder. It's all going to be replaced soon, I'm afraid I can't do anything about that now. It's a very old building."

Patrick opened the door. "Good luck, man."

"You can't leave me here alone with her."

Patrick stepped outside and waved. "Later."

Charles took a deep breath while moving in toward Matt and rested his hand on Matt's shoulder. He lowered his voice and grinned. "I have to get back to the front desk. I'm the only one here on the night shift, otherwise I'd stay here with you for a little while longer. I'm confident if you allow yourself to wind down—" Charles glanced at the refrigerator, "—you'll wake up feeling much better."

Matt eyed the gun in Charles's hand. *Just the thing I need.* He lunged for it. The cold metal empowered Matt as he ripped it away and scrambled back into the ductwork. "She's right there, staring at me. Don't you see her?"

"Drop the gun, please." Charles raised his hands as if Matt directed the pistol at him.

"I'm not crazy. I'll take care of this, if you won't." Matt climbed over the loose bricks and pushed headfirst into the hole aiming the pistol out in front. The metal walls of the ductwork clanged and chilled his arms through the thin fabric of his pajamas. Squirming forward, the darkness swallowed him.

A woman laughed from somewhere in the ductwork.

Patrick's voice boomed behind him. "Get back here!"

"She's laughing now." Matt clenched his teeth. "Don't you hear her? She's laughing at me."

"Nobody's laughing, man." Patrick groaned, then said to Charles, "Shine the light in there. I'll get him."

"No," Charles commanded, "don't shoot anything! You'll wake up the guests."

"Perfect." Matt stormed forward on his elbows. "Wake them all up, so they can see me capture this sick bastard. I'll get her."

Not enough light to see more than a few inches ahead. The woman poked her head up again.

Matt aimed and fired the pistol. The shots deafened him for a few seconds before his hearing faded back.

The woman dropped below his eyesight again.

"What the hell are you doing?" Patrick yelled.

"I think I got her." Matt scooted in further.

"For God's sake, stop shooting."

Matt continued forward. *Can't stop now.* Each breath echoed through the shaft as he came up to the edge where the woman had dropped. He stretched his arm ahead and fired two more shots into the hole.

"Dammit!" Charles yelled. "Stop!"

He spotted two holes in the metal ductwork ahead where he had missed. No blood.

"You've got to come out of there, man!" Patrick barked behind him. "I don't care what you saw in there."

Matt leaned over the edge of the shaft with his finger on the trigger. Nothing illuminated below. Something banged and scraped further down. A soft laughter filled the air. More taunts. She was there, but he had no light.

He held his breath and fired one more shot into the darkness below. Within the blast's flash he glimpsed his target. The woman's sunken, grungy face appeared with wide eyes, and a gaping mouth. Her hands gripped her throat.

Matt gagged and blasted her two more times. Both shots exploded against a pulpy rotting surface several feet further down. He fired three more times before the weapon clicked empty.

Darkness faced him.

"Good God, stop firing!" Charles yelled.

The shaft rattled behind Matt. Patrick's voice boomed, "I'm pulling you out, man. This has gone on long enough."

Matt squirmed toward the woman as far as he could without falling in. Had he missed? If he could just see the woman's face again, then he'd know for sure.

Patrick bumped against Matt's bare feet. "Take it easy now."

"I almost got her." Matt yanked his foot away and teetered at the edge of the hole before breaking away from Patrick's grip. He dropped a few feet into the darkness, landing upside down on someone's torso with his hands scraping across a scratchy cloth, until his fingers sank into a rubbery surface. His face brushed again a clump of long, dry hair, and he struggled to turn himself around. No way to get his feet under him, it forced him to embrace the woman.

"Got you!" Matt clawed at the woman's clothes until moving up to her face. His fingers gripped her cold skin and long hair. She didn't scream or resist. "I got her!"

"Just let it go," Patrick said from a few feet above. "It's probably got rabies."

*They still think it's an animal.*

This was no rat, no raccoon or stray dog. He held a human, and his fingers crawled across the woman's leathery neck until digging into the soft flesh beneath her chin. "Say something," Matt yelled at her. "Who are you?"

"Animals don't talk." Patrick's voice moved closer, inching down from above. He grasped Matt's ankles and yanked him up several inches. "I'm going to pull you out."

Matt pulled on the woman's face on the way up until the last thing he clutched was a handful of hair. He wouldn't let it go. "I got her."

"I don't think so." Patrick groaned and raised Matt another few inches. "You're not making this easy for us, man."

Matt strained to hang onto the woman's hair as he rose. "She's getting away."

"Good." Patrick pulled again.

A tearing sound filled the air, like a piece of sticky hard candy ripping away from the carpet. The clump of hair in Matt's hand separated from the woman's head and her body collapsed below.

*I ripped her hair out.* Nausea churned his stomach, but he didn't let go of the woman's hair. They wouldn't believe him without it.

They hoisted Matt up over the edge, then pulled him back out into the room again.

Rita was with them now too. She stood in pink pajamas and a concerned, desperate look on her face. "This room is cursed, Charles. Mrs. Tuttle was right."

"Rita, stop with the Mrs. Tuttle bullshit." Charles grabbed the pistol out of Matt's hand.

She broke into tears and pointed at the hair in Matt's hand. "What is that?"

"It's nothing." Charles sneered and turned back to Matt. "Are you crazy? Do you want to go to jail?"

Patrick held Matt's arms, then put him into a choke-hold and lowered him to the floor. "Just take it easy, man. We're going to get through this."

Matt didn't bother to fight him. Patrick's arms were like sweaty metal bars around Matt's torso.

Matt held up the clump of gray, grimy hair and laughed. "I got her! See? She's still down there."

"That's not human hair." Charles closed the ductwork opening, then aimed the empty pistol at Matt's chest.

Rita shrieked. "It's her hair!" She stared wide-eyed at Charles. "Why is it here?"

"Let me look at that." Patrick tried to take it, but Matt wouldn't let go.

Matt turned the clump over. Shredded chunks of skin held the hair together. An eyebrow and cheek, along with one nostril revealed the truth. A touch of rouge makeup colored the cheek.

Patrick gasped. "Oh, dear God. That *is* human hair. Is it Mrs. Tuttle's?"

Matt gazed at the clump. Long, straight black hair. "From the pictures I saw in the lobby, Mrs. Tuttle had red hair."

"Charles, tell me it's not true." Rita wept louder and extended her hand toward the hair. "This is your wife, isn't it? Poor Mrs. Redding."

"Shut up. It's not anybody's hair. You're all wrong, it's just animal fur."

Rita's eyes narrowed at Charles. "You killed her, didn't you? Mrs. Tuttle was right. The spirits cannot be silenced. You told me your wife drowned at sea, but you lied."

"I love you, Rita. I only wanted to be with you."

"Is that why you had me cover the holes? To block the spirits from speaking the truth, or to block the smell?"

Charles sneered. "There are *no* spirits, Rita."

Rita shook her head. "No, I've seen them, and you are evil. Mrs. Tuttle warmed me about you, but I didn't listen. I was so stupid to ever believe you. Did you kill her too?"

Charles turned the gun on Rita. "I did everything for you."

She backed away, her gaze locked on the pistol. "Nothing but evil. I will tell everyone."

Matt broke free from Patrick's grip and lunged at Charles.

Charles spun around and pointed the barrel at Matt's chest. The pistol clicked twice. Empty.

Rita screamed.

Matt tackled Charles, knocking him face down to the

ground. The pistol slid away and slammed against the wall. Police sirens blared nearby.

Patrick stood over them. "Give it up, man."

Charles struggled for a few seconds, then submitted. "Shoot them, Rita. We can still get away. Get your pistol from your room."

Rita slouched forward with tears streaming down her cheeks and stared at the black clump of hair and scalp in front of Charles's face. "Your wife's spirit called from the grave. There is no escaping her. I pray she can forgive you."

MORE FRIGHTFUL TALES IN BOOK 5! SEE NEXT PAGE FOR info!

# DREADFUL DARK BOOK 5
## TALES OF HORROR: BOOK 5

# HOME REMEDY

I t looked like a prank toy, like one of those rubber gag gifts you buy for someone at Halloween, but there was nothing artificial about this thing. It was all there, dried blood, torn flesh, and even manicured fingernails. Based on its waxy, pale, wrinkly skin, Jack guessed it came from an old woman.

And there was only one old couple living nearby— Charlie and Ella Anderson—but it was no reason to suspect the finger belonged to Ella. He would have heard about it from Charlie if she'd had an accident, especially in the forest between their properties, and she couldn't walk more than a few feet without help, so there was no way she could have wandered out to the woods alone. And Charlie cared for her more than life itself, always watching over her, never letting her out of his sight, so she couldn't have ventured out alone. The finger must have belonged to someone else.

Sammy was wagging his tail as he sniffed at the finger, happy as hell that he'd deposited the wretched thing there on the grass at Jack's feet. His dog's wide eyes stared up at him full of pride, probably expecting a reward for his morbid catch. *Not this time.*

"Where the hell did you get that?" Jack cringed, meeting Sammy's gaze. Had his dog ripped it clean off someone's hand? The finger was *fresh*, for lack of a better word, not rotting at all, so it hadn't been separated for long. Sammy barked a lot in confrontations, and growled plenty of times, but had only attacked once after a man tried to physically assault Jack. Just a dog trying to protect his master, and he would never have attacked anyone unprovoked. If Sammy had encountered someone dangerous in the woods, he would have raised a clamor, but it would have ended there. Sammy didn't run off and attack anyone without a good reason, much less tear off an elderly woman's finger.

There'd been no signs of a struggle in the woods. No barking, no old woman screaming, just his loyal dog prancing out of the forest like a prima donna, and dropping a severed finger at his feet. If dogs could grin, then Sammy was beaming, looking as joyful as ever in the pleasant breeze of the late summer evening. Sammy's eyes said it all: *Here's something I found for you, master. Something you'll never forget.*

The question of the finger's owner stuck in Jack's mind. A trespassing hunter? Old women sometimes hunted too, he guessed, although he'd never seen anything like that around Green Hills. Plenty of men of all ages took to the sport, and some women, but no *old* women. So did the finger belong to a homeless woman? It was possible, but unlikely, being that they were so far from the city. The only homeless he'd ever seen wandering through the area were hitchhiking along the main road through town, probably on their way to go stand by the highway exit ramps to panhandle with poorly written signs proclaiming stuff like "Homeless Anything Helps" and "Homeless Hungry Please Help". Not much benefit for a homeless person to get help out in a dark country forest.

It made no sense. *So who the hell loses a finger in the woods?*

Jack inspected the thing a little closer without touching it, although his stomach churned. All the skin and muscles leaked out from the mass of torn flesh, but one really odd thing stood out—no bones, as far as he could see.

A *fresh* boneless finger, as if someone ripped it right off the skeleton.

Trespasser or not, he would need to search the forest. If someone was injured out there, especially an old woman, he couldn't just stand around and do nothing. Grabbing a flashlight and his cell phone from the house, he headed out into the woods to search for any sign of its owner. But if someone had accidentally shot it off or had ripped it off in a fall, wouldn't he have heard the gunshot or screams or... something? But Sammy hadn't even barked lately, and nobody had stopped by the house to ask for help. Too embarrassed to tell anyone?

"If it was my finger," Jack said, heading off into the woods with Sammy at his side, "I would've picked it up and ran like hell to the hospital, so the doc could stitch it back on." *Yeah, the owner must be at the hospital getting help right now, or still stuck out in the woods. No other explanation.* Jack glanced at Sammy. "What do you say, boy? You think we'll find an old woman out there stranded beneath a fallen timber?"

Sammy licked his lips and slobbered as he pranced forward as if catching the scent of a tasty meal ahead. The finger's meat must have whet his appetite. Good thing Sammy hadn't eaten the damn thing.

Following Sammy through the trees, Jack gestured with his head. "Lead the way. Where'd you find it, Sammy? Show me where you found it."

Sammy charged ahead over toward a clearing where several trees had fallen during a recent storm. *Yes, that made sense. Someone got trapped over there in the storm.*

More graphic mental images of finding a bloody old woman pinned beneath one of the trees sprang to Jack's mind. Had Sammy yanked that finger right off the victim? That would explain its fresh appearance. But why just a *finger?*

When they arrived at the group of downed trees there was nobody around, and no sign that anyone had been there. No old lady—so far—but they didn't stop there. It could be that the victim had gotten injured and had gone off to get help on their own. The blood could have caught Sammy's nose and led him to it.

They scoured the area, and after several minutes had no more answers than when they'd arrived. But Sammy wandered off to the right, weaving between trees and heavy brush, before returning later with something new hanging from his mouth. As the dog approached, saliva dripped from his jowls and spilled out over his new catch. From several feet away, it looked like an uncooked, bare chunk of chicken with all the feathers stripped off.

Jack stiffened and gasped as he made out the shape of the object. A puffy pale palm with three fingers, a thumb, and a bloody stump at the wrist. "Looks like we found out where the finger came from."

So that solved one piece of the puzzle, but a bigger mystery remained. *Who the hell loses a hand?*

Just like the finger, the thin, feminine hand was hairless with wrinkly, splotchy skin. So the victim had lost her entire hand in an accident in the middle of the woods. But on closer inspection, the discovery made even less sense. The hand hadn't separated from the arm in a clean way, as if sliced off with a knife or a chainsaw. The skin was torn and stretched, almost shredded, at the wound as if someone had pulled it off using brute force.

Sammy wagged his tail more now as if the whole thing were some wonderful joke.

Nausea spread up through Jack's chest as Sammy didn't drop it at his feet this time, but instead nudged it closer, brushing the limp fingers against his pant legs. Jack stepped back, but Sammy moved in again as if waiting for Jack to acknowledge his prize and accept it from him.

"Drop it, Sammy." Jack winced and avoided looking at it directly. "Keep that thing away from me."

Sammy cocked his head to the side and wagged his tail more.

"No." Jack raised his voice and gestured with his palm down. "Drop the damn thing."

Sammy excitedly released it from his jaws, and the hand flopped to the ground.

The fingers landed on Jack's shoes and he lurched back. A few drops of blood splattered over the top of his shoe. If it belonged to a murder victim, then they might now suspect him.

"Damn."

But a murder in the small town of Green Hills was rare. Plenty of accidents though, and even some suicides, but not outright murder.

No, he couldn't believe it, but his heart still raced. Maybe the victim lay dead nearby. His gaze followed the path from where Sammy had just come from—a darkened area of the forest, shrouded in pine trees and thick, tall brush.

Plenty of cover to hide something sinister behind those trees.

He hesitated to move forward. If it was a murder or a suicide, then it couldn't have happened more than a day ago, judging by the condition of the victim's skin. Maybe even just a few hours. He swallowed as he considered what to do. He wasn't sure if he had the stomach to deal with a dead body, especially if the old woman's body resembled anything like the hand Sammy had found.

He would need to get the police involved after he returned home. He considered turning back then, before finding anything else, but his curiosity had taken hold. The answers were out there, and he needed to see it for himself.

Jack aimed the flashlight at the hand's wound where it had separated from the rest of the arm and tried to locate any identifying marks. The flesh was so mushy—the knuckles were lumped in with everything else—no sign of bones in any of it. Some flies now buzzed around the wounds as he kneeled down and inspected it from a safe distance while holding his breath as the bitter stench of blood floated up. Glancing under the folds of the skin, he only spotted muscle and bloody flesh. There had to be bones in there *somewhere*, right? Something couldn't have stripped out *every* bone.

Angling the flashlight higher and to the side, something sparkled, and then he spotted the glint of silver metal from between two folds of flesh. A wedding ring.

Sammy nuzzled up beside him now and pushed in.

"What's wrong, boy? Ready to head back? Me too. But

the cops won't believe this shit." Jack rubbed Sammy's fur and leaned in closer toward the ring. It was a woman's diamond ring with several smaller diamonds embedded along each side of the band.

*Ella Anderson's ring?* Something told him it could only belong to her, but he'd know for sure soon enough after he searched the woods a little more.

"Dammit." Jack stood up and stared over at where Sammy had gotten the hand. He could notify the police then, but he wanted to be sure it belonged to her before he did anything else. "If it's hers, old Charlie will be devastated... Better that I find her and give him the news." Sammy just wagged his tail.

Jack walked over to the area where Sammy had come back with the hand. He walked further and pushed through the brush and around several trees. He couldn't have gone too far—he'd only been gone for a short time.

His foot thumped into something soft within the weeds. A dead cat. Something had ripped its chest open and its innards were missing. The flies and ants had already begun feasting on the carcass. He cringed as a fresh wave of nausea flashed through his stomach.

Something else sat on the ground in front of him. Not a dead animal this time, or a fallen branch, or piece of trash. This was a human arm, but just like the hand, someone or something had torn it from its body. The torn pulpy mass near the shoulder showed the same stretched skin and more dried blood covered the wound.

Jack expected to find a pool of blood below it, or at least somewhere nearby, but it sat alone with no other signs of the body part's trauma. His stomach churned at the sight of it, but he forced himself to keep a level head. Plenty of broken branches around the area, and flattened grass where a trespasser had made their way through, but no clues who it might have been.

*So the rest of the corpse is somewhere nearby?* Staring into a darker section of the woods, he tried not to think about it.

Turning his attention back to the arm, he moved in for a closer look. The skin matched the other body parts—thin without hair. He couldn't shake the hunch that it belonged to Ella. Poor Charlie.

His heart sank further when he spotted a path of flattened brush and broken branches leading back toward Ella and Charlie's property. He followed it, and along the way, he spotted a red and orange flannel strip of torn clothing stuck to a branch. An outdated style of fabric Ella might have worn around the house, but even considering everything he'd found so far, there was no proof any of it belonged to Ella.

Sammy inched up and sniffed at the cloth, but Jack nudged him away. "You shouldn't touch that, boy. The police will need to do an investigation. Bad enough you got a little blood on my shoe."

They would search everything, all right. The woods would be swarming with officers soon and everyone would ask what had happened. It *had* to be Ella's body parts, and she was almost certainly dead. Accident or not, it was certain to stir up big news in a small town like Green Hills. They would question old Charlie most of all—interrogate him, more accurately—and if Ella had run into foul play, then Charlie shouldn't hear about it from some cop showing up at the front door. He deserved to hear news like that from someone who knew him.

There was no way—absolutely no way—Charlie could have had anything to do with her death. He was a farmer, nothing weak about him, but he loved Ella. Charlie worshipped her, and the news would destroy him... if it was her. Only one way to know for sure.

Jack dialed Charlie's cell phone number.

Charlie answered on the third ring. "Hello?"

"Charlie, this is Jack Halverson from next door. Is everything all right over there?"

"Yes... why?"

"Is Ella okay?"

Charlie cleared his throat. "Yes, of course. Couldn't be better."

"Can I speak with her?"

A pause on the other line, and rustling, as if Charlie was walking. "She's asleep now."

"Are you sure?"

Charlie chuckled. "Jack, what do you need?"

Jack hadn't expected Charlie's answers. "Just checking up on her. I remember you said last week she wasn't feeling well."

"Yes, she's feeling much better now." Silence for a few seconds.

Jack focused again on the fabric stuck to the branch next to him. It was Ella's. He was sure of that. "Ah, that's good. I hope to see you both again soon."

"Anytime, Jack."

They ended the call, and Jack turned to Sammy. "Something's up with Charlie, don't you think? What do you say, boy, you think we should pay them a visit?"

Sammy barked once and shuddered with excitement while wagging his tail again.

"I agree. Let's go."

Jack hurried back to the house and slipped his .38 revolver into the inside pocket of his jacket before jumping in his truck with Sammy in the passenger seat.

Old Charlie didn't scare him, but under the circumstances, it was better to prepare for anything.

Driving the quarter mile over to the Anderson farm, Jack prepared himself for what he might encounter. If there was any sign of trouble, any strange vehicles in the driveway, he would immediately call the police and get them involved. No sense in taking any chances. But if not, he would face Charlie himself. If the worst had happened and Charlie had gone off the deep end, then the old man deserved more compassion than any police investigator would give him. But still, even then, after seeing all the body parts, he couldn't believe that Charlie would have done something so horrendous to his wife. They were a soft-spoken, gentle couple and had always treated everyone with respect.

Still, people did *snap*.

Jack parked in Charlie's driveway, pulling in behind the old man's white Ford pickup. No sign of anything unusual, except the living room's large windows were uncovered, revealing a soft orange glow inside.

Leaving the driver's side window rolled down, Jack climbed out of his car and peered back at Sammy. "You stay here, boy. I'll be back in a few minutes."

Sammy squirmed in the passenger seat, probably desperate to jump out with Jack, but the dog did as he was told.

Jack followed the sidewalk up to the front door and knocked before waiting patiently on the cement steps. With the living room windows uncovered, he could see a short distance inside with the help of the orange glow, although the glare off the glass blocked most of his view. From that angle, the room appeared in disarray, as if Charlie and Ella had turned the place upside down looking for something, but something was *off* about the lack of window coverings. There *were* curtains over the windows, but only their shredded remnants hung along the sides and corners of the windows. Someone had torn them down.

He moved closer to the window and leaned over the railing to get a better view inside. The source of the orange glow became clear. Candles. Hundreds of them were spread out over the floor and the fireplace blazed brightly in the corner with a pile of firewood stacked next to it. Nothing inside looked anything like he remembered it from visiting Charlie a year earlier. Everything was a mess, as if a herd of cows had run through there. All their furniture and possessions were overturned and broken, the walls were cracked with the sheetrock and insulation hanging out, and shattered glass covered the floor—nothing was left untouched.

Something lying on the floor in the center of the room chilled his spine. It was unmistakable. An arm. White lumpy flesh with blood and muscle spilling out. And more torn strips of red and orange fabric next to it—the same type of cloth that he'd found in the forest.

*The matching arm to the one in the forest?*

The front door opened. "Jack?"

Charlie stood staring at him in the doorway with a confused, stern look on his face. The door was open, but only far enough for the old man to poke his face out. Sweat beaded on the old man's forehead and dripped down over his face and neck. His drenched dress shirt clung to his bony frame and his gray hair was matted to one side, sticking together in clumps. Charlie wasn't the type of guy to appear sloppy in public—he was more likely to wear a suit than shorts on a hot summer day—so it took a moment before Jack recognized him.

Jack touched the pistol concealed inside his jacket and forced a smile.

Charlie adjusted his glasses and narrowed his eyes as if he'd just awakened from a nap. "Is anything wrong?"

"That's what I'm wondering." Jack stepped toward the front door and tried to peer over Charlie's shoulder. "I'd like to talk with Ella please."

"What about? She's sleeping."

"I know, you said that, but would you mind waking her up? This is important."

Charlie scowled. "Well, what's it about? I'm kind of busy now. Too much stuff going on in the house, you know. Now's not a good time."

"I heard some noises coming from this direction," Jack lied. "Thought I should check it out, and make sure you're all safe."

"We're safe." Charlie looked back at Jack's truck, then started closing the door. "Thanks for checking on me, anyway."

Jack thrust his foot forward, jamming it against the bottom of the door. "Hold on. It'll just take a minute."

Charlie pushed the door against Jack's foot. "What's this about?"

"About Ella. I need to check on her, Charlie."

"I told you." Charlie sneered. "She's asleep. Come back another day."

"I found her wedding ring in the forest." Jack gestured toward the forest separating their properties. "You know anything about that?"

Charlie's face flushed red and his expression changed to exasperation. He stopped pushing against the door, but didn't open it either. "It can't be her ring. She's in the bedroom asleep, and she never takes it off. You must have found someone else's."

"It's Ella's. I know, because you're right, she couldn't have taken it off. Too tight."

"What's that supposed to mean?"

"Let me have a look at her ring, just to compare it with the one I got, and then I'll leave. Deal?"

"Dammit, Jack, go away." Charlie thrust the door into Jack's foot, and he almost got it latched shut before Ella's voice cried out from somewhere within the house. Charlie's eyes widened.

Her voice caught Jack by surprise. Could she have survived the trauma of getting her arms ripped off? Jack pushed the door open and stuck his foot inside. "Is that Ella?"

Charlie kicked his ankle and raised his voice. "You're not getting in my house."

Ella's crackling voice cried out Charlie's name again.

There was no mistaking it. Ella was at home—alive and well. But there was something about the *way* she called his name that didn't sound right. There was pain in her voice, and a desperate pleading.

Jack pushed against the door with his shoulder now. "I have to talk to her, Charlie. I think something's wrong."

Charlie laughed nervously. "What's gotten into you, Jack? You trying to rob me or something?"

"Open the door." Jack pulled the pistol from his jacket pocket and brandished it in Charlie's face. "I'm coming in to talk with Ella. Once I see her and make sure she's okay, I'll leave. Got it?"

"You going to shoot me? I'll call the police."

"Go ahead."

Charlie's hands shook as he clutched the edge of the door, but still didn't back away.

Jack took a deep breath. "Listen, Charlie. Whatever happened to Ella, we can talk about it. I know something's wrong with her. I just want to help her."

"She doesn't need help..."

Jack thrust his shoulder against the door, knocking Charlie back out of the way until both of them stood in the entryway.

Charlie stumbled back toward the living room and gripped the corner of a wall to keep from falling down. "Listen, I can handle it."

"What can you...?" A wave of heat enveloped Jack just a few feet in as if he'd walked into an oven. The house was broiling. The candles weren't just in the living room, they were scattered throughout the house, and they must have had the furnace cranked up to over a hundred degrees, but the temperature outside wasn't less than seventy.

Charlie stepped aside as Jack made his way down the hall, but something metal clicked behind him. The familiar click of someone cocking a gun. Jack stopped.

"I can't let you go in there," Charlie said behind him.

Jack turned around slowly while raising his hands. Charlie was aiming a rifle at his chest.

"Drop the pistol." Charlie's hands trembled with his finger near the trigger. "I wouldn't like to shoot you, but you're trespassing now, and I will."

Charlie paused to wipe a line of sweat dripping down over his right eye. When his finger left the trigger, Jack lunged forward and knocked the rifle away. The old man fumbled to grasp it even as it slammed against the floor. Jack pushed him out of the way, and within a few seconds, without any shots fired, Jack had him pinned to the floor.

Charlie didn't struggle, and it didn't take much effort to keep the old man down, but Jack still kept his pistol in full view to remind Charlie what was at stake if he tried that again.

Jack spoke in a calm, yet forceful tone. "What the hell's going on here?"

"She likes it hot."

"I don't mean the heat. I'm talking about Ella. I know you did something to her, because I found human body parts in the woods, and there's a bloody arm lying on your living room floor, for God's sake. Don't tell me you don't know what's going on. You got her tied up in her room?"

Charlie shook his head.

Scooping up the rifle and releasing Charlie, he stood and moved back, keeping an eye on him from a safe distance. "Well, something's going on in here. You trying to roast her in all this heat?"

"She likes it this way," Charlie mumbled.

Jack met Charlie's eyes as he struggled to stand. "What are you talking about? I can hardly breathe in here."

"She can breathe just fine." Charlie rubbed his arms. "Leave us alone."

"What did you do to her?"

"I didn't do anything. She's getting along just fine with me watching out for her."

"I'm not sure you're doing such a good job. Where's her bedroom?"

Charlie pointed down the hall.

"Take me to her." Jack gestured with the pistol.

"She's not in there." Charlie stared at the floor. "She's in the basement."

"Fine, then take me *there*."

Charlie sauntered ahead, still rubbing his arms, and

opened the basement door at the far side of the kitchen. Ella's voice echoed up the stairway.

Jack poked Charlie with the tip of the rifle. "You're going down first."

Charlie shook his head. "No. We shouldn't bother her. You don't understand. Just leave us alone."

"Would you rather have the police here? Get down there. I want to see what's going on."

Still, Charlie didn't move. "Nothing's going on. I'm a good husband, and you won't understand. She just needs a little more time."

"More time for what?"

"It's too difficult to explain."

"Would you rather explain it to the police? What are you so afraid of? Get down there, and if you try to run away, or make any sudden movements, I won't hesitate to shoot."

Charlie gazed into Jack's eyes and cringed before descending the wooden staircase. Halfway down the stairs, the old man spoke softly, "What noises did you hear at your house?"

"I lied. I didn't hear anything, but Sammy and I found her body parts in the woods. Hard to believe they belonged to Ella, even after finding her wedding ring—I still can't believe it—but I'm hoping you'll show me this whole thing was an accident. Please tell me you didn't do anything on purpose."

Charlie didn't answer the question as they reached the bottom of the stairs. The stench was overwhelming. A rotten smell worse than any freshly manured field. Ella's voice came from a closed door at the far corner of the basement.

"You going to tell me what happened?" Jack asked.

"You'll see. She's almost done, and then everything will be okay again. But I know you won't understand, and I never intended for things to come to this."

Ella moaned again, louder now as they reached the door. There was a long drawn out screech mixed in with her cries of pain, like an animal struggling to escape a fatal trap.

Charlie opened the door and stepped in, but Jack stopped in the doorway. It wasn't Ella in there, at least, not the woman he'd known for so many years. *Something* was lying face up on a bed. Some of it was Ella, but most of it was something else. Jack gasped.

Charlie stepped toward the bed while staring at the floor. "Hi, honey, Jack wanted to see you."

The thing on the bed met Jack's stare. It was a hideous sight. Ella's body was a dull white, like the white in a hard boiled egg, and her eyes were sunken in her head as her elongated neck stretched out over her chest as if something had yanked on it and then pulled and pulled some more like taffy. Both of her arms were there, but they weren't the same. None of her was the same. Strips of shredded flesh lay across the bed and floor. The woman was shedding her flesh like a snake, except the flesh beneath her own resembled nothing like a human. Ella squirmed within the shell of her old flesh as she shed another chunk. It dropped off and flopped to the floor.

"I meant to go back to the woods and pick up after her." Charlie sulked. "I didn't mean for anyone to find her like that."

Ella gyrated and arched her back in painful throes as another slice of flesh peeled away from her leg. Not much remained now of old Ella, except her head and her left leg.

Several smaller chunks clung to her abdomen, held on by a clear, slimy substance.

Jack wanted to run, but his legs didn't work. Nausea and icy fear pushed him to the edge of passing out, and he couldn't breathe or look away.

Charlie trembled beside him. "Now you've seen her. She'll get better soon, but I didn't intend for anyone to see her like this. She just needs some rest to help her through the process."

"What... what process?" Jack stammered. "What did you do to her?"

"It's supposed to cure her cancer. She found the home remedy on the Internet, but I think I did it wrong."

"You killed her."

Ella cried out again in pain and flailed her white, alien arms as her body shuddered.

"No, it's still her." Charlie moved a little closer. "Inside. She's just *different*."

Jack shook his head. "That's not Ella. That thing is... wrong."

Ella lumbered out of bed and sat on the edge staring at him with her sunken, dark eyes. The last pieces of her flesh slurped down over the sides of her moist, gleaming flesh as her face slipped off like a rubber mask and crumpled down onto the floor. The raw white head was as featureless and opaque as her body, appearing like an oversized, hairless newborn from another world, except that her overall shape and size were the same. Maybe Ella was still somewhere deep inside her, but this thing had shed the old woman's identity in every physical way. The form moving toward him was far from the pleasant old woman he'd lived next to for several years.

Jack turned to escape, but Charlie threw himself in front of the doorway and ripped the rifle from Jack's hand.

Jack aimed the pistol at Charlie's chest. "What are you doing? Get out of my way."

Charlie didn't move. "I can't let you leave. You'll call the police."

"Damn right, I will."

Charlie shook his head. "She's hungry, Jack. You shouldn't have come here. It's too hard for an old man like me to feed her."

The dead animals came to mind. *She's hungry, Jack.*

Jack poked the tip of the pistol's barrel into Charlie's chest and tossed him to the side along with the rifle. The old man crumpled as Jack made his way out of the room and up the stairs.

Charlie gasped for breath as he raced after him, and yelled, "No, don't go! I can't let you leave."

A deafening gunshot filled the air as Jack reached the front door. Pain shot up his spine and blood drenched the left side of his shirt. He staggered, then collapsed in the open doorway to the front door, staring out at his truck. Sammy was still out there, craning his neck out the window with his ears perked. Jack raised his hand to stop what he knew would come next, but it didn't help— Sammy jumped out of the window and charged toward the front door.

"No Sammy, just run." It was heartening to see Sammy coming to the rescue, but at the same time, Jack desperately wanted his best friend to run away. If Charlie wouldn't hesitate to shoot his neighbor, he wouldn't hesitate to shoot his neighbor's dog either. Jack continued trying to wave him away, even as Sammy charged past Jack and attacked Charlie. The old man fired two more shots—

neither shot struck the dog, but instead blew small holes into the hallway walls.

"Sammy, no." Jack moaned softly as he couldn't catch his breath. Numbness spread through the left side of his chest and it became harder to breathe. He was sure he could still make it out to the truck, but he couldn't leave without Sammy.

Charlie stumbled to the floor, landing on his back, while defending himself from Sammy and reaching for his rifle again, when Ella appeared near the basement door. Sammy growled at both of them, but charged at Ella first.

"Don't you bite my Ella," Charlie cried out, grabbing the rifle again.

Sammy jumped back to Charlie, biting at the old man's arms as he fought to aim the rifle. Within seconds, blood soaked the shirt and floor.

Ella sneered and opened her mouth wide. A single, garbled word came out that sounded like someone choking. "Delicious."

"I'll get you food, my darling." Charlie kicked at Sammy, even as the blood drained out faster from the old man's arms. Charlie cried out in pain as Sammy bit into his flesh. At the same time, Charlie clutched one of Sammy's legs and pulled him in, even as Sammy continued his attack. Charlie met Jack's gaze with a grin. "I'll feed him to her. Is that what you want? She'll eat him up." Charlie mocked chomping noises and smirked.

Several candles toppled over during the struggle and most of them went out, but one rolled across the floor and caught a towel on fire. Within seconds, the flames spread across the kitchen cabinets above it and then to the wallpaper.

Sammy yelped and broke free from Charlie's grasp.

Jack gestured toward the front door as he stood. "Go, Sammy. Get out of here."

By the time Sammy backed away and ran to Jack's side, the flames had spread into the dining room.

As they made their way out the front door, Jack glanced back. Ella was hunched over Charlie's limp body. He'd stopped screaming as the flames raged around them. Blood sprayed over Ella's virgin white chest as she tore off chunks of his flesh.

She groaned. "Delicious."

# MATILDA X

Cyclops Bar & Grill was a far cry from the cramped, isolated seat in Gary's cubicle, and a refuge from all the mind-numbing equations and constant demands of his electrical engineering job for the space program. Only a few people knew him there, and they mostly left him alone where he always sat in his usual spot at the end of the bar sipping a craft beer. He loved it.

The place usually booked a toe-tapping country band to brighten his mood on a Friday night—something he looked forward to all week—but tonight, a magician was performing. An oddly dressed woman named Matilda X. He considered complaining to Tommy, the bartender, about the poor choice in entertainment. Gary debated if he would leave or not... but he scowled instead. What else did he have to do on a Friday night? Drinking alone at home held no appeal. He could put up with it for an evening—it would only last for a couple of hours.

He smiled at Alivia, one of the servers who was busy rushing to and from the bar picking up drinking orders, and she returned his smile. All the servers knew him as the "professor", although he'd never taught a class in his life. The only thing they knew was that he was smart—super smart, using their own words—but the only advantage that he'd had in his life was getting a more lucrative, high-paying job. And the women he'd met found his intelligence interesting, to a point, but his salary... oh, now *that* was fascinating. But they were never interested in the different types of semi-conductors or what a Zener diode does. They wanted to know about his car, his house, his lifestyle —*oh, it must be so exciting*—so he avoided talking about himself entirely. It was better that way.

Tommy, the bartender, had bonded with Gary over the years since he'd discovered the place, even though they had nothing in common. Tommy was a stiff-necked ex-Marine-turned bartender, and Gary had never lifted a weight in his life. But Tommy's strength was his outgoing personality—the women crooned over him—and maybe that's why Gary stopped by at least twice a week. He wanted to see the master work his magic and flirt as he raked in the tips. Tommy was gay, Gary had learned, so no woman ever had a chance with the man, but he kept that to himself, just like he never pried into Gary's "exciting" personal life or brought up his work or marital issues, unless Gary offered to talk about it first. An ideal situation.

Matilda X started her magic act, and the woman's outfit was striking. Something straight out of an '80s music video; a puffy yellow and black skirt with fishnet stockings, and a pink and black top with ruffled edges. She could have been a background dancer in the Madonna music video "Material Girl". Besides the outdated clothes, she looked to be well into her '40s, give or take a few years, since her thick, colorful makeup helped to camouflage her exact age. Her black hair also matched the look of the '80s, fanning out in all directions, and a streak of blonde across the top revealed her true hair color beneath the black dye.

Gary looked past the distraction of the woman's outfit and followed the curves of her hips and breasts across to her hands as she performed the first trick. The audience applauded her sleight-of-hand, and it caught him off guard when he saw that she was staring right at him.

"You." She pointed at him. "Come up here. Let's mess with your brain."

The crowd laughed, but Gary didn't move from his seat, even as the patrons around him parted so Matilda X could see him better.

Tommy leaned over the bar and nudged him in the shoulder. "Go up there, Gary."

Gary grunted and shook his head. But everyone was staring at him now. "I won't"

"You have to." Tommy thumped his fist on the counter next to Gary. "Go have some fun."

Gary rolled his eyes as Matilda called out to him again. Now she used his name. "Gary, that's your name, right? Yes, it is. Come up here. I heard you have a big... juicy... irresistible..." She licked her lips. "... brain."

*Irresistible brain?* But it was the way she said it that caught his ear. Such a seductive tone, and the crowd caught it too and started chanting his name, while a few patrons nearby prodded him.

Instead of standing, he gripped his beer and stared at the sparkling edge of the glass, wishing everyone would leave him alone. He could *feel* their eyes on him.

Matilda called his name again. What choice did he have? He could escape to his car, but Tommy and the servers would tease him relentlessly the next night. *No way to get out of it, Gary.* He couldn't just sit there and do nothing.

*Go away!* he screamed in his mind, but the attention only grew more awkward the longer he delayed his response. *Dammit!*

Two servers, Alivia and Rachel, moved in beside him, and each grabbed one of his arms, pulling him from his bar stool to the delight of the crowd. They led him toward the stage and he gave up trying to fight the inevitable, but he enjoyed the moment too—women hadn't touched him like that in months, and their soft voices intoxicated him more than the beer. His face warmed within their grasp until he stood on the stage next to Matilda X.

The magician woman scanned his clothes, his hair, his face, and his eyes. "It's not so bad, is it?"

He sneered. "Yes, it is."

She gestured to the microphone on the stand in front of them. "Speak into the mic."

He leaned toward it, formed a smiled, and spoke. "Who set me up?"

The crowd laughed and applauded, and he let out an exasperated sigh. The faster he could get this over with, the faster he could get back to his beer and the solitude of the bar stool.

"No one set you up, Gary," Matilda told the audience. "We just want to have a little fun with you, my brilliant brainiac."

*Brainiac? That's good. Make fun of the smart nerd.* The crowd roared at her every word.

"We'll see how smart you are." She grinned.

The three spotlights hanging from the ceiling to light the stage helped to obscure most of the crowd's stares, but that didn't ease his nerves. Even though he couldn't see most of their faces, his imagination filled in the darkness with something worse—the knowledge that they were judging him. They were laughing at him, and anger rose up in his chest as his legs weakened.

"Are you ready for a trick?" she asked.

"I guess," he said hoarsely. *I'm ready to get this over with and get back to that golden brown ale beer.*

Matilda nudged him toward the microphone, and she gestured for him to repeat himself.

He swallowed to moisten his mouth. "I guess."

"Where are you from, Gary?"

He licked his lips. "You tell me. You're the magician."

She smirked and narrowed her eyes at him. "Looks like I've met my match. Let's do a card trick to start things off." Matilda pulled out a deck of cards, shuffled them a few times, then fanned them out, face down. "Pick one, please."

Gary plucked a card from the middle of the deck and looked at it, angling it away from Matilda. Three of hearts.

"Show it to the audience," she said.

He did, then put it back into the deck at her direction.

She shuffled the deck again, while staring into his eyes. "Don't be so nervous, Gary. This will be a night to remember, you'll see."

*Don't be so nervous...* He rolled his eyes and pictured himself sucking down a few stiff drinks after all that nonsense was over. A moment later, she pulled a card from the deck and held it up to the audience. "Is this your card?"

The three of hearts. The audience clapped.

Gary smirked. "Yes, great. I've seen that trick a million

times. You marked the card or kept your finger on it while you shuffled it."

Matilda's face lit up. "Oh? So you're saying I cheated?"

Gary shrugged. "Yeah, maybe. Am I done? Can I get back to my beer?"

She laughed. "I'm just getting started." Sliding the card back into the deck, she shuffled it again and fanned them out just as before. "This time, pick another card, but I'll do things a little differently." She turned her back away from him and instructed him what to do over her shoulder.

He picked out another card, showed the audience—the queen of spades—and kept an eye on where she was looking to make sure she wasn't cheating. Instead of handing it back to her, she instructed him to fold the card in half, and then a second time, so it fit neatly in the palm of his hand. She waited for him to finish.

He did as she asked. "Done."

"All right, now eat it."

"What?" He looked at her incredulously.

She repeated herself louder, speaking clearly into the microphone. "Eat the card that you just folded. Pretend it's a little piece of magic."

"That's ridiculous."

"Is it? This is a deck of *magic* cards. You are what you eat, Gary, so I suggest not passing up this opportunity, and it shouldn't taste too bad, considering all the beer you drank tonight."

He cringed and stared at the card. He'd done a lot of stupid things in his life, but this wouldn't be one of them. "No, thanks. I'm going to sit down now." He stepped off the stage with the crowd booing.

"Gary, wait." Her voice cut through the air.

He stopped, but didn't turn around. "I'm not eating the stupid card."

"That's fine. I'll do it then. Bring it over here and let me finish it off."

He turned around and faced her. "You'll just switch it."

"Then put it in my mouth." She opened her mouth, closed her eyes, and stuck out her tongue.

The crowd chanted his name again. He hesitated and considered throwing the card away and leaving the bar, but instead he gave in and stepped back up the stage, extending the folded card toward her mouth.

*Choke on it, then.* When he stuffed it into her mouth, she held his arm and clamped her lips shut around his fingers for a moment. She sucked on them, and a warmth passed through his body, until he lurched back. The crowd roared with laughter as he wiped his fingers on his shirt. His face was hot—*probably red as a stop sign if he could see himself in a mirror*—but he stood there with his arms folded, waiting for her to finish the act.

"What now?" he asked. "Will it pop out of your ass this time?"

She grinned and winked at him. After chewing up and swallowing the card, Matilda opened her mouth and showed it to the audience to prove that she had indeed devoured it. She really hammed it up, patting her stomach like she had just eaten a satisfying meal. "Delicious!"

"Can I leave?" Gary demanded. "Are we done?"

"Check your pants." Matilda chuckled.

Gary felt the pockets of his jeans and discovered something lumpy sitting deep near the bottom. It hadn't been there earlier. He pulled it out and unfolded a playing card, opening it slowly. It couldn't possibly be the card she had just put in her mouth, but there it was—the queen of spades, with no signs that she'd eaten it. He shook his head. "You must have planted this earlier. There's no way you could have gotten it from your mouth down to my pocket."

Matilda laughed, taking the folded card from his hands, and held it up to the audience. They cheered as Gary's mouth fell open.

"More!" the audience shouted.

Matilda nodded and stared at him. "Looks like I pulled one over on the brainiac. Maybe you're not as smart as they told me."

"*Who* told you?"

"Let's try again, Gary. What do you say?"

His beer was calling to him from the bar. He just wanted to go back to his barstool and forget any of this happened, but she was making him look stupid. She had humiliated him and he wouldn't let it go so easily without paying back the favor. He nodded and focused on her every movement. How difficult could it be to figure out a simple card trick? Even little kids could pull off stuff like that.

"Wonderful." She stepped closer to him and pressed her fingers around the sides of his head. Her flowery scent drew him in, and he surrendered to her essence. His vision blurred as she stroked the sides of his temples and soothed his nerves. Within seconds, his anger washed away, and he forgot about the crowd. He closed his eyes, taking in her soothing smell, and struggled to focus as her warm fingers massaged his scalp.

"Think of a number between one and a hundred," she said.

The tenseness in his shoulders and neck faded away. *Fourteen.*

"You have it now, don't you?" she said.

He nodded and someone in the audience shouted something, but it didn't matter. All that mattered was that this woman had connected with him in a deep, meaningful way. And it felt good.

Her hands fell away, and he opened his eyes, snapping back to the realization that everyone was staring at him, many of them laughing. *Wake up, Gary. She's making a fool of you.*

"No one's making a fool of you," she mumbled, while pulling out a small notepad and a black sharpie marker from her pocket.

His face warmed again, but now he felt a little panicked too. How had she answered his question? A lucky guess? He stared into her eyes while she handed him the notepad and instructed him to write the number in it as she looked away. He did, slowly and dazedly, then closed it and clenched it to his chest as if it held a deep dark secret.

Matilda X pulled out a second notepad and marker from her pocket while still facing away from him, and held it up so everyone could see. Then she turned to him, meeting his gaze, and focused on him intently as if drawing out the card number telepathically. "Are you thinking of the number?"

He wasn't. *And you know I'm not thinking of it, don't you?* His mind was still reeling from their intimacy a moment earlier. The number popped into his mind again without effort. *Fourteen.*

"Got it." She wrote something in her notepad and grinned while keeping it held to her chest and turning back to the audience. "Every once in a while, I find someone special in the audience, someone with an intelligent, enchanting mind who connects with me on a deeper level. Tonight, that person is Gary Jensen, and it's been an honor sharing the stage with him."

Gary stepped toward the edge of the stage to get out of the spotlight, but she put her arm around him and prevented his escape.

"Open it up and show them your number." She gestured toward the notepad in his hand.

He opened it and showed the audience. *Fourteen*.

Nearly at the same time, she lifted her notepad and revealed what she'd written in it. *Fourteen*, and she had even drawn Gary's name below it with little hearts around the number.

Holding back the nausea welling up in his stomach, the audience gasped. No more. He couldn't stand the attention, the scrutiny.

The audience cheered at the successful trick, but he rushed off the stage, avoiding all eye contact along the way, and made his way back to his open seat at the bar.

What the hell had just happened? He needed another beer. No, a beer wouldn't do it this time. He needed a shot of whiskey. No, a pint.

"Thank you, Gary," Matilda X said, "for stepping up here and bravely subjecting yourself to my magic, even though I get the feeling it was involuntary."

The audience continued clapping.

"Who's up for some more?" she called out to them.

As Gary dropped into his seat at the bar, Tommy placed a fresh beer in front of him without asking, and he leaned in. "I felt a little spark between the two of you up there."

Gary shook his head. "I think I'll head home after one more."

"What? You're running out on this opportunity? At least stick around and watch the rest of the show."

Gary sipped his full glass of beer and stared forward. "I don't know."

"You got some chemistry going on," Tommy said. "Hang around for a bit."

Gary shrugged, but stayed in his seat.

Matilda X continued with her act, enlisting a few other patrons over the next hour as she went through trick after trick. Gary glanced over at her every few minutes, but avoided eye contact. Listening to the crowd's reactions, he scoffed at each trick and dissected the mechanics of how Matilda had pulled off each one.

There was no magic in real life. No deeper connection between them waiting to be discovered. The world was illusory and only the ones keeping a subjective perspective would avoid falling a victim to its deception. The drinks had temporarily clouded his mind, but his intelligence was his greatest asset and had served him well over the years.

Gary held up his glass of beer as Tommy passed by. "Here's to an *enchanting* mind."

After Matilda had finished her performance an hour later, Gary's gaze followed her off the stage as she took a seat in a darkened booth across the room. The lights came up a little as she sat down. Their eyes met for a moment, and she grinned, but he looked away.

Tommy slapped his palm on the bar and leaned into Gary. "Now's your chance. You should talk to her. Maybe you can sweet talk her into revealing how she did that trick with you."

"I couldn't sweet talk if I tried."

Tommy laughed. "You're too hard on yourself. She's

right, Gary, you're a smart guy. You'll think of something. Just go over there."

Gary glanced back at Matilda occasionally, watching a steady stream of men approach her table and stir up a conversation, sometimes making her laugh. One man even sat at her table for a short time, but left a few minutes later. Between all the attention she was getting, her gaze jumped back to him between each conversation.

"Don't stare, Gary." Tommy clanked a glass on the counter while mixing a drink. "Staring is for nervous high school boys. Get off your stool and go over there."

Gary shrugged. He wasn't there to pick up women, anyway. Far from it. All he wanted by the end of the night was for the alcohol's sweet intoxication to drown out the incessant drone of anxiety caused by the mind-numbing demands of his job that had caused so much unhappiness in his life. The bar was his oasis from all the complications, a time to forget his troubles and fade into the cloud of "who gives a shit". *And* he was still sore after she'd humiliated him on stage.

A little later, the overhead music boomed louder. Not so loud that it drowned out any conversations, but for someone like him, it was a good excuse to avoid starting any. This was the stage of the night where all the *connections* were made, as some lonely souls discovered other lonely souls to share a phone, share a kiss, or, if you were *really* lucky, share a bed.

Tommy paused for a moment between serving up drinks, glancing between Gary and something over Gary's shoulder. "Hey, Matilda's really got her eye on you. I know when a girl is interested in someone, and I'm telling you, go over there and talk to her."

Gary followed Tommy's gaze again back to Matilda's

table where she sat grinning at him. With her '80s magician's outfit, it was difficult to see anything in that light, except her face and hair. Matilda didn't look away.

Gary turned back and took a sip of his beer. "Oh, geez."

"Right? You should run over there and get her number before she leaves."

"From a magician? No way."

"What's wrong with her?"

"What do you mean, what's wrong with her? Did you see how she treated me up there?"

"Gary," Tommy moved in closer, "are you kidding me? You've been sitting here every week for over a year now and I'm not sure I've ever seen you interact with even one lady until tonight. You should take advantage of this opportunity. How many times have you asked a woman for her number in the past year? Five times? One? Never?"

Gary grumbled. "I'm not one of those slick guys that goes up to a woman and five minutes later I'm taking her home for the evening."

"Okay, that's fine, but she's attractive. She already knows your name, so the door's open. All you need to do is walk in. Just use that *enchanting* mind."

"No, thanks." Gary finished his beer and pointed to it. "I'll have another one of these."

Tommy groaned and nodded before walking away. "Coming up."

Gary looked back. She was staring at him again now, with intense, focused eyes. Did she ever blink? She was rock solid still as if deep in thought, and he didn't want to be mean about it, but *okay, stop staring*.

He feigned a smile and turned back to the bar. Maybe

she was drunk by then and was feeling a little amorous. But that was the point, right? It was a bar, after all. A place to hang out and laugh, and maybe stir up a new relationship. But so many men had already stopped by her table. She had the pick of the litter tonight after that performance.

*I could just stop by and see* how *drunk she is. Maybe she isn't so demeaning off the stage...*

Tommy returned with another beer. "Dammit, Gary, why aren't you over there talking to her?"

"She keeps staring at me."

"Yeah, so it's a bar, that's how some people let you know they're interested in you. I know she wants to talk to you. You don't like girls who make the first move?"

Gary shrugged. "It's not that. She isn't my type."

Tommy leaned in. "Gary, listen, we've known each other for a while now. You're a regular, so take a good look at yourself. Any girl in this bar is your type."

"What's that supposed to mean?"

Tommy cringed and rolled his eyes. "Listen, I'm not trying to hurt your feelings, but this is really getting to me that you're sitting here alone every night, and finally a young woman shows interest in you. Are you going to sit there by yourself for the rest of the night waiting for the final call?" Tommy glanced over at the clock on the wall. "You've got another hour before everyone clears out. That's plenty of time to get to know her, at least get her phone number."

Gary glanced back at Matilda. Her wild, big hair reminded him of his days as a young man in college, just before the glam rock fads disappeared. He shuddered to think of how oddly everyone dressed back then, and how stupid he must have looked to women approaching them in his cringeworthy outfits. *It was a miracle that anyone had hooked up in those days.*

Matilda smiled and then laughed.

*Oh, that's good, she's definitely drunk.* She kept smiling.

Last thing I need is a loony in my life. I bet she laughs like a cackling witch too.

Matilda laughed louder, not like a witch at all, but it was cute, and he smiled for the first time that night.

"Look," Tommy said, "she's practically begging you to go over there and talk with her. If you won't do it, I'll set you up."

Gary sighed and rolled his eyes. "Oh, all right... but don't let anyone take my seat. I expect I'll return in a few minutes."

"I won't need to save your seat," Tommy said. "You won't be back. This is a new beginning for you, trust me."

Gary grabbed his drink and did his best to stand tall as he approached Matilda. She watched him step closer with that same frozen grin that she'd had on for the last ten minutes.

*She'll tell me she's got a boyfriend as soon as I sit down.*

Gary gazed at her left arm and followed it down to her hand. Too dark to tell if she had a wedding ring or not. Matilda straightened in her seat and stretched her left hand out across the table as if understanding his gaze. No ring.

Reaching her table, Gary stared into her deep, light brown eyes. He shifted his glass of beer to his left hand, wiped his right palm on his pants, then stretched free his hand out toward her. "Hello again."

"Hello, Gary." The woman's smile didn't waver.

Gary glanced back at Tommy, but Matilda pulled him closer and grabbed his attention.

"You did well up there," she said. "The audience enjoyed it. I should take you with me on the road."

"You're not local?"

"I travel around. Keeps my life interesting. You're funny."

"What do you mean, funny? They were laughing at me, not with me. No thanks to you."

"Don't be sore. It was good." She twirled a strand of her hair.

Gary looked around. "Tommy suggested I come over here and say hi. Don't mean to bother you."

"You're not bothering me. I find you entertaining and..." She leaned toward him. "... you've got an enchanting mind."

Gary's face warmed. "You keep saying that."

"It's true." Matilda laughed. "Have a seat and enchant me, Gary." She pushed out a chair with her foot.

Gary stared at the chair, but remained standing. "I'm not much of an enchanter."

"You're hilarious. Most people are very boring, but you've got a dark sense of humor. Have a seat and let me pick your brain for the rest of the night."

Gary scanned through the conversation he'd had with Tommy earlier that evening. Not much said between them that might be considered entertaining, much less contain dark humor. "You overheard our conversation from way back here?"

The woman patted the seat of the chair she'd pushed out. "Something like that."

Gary nodded slowly. "How?"

She patted the seat again.

Sitting beside her, he sipped his beer and glanced into her eyes.

"I think I'll take you home with me tonight," she said.

Gary's face flushed with warmth again. "Oh, you will, huh?"

"I'll drop you off at your house in the morning. 420 Lawndale Drive, right?"

Gary gagged on his beer and coughed. Clearing his throat, he eyed her. "How do you know my address?"

"I'm a magician, remember? I don't reveal my tricks."

Gary eyed her and thought about how Matilda might have acquired his address. She might have sweet-talked Tommy earlier, but would he have really given a total stranger his address? Tommy's words came back to him. *Go talk to her.* Yes, he must have set it up all along. "Did Tommy put you up to this?"

She smirked. "Who is Tommy?"

Gary met her eyes and studied her subtle expressions for any sign of deception. He wasn't a good poker player, but there was something deeper going on behind her eyes, a disconcerting sense that she knew more about him than she was letting on. "You must have gotten my address from someone here, or found my info on the Internet before the performance."

"No, nothing like that."

He considered the only other option. "Or you can read my mind?"

Matilda's eyes widened. "Do you think I'm capable of doing something like that?"

"I don't know..."

Matilda laughed. "Well, then." She grabbed something from the seat beside her and set it on the table. It was his wallet. "Here you go. You forced a magician to reveal her trick. Now do you think I can read your mind?"

Gary dropped his head into his hands. "My driver's

license. Oh, I'm such an idiot. You really had me going there for a minute."

She handed the wallet to him. "I slipped it from your pocket while you were on stage."

"I didn't feel a thing."

"That's the whole point."

He opened it. His driver's license sat upside down in the front pocket. "It's a good thing I didn't go home without this."

"I wouldn't have let you leave without it."

He nodded and smiled, relaxing a little after her actions became clear. "That's why you were staring at me?"

"Yes, well, and a little something more." She winked at him and took one of his hands.

His breath paused as her fingers caressed his skin. "What do you have in mind?"

"We can go back to my hotel room. It's not far from here and it's quiet. A good place to unwind."

Gary sat back in his chair and let her hand slip away from his. She looked attractive now in that space beneath the dimmed lights, but the look in her eyes reminded him of how she'd stared at him while on stage in front of all those people just before she humiliated him. "Is this part of the trick too?"

With her grin still etched on her face, she leaned forward and whispered to him. Her words were soft, but distinct. "I want you to enchant me, Gary."

*That damn word again.* But what did she see in him? With so many other guys scavenging around her table, she could have had any of them. *Why me?* He didn't ask out loud, afraid that she might suddenly realize her mistake and humiliate him again.

She chuckled and squeezed his hand. "Like I said, I find you entertaining, even intriguing."

Gary allowed himself to be pulled in closer toward her. He glanced back at the bar, but Tommy wasn't watching him now. It would have been nice for Tommy to see him finally interacting with a woman, if nothing more than for Tommy to stop pressuring him about it, but nobody was paying any attention. *Fine. I can tell him all about it tomorrow night.*

Matilda moved out from behind the table and stood up, pulling him along with her. "You're coming with me."

Gary didn't resist. Her intoxicating scent lured him closer.

She grabbed a black bag that he assumed held everything she had used during her magic act, and he left behind his half-empty glass of beer as they made their way out the door.

The cool night air did little to snap Gary from his daze. It was quiet on the street, with only a few cars rushing by, and he listened to his pulse thumping in his ears as she led him down the sidewalk toward a white minivan.

"I'll drive," she said.

*Good idea.* He'd had far too much to drink, anyway.

They drove across town with the pulsing city lights fading away behind them, but the moon's ambient light illuminated the contours of the trees and hills enough for Gary to notice he was lost.

"Soon," Matilda said before he could ask.

It took longer than he anticipated to arrive, but maybe that was just the beer slowing things down as it always did when he'd had a few too many.

Finally, they stopped at a small rundown motel just outside the city. Not the fancy hotel he'd expected, but he recognized the area. Not somewhere he visited often, but it didn't matter. He was with a woman—Tommy would be proud of him—although his eyelids drooped down, and he toyed with idea of asking her to just take him home.

By the time Matilda parked and turned off the car, he could barely keep his eyes open. She helped him out of the car, kissing his forehead several times. "No time to sleep, my enchanting little man. I can't wait to see what surprises you've got for me."

"Don't get your hopes up." Gary laughed nervously. "I'm well past my prime."

"I disagree." Matilda ruffled his hair. "You're hilarious, and I can't wait to unwrap your gift."

*Gift.* Gary glanced down at his groin. Nobody had called it that before.

Matilda's room was bare with only one suitcase opened on the floor revealing stacks of folded clothes and personal items. The bed was a king-size; plenty of room to fool around, but the large white pillow called to him. How long could he stay awake before sinking his face into it and falling asleep?

"I'll keep you awake, my little man." Matilda locked the door behind him. "Would you like a drink?"

"I've had enough, thank you."

"Oh, so polite." Despite his objections, she grabbed a pint of Jack Daniels from the mini-fridge and mixed it with a soda before offering it to him. "It will make things easier. Trust me."

"One more drink couldn't hurt." He took the drink and gazed at her body as he sipped it, slowly following her curves up and down without discretion.

"You like what you see?" She posed for him.

He nodded as she pressed her thighs and chest into

him. Her fingertips tickled his neck, then moved up through his hair.

"Let me show you a trick." She moved him back and sat him on the bed.

"Now?"

"Just one more. I'm very, very good at it."

"Oh." His heart raced faster.

She took the mixed drink from his hand and placed it on the nightstand. "Close your eyes."

He grinned and followed her instructions. "I can't promise you that I won't fall asleep."

"That won't happen as long as I'm here."

In the shifting shapes behind his closed eyelids, his head teetered with the waves of intoxication. She stood in front of him, stroking his scalp with her fingertips. "You're a computer engineer with lots of potential."

"You make it sound so interesting."

"It is, to me. It's a shame to see all that brain power wasting away in a bar."

He laughed, although he didn't know what for. The number thirteen popped into his mind. For fun, he asked, "What number am I thinking of?"

"Thirteen."

"Right!" He opened his eyes for a moment before she ran her palm over his eyes to close them again. "How do you do that?"

"Brain power. You are what you eat, remember?"

"Yeah, but maybe you can tell me how you did it. Show me the *real* trick."

"I thought you'd never ask."

She led him into the bathroom and turned on the water in the bathtub before undressing him hastily.

"Are we going to take a bath together?" he asked.

She directed him to sit in the bathtub. "Something like that. I like to wash my tasty treat before indulging myself."

*An odd way to put it.* His awareness floated in and out of consciousness, feeling more inebriated than he'd ever felt in his life. He struggled to open his eyes as he sat in the lukewarm water. Lying against the back of the tub, he relaxed and let the soothing sound of running water put him to sleep.

HE AWOKE SOMETIME LATER TO A HIGH-PITCHED whirring noise, then a loud crunch, and a sharp pain shooting through his spine like a bolt of lightning. Through blurry vision, he spotted Matilda kneeling beside him outside the bathtub. Everything was red: his hands, her hands, the walls of the bathtub, the water, Matilda's face.

He screamed, but no sound came out.

A long, gray string of matter hung between his scalp and her mouth. Shuddering almost uncontrollably, he stood in the bathtub and caught sight of himself in the mirror over the bathroom sink. The top of his head was gone as if someone had lifted the lid from a cookie jar.

Matilda yanked on the brain matter connecting them. "What an enchanting mind!" She slurped up each piece, chewing it ravenously.

"What the... the hell is..." He collapsed into the tub.

"Don't spoil the moment, Gary. I can't finish it all in one meal, you know. This will take all night."

# PUTTING HIM DOWN

Goldie jumped to attention when Roger lifted the camouflaged 12-gauge shotgun. The dog's ears perked up, and he stared at the weapon with wide eyes, as he'd always done before a hunting trip.

"Another day of hunting, right, boy?" Roger asked.

Goldie wagged his tail, still lying on the kitchen floor, but didn't jump around as he used to do years earlier. Those days were gone, and now Goldie had trouble getting outside to go to the bathroom, much less getting excited about another hunting trip.

"Yes, you can come along." Roger slipped on his hunting jacket. "This won't be an easy trip for either of us. Not like the good old days—this time will be different." He leaned down toward Goldie and stared into the dog's eyes. "Any last words?"

Goldie wagged his tail and stared back as if waiting for direction.

"I didn't think so." He removed Goldie's collar and set it on the kitchen counter while scratching the dog's neck. Goldie wouldn't need it anymore, and Roger would rather remove it now before they left to avoid getting blood on it. He would cherish the memento to remember their friendship over the years.

Roger led Goldie out to his truck and his dog wagged his tail all the way there just as he had so many times before, although now both of them moved a lot slower. Both of them had severe arthritis, but only one of them could do something about it. That's what Roger planned to do. He would take care of it.

Placing the shotgun into the back of the cab, he placed a box of rounds next to it. He wouldn't need an entire box to take care of it—he wouldn't miss—but he brought them along anyway, just in case things didn't quite work out the way he planned. *Got to have a Plan B.* No, he wouldn't miss, but Goldie was a tough Golden Retriever and might somehow survive the blast, even given Roger's marksman shooting skills. He wouldn't allow Goldie to suffer needlessly because of a miscalculation.

Roger opened the driver's side door to the truck to let Goldie climb in and step over to the passenger seat as they'd always done, except now the dog struggled to climb inside. Goldie couldn't get up far enough, so Roger rallied all his strength to lift him the rest of the way. Goldie's fur brushed against Roger's face on the way, and it brought back memories of when Goldie was a pup and used to cuddle in Roger's lap and lick his chin.

He pushed the thought away, watching Goldie limp over to the passenger seat and situate himself, then climbed into the driver's seat, finding he struggled to get in as the arthritis in his knees started acting up. Maybe after this last trip to the lake he would sell his truck and get something more easily accessible, something more appropriate for an eighty-three-year-old handicapped ex-hunter. With Goldie gone, no sense in keeping it anymore —the hunting adventures were in the past now.

"Two old dogs heading out for the last time." *But only one of us will return.* "I'll miss you, Goldie. You've been so good to me."

Goldie panted and looked around excitedly as Roger fastened his seatbelt and started the truck. He'd gone to great lengths to feed Goldie well that afternoon, giving him the highest quality last meal he could afford—they'd shared a T-Bone steak. "Nothing but the best for you, Goldie. You've been the best friend anyone could ask for."

Goldie barked once as if understanding his statement.

Roger patted Goldie's forehead. "It won't hurt. I'll make sure of that. I'll be careful and do it fast and put you out of your misery. It breaks my heart to see you suffer like that."

They drove out along the old country road at the edge of town, turning toward the forests and fields that surrounded the south end of the lake. Those were the good hunting grounds, as every hunter in the area knew, and held a special place in Roger's heart since he'd first gone duck hunting there with his father as a teenager. Most recently, Goldie had spent eighteen years of that time with Roger, accompanying him there the first time as a puppy, even if he did scare away the fowl more times than he cared to remember.

He tried to comfort himself along the way by reminding himself that everything would be fine. Lots of dogs got put to sleep every year. It was a humane, loving action that required a hell of a lot of courage. It was just the thought of what happened afterwards that bothered him. Wrapping Goldie in the plastic bag would be difficult, and then burying him there in the woods in the hole he'd dug a few days earlier. Did he have enough strength left to lift Goldie's dead weight?

Regardless, he *had* to do it.

And then how would it feel coming home to an empty house? That would be the hardest thing to overcome—the absence of his best friend. The silence. Goldie had never made much of a ruckus in the house, but Roger would miss the sound of Goldie's paws tapping along the hallway floor in the middle of the night on his way to get a drink from his water bowl in the kitchen. His eyes teared up.

Rumbling along the country roads, the gravel kicked up and dinged the underside of the truck. The setting sun was a brilliant red and orange. A beautiful epitaph to honor Goldie's faithful service all those years. The dark reddish-brown tones reminded Roger of the patches of fur around Goldie's neck.

Roger parked the truck where he'd always parked it near the lake, then helped Goldie get out before grabbing his rifle and stuffing his jacket pockets with a few extra rounds and a large garbage bag for the burial. A wooden box would have been more fitting for Goldie, but the extra weight might have been an issue, so he'd settled on the bag.

Heading off along the path leading them into the forest, Goldie's tail wagged a little slower now, but his limp had gotten a little better. Maybe the excitement of retrieving dead ducks had drowned out some of the pain.

During their previous and last hunt a month earlier, it became clear that Roger needed to do something drastic. The poor dog couldn't go on like that. Goldie struggled to keep up as Roger trudged into the forest, even at Roger's eighty-five-year-old slower speed, and it was then that Roger had known Goldie's days were numbered. And watching him suffer around the house was even more heartbreaking. The pain in Goldie's eyes was real as he limped to his water bowl and then stumbled on his way outside to urinate.

Now the fishy smell of the lake drifted through the air. Roger squeezed the barrel of his rifle. "Not far now, Goldie."

Goldie wagged his tail again and panted while moving a few feet ahead and looking around. He glanced back and met Roger's gaze, but he had to look away. It was too painful to think about what he was going to do. His heart ached deep down, but he knew it was the right thing.

Moving into the forest, they pushed through a clump of tall grass, and Goldie bounded through it like he had as a pup, but then he stumbled, crashing onto his side before recovering a few seconds later with an even greater limp.

"Take it easy, boy. Enjoy the day." Roger surveyed the forest. "No ducks today. It's just you and me."

Goldie glanced back as if not quite understanding the statement.

Roger had considered having a veterinarian put him to sleep, but he decided it wouldn't be right to let some stranger do it. He should do it himself, even if the choice was more of a *mess*. But it was only fitting that they shared their last moment together in the fields where they'd hunted for so many years. It wouldn't be too bad, anyway. Just a moment of pain, and then poor Goldie's suffering would end.

Goldie moved several feet ahead, glancing back every once in a while as Roger steered them to the clearing where they had hunkered down behind a group of fallen trees to wait for ducks to land at the edge of the lake beyond the trees. The hole Roger had dug earlier was near there too—a good spot to rest in peace. They had shot many ducks at that spot, but now the hunters were gone as the season was over, and soon the snow would blanket the ground and the lake would freeze.

Roger's heart beat faster as they moved into the clearing. Just a few more minutes and it would be time to pull the trigger.

Pain swept through his heart again. Is this really how he wanted to do it? Maybe the vet option wasn't so bad. He's shot so many animals over the years, but could he really do that to his dog? The question haunted him.

It was the veterinarian who'd suggested putting him down in the first place, making the convincing argument that it was the humane thing to do. And after so many trips to the office to treat Goldie's arthritis and other medical problems because of his old age, it was clear something had to be done. No point in allowing his suffering to continue like that.

Roger lifted his rifle and switched off the safety latch before aiming it toward the sky. He would play like they were hunting ducks until just the right moment when Goldie wasn't looking.

*He won't feel a thing*, Roger assured himself.

*I sure hope not.*

Goldie wouldn't even flinch at the sound of the shotgun blast. It amazed him that any dog wouldn't cower and run off after hearing a gunshot at close range, but Goldie had gotten used to it over the years. Was he even aware of the danger and the power in Roger's hands as the ducks dropped from the sky? It would be interesting to know what had gone through his dog's head during all those successful hunting trips.

Goldie turned back, and they stared at each other for a moment. It was time to say goodbye to his dog.

Roger lowered the rifle. "Goldie, come here."

Goldie hesitated for a moment, then limped back to Roger's side with his tail wagging. Roger tried to kneel in front of him, but found his own knee arthritis flaring up, so he leaned forward instead and scratched behind Goldie's ears. "I'm sorry I have to do this, boy, but better I do it than the doc. I'll see you on the other side."

Goldie licked Roger's hand as he stood straight and raised the rifle again.

Roger gestured toward the lake. "Stir me up some ducks, boy, for the last time."

But Goldie didn't move. He only sat and wagged his tail even as Roger acted out the same steps they'd gone through hundreds of times before.

Goldie barked, and Roger gestured again. "Go on now."

They shared another tense moment before Roger groaned and lowered his rifle. It was then that Goldie jumped to attention, but instead of moving toward the lake, he darted around behind Roger as if playing a game.

"Come on, Goldie." Roger turned to face Goldie again. "Don't make this hard on me. Just start walking away and I'll get this over with as easy as I can. You'll be better off."

Goldie charged forward, knocking into Roger's legs, then stopping in a playful pose a few feet away.

Roger stumbled backward and fell to the ground as the rifle hit a broken tree branch and blasted a shot into the grass. The world spun in his vision until he hit his head against a solid patch of soil. Pain shot through his spine. At least, it wasn't concrete.

With his head still throbbing, he sat up and spotted

Goldie panting and wagging his tail faster than ever. "What the hell, Goldie? This isn't a game."

Goldie barked and did another full circle around Roger before jumping in on top of him. Goldie licked his face, and it made him laugh for a few seconds, a flashback to the days gone by when Goldie had done the same thing to him as a puppy—maybe that's what Goldie had in mind, to just play in the fields and go back to the early years—but the gravity of the situation flooded back. He had a job to do.

Catching his breath, he stretched out his arm toward the shotgun in the grass beside him, but Goldie lurched toward it at the same time. Roger stretched as far as he could, touching his fingertips against the metal barrel before Goldie clutched the butt of the gun in his teeth, then dragged it away playfully.

"Oh, now, stop." Roger rolled his eyes. "I'm not playing with you this time."

Roger's joints and muscles ached, but turned on his side and crawled toward the rifle with one hand stretched out toward it. If Goldie intended to keep this up much longer, he would need to postpone his plans for another day. As Goldie dragged the shotgun through the grass, its barrel turned and aligned with Roger. If something even brushed against the trigger...

Roger stiffened. "That isn't a toy, Goldie. Just leave it there. Put it down, and I'll take care of it."

Goldie dragged it back further, all the time keeping the barrel aimed at Roger. Panic passed through him as he strained to move out of the blast zone in case the thing fired accidentally. Roger moved to the right, and Goldie countered him.

Goldie dragged the rifle back faster now into the long grass, and Roger stood again, brushing himself off before hurrying to retrieve it. "This isn't funny at all. Stop. I think I hurt my arm when I fell down."

A group of ducks quacked from the lakeshore as if taunting him.

Goldie hunkered down in the grass with only his head poking up and the rifle stretched out between them. *What the hell?* Did Goldie somehow understand what was going on? "We don't have to do this today, boy. I'll put it off until tomorrow, okay? Just drop the rifle and you'll win a day's reprieve."

Goldie's head shifted from side to side. Was he saying no? Did he understand what Roger was saying?

It didn't matter. He would get the rifle back and finish the job. Roger swallowed and clenched his fists before lurching toward it again. Goldie pulled back again, but Roger grabbed the barrel and pointed it away while towing it in.

With Goldie only a couple of feet away, Roger spotted the problem. Goldie's teeth were dug into the butt of the gun. That would explain his hesitation to release it and why his head had swung from side to side—he'd been trying to dislodge it from his teeth. He couldn't let go of it, even if he'd wanted to.

Roger reached out slowly toward Goldie with his palms down and spoke in a calm voice, "Okay, I see you got that thing stuck in your mouth now. I can't believe you had me going thinking you could understand me, but just stay still and I'll get you free. That's what you get for messing around, and you already caused so much trouble for me today that I'll commute your sentence for another day. How does that sound? We'll go home now and try again tomorrow." He stepped forward and reached toward the butt of the rifle, but with each step forward, Goldie also stepped back.

Goldie still didn't let go, but Roger tugged harder until it broke free. Roger took a deep breath and pointed the rifle away with it safely in his possession. "Good God, that was close." Goldie whined for a moment, then inched back deeper into the grass before turning around and running off.

"Where are you going?" Roger called out. "I said we could go home."

Goldie didn't go far. He peered back at Roger every few seconds, poking his head up from the grass with his ears perked as if expecting his master to start their usual duck hunt. His gaze jumped from the lake, to Roger, and then back to the lake as if something had caught his attention up ahead. He was running through the same actions as every other hunting trip. *Old habits don't die quickly. He's wanting me to hunt those ducks in the lake.*

"We're not out here to hunt today, boy. And now I'm too tired to go through with my original plan." Roger gestured for Goldie to come closer.

But Goldie rushed toward the lake, weaving around a fallen tree that they'd used a few times to conceal themselves while stalking ducks a few years earlier. Roger limped toward him as fast as he could as Goldie raced deeper into the forest. They circled around a group of trees and over a patch of dried, crackling branches before coming to a thick, fallen timber. Goldie climbed over it, still on his way to the lake, and Roger had no choice but to do the same. Every muscle in his body screamed and burned as he crawled over it and dropped on the other side to what he thought was solid ground. But his feet only met air as he fell into a hole.

Tumbling onto his back with the rifle in his lap, it took him a moment to realize what had happened. The hole was about three feet deep with fresh black soil on all sides. It was a familiar hole because he had dug it the previous day—the grave where he'd intended to bury Goldie.

"Damn." At least nothing was broken. He gasped for breath while struggling to stand, but he was only in up to his waist. It wouldn't be too difficult to get out, although when he'd dug the hole, he'd used a small step ladder to climb out.

Goldie grinned down at him from the top of a mound of black dirt next to the hole that Roger had created from digging it.

"Looks like our game has gone a little too far, boy." Roger scanned the area. "You might need to drag a branch over here so I can get out of this. But no more goofing around, okay? I've had enough."

Goldie turned around on the dirt mound with his backside facing Roger and clawed at the dirt for a moment before flinging pawfuls back into the hole. The dirt sprayed over Roger as if Goldie were trying to cover his poop after doing his business.

Roger leaned to the side and covered his face, trying to move out of the way as it rained down over his head and clothes. Dirt stuck to his lips and he spit it away. "Is that what I am to you? Just a pile of poop?"

He could shoot Goldie right there from inside the hole before things got any more awkward, but that wouldn't be right. Goldie was either playing or acting on some kind of animal instinct.

Despite the dirt splattering down on him, Roger struggled up the side of the hole by digging his boots into the dirt and snagging loose roots. As he inched up, Goldie inched away. By the time he'd pulled himself out, lying face down on the forest floor with his face and chest covered in sweat and black soil, he struggled to catch his breath. Every muscle was on fire, and he wondered if he could even make the short walk back to his truck.

Turning his eyes back to Goldie, he scowled. "What's gotten into you?"

Goldie perked up again, then looked away, his gaze fixated toward the lake as if something had caught his attention. There was no sound of any ducks or anything unusual, but Roger's hearing wasn't all that good anymore. All the gunfire over the years, even after using ear protection, had taken its toll. He opened his mouth to speak, but before he could say anything, Goldie hurried off toward the shoreline, disappearing into the tall grass.

After a brief rest and regaining some strength, Roger stood and called out Goldie's name a few times, pausing between each call. Nothing. If Goldie came back then, he would just leave and forget the whole thing. To hell with doing the right thing, it was too much trouble. He would let the vet take care of it.

He listened for any sounds that Goldie might return, but there was nothing now except the branches creaking, the leaves rustling in the trees surrounding him, and a few birds singing overhead while a gentle breeze blew across his face. No sign of Goldie, but he couldn't have gotten very far. The lake was only thirty feet away, just beyond the edge of the tall grass.

The rifle felt heavy now, and he lumbered with it toward the lake following the same path that Goldie had taken. Knocking branches out of the way, he spotted the clearing next to the shoreline where they had hunkered down many times to wait for a group of ducks to make an appearance. But his frustration drowned out the pleasant memories. He cursed under his breath. All he wanted to do then was get home and go to bed. The sun was low in the sky and it would be cold and dark soon. Nothing worse than the cold autumn air to exacerbate the throbbing pain in his knees. He hadn't expected to be out there so long, or to run into so many difficulties.

After reaching the clearing near the lakeshore, he spotted Goldie's paw prints in the mud along the shoreline. Most likely, Goldie had stepped into the water to get a drink, so he had to be nearby.

Roger faced the forest and called out as loud as he could manage, "Goldie!"

Almost at the same moment, something broke through the trees. With his back to the lake, he focused in on Goldie rushing toward him, bounding over the tall grass like he hadn't done in years. His dog's eyes were wide and wild, his mouth hanging open with his tongue swinging out on one side, and his ears flopping along for the ride. He couldn't believe the animal coming at him was the same dog that had limped so much earlier in the day, but there he was, jumping three feet at a time with each stride. And he was coming straight at Roger.

Before Roger could react, Goldie hit him like a bowling ball in the chest, knocking him back into the water with the rifle spinning away from his hands to slam down on the grassy shoreline.

Roger sank into the water, then came back up floundering. He knew how to swim, but Goldie had caught him off guard. He lost his breath in the collision, and his jacket and pants weighed him down in the water as he struggled to rise above it. Gagging and flailing his arms, he stood and cleared his eyes. As his focus returned, he spotted

Goldie beside the rifle on the shoreline. The barrel was pointing straight at Roger's chest. Goldie's aim was dead on.

It had to be a game. Roger held out his hand. "No, Goldie. Don't play with that."

Goldie was perched on the butt of the rifle, with the rifle lying sideways and one paw on the trigger.

Roger couldn't move. He wanted to drop back into the water or jump out of the way, but he knew there wasn't even time for that.

Their eyes locked, and sadness filled Goldie's eyes; a knowing that his best friend was doing the right thing as his paw slid slowly, meticulously against the trigger.

Roger relaxed and nodded once before the world went dark.


MORE FRIGHTFUL TALES IN BOOK 6! SEE NEXT PAGE FOR info!

# DREADFUL DARK BOOK 6
## TALES OF HORROR: BOOK 6

# ICE COLD

"Turn it up," Mr. Clifton J. Albert grumbled and twisted in his recliner in the living room. "I'm freezing in here!"

Rebecca rolled her eyes, shifted in her chair and turned back to her phone. She had wrapped three blankets over the old man, for God's sake. *Three.* She forced a smile and spoke as politely as she could. "I turned it up all the way."

Mr. Albert scoffed. "It's not enough."

Rebecca slumped and continued texting with her boyfriend, Johnny, before ending their conversation with *'Time to warm up Frosty the Snowman again.'*

She wasn't supposed to be on her phone, or do anything that might distract her from her job, which was to care for Mr. Albert's basic needs, but it wasn't like he was stuck in that leather recliner or anything. He *could* get up and walk if he *really* tried, especially if he needed something monumentally important like the TV remote. Sure, he would complain for a while, but eventually he would throw the blankets aside while bitching and moaning, and then waddle over just far enough to grab it.

Sometimes, just for fun, she would intentionally place the remote out of his reach to watch him squirm and fuss. A petty delight, but it helped break up the drudgery of her job.

Mr. Albert faced the TV, with his drooping profile outlined against a dark background. Maybe he could see her from the corner of his eyes, but he wouldn't look at her. He wouldn't take the chance to disturb the layers of blankets protecting him from the treacherously frigid eighty-two degree air. And if some part of a blanket *did* fall away from the old man's cloth cocoon, a rising wave of complaints would give her plenty of time to put away her phone. It wasn't like they paid her enough to *really* care about the old man anyway.

She walked over to Mr. Albert's side and stared down at him with her arms folded across her chest. It was better to avoid seeing him directly, as she'd learned, since his gaze would lock onto her chest and remain there for the duration of their conversation.

"What would you like me to do now?" Rebecca asked him.

He turned his head slightly toward her. "Throw more wood in the fireplace."

Two logs sat in the wood holder beside the fireplace. She tossed them into the blazing fire, on top of the other logs she had placed in there only an hour earlier, then stirred the charred wood with the fire poker.

At least Mr. Albert's crabbiness level subsided when it was hot. The sauna-like atmosphere seemed to calm him to the point of delirium. And she'd found that was a good time to bring up any important topics she had on her mind. And really, there was only one topic that kept her coming back day after day and putting up with his endless demands that would drive any other nurse bat shit crazy. The hidden cash.

Somewhere in that house, there were stacks of hundred-dollar bills and a few bars of gold. Not the little ounce bars, but the big ones. Kilo bars. She had seen the stash by accident a few weeks earlier after arriving early one morning, and he had practically lost his voice screaming at her to stay outside until her shift started. Any normal person would have quit immediately after being treated so horribly, but she couldn't shake the lingering image of what she had seen laid out on the old man's bed. So much money. She'd shaken off his verbal abuse moments later without the slightest bit of anger and with a renewed interest in taking care of him. She knew he was rich, but... damn.

Rebecca scanned the living room, as she had so many times before. That cash stockpile was somewhere in the house. Mr. Albert wasn't the type of person to take it to a bank. That wouldn't have worked for Clifton J. Albert. The old man had expressed so many times about his distrust of banks. The money had to be in one of the bedrooms or in the basement or... maybe only a few feet away. But she had never seen any sign of the cash since that one shocking morning.

She narrowed her eyes. *I will find it.*

Just like that, the old man who could barely take a few steps at a time without running out of breath had managed to tuck it away somewhere. It had to be in his bedroom or in one of the adjacent rooms but after stealthily seeking out any sign of a hidden safe or a shoebox stashed away under a bed, she hadn't located it.

But it was there *somewhere*, and she was sure as hell going to find it. It was the main motivator to continue working in that house, suffering through Mr. Albert's incessant needs. Nobody else would put up with working in his sweat factory like that. But when it was warm, then he stopped complaining, and it was time to turn on the charm.

It took another fifteen minutes for his breathing to slow enough to where she felt comfortable stepping around in front of him to chat a little. Wandering eyes or not, she would turn up the charm this time and squeeze the information out of him one way or another. Every day she had taken a little time to extract a bit of information about the fortune's location. Nothing that would give away her true motivation, but just enough to add another piece to the puzzle.

Now it was time to pry another puzzle piece out of the old buzzard.

She lingered by his side, then kneeled at his feet, reached her hands in under his blankets, and pampered him with a foot massage. Her gaze locked onto his eyes like a poker player waiting for a tell.

"How is that, Mr. Albert?" She asked in her sweetest voice. "All better now?"

He broke into a subtle, yet rare smile. "Better. For now."

She glanced around at the walls and ceiling, feigning interest. "I bet there's not much insulation in this house. Ever consider moving into a newer home?"

"Too expensive."

"But you might be a lot happier in a smaller place where you wouldn't need to heat so many rooms. I doubt you use them all."

Mr. Albert followed her gaze to a wall. "No point in

moving at my age. Too much work. Too much junk lying around."

"Nothing really heavy though. Right?" She scrutinized his eyes.

His pupils shifted down. "Not worth the bother."

*The basement.*

That made sense with all the cash in the house. Mr. Albert would almost certainly have stored it in a safe—a very heavy safe. Her heart quickened, and she tried to hold back her excitement at having narrowed down its location. Still, she hadn't found it yet, but at least she was close.

"You know..." She squeezed his feet a little harder. "I wouldn't mind giving you a full body massage, but that's not part of my regular duties as a nurse. I would have to charge extra for that. Does that interest you?"

He stared at her with blank eyes for several seconds before glancing away. "Get my checkbook."

"You know I can't take a check from you. Someone would find out. Cash only. Say... a thousand dollars?"

He scoffed. "I don't have that much."

"Can you find it somewhere?" She glanced around the room.

He shook his head. "I'll get it for you tomorrow."

"You know I don't work tomorrow. It's the weekend, remember? And I need the money to pay the rent, so maybe we could help each other out. Can we do that?"

He sniffed and scanned her clothes from top to bottom, then glanced down at the floor. "You'll need to leave the house for a while."

"What for?"

"To get the cash."

"How much time do you need?"

"An hour."

"My shift ends in half an hour."

He groaned. "It will take me too long to get it. Can't you just wait a few days?"

She shook her head. "This is a one-time deal, because I'm a little... desperate. Do you have the money in a safe?"

He shook his head slowly, but watched her without blinking. "Did you see it down there? Is that how you know?"

"I didn't see anything in the basement except the wood stove I keep running."

He narrowed his eyes. "You've been snooping."

"I don't snoop, and you don't need to tell me anything if you don't want to, but if it's somewhere difficult for you to reach, I could help you get there. Of course, I wouldn't tell anyone about it and you know I respect your privacy. If it's down there, then we can go now before I leave." She grinned. "No trouble at all."

Mr. Albert sighed. "I don't want to get up."

She nodded sympathetically. "I understand." She squeezed his feet again and moved her hands up a little higher around his ankles. "But it's for a good cause, right? And it's time for your walk anyway." She looked at her watch.

*Now the bitching and moaning.*

She stopped rubbing his feet and stood by his side again. "How about it? Might as well enjoy life and be happy."

"I'm happy under here."

She leaned in and tugged on his arm beneath the blankets. "When was the last time you went down there?"

"You know damn well the last time." He grunted. "You saw the money. That's what this is all about."

She chuckled. "I'd like to earn a little extra. That's all."

He relented and sat up, unfurling the blankets covering his chest.

She helped him into a standing position, although his face was strained as if she were subjecting him to some horrible torture. Then he started shivering, as he always did when she pried him out of his cozy chair.

"You're doing fine," she said.

He clung to her as she led him over to the door to the basement and they stepped down the stairs carefully while he clutched the handrail as if his life depended on it.

"This won't take long," she said. "And the reward will be *so* worth it."

"It better be, for a thousand bucks."

She laughed. "You won't regret it."

Arriving at the bottom of the stairs, she led him out toward the wood stove in the corner that she had agreed to keep running as part of her duties in taking care of Mr. Albert.

A stack of firewood sat beside the stove with an axe propped up beside it. Clutter blocked any chance of reaching the far walls. She doubted many people had ventured into his basement in decades.

"Alright, now. Which direction?" She scanned the nearest walls looking through every corner and shelf stocked with debris and dusty antiques. Perhaps it was behind a stack of items.

"I can get it from here. Go upstairs."

"But I should stay near you, at least. Look—" She turned away from him. "—I'll turn my back."

He grumbled. "If you turn around, you're fired."

"I promise I won't look." She laughed. "Let me know if you need help."

"I don't need help."

His footsteps scraped over the cement floor and she carefully plotted out in her mind where he was headed. He moved away, shuffling his feet and pausing every few seconds. No doubt, to look back and see if she had broken her word. An object scraped across the floor and he gasped twice.

"You okay over there?" she asked.

"Don't you worry about me. If I see even a glance back here..."

"I understand." She slipped her phone from her pocket and lifted it pressed against her chest, then switched on the camera to record the video. Maneuvering it over her right shoulder and filming in reverse with her hand cupped over the screen to block the light, she raised it just far enough to see Mr. Albert across the room. His back was turned away as she zoomed in on him, lowering it twice when it looked like he might suddenly turn and catch her cheating.

The old man removed a cheap brown section of wood paneling and spotted a massive black safe set into the wall. His fingers trembled as he pushed the numeric keypad to open the safe. She couldn't see the numbers from that far away but the pattern of his finger movements was clear. Something like... zero... six... one... nine... four... three.

The safe clicked open, and she lowered her phone with the numbers stuck in her mind. She held back a laugh. Yes, that was it. So simple and foolish since many people used the month and year of birth as their passwords. He wasn't so bright after all. June, 1943.

Her heart beat faster while dreaming of all the money that was now available to her.

She stealthily returned her phone to her pocket and listened as the crisp crinkling of dollar bills broke the silence. A moment later, the metal safe's door snapped shut and Mr. Albert replaced the wood paneling.

"Would you like me to load some wood into the stove while I'm down here?" she asked.

"That's your job, isn't it?" His footsteps shuffled closer toward her. "You can turn around now."

She faced him with a smile and stepped toward him. The money was in his hand, although it didn't matter. She would have all of it soon. After loading two logs into the wood stove, she led Mr. Albert toward the stairs. He grumbled while clutching the cash. "I don't know how the hell I'm going to get back up those stairs."

"That's my job, remember?"

"It is, but it's not as easy getting back up, and it's freezing down here."

While stepping toward him to assist him up the stairs, someone knocked at the front door. Rebecca looked at Mr. Albert. "Expecting someone today?"

"No." He groaned and shivered. "Not today. Get up there and tell them to go away, then get back down here. Probably one of those damn marketers."

Rebecca hurried up the stairs and rushed to open the door. She hoped her boyfriend hadn't stopped by unexpectedly, but was relieved to see a gangly old woman standing in a beige dress on the steps. She peered inside over Rebecca's shoulder. "Where is Robert?"

"He's doing well."

"Where is he? I have something for him." She held out a pan of freshly baked bread covered in a thin, clear plastic. The sweet smell filled the air.

Rebecca grabbed it. "I can give it to him."

The old woman didn't let go. "No, thank you. I'd like to

give it to him myself." She glared at Rebecca. "Where is he?"

"Downstairs."

The old woman formed an alarmed expression. "Downstairs? What on earth is he doing in the basement? You shouldn't have left him alone down there. What kind of nurse are you? He can barely walk."

"He's fine."

The old woman pushed her way past Rebecca. "Why isn't he in his chair? This is unacceptable."

"You don't have permission to come in," Rebecca said.

The old woman sneered. "Excuse me? I've known Clifton most of my life." The old woman stepped down the basement stairs, mumbling all the way. "You shouldn't let that nurse leave you like this."

Rebecca followed her down and came up behind Mr. Albert. "I left him to answer the door."

"Dolores," Mr. Albert said harshly, "we can talk about this another time."

Dolores looked around the basement. "What on earth are you up to in the basement, anyway?"

"It's not a good time," he said. "I'm fine."

"But I baked you some bread." She extended it toward him, but he didn't accept it.

Rebecca pushed past the old woman and helped Mr. Albert up the stairs. Dolores held out her arm toward him along the way, but he didn't take it. Within minutes, the old man was back in his recliner with a thick pile of blankets covering him.

"You just rest." Rebecca tucked him in like a child at bedtime.

Dolores grumbled and stood by Mr. Albert's side the whole time, scrutinizing everything Rebecca did.

"I'll take that." Rebecca pulled the pan of baked bread from Dolores's hands.

"He'd probably like some of this now."

Mr. Albert shook his head and closed his eyes.

Rebecca stepped over toward the front door although the old woman didn't leave Mr. Albert's side. Instead, she insisted the old man take a sip of water from a cup beside his chair, then stroked his hair before stepping over to Rebecca on the way out. The old woman moved in close to her and whispered, "You're not doing your job."

Rebecca swung the door open wide and the icy chill of the winter day rushed in. "I'm sorry you feel that way."

"Close the door!" Mr. Albert yelled.

Dolores frowned. "Are you? I think I will suggest he get a different nurse."

"Good idea." Rebecca rolled her eyes.

"You think it's all a joke taking care of him, and I'm not sure what you had him down in the basement for, but I'm going to find out."

"You do that."

"If you're taking advantage of him..."

Rebecca closed the door most of the way, leaving only an inch of space for them to talk. "Are you done?"

Dolores glared and turned away while thrusting up her chin. "I'll check on him later."

Rebecca snapped the door shut all the way and locked it. Under her breath, she whispered, "Good riddance."

Rebecca stepped over to the window and pulled back the curtain to watch the old woman walk across the street toward her home. There had always been the feeling that someone was watching Rebecca from that house. When she'd arrived every morning, the windows over there were dark yet uncovered. Maybe Dolores had a vested interest in the old man. Was she also trying to get at his stash?

*We'll just see who gets there first.*

Rebecca returned to the kitchen table and texted her boyfriend again.

*'I have a surprise for you.'*

*'I like the sound of that,'* he responded a few seconds later.

*'Meet me behind the house after my shift ends. The nosy woman across the street is watching, so be cool.'*

*'Will do.'*

She texted him the safe's combination. *'The winning lottery numbers.'*

*'Got it! See you soon, babe.'*

Only a few minutes before Rebecca was set to leave Mr. Albert's house, he started grumbling in his chair. Within seconds, he'd worked himself up to a shout. "The fire is going out. It's not hot enough. You can't leave me like this. I'm freezing!"

"My shift is done," she said.

"You're not done yet. We had an... agreement."

"Your neighbor friend spoiled the mood." Rebecca bundled up and prepared to leave before he could say anything more. "I'm heading out now."

"I need more wood!"

"No, you don't. The thing is full. It'll burn for hours."

She left Mr. Albert's house before he could make any further requests and took her time leaving to make sure that the old woman across the street had seen her leave. She would need an alibi when the questions would start pouring in the next day, and she exaggerated her movements so the old woman would see that she wasn't carrying anything besides her small nursing bag.

"See," Rebecca said with a grin, "I'm leaving. No bags

of money, and no need to worry about your precious Clifton anymore. He's tucked into his recliner like a good boy."

Rebecca took off down the road, just like she always did after working her shift, and pulling out of the driveway, she resisted the urge to give the old woman the finger. God knows she wanted to. But it was better to keep things as ordinary as possible. The sun was setting, and the fun was about to begin.

Instead of heading home, she circled around the block and turned into the alley behind the old man's house with her headlights off. Johnny's car was there, as expected.

He climbed out of his car when she pulled up behind him and approached her driver's side window. She rolled it down and beamed at him with a devious grin. He was carrying the pillowcase she had suggested he bring. They would need more than deep pockets to carry out all the loot.

"You did good this time, girl." Johnny reached in and touched the side of her face before kissing her.

"I can't stop thinking about it. We could finally afford a place of our own. Easy."

"I'm so proud of you. It'll be worth all the trouble."

Rebecca frowned. "I just don't want to go back in there anymore. I don't think I can face him again after this."

"You won't have to. Tomorrow, we'll head out and start a new chapter with all that money." Johnny turned toward the back door of the Mr. Albert's house. "Is he asleep?"

"He should be sleeping by now in his recliner in the living room. He won't get up, even if he hears a noise, but just be careful, okay?"

Johnny held his arms out and crouched. "I'm like a ninja."

"The basement door is about ten feet in on your left."
She glanced at his pillowcase. "You might need to make
more than one trip."

He grinned. "Are you serious? That much?"

"That much."

Johnny patted the car's roof, then swaggered away
toward the home's back door and she was left alone in the
seclusion of the alley.

Her heart raced while sitting there waiting for him to
return. What would she do with all that cash? It wasn't
enough to retire, but plenty to move away and live
comfortably for a few years, preferably in a warmer climate.
It was the old man's fault anyway for keeping that much
cash lying around the house anyway, and he certainly didn't
need it. Better that she take it off his hands and teach him
a lesson. Take from the rich and give to the poor.

*I'm poor.*

*Not anymore.*

She held back a laugh.

After fifteen minutes, she wondered what could be
taking Johnny so long to at least make the first trip out of
the house. Maybe he was trying to grab everything at once
and struggling with it.

After twenty minutes, she wondered if Johnny had
gotten lost inside the house or had failed to open the safe
for some reason. Had she given him the correct combination numbers? She lifted her phone and checked the
numbers again on the text message she had sent to him
earlier. Yes, that was it. So had she gotten the wrong
numbers? Her heart sank. She pictured her boyfriend
growing agitated in the darkness while trying to open the
safe. He'd never dealt with frustration very well.

After thirty minutes, she knew something had gone wrong, but she hesitated to go back inside. If Johnny had run into problems, he was more than capable of dealing with it himself, especially if it involved Mr. Albert. Still, she hoped nothing had happened to either of them.

After thirty-seven minutes, she thrust her car door open and hurried toward the house. A moment before she opened the back door, Johnny burst out and gestured for her to stop. Despite the lack of light, she spotted something on his hands and shirt. After years of working in the medical field, she had seen it many times. Blood.

She hurried toward him with her eyes wide. "What happened?" she whispered in a panic.

He held one hand over his chest while holding the door open with his other hand. "The old man put up a fight."

"What?" A sinking feeling swelled in her chest. "What did you do?"

He laughed. "He surprised the hell out of me, but I got him."

"What do you mean? We agreed, no violence."

"Get in here. He won't bother you anymore."

Rebecca followed Johnny inside and down to the basement where Mr. Albert lay on the floor huddled beside one of his blankets. Blood covered the old man's face and chest. She felt the urge to run to his side and help him, but her legs wouldn't move. Her gaze jumped from Mr. Albert's body to Johnny. "You killed him?"

"Had to. He got me with that thing." Johnny pointed to the axe lying on the floor in front of the wood stove. "I came down the stairs following your directions over to the safe and... I guess I didn't see him. He must have been down here already putting wood in the stove or something."

The doorbell rang.

Rebecca stiffened and met Johnny's gaze.

"The police?" Johnny asked.

"I doubt it."

"Still..." Johnny lurched toward Mr. Albert and pulled on his legs to reposition him near the blanket. Folding Mr. Albert's arms down at his sides, he rolled the old man up in the blanket like a burrito, then lifted one end of the wrapped body. "Grab the other end. Hide him."

"Where?"

Johnny gestured to a dark corner. "Over there."

Rebecca did as Johnny demanded. "We can still make it out the back door if we hurry."

"I haven't grabbed the cash yet."

"Not yet?"

Johnny gestured to the old man. "I had to deal with *him*. Yeah, it's probably not the police. He didn't scream or anything."

"Dolores." *Coming back to check on her, Clifton.*

"Who's Dolores?"

"The old woman across the street."

The doorbell rang again and the front door creaked open. Dolores had *walked right in.*

They dragged Mr. Albert's body into the darkness as far out of sight as they could get, and then hunkered down beside him as the intruder's footsteps creaked across the floor above them.

"Clifton?" Dolores's voice called out.

*Go the hell away. If you come down here, Johnny will kill you.*

"Clifton?" The old woman called out again. Judging by her footsteps, she went across to his bedroom and then circled around to the kitchen before arriving back near the front door.

Johnny stepped over and carefully picked up the axe near the firewood. He raised it to his chest with a hardened expression and returned to Rebecca's side.

She swallowed. This was getting way out of hand. She only wanted to get the money and get out of there.

But the basement door opened and the old woman called out again, "Clifton? Are you down there?"

Rebecca held still, although she trembled in the warm basement air as Johnny adjusted his grip on the axe.

They stood in the shadows with Mr. Albert rolled up at their feet, but if Dolores got nosey and came down, she would see them and all the blood. Johnny wouldn't have any other choice but to silence the old woman too.

*Go away! Go away!* Rebecca screamed in her mind.

But Dolores switched on the light and descended the stairs while muttering to herself. She stepped across the basement and stopped near the wood stove for a few seconds.

Rebecca expected her to scream at any moment. They could see her, and if she stared over at them, she would see them too. Rebecca's heart pounded in her ears as the room filled with silence before the old woman turned back up the stairs.

Johnny stepped forward with the axe as if to race after her, but Rebecca held him back.

"Please," she whispered, "don't kill her."

Johnny furrowed his brow and shrugged her away. "She'll call the goddamn cops."

"She didn't see us."

"We can't be sure."

Dolores's voice called out for Clifton several more times as her footsteps stomped through the rooms.

Rebecca grabbed Johnny's arm and pulled at him to keep him from charging after Dolores. "Let her go. She'll leave soon." She gestured toward the open safe where his pillowcase lay open on the floor. "Just grab the money and I'll let you know when she's gone. There's still time."

Johnny grumbled, but dropped the axe and continued filling the pillowcase with the cash from the safe.

After the front door slammed shut, Rebecca hurried upstairs and peaked out of the window facing the front of the house. Dolores had made it across the street already and would be inside her own home within a few seconds. The old woman's billowy jacket hood waved in the winter wind beneath the streetlights. The coast was clear again, but Johnny was right. Dolores would call the police after not finding Clifton. They would need to hurry.

A loud thump came from the basement. Johnny moaned and then a loud crack filled the air.

Rebecca hurried to the top of the basement stairs and called down, "Johnny? Get up here. She's gone."

An even louder crack filled the air. A sharp metal hit against cement. Then another crack.

"What are you doing?" Rebecca yelled down to him. "Let's go."

No response from Johnny.

She stepped down into the warm musty air and before she reached the bottom she spotted Johnny lying on the ground in a pool of blood. Mr. Albert stood over him wielding the bloody axe, lifting it then dropping it down against one of Johnny's arms.

Crack.

Her boyfriend's arm split away from his body and blood sprayed from the open wound.

Mr. Albert reached down and picked up the severed limb, then lifted it a little higher and met Rebecca's gaze. His eyes were glazed over and his face was drained of blood—he was dead—yet he grinned while extending the severed arm toward Rebecca. His words gurgled up through his throat. "I'm freezing. Didn't you hear me?"

Rebecca stumbled back.

He stepped over to the wood stove and dropped the arm into the wood stove's flames with a satisfied grin. "Ah, that's better."

# BIRTHDAY GIRL

Jane awoke with her face pressed down into the cool grass. Sweat covered her cheeks—or was that just dew?—and a cool breeze streamed gently over the back of her neck.

She turned over and sat up. Every muscle ached, and she groaned while glancing around through blurry eyes. It was still dark and moonlight illuminated her surroundings enough to realize that she was completely lost.

Nothing was familiar. Not the trees, or the grass, or the open field behind her. But the grass was maintained, so she couldn't be too far from a residence or a road. A crow cawed in the distance within the gentle whisper of the grass and rustling branches.

Her head throbbed as if from a terrible hangover. Had she even gotten drunk the night before? She strained to remember. It had been her birthday, but most of it was a blur as far back as the previous morning when she had come out for breakfast, flipped on the TV, and made herself comfortable on the couch in the living room. She'd had the day off and had planned a special day for...

Natalia.

Jane's heart raced as she glanced around the darkened landscape. Her friend had been with her the previous day, so where was she now?

*Jane, you couldn't have gotten so drunk that you forgot about Natalia?*

She shook her head. "No."

But trying to remember anything from the night before was like trying to break through a brick wall with her forehead. Panic swelled in her chest, but she took a deep breath. No time to freak out. She wouldn't have just left Natalia alone out in the middle of nowhere. Her friend would be somewhere nearby.

She rubbed her eyes and touched her face, remembering that she'd lost her glasses. Not a big deal. Her vision wasn't *that* bad, but the details were hard to make out.

Branches creaked and something cracked within the small group of trees nearby. She studied the shadows and shouted. "Natalia?"

A groan erupted from somewhere not too far away.

"Natalia, is that you?"

No answer. Either it was her friend unable to respond, or an animal. But *something* was moving through the brush ahead.

Whatever it was, she couldn't just ignore the danger of her situation. She struggled to her feet and a rush of fresh pain sent her vision spinning. With nothing to grab onto, she staggered forward.

She shivered, although the air was warm. Pressing her fingers to her chest to scratch an itch, she touched bare skin where her shirt should be. It wasn't just an itch. Something had ripped open her shirt and within the torn fabric she found a deep cut running the length of her finger, still wet and warm. She dragged her fingertips over the sliced flesh and winced from the pain.

*Where the hell did that come from? What did I do last night?* In any case, it would need stitches.

She wiped the blood onto her shirt and moved toward the low, guttural sounds of someone struggling nearby. The soft voice could only belong to Natalia. Had someone injured her too?

"Natalia, I'm here," Jane called out.

Who would have attacked them? Her memory of the previous night still failed her, but the injuries could only have happened after she'd passed out. No way she would have slept through such a traumatic injury. A robbery? Or sexual attack? She ran her fingers over the other areas of her body. Nothing felt different. No pain below her waist, anyway. Could an animal have caused the wound after she'd passed out on the grass? A coyote taking a swipe at her body to test her reaction before preparing to bite off a slice of her flesh as she lay defenseless?

The groans continued near the trees ahead.

"Natalia, where are you?" Jane turned her head to locate the source. "Keep talking."

"Here." Natalia whispered, her voice almost swept away by the wind. "Over here."

Jane followed her voice. "I'm coming for you."

At least the temperature hadn't dropped as low as it could be for a September night in Minnesota. If the ordeal had happened in January, she doubted either of them would have survived.

A moment later, Jane spotted Natalia's outline. Her friend was sitting up leaning against a tree, although slumped to the side with her arms folded over her chest.

Jane hurried to her side and dropped onto her knees

beside her in the grass. They embraced, although Jane avoided touching her wound against her friend. Jane wiped her friend's hair away from her face. "Are you okay?"

"I think so." Natalia looked up slowly. "I don't feel good."

"Are you hurt?"

She nodded and laughed weakly. "Everything hurts."

Jane ran her hands over her friend's clothes. "Anything broken? Cuts?"

"No. Where are we?"

Jane glanced around. "I don't know, but we can't stay here. Can you stand?"

"Probably, but my legs are so tired. Like I just ran a marathon."

"I feel the same way. Do you remember anything from last night?"

"I remember going with you."

Jane nodded. "Where? Where did we go?"

Natalia turned her head and stared into the darkness. "Not sure, but I *think* we had fun. Right?"

Jane shrugged. "Too much fun, apparently. Who were we with? Where did we go? To see friends?"

Natalia paused for several seconds. "Something like that. I remember feeling good about it, looking forward to going with you."

Jane looked around into the darkness. "Something went wrong."

Natalia fell silent.

"Someone might have drugged us," Jane said. "Do you remember accepting a drink from anyone?"

"I don't remember drinking at all, but I'm sure I did. My head hurts a lot and my mouth is dry."

"What's the *last* thing you remember?"

"Being at the apartment with you, and then we got ready to go somewhere. You were smiling."

"Were we going to a party?"

"Yes, something like that. Some sort of gathering where everyone was happy. I just remember so many smiles. Everyone was smiling at me."

Jane stared at her friend and nodded. "Yes, it was all about you."

"We should call someone."

The suggestion surprised Jane. She hadn't even thought to call for help. Checking her back pocket, she discovered that her phone was gone. Had someone robbed them? "My phones's gone. Do you have yours?"

Natalia dug into her pockets and she groaned. "It's gone! I must have left it back..."

"And that was...?"

Natalia shook her head. "Why can't I remember? This is crazy."

Jane looked around and strained for any signs of lights nearby. "We can't be too far from home." A sharp pain flared through her chest wound and she winced.

"You okay?"

Jane nodded. "For now, but I need to see a doctor. Something cut me."

Natalia's eyes widened and patted down her clothes. "You think we were assaulted?"

"I'm not sure. The cut isn't deep, at least. I might have just run into a branch or fallen over." Jane rubbed her side of her head. "I wish I could remember... anything."

Natalia groaned louder while trying to stand. Jane held her friend's arm until she stood and stabilized on her feet.

"We might not feel like it, but we have to get moving.

There must be a house around here, or at least a road we can follow, maybe wave down a car."

"What if whoever dumped us out here is still around, waiting for us?"

Jane scanned the surrounding trees. "Then we'll fight back."

Natalia wavered. "Jane."

"What?"

"I don't feel so good. Like throwing up."

"They must have drugged us. I feel the same. Do what you need to do."

Jane held Natalia's arm as they moved forward through the darkness. No plan, except to just keep moving ahead. The surrounding trees obscured the landscape, but the moonlight provided enough light to weave through the trees and brush.

After a few minutes, a light led them to the edge of a sprawling property. A house sat beyond a cornfield, with one light on over the porch, but all the windows were lit up as if someone had turned on every light in the house.

Jane gestured to the house without slowing down. "We'll go there."

Circling around the cornfield, a flurry of noises erupted within a clump of trees. Shadows moved and a rustling sound grew louder. Jane paused to stare toward the distur-bance, but without her glasses nothing stood out clearly.

"You see something?" Natalia asked.

"No," Jane answered. "Could be my imagination."

Natalia walked faster. "I want to get out of here."

The noises within the trees faded as they moved closer to the house. Maybe their attackers had returned to finish them off, but the presence of other people had scared them away.

Jane's chest ached. She touched the edge of her wound again, trying to cover it a little more with her shirt although every sensation sent a sharp pain shooting through her brain.

"Do you think someone's home?" Natalia asked. "I don't see a car."

Jane looked ahead and focused on the lights illuminating the upstairs windows. No shadows moving within the house, but that was no surprise. Everyone would be asleep at that time. "They won't be too happy about us waking them up."

A sudden urge to collapse and fall asleep in the grass swept over Jane. If it hadn't been for Natalia at her side, she might have done just that. The surging fatigue weighed on her body for a long minute before it subsided. More evidence that someone had slipped a drug into her drink?

Still, she trudged ahead while her stomach growled. She hadn't noticed any pangs of hunger earlier, but all of a sudden she craved food. Licking her parched lips, her thirst grew stronger too.

As they crossed the front lawn of the stranger's property toward the door at the side of the house, a deep relief spread through her. They were safe in the light.

Natalia arrived at the door first and glanced back while holding her fingers near the doorbell. "Should I?"

Jane nodded. "Do it."

The doorbell rang inside and they waited. Maybe the owner would call the police, but they really had no choice. And how would the strangers react to seeing all the blood on her shirt? She wouldn't blame them for treating them with suspicion. But if they could get a ride home, everything would be fine.

Jane listened for the familiar noises within the house

that someone was on their way to the door, but there was only silence. She gestured to the doorbell. "Push it again."

Natalia pushed it twice. "They definitely won't be happy about this."

"Nothing we can do about it."

But the house was still silent.

There was a tall, narrow window beside the door. Jane leaned over and peeked inside, then gasped. A long hallway led to the back of the house where the glaring lights illuminated a horrific scene. Two women and a man lay mangled in a pool of blood on the floor, their flesh torn apart as if something had attempted to devour them. Jane held in a scream.

"What's wrong?" Natalia leaned in to look.

Jane pulled her back. "You don't want to see this."

"What's in there?"

"They're dead."

Her friend's face reflected the terror welling up in Jane's chest. The wounds on the bodies were fresh, and the murderer could still be nearby.

She turned back and stared into the darkness near the cornfield and the trees. It was all darkness beyond the light of the porch, yet her skin tingled as if feeling someone watching them. Whether the noises were human or animal, they weren't alone. Whatever had happened inside the house could happen to them if they weren't careful.

Despite the gruesome scene inside, Jane glanced through the window again. The bodies were sprawled out over the floor, frozen in the horror of their last moments with their eyes wide and mouths gaping. Blood had streaked over the floors and splattered against the walls. Some of the innards were strewn over a small side table, dangling like giant worms. Muscles were stripped from the bones and shredded. Even without her glasses, her imagination filled in the details.

"What should we do?" Panic rose in Natalia's voice.

Jane hesitated to answer. Would it be safer to make a run for it or get inside and hide until the police arrived? There had to be a phone in there somewhere. But if she called the police, would they consider her and Natalia suspects? They had no alibi for their presence at the house and the bloody cut across Jane's shirt.

Without doubt, the police would arrest them.

She stepped away from the door. At least she hadn't touched the door handle yet. "We can't stay here."

"Why not?"

Jane glanced back into the darkness of the cornfield. Within the rustling stalks of corn, someone had laughed. Her heart beat faster. This wasn't an animal who'd committed the atrocities in the house, but a person out there stalking them.

"Did you hear that?" Natalia asked.

Jane nodded. "They're still here. We need to run."

Natalia stood wide-eyed, staring at Jane as if waiting for instructions. They could make it to the road—Natalia was a fast runner—but how far would they get before the murderer caught up with them?

She glanced back inside the house. There would be weapons inside, at least kitchen knives, to defend themselves. Something caught her eye. A familiar item lying next to one of the bodies.

Glasses. *Her* glasses? "No way."

"What's wrong?"

Without explaining, Jane pulled the screen door open and rushed inside the house. There was no time to wait for whoever was out there to catch up with them. At the very least, she would need to retrieve her glasses. But a greater realization hit her. If her glasses were inside the house, then *they* had been there before, and her fingerprints would already be everywhere.

*Shit.*

Natalia hesitated. "I thought we were going to run?"

"We can't now." Jane paused a moment for Natalia to catch up. "Get inside and lock the door. Lock all the doors."

Natalia stepped inside and she screamed.

"Look away from them." Jane headed for her glasses first. No blood on them, but they were bent a little as if they'd fallen from her face. She put them on and scanned her surroundings for anything they might use as a weapon.

"How could anyone have done such a thing?" Stepping around the bodies and blood, Jane stared at the raw flesh with curiosity. She tried to shield her friend from the sight of the massacre, but it was impossible.

Natalia inched toward the bodies and whispered, "They look... familiar."

"How?" Jane followed Natalia's gaze and focused on their faces. They *did* look a little familiar.

"Someone we met in town?"

Jane slowed, even as her heart pounded in her ears. But the victims were nobody she had known personally, not as a friend or relative anyway, but she *had* encountered them before.

"Doesn't matter now." Her gaze fixated on the carnage. Someone hadn't just torn their bodies apart. They had ripped away most of the innards. The remains across the floor showed signs of teeth marks as if the attacker had attempted to eat them.

"We have to call the police."

Jane's stomach growled again, louder than before. "We can't. Not yet, anyway. If we wipe down the door handles and…"

Natalia's eyes widened. "You aren't thinking of leaving them like this, are you?"

Jane folded her arms over her chest. "Someone will find them."

Natalia shook her head. "That's not right."

"Think about it, Nat." Jane pointed to the door. "Whoever did this is still out there. They're obviously out of their minds to commit something like this. We need to leave. *Now.*"

Natalia paused and stared at the body of a man nearby. His pajama top had been torn apart, leaving only his collar and sleeves to absorb the bloody mess sprayed over the area.

"We need weapons," Jane said, "then we'll run."

Natalia nodded slowly with a frown, then hurried around the corner toward the kitchen.

Jane stayed behind and stared down at the bodies. It wasn't just hunger gnawing at her stomach, but a ravenous pressure that grew more intense the longer she stared at the strips of meat still attached to the exposed bones.

*God, Jane, what's gotten into you?*

She was repulsed, not so much from the gore, but from the revulsion of her thoughts. *I'm hungry… from staring at that?* That hunger gnawing at her insides came from an attraction—a craving—for the exposed meat laid out across the floor like a delicious meal ready at the table.

She leaned toward the body of the woman closest to her and considered dropping to her knees, if only to get a better look.

A better look at what? The corpses? Or the *meat?*

The meat. Definitely the meat. A savory meal just waiting for consumption. Why waste it? It sounded like such a fantastic idea to get right down there and dig in, to pull a chunk of that muscle away like ripping away a leg from a whole roasted chicken. The desire to eat the raw flesh astonished her, but she couldn't pull away from the fixation to devour it. She salivated.

*Was I involved in this woman's murder? Did I do this?*

The question alarmed her, but it wasn't ridiculous.

Natalia returned a moment later with two kitchen knives. She handed one to Jane. "There's a cell phone on the counter. I'm not sure I agree with you that we should just run. We should call the police."

Jane shook her head without looking away from the woman's body near her feet. "Maybe we can sneak out the back... after we're done."

"Done with what?"

The front door rattled. A moment later, someone pounded against it while shouting something.

"Jane?" Natalia pulled her toward the kitchen. "Let's make the call."

Jane followed her, but before Natalia reached the phone, someone rattled the back door.

"We're surrounded." Natalia turned to face the door and raised her knife. Her friend's face was full of fear.

The hunger pangs intensified as Natalia picked up the phone and prepared to dial Emergency. Jane stopped her while staring at the phone. "That's *my* phone."

Natalia's face was full of confusion and fear. "Don't you want me to call? What should we do?"

Jane scanned the area for a place to hide, although the people outside must have seen them inside. Pulling Natalia along, Jane spotted the streaks of blood over her friend's black pants. *She* had been inside the house before as well. Could her friend also have taken part in the murders? But why couldn't she remember the events of the previous night? Had it been so traumatic she'd blocked it out?

"Which way?" Natalia's voice strained with panic.

Jane hurried across the room toward a doorway with Natalia racing behind her. Throwing the door open, Jane spotted herself in a bathroom mirror. She didn't recognize the woman staring back at her. There was more than just a bloody wound across her chest. Her face and hair were matted with blood, and small chunks of flesh had lodged in her hair and dried on her clothes.

The revelation alarmed her. Were the people at the door out for justice against *them*? A memory flashed into her mind at the same time. A disturbing glimpse of what had happened.

Instead of continuing the frantic race to hide, Jane leaned forward toward the mirror and exposed her teeth. Blood stains and bits of flesh were lodged between her gums and teeth.

No doubt in her mind. *She* had done that. And her friend had participated too.

The door to the house flew open and footsteps trampled in.

Natalia prodded her. "Jane, they're coming in. I'm dialing."

Jane grabbed away her phone. "No, don't call anyone."

"Why not?"

Jane slumped into her friend. "No sense in running anymore."

"What do you mean? We need to leave." Natalia's eyes widened while grabbing Jane's arm and pulling her toward the back door. "We've got knives. We can still escape out the back and hide outside. I'm sure we can get away."

But the footsteps thundered through the hallway toward them and stopped in the hallway near the bodies. An unfamiliar noise rose within the commotion. A slurping sound, then cracking bones, followed by joyful utterances and soft conversation.

"Jay-ane." A woman's gravelly voice called out melodically. "Come out, come out, wherever you are."

The woman's voice was familiar, and Jane relaxed as more memories returned.

Natalia's eyes widened. "It's..."

Jane nodded. "I remember now."

"Don't you like us anymore?" A man's grumbly, familiar voice rose above the others. It was her friend, Marcus. A man she had known since her childhood. He had driven them to the house the previous night. How could she have forgotten him?

She stepped out of the bathroom toward the hallway and relaxed the grip on the knife in her hand. Natalia followed her.

Coming around the corner into the hallway, her friends were on their knees over the bodies finishing the spoils of their previous night's meal.

Shannon's face and neck were also covered with blood. She looked up with a malicious grin. "Is it wearing off so soon?"

Natalia shuddered, but she didn't run. "Is what wearing off?"

Shannon laughed. "She doesn't remember yet."

"What a shame," Marcus said.

"But you will. You can never forget your first time."

Jane turned to Natalia. "Think back before they

injected you. You were so excited about going hunting with us. The amnesia side effect fades over time, but everything will come back."

Marcus groaned while chewing on the bloody muscles of someone's arm. "So delicious."

Jane didn't seem to notice Marcus's reaction to his food. She watched Natalia's face. "Do you remember now?"

Natalia silently looked over the bodies, her face full of confusion, until her gaze stopped on the blood splattered over her shirt. She smiled and nodded. "That was... amazing."

"Did you like it?" Jane pulled her friend closer. "You did very well for your first time."

"Every month," Marcus shouted. "Every full moon you can do it with us."

Shannon laughed and continued ripping off a part of the woman's arm using her teeth.

"I thought I would... transform, you know, like in the movies."

"No, we tried to explain. It doesn't happen like that. The wolf is structured completely different, so it mani-fested only the primal traits in our behavior. All the animal's survival instincts come out in full effect, and, of course, the... cravings. You became the wolf for the evening, saw the world through their eyes, but it takes a while for you to transition back to human thoughts. Did you enjoy the experience?"

Natalia grinned. "Very much!" She gestured to the body near Marcus. "Why are you still eating them? Aren't you a human now?"

Marcus shook his head and laughed with a mouthful of blood. "We came down just a little before you did, but the craving is still there. Not much left in me, but the hunger always lingers longer than the other traits. Better make the most of it while I can."

Jane nudged Natalia forward. "Have another bite. I'm sure you're still hungry, right?"

Natalia looked back at her. "I am."

"Then don't hold back. You'll regret it if you don't. You'll go home hungry and that's the worst."

Natalia stepped toward the body of the man. "I killed him, didn't I?"

Jane nodded. "It was a work of art. I'm so proud of you! It wasn't so difficult, right?"

Natalia shook her head. "It was fun. Exhilarating, actually."

Shannon chuckled. "Told you so."

Natalia touched her stomach. "It's strange. I'm still hungry, but I'm full."

"You *did* eat a lot," Jane said.

Shannon moved up beside Marcus. "You can eat a lot more than you think you can right now. Your body has changed temporarily, so might as well enjoy it before it wears off." She made a wide gesture over all the bodies. "Dig in, girl. You think we can eat all of these ourselves?"

Marcus finished the meal in his hands and tossed the bone aside. "I can try! Bon appétit."

Shannon stepped over to the man's leg and raised it up before snapping it off at the knee, ripping the flesh with ease. "I can see it in your eyes. You'll still be hungry for a few more hours."

Natalia backed away and then hurried around the corner to the bathroom where they had hidden earlier.

Jane listened while her friend regurgitated all that she'd eaten previously. "Maybe she's not as strong as I thought."

Shannon chewed on the end of the leg and spoke between mouthfuls. "I did the same thing my first time. It's only natural."

Jane waited for her friend to finish before stepping over to the bathroom and checking on Natalia. "Natalia? We can go home soon, if you'd like. We'll try again next month."

Natalia wiped her mouth and stepped out of the bathroom with a grin. "No. I'm ready now for the second helping."

# STICKY FINGERS

Julia had never really looked at the machete hanging on the wall over Donnie's bed. It had always been up there, but now she scrutinized it. Was it real? Donnie had bragged about using it to intimidate his workers occasionally, but she'd never given it a second thought before.

*She'd never needed a weapon before.*

The overhead light gleamed off the blade. It had to be real—Donnie wasn't one to possess cheap imitations—although she had never seen it up close. The blade's edge was worn yet sharp.

*Good enough to slice through Donnie's throat.*

She grinned, but turned her head away from him. Better that he didn't see the sudden expression of joy. This was the answer she'd been waiting for, and it had been right there in plain sight all along. Her heart beat faster as her mind filled with dark fantasies and her naked body tensed beside him, with her chest and head draped over his legs.

Donnie shifted, then crawled out of bed and headed for the bathroom.

Julia pretended to sleep, but after the bathroom door closed she carefully stood on the bed and removed the machete from the wall. Donnie wouldn't miss it—not in the haze of a morning hangover anyway. She doubted he would even look up from his phone long enough to notice *her*, much less his prized weapon. There were some guns in the house too, but he always kept those locked up. A machete would do just fine.

A big shipment would arrive within the hour. Donnie had said nothing about it to her—he rarely said anything, and she never asked—but they had been together long enough to pick up the patterns of his business, and something *goooood* was on its way. The incoming stash would generate more money than she could earn in several years, and he'd made it quite clear she had to leave the house for the rest of the day. With so much money exchanging hands, he wanted Julia to be safe. But that was a lie, of course. The truth was, he didn't trust her.

*Smart man. I'm not one to be trusted.*

The previous night, he had transferred the cash he planned to use for the big deal to a smaller safe upstairs. But in his drug-induced stupor, he'd made an egregious mistake by leaving several stacks of hundred-dollar bills on the dresser after counting it out on the bed, and had forgotten about some of it. Well... not so much *forgotten* about it as she had *hidden* it from him after intentionally throwing a pink lace nightgown over it, then sliding it into the top drawer after he stepped away. More like he had stopped noticing it. A wide grin crept over her face. It was more than enough cash to buy her way back home to the sunny beaches of Brazil.

*Shouldn't have left in the first place.* But the lure of easy money and a ruggedly handsome man's promises had captured her sense of adventure, if not her heart.

But money wasn't the biggest obstacle to her escape. It was the hulk of a man showering in the bathroom. She sneered at the bathroom door, but swallowed her bitterness—no time to deal with her feelings now.

As soon as she clutched the machete, she climbed off the bed and slipped the weapon beneath the sheets. Her hands trembled as she dressed in panties and a bra, but nothing else—not yet—Donnie didn't like missing the chance to watch her get dressed in the morning, and she needed to follow her morning routine and act normal or he'd suspect something. She pushed aside all the fear as adrenaline surged through her chest.

*You got this, girl.*

Donnie wouldn't go down easily. And there could be no mercy with a man like that. He wouldn't hesitate to slice her into little pieces for betraying him if she didn't succeed. It was just a matter of waiting for the right moment to strike. With the weapon hidden beside her, there was no turning back now.

Donnie came out of the shower wrapped in a white towel. The tattoos covering his arms and chest were slick over his damp skin with a cobra tattoo running down his left arm with the head of the snake ready to strike from the back of his hand. The snake's tongue ran a little further, ending like a kiss at the gold ring on his pinky finger.

He glanced up from his phone and formed a subtle grin. "How is my little doll feeling this morning? Did I leave you out of breath last night?"

"Yes, of course."

He paused and stared at her. "Something on your mind?"

"No." She forced a smile. "Nothing, babe."

"Nothing? You know that's a woman's code for something. And you got that look on your face."

She shrugged and sat on the bed. "Do I have a look?"

Donnie laughed while his eyeing her panties and bra. "Why did you get dressed so early? Going somewhere?"

"I was cold."

"And *those* will help you warm up?" His gaze dropped to her hands as if she might be concealing something. "You're transparent. Can't hide anything from me. It's the main reason I still keep you around, so what do you say if we go out for a long walk after I'm finished with today's business? Clear our minds after everything that happened last night."

"Yes, I'd like that. But it didn't bother me."

"Didn't bother you? You nearly strangled poor Alexander. He's a good worker. I can't have that, you know, it's not good for business."

"I know, but..."

"He was one of my best customers. It will take a lot of trouble to get him to return. Do you know that?"

"I know. I'm sorry."

"Sorry," Donnie repeated while stepping forward until he stood over her as she sat on the edge of the bed. He ran his fingers through her hair and across her neck. "In order to win, I can't make any more mistakes like that. Do I look like a loser?"

"No, babe."

"That's right, because I'm a winner—always a winner—and you need to learn your place here if you want to share in my victories. Do you understand?"

"I understand."

He squeezed her neck. "Do you? I think a long walk will do us a lot of good."

"I agree."

"Get dressed now. My friends will arrive soon." Donnie stepped away and turned his back on his way to the dresser.

Julia glanced over at the bulge in the sheets beside her and her heart beat faster. This was her moment, but she hesitated.

Donnie's towel slipped open and dropped to the floor as he started to get dressed in front of her.

Her fingers inched toward the machete. It was so close, and it would only take a few seconds to pull it out and lodge it into the back of his neck. But her muscles tensed as her heart pounded in her chest. She stared at his bulging muscles. If she missed...

Donnie spun around and stared up and down her body. "I told you to get dressed."

She nodded nervously with wide eyes, trying to calm her trembling hands. "I will."

"Now."

She stood and forced an affectionate smile. *I have to do it now. To grab that blade and slash it across your throat. Now.* Her vision wavered for a moment, either from the hangover or the terror surging through her body. Her legs weakened.

"What's wrong?" Donnie asked with irritation.

She gasped in a breath. "A cramp, I think."

"That's your excuse for everything."

Julia faked a laugh. "I guess it's a woman thing."

Donnie frowned and turned away again as he continued dressing.

The opportunity had arrived. Julia turned back to the bed, slipped her hand under the sheets and retrieved the machete, holding it up with both hands while fixing her gaze on his neck.

While buttoning his pants, he turned toward her again with that same sneer she had hated for so long. She met his gaze for a moment with the blade high over her head, and his cocky sneer fueled her rage as she clenched her teeth and thrust the weapon toward his neck with every ounce of strength in her.

He didn't scream, even as the blade slammed into the lower edge of his shoulder below his neck and crunched through at least one bone before stopping a few inches into his flesh. As he stumbled back, his eyes filled with confusion and terror. Watching his face felt *oh so good*.

Julia ripped the blade free and lifted it again. Blood sprayed over her bare skin and across the floor. A second blow caught him squarely in the neck, but his arm prevented the full force of her strike, giving him a moment to recover while staggering back.

Now he screamed. A torrent of curses that filled the house.

A third blow across his neck did the trick. No more cursing, or groans, or anything from his mouth except a steady flow of blood. He stumbled as his ugly feet slipped through the pools of blood, and it gushed from every wound as he dropped to the floor and reached for the dresser as if he knew she had hidden his money in it and now wanted it back.

"It's mine now." Julia waited until he stopped moving before turning away. She needed to clean the bloody mess splattered over her body and the machete if she planned to go far. She circled around Donnie's motionless body, all the time holding the machete out defensively as if he might jump up at any moment, and showered in the bathroom as fast as she could.

Returning to the gruesome scene, she yanked one of the pillows from the bed and separated the pillow from the pillowcase. She would leave the house with it stuffed with cash like Santa Claus heading out on Christmas Eve.

There was little chance of her arrest. The police wouldn't waste too much time investigating the murder of a man like Donnie, and she would leave the country within days anyway.

She opened the pillowcase with trembling hands and peeked inside the dresser. It was all there, and it had been *so* much easier than she'd imagined. Grabbing the dozens of straps of hundred-dollar bills, she threw them into the pillowcase along with her cellphone and purse. She grabbed his cellphone too. No sense in giving him the chance to call for help if he somehow survived. If her calculations were correct, she'd just acquired a few hundred thousand dollars.

*Nice.*

On her way to get dressed, she flaunted her naked body over him while staring down at him in disgust. His skin was pale, and the blood had pooled around his chest. His lifeless blue eyes stared blankly up at the ceiling.

"You lost, babe. I won."

After getting dressed, she hurried to the front door with her pulse still throbbing in her ears. Would her heart explode from the fear and elation of her escape? Grabbing the keys from the hook near the door, she hurried outside to Donnie's truck and jumped into the driver's seat while throwing the stuffed pillowcase and machete onto the passenger seat.

She laughed as the truck roared to life. She had expected a greater struggle from him. "Seriously, Donnie, that's all you had in you? Taken down by a little girl like me?" She shook her head. "All those muscles and not an ounce of brains."

Her gaze fixed on the house's front door. Could he have survived her attack? No—impossible—all the blood... And she had looked into his eyes. Dead eyes.

But she hadn't made *sure*.

*He's dead, girl.*

A figure appeared in the doorway hunched forward and heavily stained with blood. Donnie stepped out with his head cocked to one side and raised a pistol in one hand. A blast exploded into the driveway.

*Holy shit.*

Julia put the truck into reverse and barreled backwards with wheels kicking up the loose gravel as she gripped the steering wheel while desperately trying to avoid running into the ditch. Her tires hit the asphalt of the main road at the end of the driveway with a loud thump. The truck lurched up and crashed down again, coming to a complete stop sideways across both lanes of the road.

At the moment before shifting the truck into drive, she stared ahead in horror as Donnie approached. He wasn't creeping along like some half dead zombie, he was jogging toward her at a brisk speed. Despite his head flopping against his left shoulder, he still held the pistol out toward her with his eyes wide and intense.

He fired again and again. A few bullets struck the side of the truck along the passenger side door.

She crouched in her seat and turned the steering wheel. She hadn't killed him. Not by a long shot.

Pressing her foot against the gas, she sped forward

and watched him struggle to keep pace in the rearview mirror. He stopped in the middle of the road behind her as she drove away, firing shots that clanked into the truck's body around her. It was clear that if she stopped, she was dead. She wouldn't stop. No way. But wouldn't Donnie's friends be there soon? They would all join the chase to hunt her down after seeing what she'd done to Donnie. And they would succeed *if* Donnie was alive when they arrived. No, despite the dangers, she had to finish the job.

Stomping her foot on the brake, the wheels screeched to a stop, and she threw the truck into reverse.

She had to succeed this time. No room for error. She sped backwards faster and faster toward him, aligning his mangled form in her rearview mirror with the tail of her truck. He wasn't moving out of the way.

Perfect. Now just stay right there...

But he continued firing at her with his bloody torso and head slanted off to the left. His eyes bulged wider in the moments before she slammed into him. He *must* have seen he was going to die—his face so full of hate and terror. His jaw dropped open as the truck slammed into his body, and his face snapped forward against the truck's gate before dropping out of sight. Elation surged through her as the truck thudded and lurched over his body. She hadn't missed.

Accelerating past the point of her crime, she finally slowed and faced forward, spotting his mangled body lying on the road ahead of her. He lay motionless now, although she had mistaken him for dead before. She watched his body for any signs of movement. Nothing. Even so, she had to be *sure*.

She pressed her foot to the accelerator and roared

toward him again, this time aiming her driver's side wheels at his head.

His leg flopped sideways, as if struggling to move out of the way, then his hand reached up toward her as if trying to stop her from finishing her task.

*Go to hell.*

As the truck slammed into his body again, Julia bounced in her seat with a wide grin. She had forgotten to put on her seatbelt and her head almost hit the roof, but she let out a wild laugh.

*Bullseye.* He couldn't have survived the second hit. No way.

But after passing over his body, she stared into the rearview mirror expecting to see his head flattened in a bloody mass. There was blood, all right, plenty of it, but no Donnie. He was gone.

She squinted into the mirror and scanned the empty road before accelerating faster. Could she have knocked his body into the ditch? It was possible, but more likely, his body had gotten caught beneath her truck like crushed roadkill.

She cringed and sneered while weaving the truck wildly left and right across both lanes. "Don't even think of hanging on, Donnie!"

Keeping an eye on the road behind her for any sign that she had freed him, she finally gave up after not seeing any signs of him.

*Oh shit.*

Maybe he was stuck beneath her. She glanced at the machete on the passenger seat and lifted her foot from the accelerator. The truck slowed to the side of the road.

She came to a stop with her passenger side wheels dipping down into the ditch. Fortunately, there were no other cars in sight along that stretch of rural road, but she wasn't far from town. *Someone* would pass by soon, and time was running out before Donnie's friends would arrive.

Grabbing the machete before opening her driver's side door, she glanced down as far as she could looking toward the underside of the truck for any sign that Donnie had somehow, by some ungodly miracle, survived the trauma. If his body was stuck to the bottom of the truck, she would need to deal with it anyway. Nobody would hesitate to call the police after seeing something like that—*if* they recognized it as human anymore.

She stepped out cautiously, planting her foot as far away from the underside of the truck as her leg would extend as if his bloody hand might lurch out and grab her ankle at any moment. Standing beside the truck with the door open and the machete raised and ready, she leaned down and scanned the truck's underside.

His body was there, hanging off the back of the truck. Chunks of his flesh had gotten tangled around the rear axle, but most of the carnage was dragging off to the back. Even from that angle, the torn muscles and shredded flesh left no doubt in her mind. Donnie was definitely dead.

Her stomach churned. She had unintentionally hit animals before on the road, unfortunate creatures that had darted out in front of her car without warning, but the sight of his broken body sickened her.

Walking around to the back of the truck, she arrived at the bulk of the carnage, and it was even more disturbing than she'd envisioned. The twisted remains were nearly unrecognizable, but his eyes, and the puffy flesh around them, had survived unscathed. His eyes were wide open, staring off into the distance as if deep in thought, and his broken jaw gaped wider than humanly possible. One hand had somehow gotten lodged around the bumper as if he were holding on throughout her escape, and it had somehow remained attached to the rest of the bloody torso below it.

She glanced down the road in both directions. Still no sign of any cars, but she would need to remove him quickly and get out of there. She kicked the bumper hoping it might loosen him enough to ease her task, but he didn't budge. After another swift kick, more out of frustration than anything, his body shifted an inch, but not enough to drive away.

She lifted the machete and took aim at his arm. "Looks like I'll have to do this the hard way, Donnie dear."

A loud grunt burst from her throat as she struck the machete into his forearm. The blade cracked through his bone and came out the other side as the rest of the body slumped away from the severed limb.

Still, the hand's grip on the bumper remained.

With growing frustration, she peeled away the fingers one at a time, until finally the severed arm dropped to the road next to the body.

*I'm free.*

But there was still the body to deal with—she couldn't just leave him there. Despite the gore, she dragged him by one leg off to the edge of the road and dumped his body into the ditch before coming back for his arm. When she returned, it was gone.

"What the hell?" She scanned the road and the truck's underside.

It couldn't have gone anywhere on its own. Had an animal swooped in—a hawk or a vulture—to claim a tasty prize?

"Enjoy it!" she shouted toward the sky and gestured to

the body in the ditch. "The rest of him is over there. Have a free meal on me."

She climbed back into the truck with renewed energy. Now that Donnie was gone forever, she took in a deep breath and exhaled slowly before starting down the road again. Now it was just a matter of ditching the truck and getting out of town.

The cloudy skies parted as she raced away from the scene. The sunny afternoon brightened her mood, and she even found herself singing along to a song on the radio after a few minutes. Turning onto the main highway a few miles down the road, she would have danced on the car's hood if she only had time. She had made it.

But the smell of blood hung in the air after almost an hour of driving, despite her attempts to clear it out by rolling down the windows. A nauseous, disgusting stench that reeked of his presence. She would ditch the car soon anyway.

The back of her left ankle tingled. Not a numb sensation, but a gentle tickle—maybe a bug or a muscle spasm. Or Donnie had stuffed something under the seat that had broken loose in all the chaos. She slid her foot back, feeling an object against the back of her lower leg. A cup or a piece of garbage. She nudged it back under the seat, but it shifted forward again and came to rest against her skin.

She frowned. No easy way to remove it without taking her eyes off the road.

Keeping one eye on the road ahead, she reached down and ran her fingers beneath her seat's metal frame. She swept her fingers through empty space, but encountered nothing. Had it been her imagination? Nerves? Sitting upright again, the object returned, tickling the skin near her ankle this time. She strained again and reached down further, but found nothing.

"Not important," she said with a frustrated sigh and sat upright. *Whatever it is, it can wait.*

But after only a few seconds, the subtle sensation started again. Like an elusive itch taunting her just outside her reach, it moved along the back of her leg and brushed against her skin like an insect scouring the surface for food.

*Flies. Yes, that's what it is. Donnie left some rotting food down there and it's just flies buzzing around.*

She stomped her feet and threw her legs forward and back, but the tickling continued.

"Dammit!" She reached down again, this time stretching her arm so far that her muscles ached. Her gaze left the road as her fingers pushed against something soft and cold. A fleshy mass with fingers, and a ring around the pinky finger. Donnie's hand.

She lurched upright and screamed as the truck veered off to the side of the road. The wheels screeched over the asphalt as she struggled to correct her sudden shift toward the ditch. The machete slipped off the passenger seat and lodged itself between the seat and the door. Gasping for breath, she thrust her foot forward, but it was too late. Donnie's hand had already clamped around her ankle.

Panic swelled in her chest. The thing wasn't just encompassing her ankle. It was squeezing her with more force than he'd ever done since she'd known him. It was somehow *alive*.

Her heart pounded, and she screamed again while stomping her feet wildly to break free. His grip tightened like a clamp and pulling at it while driving did nothing. She would need to stop.

Red and blue flashing lights appeared in her rearview mirror. A police cruiser was speeding toward her.

*Shit.*

An icy dread spread through her as her body weakened. This wasn't just some traffic stop, the officer must have seen something. Maybe the blood on the back of her truck? This was it. The end of the road.

It didn't take long for the police car to catch up to her. It hovered behind the truck for only a few seconds before she slowed and moved off onto the shoulder hoping that it would pass her without incident, but instead it followed her to a stop at the side of the road. The officer remained in his car for what seemed like an eternity before approaching along the passenger side.

Julia kept her hands on the steering wheel as someone had recommended in cases like that. The machete was safely out of view, jarred between the door and the seat, but if the officer opened it...

Before he reached the window, Donnie's hand shifted and moved higher against the back of her leg like a giant spider repositioning itself. The pain of his fingers digging into her muscles was excruciating, but there wasn't anything she could do until after the officer was gone. It was too late to jump out of the truck and battle the thing on her own. She would just need to wait it out.

The officer tapped the window, and she rolled it down a moment later. He wasn't smiling when he peered in at her.

"You know why I stopped you?" he asked behind mirrored sunglasses.

She shook her head with her grip tightening against the steering wheel. "No, sir."

"You were weaving a little back there. Crossed over the center line. Have you had anything to drink today?"

"Not a drop. I..." She looked at the stuffed pillowcase on her passenger seat. "I thought I saw something on the road."

With mirrored eyes and a blank expression, he glanced around the truck's interior, then paused while sniffing the air. "I think you might have hit something. I smell blood."

"That's certainly possible out here."

Donnie's hand moved up further along her thigh, and she held back a scream. It had dug further into her flesh like a venomous animal that had conquered its prey and had stalled to relish its victory before sinking in its teeth for the kill. Absent teeth, it was doing a fine job of cutting into her with its nails.

"Let me see your license." The officer eyed her curiously.

Julia nodded, although she couldn't remember where she had put her purse. Had she stuffed it in the pillowcase along with the cash or left it behind in Donnie's house? Glancing over at the passenger seat, she saw the strap poking out from beneath the sack and remembered that she had left it in his truck the previous evening. She opened it, dug out her license and handed it to the officer.

He scrutinized it for a moment, then stared into her eyes before turning away and walking back to his cruiser.

Julia took a deep breath after he left, but the pain in her leg had intensified. Donnie's hand had crawled up across her thigh and around to the side of her waist. It dug in its fingernails with each advance. She pulled on the cold, dead flesh with all her strength, but the more she struggled, the more he dug in his nails.

She groaned, staring down in disbelief at the bloody

stump where she had so easily severed his forearm from his body. How was it still moving? She had heard of chickens continuing to run around after getting their heads cut off, but could human limbs do the same thing?

The hand was leaving a bloody trail along the side of her dress as it made its way up her body. Blood on the car was one thing, but this would be difficult to explain.

She swallowed. Donnie's hand crawled up a few more inches. Where was it going?

*You know.*

Touching her neck, she glanced across the passenger seat to where the machete had lodged itself near the door. She could lean over and grab it, no problem, but not while the officer was watching her. She might still get away soon if only the officer believed roadkill caused the smell of blood, and despite the officer taking her license, she wasn't under any suspicion of a crime. Maybe Donnie's friends wouldn't even report his disappearance to the police, and by the time anyone found his body, she'd be long gone.

Watching the officer in the rearview mirror, she strained to keep Donnie's hand from moving up further. Covering it with her arm, the officer might not even see it if he returned soon.

*Hurry up. Hurry up.*

But the fingernails dug in to her stomach like talons with each advance, stabbing her and drawing blood that mixed with the blood from the arm's wound.

*How will I explain this?* Her gaze jumped from Donnie's hand to the rearview mirror. The officer's expression hadn't changed since getting into his car. If she could just sit still and hide it somehow until after he left...

But it continued on its way up across her chest and she fought against it. She might still somehow hide it from the officer, even now, with all the blood streaked over her clothes, but... dammit, the officer *still* wasn't moving.

"Hurry up!" she screamed.

The officer's gaze was fixated on something below his dashboard. If she could just reach over and get to the machete, she could cut the hand away...

She stretched her hand across the passenger seat and leaned toward the machete, but the hand dashed up toward her throat, digging in inches from her windpipe. Falling sideways over the bag of money while trying to reach the weapon, her fingers touched the blade, and it dropped further out of reach.

She shrieked hysterically and clawed at the hand's grasp. "Donnie, no!"

His fingernails cut deep into her neck and blood flowed down the front of her dress. There was no hiding it anymore. When the officer returned he would see it and he would arrest her, if she survived.

Better to just run and take her chances. She didn't even bother to look back after grabbing the pillowcase of money and throwing the door open.

Stumbling onto the asphalt, she gasped for air as the country landscape swirled around her. The pain pulsed through her neck and head, and it was too late to run now. Too late for help.

With both hands clutching Donnie's severed limb, she dropped the bag of cash and turned back toward the police cruiser. Donnie's grip around her neck tightened and only a thin flow of air entered her lungs as she reached out toward the officer while trying to scream, but only a gasping shriek escaped.

The officer had removed his glasses and stared back at

her with wide eyes. His mouth dropped open as he jumped out of the police cruiser with his weapon drawn.

Pushing out the last of her air in a strained voice, she called out, "He won't let me go."

"Who won't?" The officer scrambled toward her.

She pointed to the hand around her throat.

The officer stopped a few feet away, his expression full of confusion as his gaze fixed on Donnie's severed arm. "What... what's that?"

Julia's mouth opened to beg for help, but her gaze landed on someone walking toward them along the side of the road a few dozen yards behind them.

Donnie. He was still the same bloody mass of flesh she had scraped from the bottom of the truck earlier, and even from that distance, she could smell the bloody carnage. A vulture circled overhead, probably just waiting for his dinner to stop moving.

No part of him was recognizable except for his blue eyes and the gurgling liquid pushing up from his throat as he approached. "I won."

The officer turned and stared at Donnie's living corpse faltering toward them, then let out a guttural moan while stumbling backward.

Julia clawed at Donnie's hand with the last of her strength as it squeezed through her throat and cut off any hope of another breath. In the moment before losing consciousness, she caught sight of a second vulture circling overhead.

*Isn't that nice? Dinner for two.*

Get a **FREE** short story at my website!

www.deanrasmussen.com

★ ★ ★ ★ ★
**Please review my book!**

If you liked this book and have a moment to spare, I
would greatly appreciate a short review on the page where
you bought it. Your help in spreading the word is *immensely*
appreciated and reviews make a huge difference in helping
new readers
find my novels.

Shine House: An Emmie Rose Haunted Mystery Book 0
Hanging House: An Emmie Rose Haunted Mystery Book 1
Caine House: An Emmie Rose Haunted Mystery Book 2
Hyde House: An Emmie Rose Haunted Mystery Book 3
Whisper House: An Emmie Rose Haunted Mystery
Book 4
Temper House: An Emmie Rose Haunted Mystery Book 5

Dreadful Dark Tales of Horror Book 1
Dreadful Dark Tales of Horror Book 2
Dreadful Dark Tales of Horror Book 3
Dreadful Dark Tales of Horror Book 4
Dreadful Dark Tales of Horror Book 5
Dreadful Dark Tales of Horror Book 6
Dreadful Dark Tales of Horror Complete Series

Stone Hill: Shadows Rising (Book 1)
Stone Hill: Phantoms Reborn (Book 2)
Stone Hill: Leviathan Wakes (Book 3)

ABOUT THE AUTHOR

Dean Rasmussen grew up in a small Minnesota town and began writing stories at the age of ten, driven by his fascination with the Star Wars hero's journey. He continued writing short stories and attempted a few novels through his early twenties until he stopped to focus on his computer animation ambitions. He studied English at a Minnesota college during that time.

He learned the art of computer animation and went on to work on twenty feature films, a television show, and a AAA video game as a visual effects artist over thirteen years.

Dean currently teaches animation for visual effects in Orlando, Florida. Inspired by his favorite authors, Stephen King, Ray Bradbury, and H. P. Lovecraft, Dean began writing novels and short stories again in 2018 to thrill and delight a new generation of horror fans.

www.ingramcontent.com/pod-product-compliance
Lightning Source LLC
Chambersburg PA
CBHW060950190726
48286CB00005B/1511